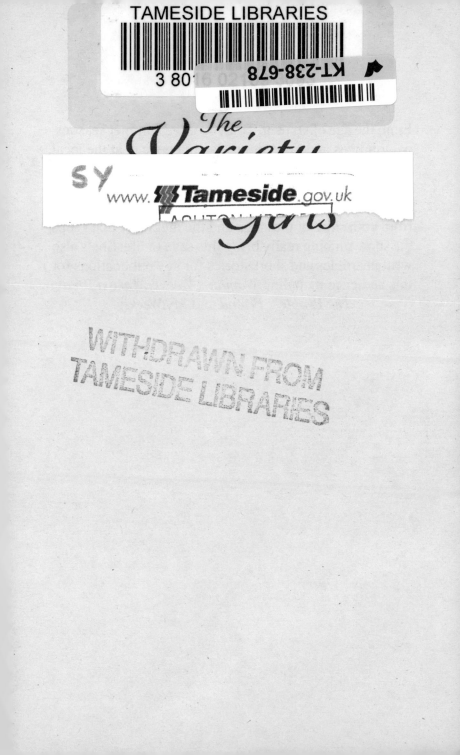

From the age of sixteen, Tracy worked summer seasons, pantomimes and everything else in between at the local end-of-the pier show. She met her husband when he was appearing with the Nolan Sisters and she was Assistant Stage Manager. Her knowledge of the theatre world from both sides of the stage and the hierarchy that keeps the show running really bring this saga to life. She's also written articles and short stories for key publications for this audience including *Woman's Weekly*, *Take a Break*, *The People's Friend* and *My Weekly*.

The Variety Girls

TRACY BAINES

EBURY
PRESS

1 3 5 7 9 10 8 6 4 2

Ebury Press, an imprint of Ebury Publishing
20 Vauxhall Bridge Road,
London SW1V 2SA

Penguin
Random House
UK

Ebury Press is part of the Penguin Random House group of companies
whose addresses can be found at global.penguinrandomhouse.com

First published in the UK in 2020 by Ebury Press

www.penguin.co.uk

A CIP catalogue record for this book is available from the British Library

Paperback ISBN 9781529103809

Typeset in 12.25/15 pt Times LT Std
by Integra Software Services Pvt. Ltd, Pondicherry

Printed and bound in Great Britain by Clays Ltd, Elcograf S.p.A.

Penguin Random House is committed to a sustainable future for
our business, our readers and our planet. This book is made from
Forest Stewardship Council® certified paper.

To Mum and Dad, Tommy and Joan Lee,
the beginning, the middle, and the end of the story.

To Neil, who makes me laugh every day. Which has
probably saved his life.

And to The Lee Sisters, Dianne and Taryn,
the richest kids in town.

Chapter 1

The house was a pressure cooker, Aunt Iris the lid, pushing down on them all. Jessie looked at the mantle clock. It clicked round; another minute. How long could a person last without air? Five minutes? Less? More? She recalled that even the great Harry Houdini had not been able to hold his breath for more than four minutes. She looked again. Another minute, please. She wriggled in the chair, stretching her arms above her head, her slender legs straight out in front of her, her toes pointed. She longed for escape, wondering how these interminable afternoons didn't bother her mum who was absorbed in her needlework. Was it only Jessie who felt uncomfortable? The silence was suffocating, and not even the wireless broke the monotony.

Jessie got up and went to the window, slid the sash open as gently as she could, and leant her head on the warm glass. The slightest noise and Iris would descend on them, migraine or not.

Grace stopped sewing. 'Don't, Jessie. You know your aunt dislikes the windows being opened in here.'

Jessie bit at her cheek. It was exasperating, having her mum kowtow to Iris and her petty rules – of which there were legion. Jessie hated her mum being feeble; it was so unlike her. It seemed to Jessie that the moment the three of them arrived at The Beeches that Grace had let out one long sigh and expelled the last remaining vestiges of courage. They'd battled on as long as they could after dad, Davey, had died but it had been too much for Grace, and in her despair she'd brought them all here, hoping for something better. It was anything but. The imposing Victorian villa sat at the end of the village, set apart from its nearest neighbour – which suited Aunt Iris well, considering that she deemed she was a cut above everyone else. Iris got involved with village matters on her terms otherwise she kept her distance. How on earth Uncle Norman got lumbered with such a harridan was beyond comprehension.

Jessie paused, allowing what little air there was left in her lungs to escape. Her aunt disliked so much that it was difficult to remember what was actually in favour. 'Just a few minutes, Mum,' she said, turning to face her.

'Don't do anything annoying, love. We really mustn't upset her. It's her house and we must do as she asks.'

Jessie sighed. The only person to upset Iris was Jessie; she couldn't help herself. The icier Iris became the more Jessie sought hot water.

Grace coughed, a small hacking sound that shook her chest, and turned back to her embroidery. Jessie watched as her elegant fingers moved swiftly, her needle glinting as it pierced the cream linen tablecloth, the coloured threads the only brightness in their life. It would be one of the many her mum had produced in the eight months since they had come to live at The Beeches; she was permitted to do little else.

Grace had wanted to take in dressmaking work to support them but Iris had been aghast that her husband's cousin could even consider bringing trade to the house. Jessie had been manipulated into taking a secretarial position at Norman's office in Holt for which she was entirely unsuited. Not that anyone else cared. She was constantly reminded by Iris how lucky she was. How it grated on her. Jessie was suddenly overwhelmed with resentment for the way in which her mum had resigned herself to life here. Grace had lost weight, shrunken so small in the armchair that it seemed she was being swallowed up. Living here had made them all so much smaller but what else could they have done?

Her dad had been ill so many times before that it was a shock to them all when he died. Since they were small children, she and her younger brother, Eddie, had grown used to the periods of darkness that overcame their dad – the melancholy, the drinking, the weakness in his chest that Grace explained was from the effects of the Great War. Jessie found it hard to understand why Davey, so mercurial, so full of music and laughter, could allow the darkness to overwhelm him. Was that happening to her mum, this darkness? Would it happen to her too?

Jessie shuddered and returned to the window. There was so much beauty outside, and so little within. A tractor moved along the fields that ran parallel to the garden, making slow progress in regimented lines, turning the soil in preparation for another crop. Beyond it were fields of wheat and barley, slowly beginning to reach towards the sun and the sky, and beyond that? Although Jessie couldn't see it, she knew every bend of the narrow road out of the village.

She leaned as far out of the window as she could, feeling the breeze, breathing in fresh air, visualising herself walking away, and a smile started on her lips. The scent of lilac blossom warmed by the afternoon sun was heavy in the air and blue tits darted through the shrubs in search of a meal. She closed her eyes and breathed in deeply again, and then out as she was overcome by a wave of such sadness and longing that she had to open her eyes to escape the pain of it all. Her heart ached for things to be as they once were.

How could her mum tolerate this day in, day out? Jessie only had to endure such purgatory on a weekend when she wasn't at work in Uncle Norman's office. However, they had no choice. When all the debts had been settled after her dad's death, they'd been left with nothing. She wanted to be angry with him for leaving them to this silent, colourless hell but she couldn't. It hurt her heart too much. She gripped at the sill, breathed in again, though this time fiercely. She should have kept singing, then they needn't be here, because she'd have kept a roof over their heads, she was sure of it, or almost. It was awful, having to rely on Uncle Norman and Aunt Iris. She was old enough at eighteen to strike out on her own. Hope stirred inside her – there must be a way for them to escape this miserable existence, and she promised herself that she would find it.

'Close the window, Jessie. Please,' her mum urged.

Jessie eased the sash down but not quite closed, and looked again at the clock. Almost four, almost time for her aunt to terminate her nap and descend on them, her pinched face certain to turn the milk sour at tea. The thought angered her, and she paced around the room. Why did everything have to be brown, the heavy drapes at the window, the walls, the floor; brown and insipid, colourless – just like her aunt, and exactly like their life.

Jessie walked to the rosewood piano, pulled out the stool, ran her hand over the dusky pink velvet, the only hint at luxury and frivolity in the house, as far as Jessie could see.

'Please, not yet, Jessie dear, we don't want to disturb your aunt.' Grace's voice held a hint of firmness this time, but Jessie had had enough. What was the worst that could happen? More sharp words, angry silences? Yes, but perhaps it would be worth it. She knew she should be grateful but Iris was so mean, so rude about her dad, so dismissive of her mum, that it was intolerable. She lifted the lid.

'I won't play anything lively, nothing of the music hall. A little Debussy, Mum, almost a lullaby, you know how you love it. I'll be quiet.' She flexed her fingers, wanting to bring some light into her grieving

5

mum's life, and placed her fingertips light on the keys. Four o'clock was the rule and, as the wooden clock chimed the hour, she began to play. In moments she was transported by the music, sensing her mum's panic fade, and the thought of Iris's disapproval dilute and disappear. Grace set her sewing in her lap, rested her head on the back of the chair and Jessie was gratified to see a smile play on her mum's lips. Music was such a blessing, her dad's gift, and now hers. She closed her eyes, leaned into the keyboard and away from it as she played, her whole body awakening and her mood changing. What was it? Happiness? Joy? Yes, she could still find it within her. There was movement upstairs and she ignored it, wanting the music to fill her up, only stopping when she felt Grace's hand on her arm. 'Shh, my love.'

Iris was in the doorway, her hands to her ears, a pained expression upon her long white face. 'What hideous noise, Jessica. You know quite well that I have a migraine.'

Her mum's grip on her arm tightened. Jessie's hand covered hers, for a fleeting second mother and daughter looked at one another, exchanging gentle smiles. Then Jessie looked towards the clock and gave her aunt the sweetest smile she could muster. 'It was after four, Aunt. I thought you would be awake.'

'I was awake but that's hardly the point.' Her aunt bustled to the high-back chair where her mum had been sitting, sneering at the embroidery and Grace, with a final squeeze of Jessie's arm, hurried to her side. It was in that moment that Jessie saw the lengths her mum was willing to go to keep the peace if it gave security to her family.

'Could I get you a glass of water, Iris? Would that help? You might be dehydrated,' Grace whispered, and Jessie's throat thickened to see her mum so submissive to this woman, a pale shadow of who she once was. Jessie closed the piano lid carefully and twisted herself around on the stool. 'I'll get it, Mum. You sit down.'

She slipped out of the room and returned with a glass of water, noticing that the window had been closed completely. Well, the old cow was strong enough to do that, Jessie thought, as she handed Iris the glass. Her aunt took it and sipped at the water while Grace stood in attendance, and Jessie hovered close by her. Iris waved her hand as if to brush them away like a speck of dirt. Jessie bit her cheek in case she said something she might later regret. Her mum hesitated.

'Do sit down, Grace.' Iris's voice was sharp. 'You're like death warmed up. And take this nonsense away.' She pointed at the embroidery.

Jessie caught the look of pain on her mum's face and clenched her fists as Grace picked up her needlework, chose another chair and, head down, continued to create roses. Was she remembering the roses that Dad had brought her when he was vibrant and full of life? Iris continued to sip at her water, the clock continued to tick, and the air became stale again. Jessie began to play imaginary piano on her thighs, finishing the tune she had been prevented from completing, her fingers playing notes she knew so well, while Iris fixed her with a beady eye. Jessie closed her eyes and continued, relishing the effect her silent playing had.

'You are too wilful by half, young lady,' Iris said, when Jessie opened her eyes again. Grace looked up. 'The child will never marry, mark my words, Grace. What sort of man would want to take on that temperament?' She picked at minute fibres on her brown skirt then brushed them away with the flat of her hand. 'An old maid if you're not careful, Jessica. Don't you agree, Grace?' She carried on, not letting Grace answer and Jessie sat on her hands in an effort to contain her fury. 'Any young man worth his salt wants a wife to be proud of – unless of course you'd be satisfied with a man of lesser opportunities?' She titled her head to one side, peering down her nose at Jessie, eyes narrowed. It was an ill-concealed dig at Davey.

'If I can find a man only half as wonderful as my dad, I'll be a very happy woman.' Jessie folded her arms across her chest. 'He was kind and he was loving, and he had the sweetest soul.' She was tempted to add 'everything you're not' and if it hadn't been for her mum would have taken great satisfaction in doing so. She saw Grace tense in her chair, her hand stilled.

Iris sniffed. 'A musician who—'

Grace's voice was steady. 'He was a very fine musician, Iris, classically trained. Before the war ...'

Iris wafted a hand. 'Before the war was a long time ago, Grace. He had a good start but to end up in the halls, playing variety.' Iris shook her head, smiling condescendingly at Jessie.

'There's nothing wrong with variety,' Jessie spat. 'It gives pleasure to lots of people. It makes them happy.' Although what would Iris know of happiness. Her aunt snorted with derision and Jessie felt the heat rise in her face and neck, her ears burning. She must think of her mum; she mustn't rise to Iris's bait. She took a deep breath, let it out, dug her nails into her palm. 'Given half the chance I'd be on the stage now, singing, dancing ...'

'Huh,' Iris huffed in satisfaction. 'Making an exhibition of yourself, you mean. You don't need to be on the stage to do that, madam.'

Jessie was all set to slice Iris apart with her tongue when the sound of tyres coming up the drive stopped her. Thank heavens, Uncle Norman was home; he at least brought a little relief with him.

When they'd first moved to The Beeches Jessie had wondered at the long hours he worked in his legal practice but it didn't take long for her to understand why. He had little of her mum about him save for his eyes, which were the same tender grey. It was difficult to believe that he and her mum were related at all.

She sat quite still and waited, hearing the car door slam shut. She had a vague memory of Uncle Norman being kind to her when she was a little girl but that was then. She had seen nothing of it these last few months. It was clear that Iris had squeezed every last vestige of joy from his life, as she did everyone's, so there was nothing for him to give to anyone else. But the car arriving meant her brother Eddie would be back, and Harry would be following too.

Jessie leapt to her feet and rushed from the drawing room, ignoring her aunt's disapproving looks but hearing her snap, 'That girl!' Her uncle was already in the hall, resplendent in plus fours, removing his tweed cap and hanging it on the hook in the hallway, then smoothing a large hand over his bald head. Through the open door she saw Eddie wrangling Norman's golf clubs from the boot of the Ford before taking them to the garage. Harry's Royal Blue Austin was parked to the rear and here he was, carefully wiping his shoes on the doormat to save a reprimand from his boss, Uncle Norman.

She moved close to him, smiling. 'They're not dirty,' he whispered, grimacing, 'but I'm not taking any chances.'

'That will do, Harry. Come in, come in,' Uncle Norman ordered. 'Where's your aunt, Jessie? We have news to share.'

Jessie gestured to the drawing room. Why on earth did he say that so often, when it was always where Iris was? Eddie and Harry loitered in the hall, but Jessie followed her uncle, unwilling to leave her mum alone with them.

Uncle Norman kissed Iris on her raised cheek.

'Did you have your lie down, darling? Did you rest?'

Iris adjusted herself in the chair. 'I tried, dear. Unfortunately, Jessica played the piano rather too loudly and I awoke with a start.' She let out a breathy sigh. 'I'll be all right in a little while.' Her tone was frail and weak, the voice she used for Norman, not the voice she used to pierce Grace and Jessie's world. Oh, she was clever, Jessie had to give her that. Norman looked at her, not in reprimand, she thought, more a weariness that she had added to his burden. She hung her head.

Norman turned to Grace, his voice soft. 'You seem so much brighter today, my dear. I do believe this country air is doing you good.' He patted her hand and Grace summoned a weak smile. 'Harry,' Norman called into the hall. 'Let's share our good news, young man.'

Harry entered the room and Norman slapped him on the back. 'Ladies, allow me to introduce the new junior partner of Cole's Solicitors. Mr Harry Newman.'

Harry didn't look at him, but at Jessie, and smiled, proudly, but there was something else in his eyes and Jessie sensed his recognition that the net was closing in on him, and that darkness made her love for him intensify. Before Jessie could speak, Grace rose to her feet and hurried to take his hand in both of hers.

'Why, that's wonderful news,' she said. 'Oh, well done, Harry, and much deserved. Good news at a time like this, with the world so dreadfully tense.'

Norman nodded his agreement.

Jessie followed and hugged him. She heard Iris tut at such an outward display of affection, which made her want to hug him more. He held her close. 'Sweet darling, Jessie,' he whispered into her hair. She gripped his hand, squeezed it, then let it drop.

'Of course, I knew before you did,' Iris whined. 'Norman informed me during the week of his intentions.

11

As Grace has already said, congratulations, Harry. I'm sure you will prove to be an asset to my husband's well-respected practice and let's hope Jessie will handle the increasing workload, for there will obviously be more contracts to type.' She looked piercingly at Jessie, her hands folded in her lap. There would be no handshake for Harry from that quarter, that's for sure. 'Or at least, as a partner, that should be your primary aim.'

Jessie's shoulders sagged. Damn the woman. Did she not possess one ounce of grace?

Harry smiled. 'I will endeavour to repay your husband's confidence in me,' he said, tipping his head in a little bow. Jessie hated to hear him being so subservient, but, of course, he had to be. She knew Harry didn't believe it; it was all a pretence.

'And his investment,' Iris added, eager to labour the point.

Harry's smile became fixed as he looked from Norman to Iris. 'Of course, without a doubt. I will always be grateful for the opportunity and faith you and Mr Cole have shown to me. I know quite well that at twenty-two I am fortunate indeed.'

Jessie sighed, loudly, and her mum shot her a look before returning to her chair. Jessie forced a smile. *Grateful*: the very word set her teeth on edge.

Eddie sidled into the room and stood behind the sofa, his brown hands stark against the white antimacassar. The sleeves of his blue shirt were rolled back to the elbows and he was burnt from the sun out on the golf course where he'd been caddying for his uncle.

His wavy brown hair, the same colour as Jessie's, was sticking up at the front and he ran a hand over it in an attempt to tame it. He at least seemed able to shrug off the atmosphere of the house and wend his way heedless of it all.

'Now, now, Iris. Harry has more than earned his good fortune,' Norman said, stepping in to smooth the way, something Jessie had noticed he did quite often for Harry. 'Eddie here, at fourteen, is a long way off being able to step up, and it is only sensible to have this wonderful young man on board.'

Another pat on the back and he gestured for Harry to sit down on the sofa. Jessie sat back on the piano stool and dug her nails into her hands; Eddie's life already mapped out for him, and hers too, as a typist. Indeed, the net was closing.

Tea was quickly served by Nelly, who Iris liked to call the maid, but who was really a girl from the village who did a little light cleaning and brewed a cup of tea. Nelly put the tray down on the oak side table with a bang, turned, winked at Jessie, sniffed, and slammed the door shut behind her. Jessie saw that the milk hadn't curdled, which was a miracle given Iris's stony look. 'That girl might have to go, Norman. She has no finesse whatsoever.'

It was all nonsense of course, because Nelly was the only one who had stayed more than a month or two and that was because she nicked the sugar and whatever else she could slide into her bag. Jessie didn't blame her one jot.

She got to her feet and poured the tea, Eddie wordlessly slipping beside her, taking the plate of ham sandwiches and offering them round. He grinned at Jessie when he returned and she handed him the milk jug, their silent unity calming her. Norman settled on the sofa with Harry and chatted about the golf game, his best shots, his worst. 'Of course, Harry here let me win.'

Harry nearly choked on his tea. 'I did no such thing, Mr Cole. It just wasn't my day.'

'Norman, please. No more Mr Cole. We're partners, remember.' He leaned across to Jessie, who sat on the spare upright chair, which Eddie had brought in from the dining room. 'He's a fine golfer, Jessie. A fine young man all around, don't you think?'

Jessie nodded; she couldn't and wouldn't argue with that because she'd known from the start he'd be a bright shining star in this miserable existence. He'd been so kind to her when she'd started pounding the typewriter at Cole's and it had made it all more bearable, so much so that she loved him, but enough to spend the rest of her life with him? She wasn't sure. But was that because Uncle Norman felt it would be the ideal solution to Jessie's restlessness to make a good marriage and settle down with him? Or was she doomed to be an old maid as Iris had so spitefully suggested. She sipped at her tea, then replaced it on the small table to her left, unfinished. Just like her life. If she was to be a spinster she wouldn't be spending her days here. The very thought made her shiver.

Norman sank back into the cushions of the sofa, his hands folded across his ample stomach. 'I think you youngsters should go out and celebrate Harry's good news, don't you?' It was an instruction, not a suggestion, and Jessie snatched a look at Harry. She saw the relief on his face and leapt to her feet. Oh, yes, to breathe some air, to hold his hand, to be a person, to escape, even if it was only for a moment. But what about Eddie?

She turned but Eddie shook his head, knowing her thoughts, just as he always could.

'I said I'd clean Uncle Norman's golf clubs this evening. I can do yours too, Harry, if that helps?' He winked at Harry and just as Eddie could read her thoughts, she could read his. Clearly the two boys had arranged this. It would be just the two of them then.

Jessie wound down the window of the Austin before Harry had put the car into gear. It was wonderful to be going somewhere, anywhere. She'd never sat down as much as she had these past months – with Dad, with Eddie, with her mum, and now her aunt. Even at work she sat down most of the day. She could feel her muscles slackening, and was becoming increasingly restless from being indoors so much. The days of dance and movement seemed further away every day, but she did as she always did, and told herself that her dreams of a singing career were merely interrupted, that what she had paused in her life could be restarted.

Harry reversed out of the drive, and headed towards the main road, whistling to himself, and grinning at her. She grinned back, but her head was full of what she had lost. Her singing had been paused but her dad was lost to her forever. A surge of sadness made her chest tighten and it was hard to breathe, harder still to bear and yet she knew she must suppress her grief because her mum could not shoulder anything more than she did already. She shouldn't have snapped at Iris. It only made things worse for all of them.

Harry turned left at the crossroads, and out of the village.

'Where to, Miss Delaney?'

Jessie took the pins from her hair and shook it about her shoulders, the copper tones caught the late-afternoon sun and she felt the chains of the Cole household left far behind. 'It's your celebration, Harry. You choose.'

'I'd rather you did. I think you'll choose something far more exciting than I would. I'm rather new to all of this. Besides, think of it as a reward for your afternoon of penance.'

She turned and smiled at him. His eyes were steady on the road ahead as it snaked through the burgeoning hedgerow on either side of them. She tipped her head back and rested her neck on the cool leather of the seat while she ran through their options.

'Let's go into Cromer then, and see a show,' she said at last. 'There's bound to be something on the pier.' The thought of it made her half laugh with anticipation and she turned suddenly, put her hands either side of the window and leaned out as far as she could. The breeze blew at her hair and whipped it across her face. Opening her mouth wide she gulped in the cold air as the car rushed along. She tilted her head back to let her hair flow behind her until she felt Harry's arm on hers.

'Get in, you crazy fool. You'll get your head knocked off.'

She pulled in, liking the feel of his hand, because it was gentle. He wasn't ordering; he was protecting her. As she settled back into her seat his hand returned to the steering wheel.

They drove down towards the west promenade, and Jessie thrilled to see the swarms of people out enjoying themselves in spite of the news from the continent. Italy had aligned itself with Germany, the two bullies committing to support each other if it came to war with France and Britain, and Hitler had made clear his intentions to move in on Poland. War seemed inevitable but there was still a sense of hope. Bodies moved along the esplanade like waves on the ocean and Harry braked the car to a halt outside one of the large hotels. While she waited for him to walk round and open her door she watched a family on the other side of the road. A mother and father were holding a small girl between them, swinging her by the arms, her face shining with delight, her happiness a reflection of theirs.

She longed to feel that safety and strength again but knew she must find it within herself from now on. She got out and pulled her cardigan about her shoulders. The seaside air was fresh and smelt of fish and chips and candy floss, sweet and salty. Harry closed her door behind her and guided her across the road, finding a place where they could quickly mingle into the crowd as they dropped down onto the wider esplanade. People surged down towards the beach, and noises of laughter and squeals of delight mingled with the sound of merry-go-rounds and bangs and whistles from the kiosks that lined the promenade. On the beach children gathered round a Punch and Judy tent, their necks bent, looking up at Mr Punch whacking the crocodile with a truncheon as donkeys plodded along the golden sands, the bells on their halters jangling as they went. Well-fed fathers snoozed in deckchairs while mothers fussed about their children who raced down to the waterline, splashing the water at each other and skipping over the gentle waves that lapped along the shore. They strolled past carts selling fresh crab, cockles and mussels.

'Fancy some?' Harry said, catching her hand. She nodded, smiling, and suddenly the misery of The Beeches felt a million miles away. Harry queued, she beside him, and they ate vinegary cockles from a paper cone as they walked, then idled on, looking at postcards, trying on straw hats, posing for a photograph that would be sent on to them. The sun was still shining as it began its slow descent in the sky, and she felt as free as the gulls that wheeled and screeched above them.

Her pace quickened when she saw the playbills in the distance, plastered on lampposts and hoardings. Would there be any big names, would there be anyone she knew? They walked along, swinging hands as they went but as they got closer she saw the Sold Out board had been put outside the pier entrance. She let go of Harry's hand, her pace slowed. He sensed her disappointment.

'Hey, grumpy face, let me ask, they might have one seat left at least.' She laughed as he walked over to the box office and watched him bend his head to speak to the girl at the window. She studied the poster at the pier entrance, hoping that when she turned he would be holding tickets, but when he came and stood beside her she knew he hadn't been successful.

'I'm sorry, Jessie. I tried everything bar bribery but there's not a seat left. The girl said they'd never been so busy.'

She looked longingly up at the pier as people came and went. Three girls, their bare arms linked, walked towards them and a couple of lads whistled as they passed. The girls giggled and preened. Jessie turned to Harry. 'Perhaps everyone feels as I do, that this is the last summer we will know before war, and are taking every grasp at happiness they can.'

'I know the feeling. All this "will we, won't we" is driving everyone ruddy crazy. It's the uncertainty of it all.' He struck out with his heel. It was her turn to cheer him up.

'It's not your fault, Harry. We can always walk along the pier anyway. It's a lovely evening.'

They strolled along at an easy pace, stopping at intervals, leaning on the railings, staring down onto the beach. Children were building sandcastles or digging holes and she laughed and pointed at two little boys who were burying their father in the sand, his toes and head the only parts of him peeping out. Out on the sea, sail boats tacked through the water.

'Do you think there will be a war?' she said, eventually, shaking her head at the cigarette he offered her from his case. The breeze snatched at the lighter flame so he cupped it, inhaled, exhaled, and dropped the lighter back into his pocket, only then replying, leaning on the railings again. 'It's beginning to seem more likely. I don't think Mr Chamberlain's so confident these days. It all seems a pretty poor mess.'

'What will you do, Harry? Will you sign up? Or will you wait?'

'Hey, slow down,' he murmured. 'You've got me fighting for my country and I haven't even had one day as junior partner at Cole's yet.' He raised an eyebrow. 'What would your uncle say?'

She laughed. 'I'm sorry, Harry. I forgot: it's your celebration. You've done ever so well, and you'll be good, I know you will. Just don't become like him, for goodness' sake.'

Harry shook his head. 'Not much chance of that with you in the picture. Any move towards Uncle Normanhood and you'd wrench my head off. Come on, Miss Delaney, let's keep walking, not thinking.'

'But it's the time to think, isn't it, Harry? You with your partnership, Eddie and Mum stuck with Norman and Iris, the world ...'

He took one last draw on his cigarette and rubbed it out under his foot, taking her hand, and walking along. She matched him stride for stride.

'You're right. And yes, I have the partnership, but, Jessie, life needs some security while things are as they are. I know you don't want to hear it, but your uncle is good to work for, he knows his stuff, and I'm learning such a lot. Soon I'll have something to offer—' He stopped, kissed her hand, her heart twisted. He looked into her eyes and smiled. They said nothing, just stood there as others passed either side. At last they strode along. 'What I'm trying to say is that soon I'll have something to offer you other than life with a fumbling trainee solicitor who doesn't know his arse from his elbow, and don't tell your uncle I said that, or I'll be out on my ear.'

She laughed, and looked away, over his shoulder, at the sea, the clouds floating across the sky, seagulls soaring far out over the water. She loved him, of course she did – but was she in love because that was some-thing different, wasn't it? That's why her mum had mar-ried her dad, that's what the books and songs said. But how did you know when it happened? And look at her mum's life with her dad, such a struggle. Love wasn't everything, was it?

Suddenly, in spite of her words, she didn't want to think; she just wanted to be with him, holding his hand, walking and laughing with him for there was so much life left to live, so much she needed to do for her family. She turned to look at him, his dear face, his eyes so earnest, then back at the theatre. At the sea, at the sky.

'Well?' he asked.

She reached up and stroked his face. 'I'm not sure what I want, dearest Harry. The only thing I know is that you are my anchor when everything else is so horrible.'

He gripped her hand, kissing it. 'Then let's cross over to that café and we'll have a drink and see if we can find one of those spivs who seem to have tickets tucked up their sleeves like a dodgy magician. I will get you to the ball, Cinderella. Or at least to the theatre. It might help, whaddya say?'

He hurried her along the promenade, and over to the right, by an alley at the side of a café, was a fat man with greasy slicked-back hair leaning against the wall. 'Looking for tickets, gov?'

Harry grinned at Jessie. 'There you are, Jessie, meet your fairy godmother. Yes, let's have a couple. My girl-friend's happiness depends on it.'

Chapter 2

Harry grabbed her hand and pulled her along the parade, the pair of them laughing as they went.

'Come on, slowcoach or we'll miss the opening.'

She could barely keep up as he weaved through the crowds, taking her with him as they headed for the pier. Squeezing through the slender gaps that appeared in the crowd, Jessie felt her worries fall from her shoulders, leaving them behind on the promenade along with the discarded wrappers and cigarette stubs under their feet. At last something wonderful was happening, a slice of her old life brought into the new. Dearest Harry. He could never disappoint her. At last they reached the pier and Jessie stopped to catch her breath, her hand to her heart, her chest pounding with exhilaration.

'You shouldn't have paid so much, Harry,' she berated him as her breathing steadied, secretly pleased he had, that her happiness meant that much to him. 'You must be out of your mind.'

He grinned. 'Maybe I am but it was worth every exorbitant shilling to see your face.' She stayed close to him as they walked up the pier, their footsteps clattering on the wooden planks.

'Thank you so much, Harry,' she said again. 'I can't tell you how excited I am.'

'Tell me later.' He smiled, cupping her chin and tilting her head up towards him, kissing her lightly on the mouth. 'We'll have all the time in the world after the show.' They clasped hands again and swung them as they walked towards the concert hall entrance. The queue was already forming for the second house and they got in line, Harry holding the tickets in one hand, hers in the other, as they shuffled closer to the front.

He laughed at her. 'You chump; if you keep smiling like that your face will ache like merry hell in the morning.'

The man in front of them turned around. 'Yes, love. I'd pace yourself if I was you. From what I've heard the comedian's a corker.' Beside him his plump wife giggled, and Jessie watched her upper arms wobble.

'I don't care,' Jessie said. 'I want to laugh until my head falls off.'

'Now, now, miss. Nothing so drastic if you please,' he said, putting out a warning hand. The woman turned her head and smiled good-naturedly at the two of them.

'It's grand to get out and have a laugh, lovey. Make the best of things while we still can.'

Jessie nodded her agreement. She only wished her mum could be here to enjoy it too. A little laughter would lift her spirits so much. Jessie stared out over the pier and watched people milling along the esplanade. Little lights had begun to appear on the stalls that were dotted along the promenade selling candyfloss and rock.

The woman's words were jolting in her head. While we still can. She pushed them away, up, up into the clouds that were scudding by in the darkening skies above them. She wasn't going to think about what the papers said or the gossip in the office. Miss Symonds had the right idea: she refused to speculate; refused to get into lengthy debate. 'What will be, will be' was all she was ever drawn to.

Harry grinned at her as she turned back to him and she tried to catch up with the conversation. It seemed everyone was chipping in with their two penn'orth now.

'I shouldn't think the shows will go on much longer,' the plump woman said, her voice wistful.

'Nah, this ruddy government don't like any of us to have fun,' someone behind them chimed in. 'It'll be the first thing the blighters do.' The others around them laughed but Jessie couldn't bear to think of it. She turned to see an older man with a red shiny face and head to match from too much time in the sun. He should have knotted his hanky. The line shuffled forward, and Harry put his hand to her back and gently guided her.

'They won't stop the shows,' she said, quite adamant. 'If it does come to war, we'll need to keep our spirits up. We have to, don't we?' she said, soliciting opinions from either side. The laughter had subsided now, and the conversation took a heavier tone. The first man considered it.

'I'm sure you're right, Miss. But I shouldn't think they'll let the piers stand. Not as they are. It's almost an invitation to Jerry to step right up an' 'elp 'imself.'

Jessie's face tightened in a frown. Close the shows. The whole country silenced of music. Wouldn't Iris just love that? A wave of hopelessness swept over her.

Harry shook at her hand. 'I can see your point about the piers,' he said with a nod to the chap, 'but I can see Jessie's too.' He smiled at her. 'We'll all need to keep our chins up, won't we?' Jessie looked up at him, her eyes shining. He believed in her and it warmed her heart.

'We will, young man. We'll need something to keep us all going.' Someone else had joined in. 'We needed it the last time round so we'll sure as damn it need it this.'

'Ah, love's young dream.' The chap nudged his wife as the queue began to move again. 'Ain't it great. You hang on to him, lass. He's fighting your corner good an' proper.'

Jessie gripped Harry's hand tightly.

'I will,' she said, feeling her cheeks redden. Harry fighting for her was one thing; to think of him out fighting in uniform was something else entirely. It changed everything. Dad had never been the same again. Her mum said war had ruined him, the man he was; his hearing was damaged by the shells, so he couldn't hear his beloved music with clarity, and he'd developed tremors, so much so that at times he couldn't play. It was the reason he drank, to calm himself, nothing more. She didn't want Harry to change, she liked him as he was. She wasn't going to think about the war, or anything else for that matter. When she walked into the theatre she knew she would forget everything. Wasn't that what Dad had said theatre was all about? Forgetting and remembering – and both at the same time.

The queue surged forwards and as they neared the doors her shoulders tensed with delight. Harry bought a programme from the petite usherette with chipped red nails who tore their tickets and handed the halves back to him.

'Down the centre aisle and on your left' she instructed before turning quickly to the next person in the queue. Jessie hurried towards their row, Harry amused by her eagerness. She felt like a little child, waiting for her birthday surprise as she pushed down her seat. She could hardly believe she was here when just a few hours ago she had been gasping for air.

'Happy?' he said, sitting down beside her.

'Delirious.' She leaned over and planted another kiss on his cheek. It was so good to be in a theatre, to be where she belonged.

Her heart was beating hard with excitement as she drank in the deep-red interior, the plush luxury of the stage curtains, the glow of the lights overhead. All around them people were taking their seats, a constant wave, up and down as they shuffled into place. Little pillars of cigarette smoke rose up about them and a low cloud floated in the still air.

They barely had time to look at the programme before the usherettes drew the curtains over the doors and the lights were dimmed. The babble of the audience became a hush as the orchestra began the overture, and as the music played, the memories came flooding back to Jessie, of being backstage with her mum watching her dad perform, the music, the soft notes and crescendos, all to lift the audience and sweep them on a journey. Jessie shuddered with delight and wiggled in her seat as the ruby curtains drew back with a swish to reveal eight dancers gliding across the stage to 'Embraceable You'.

Four tall handsome men in evening suits led four leggy girls across the stage, sweeping them into their arms, the girls' shapely thighs showing through the splits in the skirts of their diaphanous pink dresses. How her mum loved that particular song; Jessie would play it for her parents in the rooms they had in Lowestoft, before her dad became too ill to stand, her mum light on her feet, her face glowing with happiness as she stared into her husband's eyes. What love they shared; what happy times. The song came to an end and, brought back to the present, Jessie found herself applauding. Harry nudged her and she smiled. Would they dance together; would she look at him with the love in her eyes that Grace had for Davey? Did she love him enough?

The inner gold curtains came across and the compère, smart in his black suit, half ran, half skipped to centre stage. He took the microphone in his hand and beamed at the audience.

'Ladies and gentlemen, boys and girls, welcome to Cromer Pier. Have you all come to enjoy yourselves?' There were a few mumbled yeses from parts of the audience. The man put his hand to his ear. 'I can't hear you. Have you come to enjoy yourselves?' This time everyone shouted 'Yes' in unison, then burst into laughter.

Jessie looked at Harry. His face was glowing with happiness and she knew it was partly because he was enjoying himself but mostly because he had made her happy.

'That's better,' the compère roared. 'Let's get on with the show. Put your hands together in a big warm welcome for Mr Magic, himself, The Great Valdini.' He held out his hand as he walked backwards into the wings, in time with the opening of the gold curtains.

The Great Valdini wore top hat and tails and began by pushing up his cuffs, opening his fingers wide, turning his hands back and forth in time to the music so that the audience could see that he had nothing up his sleeves. He produced cards from thin air, or so it seemed, and deftly weaved them between his flexible fingers, dripping them onto a small table to the side of him. The audience applauded politely.

'They're not warmed up yet,' Jessie whispered to Harry. 'It's always tough being first on.'

Harry took her hand. 'Ever happen to you?'

'Frequently.' She wished that she was up there now, first on or not. She knew she would conquer her nerves once the music began. It was always the same, the churning stomach, the hesitation, but, once the music played and she stepped out into the light, everything fell away. Nothing else mattered.

Valdini took off his top hat, showed the inside to the audience, dipped in and produced a white dove and settled it on the perch on the table. The audience clapped in appreciation as he then produced another and sat it alongside its companion. It was a bit old-fashioned but Jessie loved it for that very reason. Then came the rainbow of knotted handkerchiefs, Valdini pulling the ribbon of them on and on. He stopped momentarily as one of the doves left its perch and flew out into the audience. The orchestra carried on playing and the magician attempted to continue with his tricks, but the audience were ducking, ladies putting their hands over their heads to protect their hair, their clothes.

'Watch it, the pigeon's made a break for it,' a wag called from somewhere towards the back and the audience erupted with raucous laughter. The dove made a tour of the auditorium and settled back on its perch and the audience cheered.

Harry leaned across to her, whispering, 'He ought to build it into his act, and the comedian had better be ruddy good after that performance.'

They weren't to be disappointed. As soon as Will Green bounced onto the stage in his green plaid suit and yellow shirt, he had the audience in the palm of his hands. He rattled out jokes like machine-gun fire and Harry threw his head back in laughter. Jessie felt her sides would burst. It was a relief when the interval started. They needed a rest.

While Harry queued for ices, Jessie read the programme, poring over every detail and working out what she would use for her bill matter when she took to the stage again. Because sitting here she knew she would. It was important to entertain, to lift people away from their worries and troubles. She knew it – she felt it – here with Harry.

Did her mum still have some of their old programmes? Where on earth had she put them? There had been so many things that Dad had collected over the years: his music; the playbills. There hadn't really been time to think when Davey died. Grace had been distraught, weakened by the constant care of her ailing husband, and Eddie's care had fallen on Jessie. They had struggled on with little money as long as they could, but in the end Jessie realised that the only sensible option was for her to stop singing and stay in one place. If only she'd been able to secure a long theatre season it could all have been so different. She should've held firm; something would have come up, it always did, and the money was three times what she was earning now.

Harry handed her an ice cream slice and she put the programme on her lap, folded the wrapper into neat squares and placed it in the ashtray on the back of the seat in front of her.

'We should do this more often.' Harry settled back in his seat.

'Yes, we should,' Jessie agreed as the lights came down for the second half. How could she explain to him the sense of completeness she experienced not only when she was watching but when she was the one up there, performing, singing as if her heart would burst with the pure pleasure of it, of sharing something special? She was scared he wouldn't understand.

It was soon time for the top of the bill and the mood in the theatre changed to one of high anticipation. There was a reprise of the overture and the ruby curtains opened once more to reveal a starlit night on the Riviera – or as close as could be created with the magnificent artistry of scenery and props.

Daphne Shearer appeared centre stage and walked to the front, tall male dancers in evening dress, one either side, holding her hands. She blew them both an exaggerated kiss, came to the microphone and began to sing 'Love for Sale'. The audience were with her from the beginning and remained so until the end as she sang old favourites and songs that they heard on the wireless. Jessie drank in every movement, the way Daphne held the notes, the way she moved across the stage and leaned towards the audience, drawing them in, holding them with her; they wanted to be led and gave themselves over to her. The audience were hanging on to every note she sang. Jessie looked around her, at the men and women who may have already accepted that their loved ones would be going off to war, some for the second time. They'd left their worries behind them for that magical hour.

Now they were swaying along to the familiar tunes and when Daphne finished with 'Thanks for the Memory', the seats clattered as the audience rose as one to applaud her, their programmes slipping onto the floor. Jessie and Harry leapt to their feet along with them, grinning at one another. Then Harry leaned over and kissed her mouth. 'I'm so glad that you're happy,' he said against her lips. He drew away and she leaned against him.

'I can't tell you how much, dear, darling Harry.'

As the applause rang on and on, she knew that this was what she must do in turn – make people happy, and not just 'people' but her own family. They must all move away from life's Aunt Irises and Uncle Normans and the endless dreary brown.

When the show ended they filtered out onto the pier, the voices drifting in the night air, full of excitement. Lights were shining from the Hotel de Paris in front of them, high up on the clifftop, and couples sat cuddling in the ornate Victorian shelters either side of the pier, whispering sweet nothings. She and Harry passed the stacked deckchairs that had been collected at dusk. The ropes of lights along the pier swayed a little in the breeze, and the surf rushed across the shingle. Harry put his arm around her shoulder and she nestled close to him.

'Cold?'

'Only on the outside, Harry,' she whispered, leaning her head on his shoulder. Once again Jessie acknowledged the power of good entertainment. It was a wonderful gift, Davey had always said that, and it was true, wasn't it?

'Dad said that one of the greatest gifts was to be able to entertain,' she murmured. 'It takes people out of their lives.'

Harry slowed. 'That sounds serious, as though you're thinking of yourself. Are you? Is life that bad?'

She had no idea how to answer him; what if he told her uncle how she felt? But would he? Her Harry? For a moment she wasn't sure, and after a moment she said, 'Oh, Harry, if there's to be war ...' her voice tailed off.

She slowed so much that Harry dragged at her arm, then stopped with her. He stared, worried. She saw her dad, so damaged by war, and all of his friends who had not returned. She looked at those passing them, talking of the show. It all seemed so fragile, and Harry most of all. War was surely coming. Everything would change; everything they held dear would be threatened by a war no one wanted. And yet one couldn't stand by and let things happen. She must do something; she owed it to her dad, to Harry, to all of those people walking along, under swaying lights.

She shivered and leaned into him as people passed by, heading for their boarding houses or dashing to catch the last bus. Yes, she must do something, no matter what Iris and her uncle thought, no matter how many obstacles they put in her way.

In the car on the way back she started to sing 'Little White Lies'.

'You have a wonderful voice, Jessie,' Harry said, taking his eyes off the road for a moment to look at her.

'Sing with me,' she said. 'We could do a duet. Jeanette MacDonald and Nelson Eddy.' She began to sing 'Will you Remember'.

'I'd rather listen to you,' Harry said, changing gear as they reached a crossroads. They idled there, waiting for a bus to pass before Harry could turn right.

'My heart, la di da, will remember,' Jessie sang, purposely over-dramatic, holding her hands across her heart, a forlorn expression on her face.

'Idiot,' he said, laughing. She loved making him laugh.

He stopped at the bottom of the drive to The Beeches, left the engine running, and opened her door. Jessie leaned forward and started to sing 'On the Sunny Side of the Street', holding out her hand, urging him to take up his hat and coat and leave his worries behind. He took her hand in his and eased her out of the car.

'Shh, darling girl. You'll wake everyone up.'

She looked at the house; a lamp was lit in the drawing room, the glow from the bay window at the front so welcoming. She turned to Harry, her eyes sparkling. 'Mum will be waiting to hear all about our evening. We always waited for Dad to come home. It was such a special time.' She looked towards the window again. Her mum and Eddie would want a blow-by-blow account; she would sing some of the songs, tell them of the dove's break for freedom, of her yearnings to do the same. But that would only happen if *they* had gone to bed. At the thought, her joy began to seep away, continuing even when Harry pulled her close and kissed her, his mouth warm against hers, his hand in the small of her back.

'I'll ask you again, Jessie Delaney,' he whispered. 'I'm not going to let you slip through my fingers.'

She pulled away from him, holding onto his hands. It was too soon to have an answer for such a question; they had only been dating a few short months, yet she felt sure that her uncertainty would fade with time. His face was half in shadow for there was barely a moon that night. The leaves of the oak and beech were rustling in the breeze and in the distance a vixen shrieked. Jessie heard the front door open and she saw Eddie silhouetted in the doorway, the light from the hall spilling out onto the path.

'I'd better let you go,' said Harry. He released her hands and got into his car, almost whispering. 'One day I'll marry you. One day, but only when you're ready. In the meantime, be happy, my little songbird.'

'It's been the most wonderful night. Thank you, Harry,' she called in a low voice, watching him drive away, feeling relief, and then the return of her joy because Harry had said to be happy. She almost danced up the path, holding her skirt, swaying along to the tunes that were returning thick and fast as Eddie stood back to let her in, closing the door quietly behind them.

As she swayed into the drawing room, she hesitated, seeing no smile on her mum's face, and her eyes flashed a warning. Instantly, Jessie fell silent and sought Iris, who must still be in the drawing room. And there she was, stony-faced in the high-back chair, her glasses on the end of her nose. Without looking up, Iris closed the book she had been reading, put it on the side table, removed her spectacles and placed them on top.

'I hope you're pleased with yourself, Jessica – waking half the village with your noise. And I can't for the life of me imagine what Harry was thinking of; or perhaps he didn't know how to cope with such behaviour.'

Jessie steeled herself, wanting to shout out that he had enjoyed every minute of the show, and her singing, but she mustn't spoil his prospects or their opinion of him. Much better that they blamed her.

'It's Saturday, Aunt Iris,' she replied calmly. 'There's no work tomorrow.'

'And no sleep for some either with you carrying on. Your poor mother is exhausted waiting up for your return, and so am I, after keeping her company.'

Grace remained silent, sadness in her eyes. Jessie held her tongue but fisted her hands with the effort. She wouldn't add to her mum's misery by responding to Iris as she ranted on and on. It was like being back at school again, pulled out in front of 4C while Miss Renshaw asked her why she hadn't completed her homework, only it was worse; suddenly she felt her throat thicken and she shook her head slightly. She wouldn't cry, never, in front of this woman.

Iris got to her feet and walked over to Jessie, leaning into her, whispering hateful things, contorting her face; such an ugly, bitter face it was too. Jessie glanced down at Iris's hand, the palm flattened. Was she going to strike her? Is that what she wanted? Let her dare.

Jessie tensed her body and looked at her mum again. Her eyes were bright with fear, her hand at her throat. She mouthed, 'Don't', and gave the slightest shake of her head before looking down at the ground. It was the slightest of movements but enough to make Jessie reconsider and she swallowed hard and forced herself to say, 'I'm so sorry, Aunt Iris.'

Her mum looked up, relieved, because Jessie knew she had expected her daughter to defend herself, knowing they would all suffer if she did. 'It was selfish and thoughtless of me,' Jessie continued, making sure she looked suitably apologetic. 'It was good of you to wait with Mother. Thank you.' Did she sound sincere? She hoped so. Iris wasn't sure, Jessie could tell by her expression. 'I'd better let you all get to bed. I'll turn everything off and lock up.' It had taken the wind out of Iris's sails and they both knew it. Eddie stifled a yawn, and Iris glared at him.

'Let's hope we don't wake your Uncle Norman. He and Eddie are going out on the boat tomorrow, though what good Eddie will be to him is debatable. He's as tired as your mother and I, but he insisted on keeping us company. What a gentleman he is turning out to be.'

Eddie kept his head down, not wanting to invite comparison, and Jessie loved him for it, feeling exhausted when only moments before she had felt so vibrant and alive. How could they all carry on like this, afraid to be who they really were, slowly being shaped into the people Iris thought they should be. She felt a deeper anger and gritted her teeth. She apologised again, all the while wanting to scream at the old battle-axe.

Iris swept out of the room and Grace got up and rushed to Jessie's side, clasping her hands in hers, whispering, 'Did you have a lovely time, darling?'

'Wonderful, Mum,' she said. 'Harry tried everything to buy tickets for the show and kept on at it until he did.'

Grace smiled, her eyes twinkling in the dim light of the room.

Iris called from the hall, 'Are you coming to bed, Grace?'

Grace kissed Jessie on the cheek and whispered to her, 'Clearly she's not so worried about waking Norman now, is she? Was that a foghorn we just heard?' She and Jessie shared a triumphant grin.

So, her mum was not beaten entirely and, while there was a glimmer of her old fire, there was hope.

Grace brought her hand to her mouth and coughed, then put her arms out to hold Jessie close. As they hugged, Jessie felt Grace's shoulders sharp against her.

'I'll tell you all about it in the morning,' she said. Eddie moved to the corner and turned off the standard lamp.

'I'll lock up, Jessie. You go to bed.' He walked back to her and she ruffled his hair, he was almost as tall as she was now, and losing some of the gangly thinness that made him awkward. He was indeed growing into a fine young man. At least she and her aunt agreed on something.

Jessie left the curtains open and laid on the bed, fully clothed, staring out at the moon and the stars. The three of them shouldn't have to suffer this silent house; her mum deserved so much more than this. She thought of the people in the queue, and felt herself slowly untangle, and as she stared at the moon she realised it was not just because she was in the privacy of her room, but because this evening had woken her from the stupor in which her dad's death had left them. Tonight had given her happiness because of Harry, but also because she had been in the world she loved, a world that could help the war, and her family. She got up and went to the window, looking at the trees moving in the wind, the moon lighting up the garden. Would such a moon help the German planes? Would bombs drop? Would Harry go to war?

She shook herself free of the questions. For now she had to concentrate on the possibilities that she could create herself. And what were they? She heard the call of an owl. Well, tomorrow she would write to Bernie, her dad's old friend and agent. He'd have work and she would take anything, anything at all to make her life worthwhile, her family free ... and Harry ...?

'Oh Harry, will you ask me again, later? You see, I have work to do.' It was only a whisper, but it was a promise too.

Chapter 3

It had been almost a month and no news, not even the briefest of notes from Bernie. Jessie had been certain that he would've got in touch but as the days turned into weeks, she became more despondent, until every residue of hope had diminished. Her only consolation was that she'd kept it to herself. Even when she searched in the garage for her practice clothes and shoes, she had done so in the pretence of looking for a particular piece of music of her dad's. She'd found them at the bottom of a tea chest, one of four that were stacked along the back wall. Her shoes were worn but they still fitted, and she had tapped out a little routine in the cool darkness of the garage, delight fluttering like a butterfly. She had smuggled them into the house and squirreled them under her bed, waiting for the time they would be needed. What an idiot she would've looked to everyone if she'd told them of her plans. The thought of Iris's gloating satisfaction turned her stomach. She'd been a fool to imagine that Bernie would remember her. Things moved on, especially in the theatre. People were looking for something new; fashions changed, stars came and went. An act could be top of the bill one year and on their uppers the next. Nothing was secure; a good week could be followed by a bad month with no work at all.

A long summer season and even longer pantomime was the best she could hope for. She let out a long sigh and as the church clock chimed five, Miss Symonds pulled the cover over her typewriter and signalled for Jessie to do the same.

'Anything else will wait until tomorrow, Jessie.'

Jessie made a small pencil mark on the list of invoices on her desk, slid them inside a buff folder and pushed her chair back. She didn't need to be told twice, only too glad that another day was over.

Miss Symonds placed her neat handbag on her desk while she fetched her dark-grey jacket and hat from the stand in the corner.

It was Wednesday, Norman's half-day when he would see clients throughout the morning before leaving for meetings with the Chamber of Commerce and other worthy committees. Jessie had already taken the post and checked the waiting room was tidy so there was little to do before they left. The main reception office where she worked with Miss Symonds was always in order – Miss Symonds was a stickler for it – and it made it easy at the end of the day to simply get up and go. There was a place for everything, and Jessie was at last beginning to grasp where those places were.

'Mr Cole will no doubt be pleased with the progress you've made, Jessie. When you apply yourself you really are most efficient.'

Jessie closed the ledger on her desk and popped her pencil back into her pot. 'I do try, Miss Symonds, even if I don't always succeed.'

'But you will succeed, Jessie. I can tell you have it in you. You're that sort of girl.'

Jessie walked over to the cabinet behind Miss Symonds desk and stored her files while Miss Symonds pulled on her jacket and secured her felt hat with a large pin.

'I'm not sure whether that's a compliment or not.' Jessie grinned and Miss Symonds raised her eyebrows. She liked to tease now and again, and the old girl took it in good part even if she didn't join in.

'It is, and while I appreciate your attempts at humour, Jessie, it's best not to get in the habit of using it in the office. You might very well forget when there are clients present and Mr Cole would not be best pleased.' She took her gloves from her bag, snapping it shut.

Jessie slipped her chair beneath her desk. 'Bye, Miss Symonds. See you in the morning.'

'You will,' she replied, slipping her bag over the crook of her arm and patting her hat into place with a free hand. 'Have a pleasant evening, Jessie.' She left the office and rapped on Harry's office door that was the other side of the corridor. Jessie heard her say, 'Goodbye, Mr Newman', then the click of her footsteps as she moved down the short hallway. The bell over the door to the double-fronted offices of Cole's Solicitors rang out as she opened it; there was the brief noise of cars and horses in the street before the bell tinkled again as the door clicked to. Jessie pulled on her red jacket, flicking her hair out of her collar and went to get Harry. She peered around the door to his room that was barely more than a cupboard but a nod in the direction of his new status as junior partner.

'Nose to the grindstone, Mr Newman.' His desk was covered with stacks of papers and around him on the floor were more of the same. There was barely room to stand, Harry adrift in an ocean of paperwork. He continued to read, head down.

'I have my mark to make, Miss Delaney, a crust to earn.'

Jessie leaned over his shoulder. 'Looks like gobbledygook. But as long as you understand it.'

'I'd better or the Messers Huntley will be the poorer for it. And your uncle wouldn't be too pleased if I lost him one of his best clients.'

She took his jacket from the back of his chair, shook it gently and held it out for him in a signal to stop and turn his attention to her. He didn't disappoint. He slipped his arms in the sleeves, tugged on his lapels and planted a kiss on her nose.

'Why, Mr Newman, how very forward of you.' She laughed and he put his arm around her waist. 'Ready to go?'

They stepped out onto the high street, tucking themselves to one side to allow a woman pushing a pram to pass by. Further down Jessie could see the queue forming for the bus, and if it was any other day she would be with them but on Wednesdays Harry drove her home because Norman had collared him into tutoring Eddie through his exams. Not that Eddie was interested but at least it meant they could all benefit from Harry's company. He had a special way with Iris that seemed to curb her sharp tongue; Jessie had no idea how he managed it but was grateful all the same.

Harry locked the half-glazed front door that bore the name of Cole's Solicitors in gold lettering, tugged at the handle, then put the newly cut set of keys into his pocket. He made a sweeping arc with his arm. 'Your carriage awaits, Miss Jessie.' He held out his arm and she took it as they walked down the high street.

Holt was a pretty town with many Georgian buildings gracing the main street, their balanced proportions giving a sense of order and stability. The brick and flint walls of houses and shops that dotted the lanes and courtyards presented a sharp but pleasing contrast, and Jessie tried to imagine spending the rest of her life here, squashing down the surge of disappointment such thoughts generated.

They were in no rush and they dawdled along together, chatting, peering in shop windows as butchers and bakers emptied their window displays, blinds being pulled down in some windows, awnings pushed up on others. They passed Byfords, the ironmongers, and the pair of them glanced over to The Feathers where Uncle Norman would end up after his meetings. It was a sharp contrast to the grimy towns and cities they had visited in the old days when her dad was performing. She should enjoy being here; it was beautiful – the trees, the greenery, the pace easy – but she couldn't settle. Perhaps if her mum had a place of her own, if they didn't have to suffer the misery of each day with Iris, she could love being here, but as it was she only felt trapped.

The Austin was sluggish and back-fired, causing Jessie to jump in surprise. Harry gave a wry smile. 'I'm hoping Eddie will have a look it for me. He's very good at working out what's what.'

'He's been like that since he was a small boy.' It made her puff with pride. He was forever tinkering around with the props backstage, fiddling about with the mechanics of the curtains and the lighting rigs. 'Why on earth Uncle Norman wants to spend money getting Eddie articled I'll never know. His heart isn't in it. He'd be the first to say how much he hated it all. His passion is cars, engineering. He'd be far better suited to being apprenticed at the garage. That's what he really wants to do, that's what he's good at.'

Harry slowed down at the junction. 'Your uncle is only thinking of the best for him, Jessie. Eddie's very fortunate.'

'As am I.' She tried not to sound churlish, but Norman and Iris seemed intent on shoehorning them into things as they felt fit, rather than what Eddie and Jessie wanted. It was all so worthy, and she loathed it.

'No, I'm the fortunate one because I have you with me every day,' Harry said, putting the car into first and moving off down the Norwich Road. 'Or I do until you've made your decision, then we'll set a date and you won't have to type invoices day after day because you'll be making a home. Our home.' He turned to her, caught her hand. 'I hope?'

Jessie looked out of the window as they waited in traffic. Mr Chapman, the greengrocer, was dressed in his familiar brown overall, carrying in the boxes of vegetables that he set out every morning come rain or shine. His boy Sam was sweeping up the cabbage droppings behind him. How much longer would they be able to do that? Would things stay the same when war started, or would there be rationing again? It was all Iris went on about. How they needed to cut back on everything, and yet she didn't appear to apply the same rules to herself. It was plain that Iris resented every inch of space they occupied at The Beeches. As for making a home, their own home, she couldn't think about it no matter how much she wanted to. Not yet. It was what Mum had always longed for, a home of her own, and Dad had dragged them from town to town so that Grace never really had what she dreamed of. But she loved him and that had always been enough, or so it had seemed to Jessie. Dad wasn't here now, to give Grace her dream but Jessie was. It was unfair to ask Harry to take on all three of them.

She began to sing 'On the Sunny Side of the Street' and Harry joined in with her. She paused. 'It's impossible to be sad when you sing a happy song, isn't it?'

'And are you sad?' He indicated, turned his head to the right, then left.

'No, not sad. I was simply thinking that it is, isn't it? Singing makes you happy even if you don't start out that way.'

He mulled it over, pushing out his bottom lip. 'I've never given it a thought but you're right. I'll have to remember that when I'm feeling blue.' His hand rested on the gearstick and she squeezed it.

'I hope you never feel blue, Harry, or not very often, anyway.' Could she say that and believe it when all the talk these days was of war? Not if, but when. Well, she had to, because it was what she believed in, and they would all need to believe in something.

As they walked up the garden path, Eddie was by the back door soaking the inner tube from his bicycle in a tin bucket full of water, pushing down, watching for bubbles. The garage door was open, Eddie's bike balanced upside down minus one tyre. He beamed when he saw Harry. 'I'll be finished in a few minutes.'

'Drag it out as long as you like, Ed. I'm in no rush.'

Harry stood beside him, watching Eddie move the tube around. 'I was wondering whether you could take a look at my car later. It keeps backfiring. Must have a bit of dirt somewhere.'

Eddie stood upright puffing his chest out. 'You betcha.'

Jessie watched them for a moment, their heads together, chatting easily. To have two such men in her life was more than a girl could hope for.

In the kitchen she found Nelly washing and her mum drying after a baking session. A large fruit cake, light-as-air scones, and generously filled jam tarts sat cooling on the scrubbed pine kitchen table. Grace turned to greet her daughter, her hands busy drying a cake tin, a smile on her face that made Jessie question whether they couldn't find happiness here after all. If her mum and Eddie could adapt, then so could she. Perhaps it was just a matter of time.

'You've been busy. Smells scrumptious.' Jessie picked at a crumb and Grace tapped her hand playfully.

'You can wait like the rest of us.'

She kissed her mum's cheek. 'I bet Eddie didn't wait.' It was good to see her mum so relaxed; she'd obviously enjoyed a couple of hours in the kitchen while Aunt Iris reclined like Garbo on her bed for the afternoon.

'You're too old to lick the bowl, Jessie.' Nelly was passing Grace another bowl to dry.

Jessie rescued a sultana that had fallen through the cooling rack. 'But not too old to still want to.'

The grin went from Nelly's face when Iris entered the kitchen. Head down she turned back to the sink. Old hatchet face ruined everything. She looked like she had a permanent funny smell under her nose. Nelly dried her hands and went to get her jacket from the back of the kitchen door, and it was then that Jessie realised that Iris held a telegram in her hands. She held it out to Jessie.

'It arrived this afternoon.'

Jessie took it from her, holding it, reading the address, feeling excitement swell, or was it disappointment? She could hardly wait to tear it open, but mustn't, not here. Not in front of everyone, in front of Iris. Of course, she should have known; Bernie wouldn't do anything so subtle as to send a letter.

Grace was suddenly tense. 'What is it, Jessie?' Jessie looked at her mum, her gentle face pinched with worry. Jessie realised she should have told her a little of her intentions, but she hadn't wanted to worry her needlessly, in case nothing came of it. Her hands were trembling. Nelly was pulling on her jacket as slowly as she could, eager to eavesdrop, wondering whether it was good news or bad, and it gave Jessie courage. She needed to take the advantage. It would neuter Iris to have her there.

'It'll be from Bernie, Mum.' Her voice was wobbling now, and she took in a deep breath to steady herself.

'Oh,' Grace said, understanding immediately as Jessie knew she would. Her mum shook the tea towel and folded it squarely, holding Jessie's gaze, knowing, or perhaps fearing what was to come. The tap dripped and Jessie stared at it, droplets falling into the sink in a tattoo. She felt like she was falling too. Nelly moved and gave it a turn, grabbed a cloth and wrung it out. It gave Jessie the jolt she needed. She ran her finger under the envelope, grateful that today had been baking day and Iris unable to come into the kitchen and steam it open, because Jessie was certain that she wouldn't have waited otherwise.

'Who's Bernie?' Iris was clearly irritated by the silent connection between mother and daughter.

Jessie ignored her and read the telegram. Reading it again to make sure she was right. That Bernie had not let her down.

'It's Davey's friend, from the army. He was Davey's agent,' Grace said, filling the silence, allowing Jessie time to compose herself. Jessie looked directly at her mum. Grace understood, smiled, then sighed. It was the sigh that hurt Jessie so much. If only Iris hadn't brought it in, if only she and her mum could have had a private moment.

Beside her, Nelly was fussing about at the sink, giving it another wipe. It had never been so clean. The window was open to dispel the heat from the oven and she could hear Harry and Eddie outside – and a third voice – Uncle Norman? Yes, it must be. Well, she had a full audience so she might as well get it over with.

'He's my agent now, Mum. And he's offering me a job.' Her mum's expression did not change, and Jessie felt her courage return. Faced with a difficult situation Grace always said it was like lancing a boil. Best to get it over with and get the poison out. 'It's a variety show further up the east coast. I start next week.' She grinned, unafraid now because here at last was escape.

Iris gasped, her hand to her throat, but her words when they came were measured.

'Ridiculous girl. You already have a job, Jessica. A very good job for which you have been trained. Training that was costly to your uncle and myself.'

Jessie turned to her aunt whose eyes were dark now, and narrowed, her chin held high. No, Jessie told herself, her shoulders back and her head up, she would not be intimidated; not this time. She had a job, God bless dear old Bernie, and she would be leaving in days.

'I'm very grateful for the opportunity that you and Uncle Norman have given to me, Aunt Iris, and I will always have those skills, thanks to you.' She rubbed at her palm with her thumb, pressing hard, gripping the precious telegram, and all the time wanting to leap with joy and dance around the kitchen with her mum. 'But it's a chance to—'

'Ah, there we are ... a chance,' Iris spat, raising her voice to pierce Jessie. 'The theatre is full of chancers and dreamers. People like your father. Well, I have no idea what Norman will say.' Iris tugged at the cuffs of her blouse.

'No idea what I will say about what?' said Norman, striding into the kitchen, eyeing the cake and sniffing appreciatively. He removed his trilby and placed it on a chair. 'Still here, Nelly?' he said, peering over Grace's shoulder.

Nelly had been rumbled and she didn't like it. She'd have to leave just as the fireworks were starting. 'Just leaving now, Mr Cole.' She pushed past Iris, giving Jessie a thumbs up from behind her back. Jessie heard her chattering to Harry outside while she waited for Iris's next shot. She dearly hoped she wasn't telling him, for that was for Jessie to do, because she feared it would hurt him, and it tore at her heart but there was no other way.

'What will I say? Is anyone going to enlighten me?' He looked at the three women.

Iris took the lead as Jessie knew she would. Why waste her breath explaining? She glanced across at her mum – would Grace forgive her? Would Eddie, and, more importantly, would Harry? That was all that mattered and would ever be, that Grace would know that she was doing it for all of them. It was a chance to carry on her dad's legacy, to have the Delaney name written large upon playbills once more.

'Jessica here is throwing your kindness back in our faces, Norman,' Iris staggered to the chair, feigning weakness. If ever there was an actress in this family, it was Iris, Jessie observed. She could turn it on like the damned tap. 'She has taken another job. Not a steady, reliable job I might add.'

'Jessica,' Norman frowned, 'what does Iris mean?' He put his thumbs into his waistcoat pockets and leaned back, eyeing Jessie with suspicion.

'I haven't taken another job as a secretary, Uncle Norman. I have been offered one. In a theatre.'

'A theatre.' Norman twisted his mouth, dipped his head, shaking it in deliberation, as if he was in court and she the criminal, mulling over his words before he lifted his head again. 'So, you would give up a secure job for the precarious living that was your father's ruin?' He stepped forward, leaned into her. He was far too close, and she could smell his stale beer breath, but she wouldn't move back. How dare he try and bully her, and how dare he bring her dad into this.

'It was not my father's ruin; it was the joy of his life.' She felt her throat tightening and her voice was high. 'We were happy, all of us.' She turned to Grace who was standing so calm, being there for Jessie like the rock she was. Jessie saw the sadness in her mum's eyes. Was she the cause of it? Well, if she was, she would make it up to her, she would show Norman and Iris that her dad was right. If it hadn't been for the war ... The thought made her waver. Would she be damaged too? Wouldn't they all, when war came? Did it make any difference to try and change things, if Hitler was to march in at any moment? She saw Iris glaring at her, and her uncle's furious eyes and straightened herself. They would not win; she wouldn't let them.

'Hot-headed, just like your father.' She felt Norman's spittle, then he shook his head, turned, picked up his hat and strutted towards his wife, placing a comforting hand on Iris's shoulder. Iris pursed her lips in satisfaction. 'As if your poor mother hasn't suffered enough, and now you want to add to her distress.'

'I don't want to make Mum suffer, not like you, Iris.' Damn the formality, she wasn't her proper aunt and didn't deserve a title that indicated familiarity. She glared at Norman. 'I am not hot-headed, and neither was Dad; he was kind and gentle.' She longed to add, not at all like you and Iris, but Grace was standing there, so calm, so steady, and Jessie gained strength from it. This wasn't the time or the place. She mustn't shout, she must not raise her voice. She yearned to talk with her mum, alone, just the two of them so she could explain why, and how, and when. It had gone quiet outside. Nelly had left the back door open. If she hadn't told them already, had Harry and Eddie heard all this anyway? Damn. She'd gone over and over it all in her head and had intended to tell Harry in particular when there was something to tell, and but for Iris she could have done that. As it was, she felt the ground had been taken from beneath her feet.

'Don't interrupt, child. Norman, I was right, wasn't I? I should have known we would have to deal with the histrionics that come with theatricals, making an exhibition of herself, just like her father.' Iris reached up for Norman's hand.

Jessie balled her fists, the telegram crumpling, her sweat seeping into the paper. 'Well, you won't have to put up with theatrical me much longer. I'll be earning far more than I earn now.'

'Jessie,' her mum gasped. 'Please, don't.' The colour had drained from Grace's face but there was no going back. Jessie knew it was ungrateful, knew she shouldn't have said it, but her dad wasn't here to defend himself. He wasn't here to look after any of them, and Jessie had promised that she would do it for him. She felt hopeless, suddenly, but then drew in a deep breath and steadied herself, wishing she was nearer a chair so that she had something to hold on to. She would not give them the satisfaction of thinking they had crushed her.

Norman took his hand away from Iris and came towards Jessie. She stood square as he loomed over her, breathing that smell into her face again. He was ridiculous, and she wasn't scared; well; perhaps a little part of her was, only there was no way that she was going to show it. She concentrated on the black hairs that came from his nostrils, so many there and so few on his head.

'Tell me, Jessica: what makes you think you can support your mother when your father, a grown man, couldn't?' He folded his arms and waited for an answer. How she wanted to slap him on his big shiny nose as he stood before her but realised that that was what he wanted, and Iris too, so they could prove themselves right, that she was making an exhibition of herself. Her mouth was dry, her throat restricted.

'He was ill.' Her voice was quiet now; she was finding her equilibrium. Her dad knew she had the strength to look after Grace and Eddie. He'd had faith in her and she needed to have faith in herself because one day her mum would find her courage too, but not here, not in this house with these bullies.

'If that's what you want to call it,' Iris sneered, getting to her feet, her chair scratching on the tiled floor.

'Why, you spiteful—'Jessie was shaking with anger, the veins pulsing in her neck, her head.

'Jessie.' Grace's voice was sharp, and she barged in front of Norman, speaking directly to Jessie, taking her hands in hers, her grip strong and firm but her body was trembling. 'Let's talk about this later, when we're all calmer.' She held Jessie's gaze with hers and Jessie knew then that it was over, that there would be no more fighting.

'I am calm,' Jessie said flatly, wanting to weep, wanting her mum to hold her, knowing that she must be strong because she had to leave Grace behind and she couldn't make it more difficult for her. How long would it be before she could come back for Grace and Eddie?

'You most definitely are not.' Iris had got to her feet and was gripping the back of the chair, her knuckles white.

'Let's get some air, darling,' Grace said, her voice soft. 'Would you get my coat for me? I left it on the bed.'

Jessie let go of her mum's hand and left the room. She held on to the newel post, her heart pounding leaning into it to steady herself. Her legs were shaking, and she gripped the oak banister, hauling herself up the stairs, hearing the voices in the kitchen, her mum placating. 'Iris, she's young. We were all young once.'

'Young, yes; insolent, never. It's a good job she is going. I couldn't bear her here for one more minute. She's wild, Grace, and you need to tame her.'

Jessie gritted her teeth. She wasn't a bloody lion at the circus. She sensed that Iris was building up steam, relishing the chance to give full vent to her thoughts. 'That child doesn't appreciate all that Norman and I have given to her. And on a plate, mind you. When has your family ever had such a beautiful home to live in? And all the comforts and security that goes with it. Not to mention a steady, respectable position at a highly regarded solicitor's office. She's a little madam and no mistake.'

'Now, now, Iris.' Her mum again. 'Jessie is passionate—'

'Theatrical, as I so rightly said.' Iris sounded smug and self-satisfied and Jessie hated her.

'I'll have to get a replacement of course,' Norman chipped in. 'It's a damned inconvenience.'

Jessie reached the landing; well, she was glad she was an inconvenience. She went into her mum's room, took her faded coat from the bed, hugging it to her, and went over to the window. Down in the garden Eddie was fitting his newly repaired inner tube. Harry was steadying the bike while Eddie prised the tyre back into place with the aid of two soup spoons. She hoped they were Iris's best silver ones. Serve the old cow right. She suddenly felt utterly miserable at her outburst. Harry wouldn't want her now, would he? He'd think her hot-headed and hysterical, but he didn't know what it was like living here, being suffocated when all she wanted was to be allowed to be herself, to help her family to be themselves, to stand on their own feet, to stop being grateful but knowing all the time, that without this roof, for which they should all be *so* grateful, life would have been so very difficult, until they got it sorted. In her heart she felt it would have been the making of them all to do just that – sort it. Today had to come. And now it had.

She must make Harry understand that as much as she loved and wanted him, she had things to do. Leaving was the first step, one of many more ahead of her but she wouldn't turn back now. Nothing could be worse than this moment.

The boil was lanced, and the thought gave her energy. She slowly descended the stairs, calmer now. Her mum was waiting in the hall, her face expressionless. It must have been such a shock, such a disappointment but what else could she have done? She handed her mum her coat and Grace slipped it over her arm, opened the front door and stepped outside. Harry and Eddie were now on the lane outside the house, the bonnet of the Austin was up, and Eddie was leaning over the engine. Harry stood beside him, an oily cloth in one hand and he briefly looked at her and then away again. Her stomach tightened and she felt weak, all the energy that had been coursing through her veins sucked away in an instant. He had heard every word; of course he had.

'Come on, Jessie,' her mum said. 'We need to walk.'

Jessie followed her out into the tiled porch, pulling the door to a close, glimpsing Iris walking imperiously towards the drawing room as she did so, her face twisted in disgust. Jessie hoped she had given her a migraine, a real one this time instead of the fake ailments she peppered her day with. As she turned, her mother was holding out her arms and Jessie walked into the warmth of her; Grace hugged her with everything she had, kissing her forehead. When she released her, she touched Jessie's face with her fingers, wiping away the tears that Jessie had been unable to hold back. Jessie gripped her mum's hand. She longed to be a child again, when there had been just the four of them, but it was no good wishing. It was up to her to make a different life for them.

'It'll be all right, darling girl. Such exciting news for you ... for us.'

'Oh, Mum. I'm so sorry. Truly I am. I thought I'd have time to tell you—'

Grace put her fingers to Jessie's lips, shaking her head. 'You can tell me later but I think it's Harry you need to talk to now.'

Jessie sighed, where would she start? Harry was still beside Eddie; he hadn't looked at her again.

'Help him understand, Jessie.' She pushed the strand of hair from Jessie's face and tucked it behind her ear. Jessie squeezed her mum's hand one last time and walked down the red-brick path, opened the gate, closed it behind her. Grace watched, urging her to go on with a flick of her hand and an encouraging smile.

Harry looked up as she came and stood by the car. She could see the pain in his eyes. Eddie kept his head down twisting the radiator cap back and forth. Harry said nothing but she'd dealt the blow so she must take the lead to set it right.

'Will you walk with me, Harry?' He rubbed his hand on the oily rag and laid it on the engine beside Eddie who remained as he was. She placed her palm on her brother's back and kept it there. 'We won't be long, Eddie.' He nodded. Harry stood waiting for her to make the first move, so she started to walk along the lane towards the village and he got in step beside her, his hands thrust in his trouser pockets. She was suddenly flustered, not knowing what to do with her hands, she held them behind her back then let them drop to her sides, but it all felt so awkward. She held them in front of her, fingers linked, her thumbs a steeple. Where to begin?

The hedgerows were blousy with nettles and cow parsley, white fronds bent over towards the path. Poppies dotted the verges and swayed in the breeze. Jessie felt as if they had all been seeds, blown about in the winds since Davey had died. Her mum couldn't bear to look at them. Grace said they reminded her of her brothers, Sam and Albert, who she had lost in the Great War, and friends, so many of them. Jessie shuddered; please, God, it wouldn't happen to Harry if the time did come. She longed to pull his hands from his pockets, but what right had she, when she had gone behind his back.

Not knowing quite how to start, she began, 'I'm sorry, Harry. I wanted to tell you.'

He stopped. 'When?' he said, his voice fractured. She faltered; how would she find the right words?

'When I had something to say but the telegram came and—'

'I heard,' he said, walking again and she kept at his side. He kicked at a piece of gravel and it bounced along in front of them. 'You don't have to go, though. It's just an offer.' He turned to her, smiled, hopeful. 'We were making plans, for our future. What's the rush?'

'And we still can, Harry.' She frowned. How could she explain how crushing Iris was, how cruel? He wouldn't believe her, would he? No one would. Iris was sly, like a fox. Even Norman had no idea. 'I want to try though, surely you understand. Cleethorpes isn't that far away.'

'Why there? Why not Cromer, or Great Yarmouth? You could still do what you love and be here with me.'

She shrugged. 'It's all I've been offered.'

'Then wait. Wait for something nearer home.'

'I can't, Harry. I might never get another chance. Bernie is my only contact. If I turn this opportunity down who knows if another will come my way.'

She was shaking her head, ever so slightly, but he saw it and he looked away.

'When do you go?' He pulled at the grasses along the hedgerow and threw the heads onto the lane, avoiding her gaze when she longed for his eyes to meet hers, wanting his hand, his touch.

'Sunday.'

He stopped again, obviously shocked by how soon she'd be leaving. She couldn't bear the way he looked at her with such hurt in his eyes. She waited while the words sunk in; he nodded to himself, swept his hand across his face.

'Why didn't you tell me that you were even thinking of it? Where will you live, for God's sake?' His shoulders sagged and he seemed crumpled and defeated. 'You haven't thought this through. I know you haven't.'

What could she say? That she thought he might try to talk her out of it, that he would stop her, or tell Norman? No, he wouldn't have done that; she should have trusted him. He loved her. Did he still? Did he think she was hot-headed and hysterical as Iris did? In the distance buzzards circled the fields. Round and round in perfect circles and her head was spinning, round and round too. She didn't want to talk, she wanted him to hold her, as her mum had done, to tell her it didn't matter, that he would be there for her.

'Oh, Jessie.' He shook his head and walked off towards the church.

She watched him striding away from her, so strong. For a minute or two she couldn't move, unsure of herself, of what she wanted and then she was half-running towards him and she grabbed his hand because he had released them from his pockets at last and she held onto it, onto him, the tears falling freely. Holding onto Harry gave her strength.

She stopped, digging in her heels, gripping his hand so he couldn't release it. He stopped and she grabbed hold of his other hand, making him turn to face her. Her eyes glistened with tears but there was hope now, mingled with the sadness of hurting him.

'I'm doing this for Mum and Eddie. We need a place of our own, somewhere they can grow and be themselves, and I can do that, Harry. I can buy that for them, by being at the theatre. Do you understand?'

He shrugged. 'Not really. I can't see how you can sustain it. It's all so unpredictable. War is biting at our heels, Jessie. They've already called up the twenty and twenty-one-year-olds for national service; it's only a matter of time before they call the older men up, before I get called up. None of us will be safe.'

'But don't you see, Harry? There are no certainties, not ever. And how else can I help them, and myself?'

He pulled her close and she melted into his strong arms and when he kissed her, she knew it would be all right, that they would work it out.

'I had a plan,' he said. 'I was looking at places for us to rent. Together.' His voice trailed off.

'And we still can, Harry. But first I have to take care of Mum and Eddie. It's what Dad would have wanted.' The buzzards had gone now, the sky empty save for clouds that moved slowly onwards. 'It's not your responsibility, it's mine. I can't burden you with that. It's not fair.'

He put his hand to her face, and she took it and kissed it.

'It's not about fair, Jess. It's about love. If that means providing for your mum and Eddie, then I just need to work on a different plan.'

Would she ever love him more than this moment? She doubted it, for he could forgive her and still love her, and not only that, love Grace and Eddie too.

'*We* need to work on a different plan,' she said, suddenly full of optimism.

He put his arm around her shoulders, and she leaned into him as they began walking back to The Beeches, Jessie bracing herself for an icy blast from Iris that couldn't hurt her any more. She had Harry and that was all that mattered; everything else would work itself out in time. And they had all the time in the world.

Chapter 4

Eddie and Harry stood back as a gaggle of children piled onto the train with their parents close behind, apologising for their offspring's exuberance. A porter laden with cases and boxes tied with string followed them, and, as the father got on the train, started passing them up to him.

Grace smiled at the mother as she scooted the children to their seats and tried to get them to settle. It was good to see her smile; it had been so rare since Dad had died and it filled Jessie with a renewed sense that she was indeed doing the right thing by leaving, hard as it was. Living at The Beeches had not lessened their misery, merely added to it. The last time they'd been at the station was when the three of them had arrived less than a year ago. And now there would be only two of the Delaney family left together.

'You need to get your seat, Jessie,' Grace urged, coughing into her handkerchief, blaming the smoke that lingered around them. All along the platform people were stepping up into the carmine and cream carriages. A red-cheeked young couple wearing bright-coloured hats, their trousers legs tucked in their socks, were loading their bicycles into the guard's van and an elderly woman with a heavily laden basket was being helped onto the train in the next carriage. The air smelt of coal, and smoke hung about the platform.

Jessie hadn't expected to be in such turmoil. Although happy she was going, she was sad to be leaving loved ones behind, as well as fearful of being on her own. It had always been the four of them, there had always been someone else to rely on, but not any more. Life would be difficult but at least it was peppered with the hope of something better. She pitied her mum and Eddie going back to The Beeches. Iris had not spoken to her since the argument, not that it had bothered Jessie, but the fall-out would affect Eddie and Grace, not her who had been the cause of it.

The last two days at the office had been awkward. Norman had been curt, mostly communicating through Miss Symonds, who had been an absolute darling to Jessie. It would have been tortuous had it not been for her quiet and stoic support. This had surprised Jessie, for she'd expected Miss Symonds to have been of the same mind as Aunt Iris.

'Happiness is fleeting, Jessie, and you must take every chance you get to find it, and once you do, hold on to it with everything you have.' Her parting gift had been a lace handkerchief with Jessie's initial on it that she had embroidered herself. 'I hope if you have need of it that it's for happy tears and not sad ones, Jessie.' On Friday she had hugged Jessie so tightly that she'd been near to tears. 'I shall miss your cheery little face of a morning, Jessie.'

'And I shall miss yours, Miss Symonds.' They had both laughed and as she held the handkerchief now; she knew there had already been too many sad tears.

Harry opened the carriage door and put Jessie's brown leather suitcase inside. It had belonged to her dad and had travelled far more than she ever had. Before the Great War, Davey had played piano with orchestras in the grandest opera houses and concert halls all over the world. That world had been lost to him when he returned from France and could no longer sustain the arduous days, the hours of practice before a performance. In time, he'd grown to love the variety theatre and Jessie had known nothing else. Her love and passion for it had always been constant, a reminder of happier times. Harry stepped back onto the platform.

The station master was walking towards them, banging the doors shut and checking all was secure. Steam billowed from the undercarriage and leaked onto the station and the train creaked as it built up steam.

'Now, now, darling,' Grace said, as Jessie mopped her face. 'Today is a happy day, not a sad one. This is the first step of a wonderful adventure. Your father would be so proud of you, Jessie—' Grace's voice started to crack a little, which made Jessie pull herself together. Her head was swimming with Grace's instructions that she had drip fed over the last few days as she sought to protect her daughter as best she could from a distance.

Jessie repeated them silently now: Go home straight after the show, no parties; never go into a man's dressing room alone; never let a man in your dressing room; always take your make-up off before you leave the theatre; always give of your best. And no matter what: smile, smile, smile. It was hard to smile now but she would find it from somewhere, before she said goodbye. It wasn't as if she was starting at the top, merely part of the chorus, but she had taken that first step and she was determined to rise through the bill until she could earn enough to look after them all. Always.

Eddie threw his arms around her and held her tight. He'd changed since the telegram arrived and it all blew up, sensing perhaps that he would need to step up now that Jessie was going. He'd put on his smart shirt and tank top to see her off, but his hair was still tousled waves, the only unruly part of him.

'Look after Mum, Eddie,' she said, keeping her voice steady. She kissed his cheek and squeezed his hand, and he nodded.

'Of course I will, Jessie.'

Her lips trembled and she bit down on them to prevent the tears that were brimming again. What was she thinking of? He was still at school. What could he do but give of his best like her.

Grace took his hand, standing tall, as if Jessie was making a fuss about nothing. 'We'll look after each other, won't we, Eddie?' For a fleeting moment Jessie wondered if her going was a good thing after all. It was as if her leaving had revived something in her mum, that quiet inner strength that had been hidden these past few months, and Jessie took heart in it. The spark might yet become the flame.

Steam was coming from beneath the wheels and the sound of doors slamming was getting closer; she looked at the clock. Two minutes. Grace gave her another hug, 'Be careful, darling, remember what I said. The theatre will not be the same without your dad to watch over you.' Grace's tone was still positive but guarded a warning of the vagaries of being a single woman away from home, in a place that had a reputation for loose morals.

'But he will be watching over me, Mum,' Jessie said, confident that he was, that he would always be with her. Another kiss and Grace stood back.

'Come on, Eddie. Let's give Harry a turn to say goodbye.'

They walked towards the small bench by the station waiting room; Grace began reading the timetables with great intensity and Eddie had struck a conversation with the porter now that the passengers were all on board. The crush on the platform was easing as people left the station or stood back ready to wave goodbye.

Harry held her close and at that moment, if he had asked her to stay, she would have wavered because it felt so wonderful to be with him, to smell the freshness of his skin against hers. He lifted her face to his and kissed her and she longed for him to be coming with her.

'Oh, Jessie. I don't know if I can bear to let you go.'

She grabbed both of his hands and gripped them so fiercely that it hurt her fingers. 'I don't want to live a life of regrets, Harry. I want to try and make a success of my life, and God bless you for understanding, for making it easier for me.' He had been incredible since that awful evening when she thought she might have lost him. They'd talked and talked at every available moment, and even though he hated for her to leave, he knew she must.

'I'm busily adapting those plans I had, Jessie.' He kissed her full on the mouth and his lips were hard and warm. 'We'll work on a way together, so that we're both happy.'

She nodded, the words escaping her when she needed them most, but if she spoke there would be more tears, and this time she might not be able to stop.

The station master walked along to other carriages and said as he passed them, 'You need to get on that train, miss, or we'll be leaving without you.'

She saw the yearning in Harry's eyes, saw how much he wanted her to miss the train and stay with him. He kissed her so hard that she could scarcely breathe with longing, then pulled gently away from her, taking her hand while she stepped up onto the train, closing the door behind her. She pushed down the window and leaned out, held his hand.

'Make sure you write, Jessie Delaney. I want to know everything, and I'll be coming to see you on opening night. We all will.' Grace and Eddie came to stand behind him, and she fought back more tears. She would miss them all so much. She had no idea of what lay ahead for her, but she would make a success of it, for all of them and for herself, and then this tearing pain of parting would have been worthwhile.

The station master blew his whistle and waved his flag; there was a loud hiss as the brakes were released and the train slowly began to move off.

Grace and Eddie stood waving and Harry ran along beside the carriage until the platform ended and she watched him, standing there until the train curved the bend and they were all gone from sight.

She found a seat, stowed her suitcase, sat down and leaned her head on the window, watching the familiar landscape fade and blend into the new. Had she done the right thing? She bit back tears. Too late to turn back now. She would make a success of this opportunity and then the only way was up. Harry had a plan and so did she, and they would meet somewhere in the middle.

Chapter 5

The train was delayed at Doncaster and they spent two hours in the siding while another engine was found and linked to the carriages. It was hot and stuffy and people started to moan and grumble, the children becoming fractious.

She was grateful for the bottled lemonade and wrap of sandwiches her mum had prepared, along with a generous slice of the fruit cake that had been baked on that onerous Wednesday, when the telegram had arrived. Everything had happened so quickly that it was only during the train journey that she'd had time to reflect on the momentous decision she'd taken when she wrote to Bernie Blackwood. It wasn't quite what she'd envisaged but it was a step in the right direction.

She wondered now whether she should have waited for something that paid better: soubrette, perhaps; a crooner. Had she been too hasty? Iris's words tumbled about in her brain. Hot-headed. Wilful. Unsuitable. It was unsettling.

She reached into her bag for the lemonade. She forced herself to think of her dad. Mum said he'd be proud. Would he? Would he be happy that she'd left Grace and Eddie behind? It was too late for second thoughts now. It felt as if the whole country was holding its breath for something to happen and she wanted to breathe. She pulled the stopper from the bottle and took a swig of lemonade, then licked her lips. It was warm but still refreshing.

It was all behind her now and the only way was to go forward and make a success of her new life. There had been tears, of course there had, and even though she felt the wrench of leaving them to suffer Aunt Iris, she knew in her heart they would be better off without her. Things would be more settled because her mum could tolerate Iris's petty ways whereas she could not. And Eddie was Eddie; he was a different temperament to Jessie, calm and measured. He got on well with Uncle Norman, who seemed to like him too. It was Jessie who was the square peg.

Jessie watched the mother valiantly try to restore order with her brood and debated silently whether to offer them some of her lemonade. She clutched the bottle. What if they had chickenpox, though, or something else? And their little mouths would be wrapped around the neck. The last thing she needed was a tummy upset. She scolded herself. How could she be such a snob?

She held out the bottle to the mother who looked like her nerves were shredded already. 'Would the children like a sip of lemonade?'

The mother smiled and shook her head.

'That's really kind of you but I have water somewhere in the cases. I've sent their father in search of it.'

Jessie laughed to herself. Perhaps the mother didn't want her children getting Jessie's germs. The minutes ticked by and still they waited. Jessie stared out at the sidings, watching sooty-faced men jump up and down from a line of trucks. The mother sang gentle nursery rhymes and jiggled the little girl on her lap. Her other blonde-haired daughter, who Jessie guessed was about five or six, huddled to her mother's side and watched as Jessie began to unwrap her cake. Jesse smiled as the child's eyes grew round when she saw the plump fruit fall onto the napkin that was spread about her skirt.

'Would you like some of my cake? My mummy made it for me.' She looked askance to the mother, and she smiled and nodded that it was okay to share her bounty this time. Jessie broke the cake into pieces and offered them from the napkin.

'Where are you going?' Blondie asked.

'Shh, poppet, don't be so rude. The lady might not want to share her business.'

It was a welcome chance to talk, to break the monotony as time continued to drag. 'I'm going to dance on the stage. It's in Cleethorpes, at a theatre called the Empire.'

There was a snort of derision from the woman in the seat by the aisle. She was wearing a buttoned-up tweed suit that was far too unsuitable for the time of year and looked at Jessie as if she was the dirt on her shoe. There were far too many Irises in the world. Did she have to meet them all?

'Why that's a wonderful thing to do,' the mother said, loudly in Jessie's defence. 'Good for you. We all need a bit of cheer these days.' She took Blondie's hand.

'We'll have to save up and see the show, won't we, girls?'

The father returned bearing bottles of water and a flask, which made his wife's eyes shine with relief. She unscrewed the cap and poured steaming hot tea into the cup, sharing it with her knight in shining armour. Minutes later the train moved off and Jessie sat back in her seat, her head full of dreams.

The train stopped briefly at Grimsby, then again at Grimsby Docks. Freight wagons lined the sidings and Jessie held her scarf to her face to filter the rank air that reeked of fish and coal. They pulled into the station at Cleethorpes soon after and she had been surprised how swiftly the landscape had changed, from warehouses and terraces to reveal the crowded promenade and the pier stretching way, way out, into the middle of the sea, the late afternoon sun glistening on the water.

She waited for the train to come to a complete stop before getting to her feet, allowing the other passengers to lift down their cases from the luggage racks, children jumping up and down in excitement now that they were home again. It felt good to stretch and stand. Passengers bustled down the corridor, lugging their cases in front of them, dragging their children behind as they headed for the doors. She felt a gentle tap on her arm and found little Blondie standing before her, a penny in her out-stretched hand.

'It's for you,' she said shyly, swinging herself from side to side. Her cheeks were pink and she fluttered her eyelashes. Jessie bent towards her.

'I couldn't possibly take your penny, but you are a very kind little girl.' The girl remained steadfast, the penny bright in her tiny fingers. The mother clasped the child on her shoulders.

'Yes, keep it.' She smiled. 'You never know when you might need to spend a penny.' The two women laughed, and Jessie took the coin from the child.

'I will keep your penny as my lucky charm and always remember that you gave it to me on this special day. Thank you.'

Jessie picked up her vanity case in one hand, her suitcase in the other and stepped out onto the platform. The sun was shining and there was still warmth from it even though it was early evening. A stiff breeze blew in off the sea, lifting discarded tickets and scraps of paper, sending them skittering along in front of her. The bustle of the station had eased, most of the passengers had already poured past the station guard, holding out their tickets. She stood on the platform, watching as cleaners boarded the train, doors slamming behind them. A whistle blew on the other platform and the train pulled away, billowing smoke as it chugged forward, galvanising her to move.

She walked along the platform hoping that the theatre wasn't too far away, for she was weary now and her case heavy. How many times had they arrived as a family on platforms around the country, her dad leading the way giving instructions to the porter, her mum holding on to her and Eddie as they found their bearings? It was all but fleeting shadows now; she was stepping out alone and she needed to get her bearings too. She handed over her ticket and stepped into the station where people gathered around the buffet and ticket office. The station walls carried posters of shows and cinema performances on every surface along with adverts for Lifebuoy and Pears soap. Was one of them advertising the Empire? Porters leant on trolleys stacked with cases, and a fat man with the curliest moustache Jessie had ever seen sat on his trunk reading a newspaper. Everywhere was hustle and bustle. It was hard to believe it was Sunday at all. Her thoughts skipped to her mum at The Beeches, the interminable silences of her days.

'Carry your bag, miss?'

A boy of around eleven stood by her with a cart that looked not much more than a box on pram wheels. She would've loved to hand her case over, but every penny must be accounted for. And never would she spend her precious penny from ... oh, she hadn't even asked her name. Well, she would give her one. She recalled the child's sweet face, her gentle blue eyes, and smiled. She would call her Hope; it seemed fitting. Hope's penny.

'I can manage, thank you,' she replied. 'How far is it to the Empire?'

It was all the invitation he needed. 'I'll show you. It's tuppence.' He loaded her case on the wagon, took the handles and began to walk. 'Are you for the show? Yer look pretty enough'.

She smiled at his cheek. She could go to tuppence and if it would save the case banging against her legs and laddering her stockings it would be worth it. He started walking. 'Are ya cummin' then?' He had already weaved along the platform and through the barrier and she hurried after him as he snaked amongst the travellers ahead of them.

'D'ya want the quick route or the scenic route?' he called over his shoulder and Jessie hurried a little so that she came to walk beside him.

'How long will the scenic route take?' She was already delayed by two hours so a few minutes more wouldn't hurt. It would be good to see the nicer parts of the resort.

'Same as the quickest.' He grinned. 'Scenic it is then.' He hitched up the cart and turned left out of the station and down the ramp to the promenade while Jessie took the steps, squeezing past people pouring back into the station. He pulled the cart onto the parade and once again tacked through the hordes calling, 'mind yer backs', at intervals as the crowds parted to let them through.

The clattering of machines in the penny arcades sounded thunderous after the steady thrum of the train, and the air held the tang of salt from the sea mingled with sugar from the shops, which sold sticks of rock and filled the gaps between the amusements. Windmills, buckets and spades were stacked outside gift shops while the window displays were crammed with egg timers, ashtrays and perpetual calendars with Cleethorpes painted on them; cheap souvenirs that would be taken back to family and friends when holiday time came to an end.

She followed the boy until he turned right at the pier, stopped, then nodded towards the top of a small incline where she could clearly see the Empire facing them. It was an elegant building, windows across the top and what looked like a balcony over a wrought-iron canopy that arched over the doorways into the building. Empire Theatre was written in large white letters on the end wall to the right so it could be seen way across the promenade, advertising its presence to anyone who cared to look away from the sea.

The hairs bristled on the back of her neck. This was her beginning and she drank it all in so that she would always remember this moment, the moment she had taken her destiny into her own hands. The boy nipped across the road and Jessie followed, taking in the floral displays that ran down the centre of the road while avoiding the bicycles and cars that were heading down to the promenade. No wheat or barley here, no brown fields, only artfully clever plantings of begonias and bizzy lizzies in a riot of colour. Oh, to at last have a life with colour. Once again, she was reminded of the quiet Sundays back at The Beeches. This was much more to her liking.

She quickened her pace and caught up with him, feeling a renewed sense of energy. Car horns tooted and startled her. She would have to get used to the noise. They waited for a bus and two charabancs go by then crossed the main road and came to a halt outside the row of glass doors that ran along the theatre frontage. Light bounced off the brass finger-plates and handles.

At either side of the doors glass display cases held photographs of stars who were booked or had already performed there. She quickly scanned the playbill; a comedian, an acrobatic act, a magician, musical act, singers, and towards the bottom The Variety Girls. She felt a tingle in her spine. There she was, albeit hiding in plain sight at the bottom of the list. The only way was up, and she was ready to make it happen.

'D'ya want yer bag 'ere or round back?'

She pulled at the doors in turn. They were all locked. She leant forward and peered through the glass, but it was dark and there was no movement or light within.

'Round the back then.' He began walking to the end of the road then turned the corner. She pulled a handbill from the display on the wall, tucked it in her pocket and went after him, taking note of the café and sweet shop as she did, the Dolphin Hotel on the opposite corner. She saw him walk past a few more shops on the small side street that led towards a market square and then turn to a street than ran along the back of the theatre. She looked up; Dolphin Street. The first thing she noticed was the sign for the stage door protruding between what must be the backs of the shops and cafés that were situated on the main road. On the other side of the street ran a row of terraced houses. He stopped his cart and took her case off by the stage door, rattled the door, knocked loudly. They waited.

'Sunday, innit. No one here.'

'But there must be?' There had always been some-one around on a Sunday when she was with Dad. It dawned on her how much she didn't know, and how Davey had taken care of so many of the small details that this life involved. There was so much to learn. She berated herself. How stupid she had been not to make firm arrangements.

He shrugged. 'I knocked, the door's locked. Ain't no one here. George would have answered it by now, slow as he is.'

She ran her hand through her hair; she had been relying on the theatre to get a list of digs as Bernie had not been forthcoming. She'd have to walk the streets in search of a Bed and Breakfast in order to find something for the night. She sat down on her case, exhausted.

The boy left the cart and dashed across the street, past the first couple of houses, leapt over the low wall and hammered on the window. Seconds later a short, stout, elderly man with a shock of white hair stepped outside. He was in his shirtsleeves, braces over his chest attached to grey trousers that puddled a little about his slippered feet. He pushed his glasses up the bridge of his nose with one finger and peered at her, beckoning her over with a wave of his arm.

Her body sagged with relief but then she hesitated – should she waltz off into a stranger's house without a second thought, just because she was tired? She looked again, he looked safe enough – and he was in his slippers. Realising she was short of options, she picked up her suitcase and walked towards him. The old man gave the boy a nudge and he ran back and took it from her.

The man was smiling as she walked towards him and he put out his arm and gently guided her to the house.

'Come in, come in, lovey, and let's get you sorted. The missus is through the back.'

Jessie hesitated, her relief vying with her mum's words. Should she go in? He looked kindly enough, but you never could tell, and her mum had warned her to keep her wits about her.

'I couldn't impose,' she stuttered. 'I thought the the-atre would be open; there's usually a list of digs.' Her voice trailed off; she felt like an idiot. She should've made plans and if she couldn't make the simplest of them what chance would she had of making bigger ones. She ached all over.

'Still is, lovey, all a bit up in the air at the moment,' he said. 'New owner and all that. Only just taken over, he has. Gets a bit confusing at times.'

The boy dropped her bag by her feet. 'This is George, stage doorman over road.'

George shook his head, patting the boy on his back. 'Thank you, Alfie. I should have introduced myself, Miss. Do forgive me.'

Jessie relaxed a little. He was connected to the the-atre so he would know of lodging places or at least a boarding house that would be suitable. She opened her purse and paid Alfie and he slipped the pennies into his pocket, took the handles of his cart and did an about turn. George picked up her suitcase and placed it in the narrow hall then led her through a door near to the bottom of the stairs that opened into a sitting room and then a kitchen. Light flooded in from the large bay window at one side that had a table and four chairs set inside it. A slip of a woman was settled in a chair, knitting bootees in lemon wool, her fingers busy, her head tilted towards the wireless. She leaned across and turned it down low when she saw Jessie. Her salt and pepper hair was set in neat curls and her eyes were bright blackberries that almost disappeared when she smiled.

'Take a seat.' George gestured to a chair opposite the woman at the other side of the fireplace. Jessie sat herself down and adjusted the plump green cushion at her back. George patted his wife's shoulder. 'This is Olive, the missus. Now can I get you a drink? A nice hot cuppa, there's already one in the pot, or a glass of water?'

'Tea would be lovely, thank you, George.' She quickly glanced about her. The room was plainly furnished; pictures, paintings and little photos were placed here and there and it was homely and cosy. The rag rug at her feet was full of colourful scraps. So different to the museum that Aunt Iris curated.

Olive reversed her needles and started another row, drawing the wool with deft fingers. 'Have you just arrived, lass?'

'Yes, my train was delayed.' Jessie slipped off her gloves and laid them on her lap. 'It was a bit short notice. My agent got me the job last minute, so it's all been a bit rushed.'

Olive nodded, her hands busy with the wool and needles.

'Our Dolly will be able to help. She'll be back soon enough. She's been babysitting round her sister's.' She tugged at the wool that was balled at her side and Jessie noticed a walking stick propped beside the chair.

'My mum was always knitting,' Jessie said, remembering. 'She doesn't do it so much now. She sews.' As Olive continued to knit and chat, it dawned on Jessie precisely why her mum chose to sew these days. The close attention it warranted didn't invite conversation. Not that any had been forthcoming, because Iris liked the sound of her own voice or none at all, and the constant click of needles, no matter how quiet would have no doubt given her a migraine. Her mum was cannier than Jessie had ever realised. Why did it all seem to clear now that she was so far away?

Olive was talking again. 'I always seem to be knitting bootees and matinee jackets. I've another grandchild on the way. That'll be six,' she said proudly.

George brought a tray laden with the tea things and placed them on the footstool, putting Olive's knitting bag on the floor beside her. He placed three cups on saucers and poured from the brown glazed teapot. 'Milk?' he asked. Jessie nodded and he poured a splash, handed her the cup and saucer and pushed one in front of Olive. He pulled a chair away from the table in the window and sat astride it then drew his large hand around his chin and pulled at it. Jessie noticed his swollen knuckles and wondered if they were painful, they certainly looked it.

'What's your name, lass? We didn't even ask, did we, Olive?'

Olive carried on knitting, the needles clicking a steady rhythm.

'It's Jessie, Jessie Delaney. I'll be one of the Variety Girls.' It made her smile to say it aloud; it was if she already belonged somewhere else.

Olive nodded. 'Thought you might be. Tall girl like you.'

'Are you staying put then? The girls tend to stay a long time.' George leant back into the chair. 'Steady work's not always easy to come by.'

'I have a contract for three months and then, who knows. They might not like me.'

'I'm sure they will.' George was encouraging. 'You might not like us.'

Jessie shook her head, put her cup back on her saucer. 'Oh, that's not in question. I've only been here a short time and already you've been so kind.'

The back door opened into the kitchen and a blonde girl walked in.

'Here's our Dolly now,' George said.

The girl kissed him on the forehead and kissed Olive who put down her knitting and her hands went up to Dolly's shoulders. 'Dolly's our youngest. Only one left at home now.' Jessie noticed how blue her eyes were. She had the most beautiful complexion and her lips were full and pink. 'Dolly works at the theatre front of house of an evening. This is Jessie, Dolly; she's one of the Variety Girls.'

'Nice to meet you.' The girl flashed a smile that made her eyes sparkle and Jessie warmed to her as she settled herself on the arm of her mother's chair.

'Jessie needs somewhere to stay tonight, Dolly,' Olive said over her shoulder. 'Didn't have time to sort things out before she left home.'

Jessie felt her ears burn at her inadequacy, ruing her impulsiveness.

'My agent, Bernie . . .' She paused. 'Someone dropped out and—'

George put a hand to her knee and tapped it. 'No need to explain, Jessie; you can stay with us tonight, give you a chance to sort something out tomorrow when you're not so tired.'

'I couldn't possibly,' Jessie was flustered faced with such kindness.

'Course you can,' Olive said. 'We're always having theatre people to stay. You're not the only one who turns up last minute. No arguing. And Dolly will like having someone of her own age to talk to instead of us old biddies.'

Dolly nodded and Jessie noted that she did seem pleased, as she was herself. She hadn't known anyone young in Norfolk, save for Harry, and the Delaneys had been on the road so much before that that friendships were fleeting.

'That's settled then.' George got to his feet. 'You girls get the table ready and Dolly will help you sort the bedroom later.'

Olive reached for her stick, stood up and shuffled to the kitchen. Jessie watched as she and George worked together, passing plates, giving instructions; it was an echo of what her mum and dad were like, working as a partnership, all of them together, not solitary as it was with Iris and Norman. It hadn't dawned on her until now that they were so separate. Did Iris and Norman ever do anything together? She couldn't think of a thing.

Dolly pulled the table away from the bay and Jessie sprang to her feet to help. 'I've done this more times than I care to remember.' She squeezed through the gap and round to the other side of the table. 'Good job I'm not much bigger.' She smoothed her hands down her skirt checking for snags. 'Escaped again,' she grinned. 'Always catching myself on something or other; proper clumsy.' She flicked a checked cloth over the table and set place mats around it.

'Your skirt is beautiful, so pretty,' Jessie admired the clever waistband that swept into a V and accentuated Dolly's already tiny waist.

'Made it myself,' she said proudly. 'At least I'm good at something.'

Olive held a plate of freshly cut slices of bread. 'Don't you sell yourself short, our Dolly. You're a very talented girl if you could but see it.'

Dolly smiled awkwardly, took the plate and passed it to Jessie with a nod in the direction of the table. 'Put that there, Jessie. You sit yourself down, Mum; I'll help Dad do the rest.'

Olive sat down and Jessie joined her and in no time at all they were all enjoying bread and butter and ham followed by tinned fruit salad and condensed milk.

'I've got a cupboard full of this, Jessie,' she said with a twinkle in her eye. 'Yon cupboard under the stairs is filling up nicely. There'll be shortages before too long, no doubt about it, so I'm making a start and putting things by.'

'There'll be no supplies if you keep dipping into them, Mother.' George teased, while Dolly collected the dishes and put them by the sink.

Olive shrugged her shoulders. 'It's Sunday. We always have fruit and cream on Sunday.'

George reached across and took his wife's hand. 'We do indeed.'

Jessie was warmed by their affection for each other. She thought of Harry, how kind he had been these last few days, helping her to leave when it was the last thing he'd wanted. Would they be together in years to come?

'You said that the theatre had new owners,' Jessie said now, slipping from the table to help Dolly with the washing-up. Dolly handed her a tea towel and Jessie began drying the plates resting on the draining board.

'The theatre's been having a bit of a rough time these last few years – owners ran out of money then it closed, opened as a cinema for a few years, closed again – but I reckon this show will bring them in. Folks love a variety show hereabouts.' George eased back into the chair, resting his arm on the table. He watched Olive protectively as she went back to her chair by the fireside and when she was settled, he continued. 'The new owner is a hands-on sort of chap. Jack, his name is, Jack Holland. He seems all right. Directing the show as well, so I hear. Suppose he's trying to save money where he can – until he knows what's what, like. We'll have to see what happens, can't do much else.'

'Well, let's hope it can manage to struggle on,' Olive said, taking a small bag from the mantelpiece and taking out a Nuttall's Mintoe. She offered them around but there were no takers. 'Too many of them have been turned into cinemas these days.'

George shrugged. 'You can't blame the owners, love; they're in it to make money when all's said and done.'

'It's not the same as a live show though, is it, Dad?' Dolly chipped in. 'With films it's the same every night. It's not like that when the acts are on stage. Singers, dancers—' she grinned at Jessie '—dogs acts, acrobats, jugglers, magicians. That's why I love it. Anything can happen.' Jessie thought of the dove that had made a break for it in Cromer.

'And it frequently does,' Jessie agreed. The two girls shared a smile and Jessie felt she'd made a friend.

Dishes dried, Dolly began putting them away on shelves and in cupboards, and Jessie went back to the table. George gestured for her to sit back in the armchair opposite Olive, which she did, adjusting the cushion behind her back and settling into it.

'How long have you been dancing, Jessie?' Olive picked up her needles.

'I'm not really a dancer,' she confessed. 'Although I can dance,' she said hurriedly to qualify. 'I've appeared in pantomimes and shows since I was tiny, but my dad was a classical pianist and he taught me to play.' She was instantly reminded of the hours and hours he had

sat with her, the encouragement, the patience he possessed, his beautiful long fingers that had danced across
the keys to illustrate technique. He'd given her so much.
She smiled at Olive. 'But mostly I love to sing.'

Dolly wiped over the table. George got up and together
they nestled it back into place. 'I'd love to be able to
play the piano,' Dolly said. 'It must be wonderful.'

'It is,' said Jessie, thinking of the comfort it gave her,
and the way it soothed Grace. It felt like the only thing
Jessie had ever been able to give her mum.

They spent the evening chatting companionably
and Jessie relaxed for what seemed like the first time
in months. It was so easy here, being with people who
were not trying to catch her out, who took her for what
she was. They'd invited her into their home without a
second thought and with such warmth and generos-
ity that she felt she had known them half her life. The
rhythmic sound of Olive's needles soothed her, and her
eyelids became heavy; she fought to stifle a yawn.

'Time you got your rest, lass, you've a busy day ahead
of you tomorrow.' George took off his glasses and
rubbed his eyes and Jessie felt humbled by the kindness
they had shown her. They must be tired too.

She said goodnight and Dolly showed her to the
spare room. It was long and thin, a single bed pushed
against one wall, a dark wardrobe on another, a window
looking out onto the yard at the back. The wallpaper
was sprigged with ribbons and roses; soft light glowed
from the damson-coloured shaded lamp on the bedside
table. Dolly ran her hand across the bed and patted it,

smiling with satisfaction that all was as it should be. 'I pulled the sheets back earlier to air it for you.' She peered around the door before pulling it shut. 'If you need anything, I'm only next door.'

Jessie sat on the bed. She could hear Olive and George making their way up the steep stairs, their low voices, their sweet kisses on Dolly's cheeks as they went to their rooms. Her thoughts turned to Grace. How long before she would kiss her mum goodnight again? She listened as lights were turned off, the creak of the mattress as George and Olive got into their bed. Tonight, she was fortunate; she had been taken in by a family who made her heart pinch with longing for her mum's arms. But what would tomorrow bring?

Lying in bed, she thought of Harry. How she missed his steady presence in her life. He gave her courage and self-belief and she longed to be able to talk to him now. Was Iris right? It had been embarrassing not to have at least planned where she would stay; George and his family must think her simple. Fear caught at her again as it had done since the telegram had arrived, but she forced it away. She would not go back; she wouldn't give Iris the satisfaction. A cat screeched, then a dog barked until a gruff voice shouted for it to shut up. She turned on her side and studied shadows on the bedroom wall, listening to footsteps as someone walked down the alley outside. In the morning, she would get herself organised and find somewhere to stay; this was no time for self-doubt and when Grace and Eddie came it would be to a home like this. A real home.

The thought comforted her then disturbed her; oh Lord, was she completely foolish? She sat bolt upright. She hadn't even mentioned money to Olive and George, and would she have enough? They had been so generous, so welcoming, and she hadn't offered them anything in return. Her face burnt with the shame of it. What on earth must they think of her? In the morning she would broach it, first thing. She threw off the blankets and went to her purse, and took out Hope's penny. She must always remember the pennies. Always. She kissed it and placed it under her pillow.

Chapter 6

Neglect and lack of investment over the last few years had rendered the Empire shabby. No longer did it shine like the jewel it once was. The plush red furnishings had faded and worn through in parts and the gilt that decorated the ornate arches, the balconies and proscenium arch were chipped, the broken parts shining out like pimples on an otherwise smooth face. It was still beautiful, Jessie thought while standing centre stage, looking past its many faults, glad to be somewhere that felt familiar.

'It's a pretty little theatre, big enough but not so big that it's not cosy.' George was standing next to her, thumbs under his braces. He had slicked his hair back this morning and was wearing his outdoor shoes. Jessie had broached the subject of payment for her night's stay, but George and Olive wouldn't hear of it. They'd been almost offended, and Jessie didn't press the point but consoled herself with knowing she could return their kindness when the first opportunity presented itself.

'Yes, pretty describes it perfectly, George. It must look wonderful when the sets are in place and the seats are filled.' She imagined the rows full of smiling faces and closed her eyes. One day, one day soon, she would take this centre stage and hold it, singing her heart out and taking her bow, but for the moment she had to be content with being part of a chorus of dancing girls. She opened her eyes. She didn't mind sharing for now.

A stockily built man came and stood mid-stage, shouting instructions up into the flies. He was wearing a dark-grey waistcoat that matched his trousers, his striped shirtsleeves rolled up to the elbows, showing arms as freckled as his face, his red hair stuck up like the bristles of a toothbrush.

'Ah, this is Mike, Jessie. He's the stage manager.' Behind them backcloths were being flown in and out. Mike shook his hand in a brief wave but didn't stop. Now and again other members of the stage crew drifted on stage, busying themselves with bits of maintenance and checking the tabs flowed open and shut smoothly, that the ropes were not tangled.

'Let's hope these seats are filled for every show from now on, lass,' George continued. 'The theatre's been through a bit of an up-and-down time lately, as I said.' He moved closer. 'Bad management, if you ask me, but I do believe Jack is a different fish.' He squeezed her arm. 'Now, I'd best be getting on, and remember, if you don't get sorted tonight you're coming back with me.' She was about to protest but he held up a hand. 'No argument,' he said, and walked offstage.

She stepped down into the auditorium. The seats were fixed and slightly raked, and she wandered down the centre aisle, slid into the seat at the end of a row, tipped the cushion forward and sat down. She took her practice shoes from her bag and slipped them on.

They pinched in places but she felt certain they'd be all right. They had to be; she couldn't afford a new pair. She waited, already in her rehearsal clothes, for the other members of the cast to arrive and closed her eyes. She had barely slept even though the bed she had been given was comfortable and the room cool. Through the open window she'd heard the sounds of the street, the milk floats, the clatter of glass bottles and crates being lifted into position as the load was emptied. It had all seemed so easy, planning her future in her room at The Beeches, but reality had been like a slap in the face, and it stung.

There was a murmur of voices and light flooded in as the theatre doors were opened behind her. Jessie got to her feet. A bottle blonde, hair in a ponytail, was issuing orders to the girls behind her as she came down the aisle towards the stage, her head high, shoulders back and chin jutting forward, and Jessie knew in an instant that she was the choreographer. She was clutching a wad of sheet music to her chest and her dance bag was slung over her shoulder; it bounced on her back as she walked, her ponytail swaying from side to side. Three younger girls followed in a line behind her like ducklings and a fourth, a slender girl with black hair, was wedging the doors open to let in more light and air. Through the opening, Jessie saw one of the cleaners busy in the foyer with a duster. Everything was starting to come alive and she smiled broadly at the girls as they came close.

'Stage,' the older girl said to Jessie without stopping and Jessie followed, the black-haired girl coming up behind her. She whispered over Jessie's shoulder, 'She's a little ray of sunshine, isn't she.'

Jessie grinned. It was going to be all right.

They stepped up onto the stage using the stairs that were either side, putting their bags down by the wings. The older girl dropped the music on top of a battered piano that was stage right while the ducklings flopped onto chairs and began changing into their practice shoes.

'As some of you already know—' she looked at the three ducklings '—I'm Rita and I'm choreographer and head dancer. We're rehearsing at the theatre while they make some changes – it saves time and money.' She paused. 'Some of you I've worked with before, obviously some I haven't, so let's all introduce ourselves and get it out of the way.' Rita sat on the piano stool and changed into her battered black dance shoes while the girls did as she had instructed.

'Kay Steele,' announced the first duckling, turning to the next along.

'Virginia Thompson.'

'Sally Brown.'

The black-haired girl said, 'Frances O'Leary', in a soft Irish lilt. Jessie spoke last. Rita came back onto full stage to face them, hands on hips.

'Now we all know each other, let's get a few things straight. There are plenty of girls out there who would love this job and they have the talent to do it, so let's make sure you all know from the start that you'll have to work damned hard to stay in this show. You can be replaced at any time.' She gestured to Jessie with an outstretched arm. 'As Delaney here knows; she got the job last minute.'

Jessie felt her cheeks burn and looked straight ahead, into the darkness of the theatre, the light streaming in through the two doors that had been wedged open. The message was for them all, but she felt it keenly. She couldn't afford to lose this job and she was damned if she was going to fall at the first fence.

Footsteps came from behind them and Rita smiled. A man in his early thirties took off his tweed jacket and laid it across the top of the upright piano, lit up a cigarette, inhaled, then tilted his head and blew out a plume of smoke.

Rita mouthed, 'Hello', to him and continued.

'The rest of the cast won't be arriving until next week, as will the rest of the orchestra, so until then we will rehearse with Phil.' She put out her right hand to introduce him. Phil sat on the stool and nodded towards the girls. A couple of them gave a little wave, their hands still by their sides. Jessie was reminded of her dad once more; he would always drape his jacket over the piano before he began to play. The thought soothed her.

'We're going to rehearse five routines ready for opening night next week,' Rita continued, 'on the fourteenth, then another five during the run. Some of you might be needed for sketches, depends what Jack wants, but I will expect you to be at rehearsal promptly. No excuses. Right, carry on with your warm-up stretches.' She turned away. 'Phil. A word.'

He turned on the stool to face the girls, hands splayed out across his knees. 'Only one?' he said wryly and winked at them. Rita began talking through the music, turning the pages and placing the songs in the order she wanted to rehearse them.

Frances stood beside Jessie and began to bend to the left, her right arm outstretched over her head.

'Don't worry about her,' she said in a low voice, reversing her stretch. 'The other girl left because she was in the family way, not because she wasn't any good. She's just trying to keep us on our toes.'

Jessie wasn't so sure. Even though she had kept herself fit, she'd wished she'd danced regularly, for her knees felt weak and her ankles stiff and inflexible, and when she saw the ease with which the ducklings pointed their toes back and forth and the fluidity of their bodies she knew she had a lot of catching up to do. How long had it been? Jessie shouldn't have taken the first job Bernie had sent her. She was bound to make a fool of herself. She couldn't bear the humiliation, but Iris's smirking face swam before her and she dug deep into her resolve.

Sally put her hands on her hips and twisted from side to side. 'Five routines before Friday. I've got a terrible memory, I'm bound to get it wrong.'

Jessie rolled her neck around one way and then another to loosen her muscles. 'We're all in it together, Sally. We'll have to help each other.' The girl brightened and Jessie felt a little bolder. They were all worried, weren't they? It was natural to be nervous so perhaps it wouldn't be so bad after all.

Rita clapped her hands and returned centre stage.

'Right, first number is "Let Yourself Go"; Jack wants a good upbeat song to start the show, so—' she eyed the girls '—get into a line so I can work this out.' The girls obliged and she scrutinised the line-up. 'This is fixed.' She pointed to Kay and Virginia. 'You two in the middle.' The girls stepped into place. 'I'll be next to Kay then Frances, you'll be next to me so leave a gap that I can step into.' Frances got into position. 'Sally next to Virginia, then Jessie you're on the other end. Got it?'

She turned her back to them and demonstrated the first steps as Phil began to play and as he did the memory of Jessie's dad came right back to her; he was with her, wasn't he? Always. She had to remember that when fear came calling. Rita twisted herself back to face them and they repeated her moves, committing them to memory. Rita counted the beats, clapping her hands, pointing, shouting above the music, walking between them as they went over and over the first two routines.

Jessie was starting to perspire, the sweat beading on her forehead even though it was cool in the theatre. It was obvious how easily the others grasped the routine and she didn't. The effort of keeping up was starting to tell on her body and she kept missing beats. She gazed into the darkness of the dress circle and imagined her dad sitting there, his arms resting on the brass rail, watching, urging her on. It helped a little.

'Delaney,' Rita called out, 'what are you doing, for pity's sake? To the left. Left!'

Jessie listened to the music and fell back into time and continued. It was hard getting into the rhythm; her arms and legs didn't move the way her brain wanted them to, and even though she was certain her limbs had fluidity, Rita was certain they did not. 'You look like a ruddy elephant girl, glide, glide.' And so it went on, Jessie the unavoidable target as she was noticeably out of shape. In the end she stopped looking at the other girls' faces, she couldn't bear to see the pity as Rita barked commands that Jessie tried desperately to follow.

After two hours of repetition she was furious with herself. The balls of her feet stung, and she could feel blisters rubbing at her heel. She should have stretched and danced in the fields to keep herself supple and the thought of Iris seeing her dancing amongst the hedgerows and 'what would the village say' cheered her. It was ridiculous of her to think that she could just fall into a routine when she'd not danced for so long. She could only improve, and improve she would, for she was damned if Iris would ever be given the opportunity to gloat at her expense.

Rita barely broke into a sweat throughout the entire session and strutted over to the piano, peering at the sheet music on top of it, making sure her pert bottom was angled perfectly in Phil's direction. 'Right, that's enough. Break for fifteen,' she called.

As the girls fell out of line, Kay touched her shoulder. 'She's not that bad really, Jessie. And while she was watching you she couldn't see that I was getting things wrong as well.' Jessie gave her a quick nod, unable to speak and went over to her bag so that her back was to everyone and they couldn't see the tears glistening in her eyes. She took out the bottle of water that Olive had filled for her that morning and sat on the floor.

Frances flopped down beside her. They watched Rita flirt with Phil, her exaggerated laughter as they chatted, tossing her hair back so that her pony tail swung like a frenzied pendulum.

'Rita, the man-eater,' Frances said, observing the blatant way in which the girl was leaning into the piano so that her breasts appeared more fulsome. Phil was lapping it up. He couldn't take his eyes of her. Jessie hardly dare look up.

'She must have saved her soft side for Phil. I certainly didn't see any of it.'

Frances stretched her legs out in front of her, bent her feet forward and back a few times, rotated her ankles in circles, this way and that. 'I wouldn't worry about it. It'll be my turn tomorrow. I'll say one thing about Rita: she's fair.' Frances swigged at her water and wiped her mouth with her fingers 'I've had worse.'

'Have you worked with her before?'

'Briefly. A couple of years ago. The Floral Halls in Scarborough. Do you know it?' Jessie shook her head. 'The other girls have been with her for a few months. They're her little entourage but then they're a lot younger than I am. I was the odd one out until you came along. You've given me a break.'

Virginia, Sally and Kay had settled themselves at the other side of the stage by the piano and were talking animatedly while keeping a weather eye on Rita and Phil.

'Not sure whether I want it,' Jessie mumbled, hoping Frances was right.

'Well, you'd better get used to it. The three little maids are sharing a flat with Rita so are a bit pally pally. No doubt she'll have bagged the biggest bedroom.' Frances picked at a wood splinter and tossed it back into the wings. 'Where are you staying?'

Jessie told her of the last-minute booking without going into the details of her lack of recent work.

'When we've finished here I need to get something sorted. George and his family put me up last night, bless them, but I can't take advantage.'

Frances considered for a moment, tracing a finger over the floor. 'There's a room at my digs.' She paused. 'It's no palace – the rooms are basic, but they're cheap. Most of all, Geraldine, the landlady, sort of, is lovely. You might want to take a look.'

Jessie stuck the cork back in the water bottle and gave it a bang with the flat of her hand. 'Cheap is good. I'm not here to be frivolous.' It was the reminder she needed of exactly why she was here. She would get over her lack of skill by working harder to catch up. Her head was beginning to clear. Another thing could be crossed off her list. Rita clapped her hands to get them started for the next session and Jessie almost bounced to her feet. It was all achievable, wasn't it, if she didn't give in to despair.

*

When they broke for lunch, Frances and Jessie left the theatre by the front entrance and walked along the main road so that Jessie got a chance to see more of the town. Gift emporiums, bazaars and chip shops populated one side and on the other ornate gardens with floral displays and a crazy golf course smack in the middle. Holiday makers were strolling through the paths that wended their way through the shrubs and low trees even though it was quite overcast. Buses ran past them at regular intervals and they walked up the small incline to the top of the road, taking in the view over the horizon. The sky was clear and cloudless, and they could see the lighthouse at Spurn Point on the other side of the water. Jessie stopped in front of the Cliff Hotel.

'I've never been any place where the sea went out that far.' Jessie took in the large expanse of dark sand and the thin sliver of water in the far distance.

Frances came beside her.

'It's not the sea; it's the River Humber. That's Hull over the other side.' They watched the steady stream of trawlers heading in and out of port. 'It's a prosperous resort,' Frances continued, starting to walk on. 'Fishing brings in good money and they like to spend it as well but when the wind's blowing the wrong way, you'll know about it. Everything has a downside.' She began to walk on, and Jessie fell into step beside her.

'As long as the downsides don't outweigh the up.' It wouldn't do to dwell on what hadn't worked so far. Things that had gone wrong today could so easily be put right. Away from the theatre, with the wind fresh on her face, she could forget about how bad the morning's rehearsal had gone, for her anyway. It was something she could resolve with practice given the chance to do so. She was determined to put in the hours of graft needed until she caught up with the others and Rita was happy with her performance. It would give her something to build on. And then she could think about the next thing.

They rounded the corner and the road sloped down again, and Jessie could see the outdoor bathing pool and a glass building on the opposite side of the road. It wasn't a huge promenade, but she liked it. It was friendlier somehow, like the people she'd met so far. Frances put her hand out to indicate for them both to turn right down a side street. The houses got smaller, tighter together as if huddling for warmth. The shadows were long and one side of the street was dark even though it was little past midday. Jessie folded her arms around herself as Frances led her along terraces and down cut-throughs.

'We're almost there,' she said. 'There is a shortcut but the way we've come is a nicer walk.'

'It doesn't seem as if we've been walking too long anyway,' Jessie replied. What had it been? Ten minutes. That wasn't half as bad as she had expected it to be for somewhere in her price range. Cheap usually meant miles away from the theatre and what she saved would be spent on buses or shoe leather.

'Well, here we are.' Frances came to stop outside a house on Barkhouse Lane. Dark-brown paint peeled and blistered on the large bay window and a grey net covered the glass. Dandelions and tufts of grass protruded from the cracks between the tiles. Above the doorknob was a grimy smudge of fingerprints, all that remained of the itinerant lodgers. Jessie tried not to wince, failing miserably.

Frances nudged her and grinned. 'I warned you,' she said, opening the door. 'Is cheap still your preference?'

Jessie nodded. No need to say that it wasn't her preference, more a necessity. She reassured herself with the thought that she wouldn't be in it for most of the day. It was primarily somewhere to sleep, somewhere to leave her belongings. Did she dare?

'Geraldine has only just taken it on. It needs a lot of work.'

'Mainly elbow grease by the looks of things,' Jessie said as cheerfully as she could.

The hallway was dingy and Frances told her to leave the front door open to give them some light. The walls were painted brown below the dado rail and possibly cream above, although it now looked a dreadful tinge of coffee. It had strange echoes of The Beeches, and she smiled ruefully. Had she swapped one house of brown for another? A pile of letters were a collapsing mountain to one side, the envelopes covered in dirt from boots and shoes. Above her, thickly matted cobwebs danced in the breeze that came in from the door. She quickly lowered her gaze. They passed the first door and Frances opened a second that led into an excuse for a sitting room with two battered chairs and a table that leaned to one side. The fringe of the shade on the centre light fitting was coming away from the edges. 'There's a kitchen, somewhere to wash.' She pointed through a doorway that had been relieved of its door. It was all very basic but remarkably clean and Jessie didn't bother to look any further. What was the point? It would be temporary, it had to be because she couldn't possibly get Grace to leave the comfort of The Beeches for this. Her mum, all she could think of was her mum. She had wanted to rescue her, rescue them all and this was where she would be starting from. It would take longer than she had expected and as Frances chattered on she knew now why Grace had tolerated Iris and Norman – for what was the alternative? This? Shabby rooms in shabby houses. Her thoughts flicked back and forth, Grace at the station, Grace when she had the telegram. Her mum had been protecting them all the best she could, with what little spirit she had left after Davey had died. And Jessie had been an added burden to her, hadn't she, Grace placating her as much as she placated Iris and Norman. She winced at the truth of it.

'All the other rooms are bedrooms, including the one downstairs at the front,' Frances said, without a trace of apology in her voice. 'Geraldine only moved in at the beginning of last week, so she hasn't had time to clean up, and neither have I. It's just the two of us, and it is what it is. The owner's not got any plans to come back anytime soon, and all the rooms will be let eventually. Come upstairs and I'll show you my room.'

Jessie was about to put her hand on the rail but decided against it as Frances went ahead. On the landing she turned right, pulled a key from her pocket and unlocked the door. Jessie was surprised by how neat and tidy the room was. Frances had cleaned the sash window and plain cotton curtains hung from a rail. 'They're mine,' Frances said. 'Got to make it a little homely. I don't want to wake up feeling any worse than I have to and that's the first thing I see.'

Jessie nodded her agreement. 'It's a good idea. I'll do the same.'

Frances raised her eyebrows. 'You're not put off then?'

Jessie shook her head. 'How much is the rent?' She moved to the window and peered out onto brown yards, and brown walls. Well, it wasn't The Beeches but it had potential. She could save where she could and if it meant being uncomfortable for a time, so be it. It was only what she deserved for being such a pain to her mum.

Frances told her the price.

'What do I need to do to get a room?'

Frances grabbed an envelope from the bedside table, pulled the letter out, took a pencil and wrote on the back. 'I'll leave a message for Geraldine. She'll push the key under my door; we can sort the rent book out tomorrow.' Frances scribbled a quick note and put it in her pocket. 'I'll push it under her door on our way out.'

'Thanks, Frances.'

'Not sure you'll be thanking me much after a night in the bed,' Frances called over her shoulder as the two of them went down the stairs. 'If it's the same as mine it'll be like sleeping on a plank, but it's safe enough and at least we can walk home together after the show.'

Out on the pavement, Frances linked her arm through Jessie's and the two girls walked back down the street. 'We'd best get back,' Jessie said, grinning, 'before Rita devours Phil.' Above them the clouds had thinned and patches of blue were breaking in through the gaps. There was much to be thankful for. It might not have the comfort of The Beeches but she wouldn't change a thing. Her destiny was in her own hands at last and she would make the most of every opportunity that came her way.

They went in through the front of the theatre, waved to Dolly who was taking a turn in the box office, and walked into the stalls. Rita was already on stage and they leaned on the back rail watching her go over the routines, working different things out, trying, changing, adapting, getting cross with herself, changing a step, an arm movement, her satisfaction when she discovered the new way of doing something, the relentless search for improvement. Frances leaned to Jessie. 'She's hard on us, Jessie, but she's even harder on herself.' It couldn't be argued with and something shifted in Jessie, like a small butterfly settling on a flower and taking a rest in the warmth of the sun. She could let go of the feeling of not being good enough because there was Rita, her whole life dedicated to dance and she wasn't happy with her performance either.

Rita worked the girls hard that afternoon, accommodating the new steps into the routines that Jessie and Frances had seen her perfect. The work was just as arduous as the morning had been, but Jessie didn't feel so hopeless. Now that she had somewhere to stay, her mind was less cluttered and her movements became more fluid. Was she at least gaining some confidence? She dearly hoped so, but her legs ached like billy-o, the muscles unused to so much punishment in one day.

'Better, much better.' Rita stretched out her arm to direct the rest of the girls' attention to Jessie. Jessie felt as if she could glide off the stage with that one piece of praise. It was an exhausting but exhilarating afternoon and it seemed counter intuitive to blend in when her dad had trained her to stand out, but she was part of the Variety Girls and not a solo artiste. The time would come for her to step out of line, but this was not it.

Rita dismissed them at six. Jessie ached in every bone and muscle, her head thudding, and she steeled herself for the walk home, ready to drop onto her bed. Frances walked with her to Olive's to collect her case. Jessie was so happy to see her again. How blessed she had been that Sunday afternoon to find them.

'I'm glad you found somewhere, lovey, but I hope you'll still pop in and see us now and again.' She put her hand in her pocket and pressed something into Jessie's palm. 'You left it under your pillow.'

Jessie folded her fingers over Hope's penny, how careless she had been. She wouldn't be so lackadaisical again. She leant forward and kissed Olive's cool cheek, picked up her bag and the two girls headed for Barkhouse Lane.

Frances handed Jessie the key to her room. Jessie clasped the cold metal in her hand, the first key of her first room. She opened the door and stepped inside, followed by Frances. The room was square whereas Frances's was long but the view into the alley was the same. It was a tad grubby and after a long day in the theatre the last thing she wanted to do was start cleaning but working together the two girls made it passable. It couldn't be called homely by any stretch of the imagination, but it was a place to lay her head, and Frances was only down the hallway. Geraldine occupied the large upstairs room that faced onto the street.

When they felt they had done all they could, the two of them walked to the nearest chip shop. They bought two wraps of chips loaded with batter scraps and coated them liberally with salt and vinegar; they ate them with their fingers as they walked home. The moon was high in the sky and the clouds scudded slowly by. Jessie searched for the north star and found it. Her dad had always pointed it out, the two of them searching the sky wherever they happened to be. 'Follow your star, Jessie. It shines for you.' A tear threatened but she held it back.

They finished their chips sat at the wonky table in the back room in Barkhouse Lane, tired and weary, dirt under their nails, and Jessie couldn't have felt happier.

Chapter 7

Harry tried to concentrate on the meeting, but his thoughts kept straying to Jessie. He leaned over the highly polished mahogany table, twisting a pencil in his fingers. Was she thinking of him? He frowned, biting the inside of his cheek. In the three days since she'd left two letters and a postcard had arrived, full of the people she had met, the room she had rented, the demands of the routines, how she felt she was failing and succeeding – and both at the same time. He envied the newness of everything she was experiencing without him and was counting the days until he saw her again.

This was the first meeting he'd attended as a partner and not a clerk. Norman, Stan, Ambrose and Ted all had premises on the High Street and as war looked ever more likely they had taken to meeting up once a fortnight to pool ideas and resources.

The other voices in the room drifted in and out of his consciousness. He hadn't really been paying attention, feeling he'd been brought in by Norman to make up the numbers. The silence in the room made him look up to find all eyes upon him, waiting for a response to a question he hadn't heard. He felt the hairs bristle on the back of his neck. What had they been talking about? He sat up straighter, stared at each of the men in turn, playing for time. The walls in front and to the side of him were laden with dusty gold-lettered tomes of legal expertise of which he realised he knew little, and a mahogany-framed portrait of King George VI glowered at him. He reached for the water jug and poured himself a glass, pointing to his throat apologetically.

Miss Symonds cleared her throat. 'Could you repeat the end of that question, Mr Cole? I didn't quite get it down and it must be correct. You said something about it being good to get a younger man's perspective on—' She tipped her head to one side, her pencil poised over her shorthand notebook.

Harry flashed her a smile, topped up his glass and sipped. He would thank her later. Norman leaned back in his chair at the head of the boardroom table. The leather sighed under his weight. He made a steeple with his fingers and pressed them to his chin. 'Harry, what do you think about storing our legal records out of town? We had previously thought the basement adequate; personally, I'm not so sure.'

Ambrose Gale, the accountant, folded his hands across his ample chest and rested his elbows on the arms of his chair. He stared at Harry, pursing his lips as if Harry had nothing much to contribute and Harry immediately wanted to prove him wrong. How should he answer? He needed to show that Norman's faith in him was warranted, that he wasn't simply there to take up space.

Harry leaned back a little, put his pencil onto the pad in front of him. He had been scribbling notes to begin with, but his mind had been on Jessie; it was always on Jessie.

'I agree with you, Norman,' he said, choosing his words carefully. 'If there is to be an invasion it will come from the air. I would be inclined, initially,' he said, looking at all the men in the room, 'to consider the effects of aerial bombardment and fire as priority.'

Miss Symonds winked at him.

Ted Morris was picking at the skin around his thumb and didn't look up but said, 'Fair point, young man. We only need to consider what has happened in Spain. They bombed Guernica until there was hardly a building left standing. This time round, the war will affect this nation in different ways to the last.'

'Chamberlain is still piddling about and if we're not careful we'll be got by the short and curlies, Norman.' Stan Porter said, blunt as ever. 'Bombardments will bring more than death and casualties. We'll have housing shortages as well as being short of men when they've signed up.' Spoken like a true estate agent, thought Harry as Stan waffled on. 'We need to go through the insurance practicalities as well. Our paperwork will need to be in good order but, more importantly, it must be safe.'

Harry relaxed; he'd deflected the attention, thanks to Miss Symonds, and had contributed to the meeting. He might not have experience of war as the older men did but his opinion counted; mostly, he surmised, because this war would be fought by men like him. He half thought that it was all a bit over the top to think bombs would be wasted on a market town like Holt.

Wouldn't the primary targets be factories and airfields – one never knew how it would all pan out, himself least of all. Norman nodded his approval at Harry.

'I believe this must take priority, all things as they are. I don't think we ought to wait until our next get-together.' He paused. 'What about Friday the fourteenth; we could meet in the Cons Club?'

Harry blanched. That was Jessie's opening night and he'd said he would be there, and, not only that, he would be taking Grace and Eddie.

'I think we'd be better off using next Wednesday,' he suggested. 'Then we have two working days to get the ball rolling. A few days won't make much difference.'

Norman shook his head. 'I have to be at a committee meeting and so do Stan and Ambrose.'

Of course they did, how could he forget. Harry pursed his lips. Would that be the next thing he'd be shoehorned into – a member of the honourable Chamber of Commerce? He shuddered.

'But if we had the meeting before you leave, we'd get everything sorted in the hour,' Harry suggested. 'It would focus our attention, and everything could be wrapped up on the one day.'

Stan agreed. 'Good point, Harry. These meetings can go on for as long as you let them. I for one think that's the best option.' There was no dissent and so, as Harry fought not to smile with relief, Miss Symonds was instructed to mark the day as the nineteenth.

The four older men got to their feet and left the boardroom while Harry lingered until he and Miss Symonds were alone. He heard their muffled discussions as they descended the stairs, and he turned to look out of the window onto the street below. There was a small queue outside Archers bakery; two middle-aged women stood chatting, baskets over their arm and an elderly gent passed, tipping his hat in greeting. It appeared that life was going on as normal but without Jessie it was anything but. He rarely came upstairs. The boardroom took up most of the front of the building and a large room to the rear was where all the records were stored. There was also a small washroom and two empty offices. He knew that Norman's father and uncle had set up the firm almost half a century ago. Their sister was Jessie's grandmother. They had four sons between them. Two had been lost in the Great War, one had died of the Spanish flu the following year. Norman had been left to carry the firm. Sad that such hopes and dreams were gathering cobwebs in rooms that might once have held young promise.

He spoke when he was certain that he could not be heard. 'Thank you for saving my bacon, Miss Symonds; I was lost in my thoughts.'

Miss Symonds collected her notepad and pencil. 'I'm sure I don't know what you mean, Mr Newman.' He stood back to let her pass. 'Changing the date was nicely done; I wouldn't want Jessie to miss out on having you with her on her big night.'

He held the door open. 'I think I would rather have lost my job than not be there for her.'

She smiled at him and it was good to know that she had some idea how he felt.

'I think so too. It's very dull without her, isn't it?'

'It is,' he said, following her downstairs. He wanted to add how achingly dreary life was in the office and out of it, that his every waking hour was filled with her voice, her sweet face, the way she moved. He wanted to tell this lovely woman how he lay awake most of the night, every night, wondering if she was out with the other dancers or if she was at home in the little room she had taken. He felt sure she would understand his loneliness.

Iris was fussing around the men as they lingered in the entrance hall. Harry slipped into the main office before she could collar him. Grace was standing at Jessie's old desk. She was wearing a summer coat in powder blue and Harry noticed that her hair had been cut shorter and set in waves. It suited her, but she was still so thin, and her cough had lingered in spite of the warmer days.

Miss Symonds slid back behind her desk and began typing up her notes. The room hummed to the sound of her keys flicking along at lightning speed.

'Hello, Grace,' Harry said, taking her hand and shaking it warmly. 'It's good to see you.'

'And you too, Harry. It's good to be out and about.' She coughed, put her hand to her chest and turned to Miss Symonds. 'We've been to an Air Raid Precaution meeting. We've heard that there will be a test blackout in southern England next week; we thought we'd better get a move on in case we're next. Iris and I have been to buy blackout material, paint and tape. Torches.' She leaned closer into the room and lowered her voice. 'Iris has been very precise. Nothing has been left to chance, as you can imagine. Do not sit still too long, young Harry, or you will be painted black for certain.'

Harry saw a smile play on Miss Symonds' lips. She might very well be industrious, but she didn't miss a thing.

'You look rather pleased with yourself,' Grace continued, slipping off her gloves and putting them into her handbag. 'Let me guess, a letter from Jessie this morning?'

He grinned, retrieving it from his pocket. 'And a postcard.' He handed it over for Grace to see the picture of the pier and promenade. She smiled, handing it back to Harry, too polite to read the reverse. 'I had one of the theatre. Quite near the promenade, I believe.'

Harry nodded. 'It sounds like she's really busy, struggling a bit, but working hard to catch up. I don't know how she found the time to write but I'm glad she did.'

The two women smiled at each other.

'We women know our priorities, don't we, Miss Symonds?' She squeezed Harry's arm. 'I expect we'll get another sooner or later, and in the meantime at least we know she is doing well.'

Harry spread his hands and shrugged. He didn't want to know that Jessie was thriving without him, he wanted to think that she was missing him as much as he was missing her. They hadn't found a replacement for her yet; Miss Symonds was keeping them all afloat for the time being. Grace sat down in Jessie's old chair to wait, and Harry wandered over to the window. The lower half was frosted glass and the upper part had Cole & Sons in an arch of gold lettering. Iris was stood with Norman and the other men who were now outside, blocking the pavement. People stepped out onto the street to avoid them but they were oblivious of the obstruction they caused, and no doubt wouldn't move if asked. They were men of influence and as such stood their ground.

'She sounds happy enough,' he said, turning back to Grace. 'I think she's found it hard though.'

'She would,' Grace considered. 'She's not really a dancer, Harry. She should've waited for something that was more her thing but that's not Jessie's way.'

'No.' Harry was quiet. He wished her impulsiveness had worked in his favour. She had rushed away to the theatre, but she had not rushed her answer to him. These were the thoughts that filled his head on sleepless nights, and he didn't want them to fill his days as well. He frowned and sat on the edge of Miss Symonds desk, stretching his legs out in front of him.

'Don't worry, Harry.' Grace put her hand on his and squeezed it. 'We had to let her go this time. If we hadn't, she would have been restless until another opportunity presented itself. She'll come back.'

He forced a smile. 'At least she's working hard and enjoying herself.' Her letter had run to several pages, both sides spilling with words full of the theatre, the girls, and the room she had secured with her friend Frances's help. Her love of the theatre was clear on every page – did she love it more than him? It was hard standing back, letting her find her own way. The clock on the wall behind Miss Symonds chimed the hour.

'She's a bright girl, sometimes too bright for her own good,' Miss Symonds said, over the top of her typewriter when the clock stilled. 'That's why she lands herself in so much trouble. We were saying earlier how very quiet it is without her.'

He let out a long sigh. 'I'd say tedious is the word, Miss Symonds.' He leaned towards her. 'But please don't tell Mr Cole I said that.'

The older lady leaned into him, their heads close and whispered, 'Your secret is safe with me, Mr Newman.' She resumed her typing, keeping an eye on the door.

'You'll see each other soon enough. It's only a few days until opening night.' Grace picked at a piece of glue on the desk, quite possibly some residue of Jessie's cavalier exuberance when putting the files together. She stopped herself and folded her hands into her lap. 'I'm so looking forward to seeing a good show again – and not having to work in it.' She smiled ruefully. 'It's such hard work for a few minutes of glory, Miss Symonds.'

Miss Symonds took the letter from her typewriter and began loading another sheet, placing carbon paper between the headed paper and the copy with precision.

'If it hadn't been for Harry's quick thinking, you might not have been seeing it at all.'

Harry told her about the quick swerve he'd managed around the date of the next meeting. Grace tutted.

'Jessie may be full of bravado, Harry, but she desperately needs our support. It's a crying shame that Iris and

Norman don't understand that.' Grace stopped speaking as the office door opened and Iris marched in, followed by Norman, who slapped Harry on the back as Harry scrambled to his feet.

'Great meeting, Harry. You brought up some very good points.' He slipped his hands into his pockets, his belly burgeoning out as he bent his knees. 'Very good indeed. I think the others appreciated having you there. As do I.'

Harry folded his arms across his chest. 'I'm glad to have been of use.' He was even more glad that he'd been there to defer the meeting until after Jessie's opening night.

Iris stared at the letter and postcard in Harry's hand, making him uncomfortable.

'From Jessie,' he said, sliding them into his pocket. He decided to put Norman and Iris on the spot, hoping it would lead to a thawing of the relationship between the two families. 'Will you be going to her opening night?'

'I will not, and neither will Norman. Sorry, Grace, but if that child wants to swan around in some godforsaken seaside town flashing her legs to all and sundry that's up to her – but at a time when we need to be thinking of preparations for war? No, we will not be going.' She spat out the words and Harry felt himself draw back. He walked to the filing cabinet and pretended to search for papers so that he could turn his back. That would be an emphatic *no* then.

'Now, Iris—' Norman began, indicating for his wife to follow him with a flick of his head. The pair of them went across the corridor to his office. The door was left open and they could all hear Iris's high-pitched voice. She was busy pulling not only Jessie to shreds but managed to include Norman's cohorts.

While Miss Symonds tapped away at the keys, Grace and Harry loitered awkwardly as Iris droned on, finally sweeping back into the doorway of the main office.

'Are you ready, Grace? I will drop the order in at the greengrocer and we can be on our way. We don't want to keep the men from their work.'

Grace said a brief goodbye to Harry and Miss Symonds and followed her out, closing the door quietly behind them.

Miss Symonds bore her usual neutral expression and Harry dipped his head to hide his smile. He went back into his office and closed the door. He propped the postcard up against his desk lamp. His promotion was a reality now and had already lost its lustre. Would the shine of the stage dim for Jessie too, or would it shine brighter and keep her away?

Chapter 8

By the end of the first week of rehearsals, the nails on Jessie big toes were black and the skin had rubbed away from her little ones after she had popped the blisters with a clean needle; the soles of her feet stung as she walked. Each night she rubbed liniment into her legs to try and ease the pain of overworked muscles and every morning she strapped her feet with makeshift bandages, wincing as she forced herself into her shoes. Frances sympathised. Dancers didn't have pretty feet.

On the Monday morning, as she was getting dressed, Frances knocked on her door. 'Leave your shoes off.' Frances nodded to where they were positioned underneath the window. 'We'll walk to work along the beach. The salt water will be good for your feet.'

Jessie wondered whether she would still be here if it wasn't for Frances. Not only had she found her a safe place to stay but each night, after they had eaten, they had rolled up the rug in the small room downstairs and gone over the routines. Not that Frances needed to – she was a wonderful dancer – but Jessie needed all the help she could get.

They ate a good breakfast and strode down Brighton Street towards the slipway. It was a mild but overcast morning, the water lapping along the shore leaving a scattering of seaweed and a ribbon of shells that they hobbled over, laughing as they went, to reach the smooth bank of sand. The water was cool on her feet and the two of them walked along, side by side.

'Better?' Frances asked, her shoes in one hand, her bag in the other.

Jessie nodded, smiling. 'Much.'

Frances stopped walking and Jessie turned to face her. Her hair was so black, her face so milky white against the vivid red lipstick that she wore, a stark contrast to the grey morning.

'Look, Jess.' She paused, considered, then said, 'You don't have to put on a brave face for me.'

Jessie stopped, taken aback, 'I'm not. I ...'

Frances put a hand on her arm. 'I don't need explanations either. It's ... well ... it's obvious you're out of condition.'

Jessie's shoulders sagged. 'Obvious to everyone?'

'Virginia, maybe. Rita, definitely – but she can see how determined you are.'

Jessie began to walk on. 'What if determination isn't enough?' She looked up at her friend.

'You didn't let me finish.' Frances laughed. 'How determined – and how hard you work.'

Jessie watched the water run around her feet as the tide lapped along the shoreline then slowly pulled back again.

'This is my first theatre job, Frances, and I can't afford to lose it.' She sighed. 'I didn't realise how hard it would be. I thought I'd be able to keep up with the pace, that it would all come flooding back the moment I stepped on stage. I haven't been in a chorus since I was one of the babes in a panto when I was twelve. I'll bet it shows too.'

She'd been deluding herself, hadn't she, even with all the extra work? Had Rita spoken to Frances? Was she forewarning her? She'd tried not to appear vulnerable, knowing she had to toughen up. She trusted Frances. The girl might be a closed book but she was kind, and Jessie was glad that she was on her side – or was Jessie deluding herself about that too?

Frances must have guessed what she was thinking because she said, 'Hey, you chump. No need to worry. It will suddenly kick in, and then it'll flow.'

'Just like that?'

'Yes, just like that.' She linked her arms with Jessie's and the two of them walked under the pier to the slipway and made their way off the beach. 'I wanted you to know that I understand. You'll soon catch up.'

The two of them found a bench and sat down and Frances helped Jessie strap up her feet.

'Thanks, Frances,' Jessie said, as the two of them stood up and walked up towards the theatre. 'That feels better already.' Her feet certainly did but so did the fact that she had confided her fears to her friend. Frances caught her arm again.

'A trouble shared and all that.'

Jessie grinned. They had indeed been halved.

*

The morning was punishing. Last week they'd had the stage to themselves but now the other turns on the bill would be arriving and they would want the stage to pace out their own acts. It was all getting much more intense and Rita worked them hard, knowing that opening night was only five days away.

'New number, girls. Pay attention.' Rita barked. When had she last smiled? Jessie rolled her head to ease the tension in her neck. Would she last the week? Would she make opening night? Phil began to play the opening bars and Rita counted them through the steps. ' ... five, six, seven, eight.'

Jessie watched her closely, they all did, each girl memorising the moves as Rita demonstrated. It would all be committed to memory – in their head and in their bodies, their muscles remembering the position of their arms, their legs, their torsos.

'Better, better,' Rita shouted over the music. 'Virginia, Jessie – to the left. You three come to the front, make a space, that's it, now, on the refrain, you come forward, yes, yes, now all to the left, beat, all to the right, beat, centre, beat, kick, beat. Yes, yes, lovely, that's good.' The girls carried on to the end of the song and finished as one. Rita applauded them. 'It's all coming together now.' Her voice was eager, the relief beginning to show on her face. 'Good work, all of you. Delaney. A marked improvement on last week.'

Frances winked at her and Jessie could've wept.

They had a break of sorts when they were called for costume fittings. Phil picked up his jacket and left the theatre by the stage door while the girls fetched their costumes from upstairs, space being too cramped for them all to gather in Wardrobe. They took it in turns to stand on a chair at the side of the stage. It was Jessie's turn to pose there while Mary, the wardrobe mistress, bent at her knees, mouth full of pins, glasses sliding down her nose.

Jessie felt a sneeze building but held it back, managing to remain ramrod straight while Mary adjusted the hem of the costume she'd be wearing for the routine that would close the first half – a bold blue bodice with an organza skirt that skimmed her ankles. Most of the costumes were on hire, shabby and aged; under the lights they would shimmer and sparkle, creating a glamorous illusion.

'I'll only be a couple more minutes, ducky,' the older woman said, tilting her head to smile at Jessie. Jessie wondered if Mary was full of pins that had slipped down her gullet unnoticed, if that was at all possible. She was almost as round as she was tall, which wasn't more than five foot, and her grey hair sat in tight curls about her head. She brooked no nonsense from the girls and had a reputation for 'accidentally' stabbing them with pins if they gave her too much hassle. She was the same with the men, Jessie noticed, although she did like to flirt with them, and they with her, only there was never much to do for them really, other than take in or let out their suits according to their indulgences. It was all good humoured, but they crossed her at their peril.

'It's a bugger having to do it out here but it's that cramped in my room I can't get around properly.' Mary slapped Jessie lightly on the leg. 'That'll do, hop off and I'll do the next one.' Jessie stepped down and found Frances, slipping the dress from her shoulders and standing in her leotard while she hung it back on the hanger. She wrapped her dance skirt around her waist, tying it in a bow.

Mary shouted for her next victim. 'Sally?'

'Sally, pride of our alley,' Frances and Jessie sang the first line of the famous song back to Mary and Jessie continued with the rest of the opening verse, raising up her arms and imitating Gracie Fields. Mike and Bob, the stage carpenter, gave her a ripple of applause and she responded with an exaggerated curtsey.

'Not bad at all.' Mary nodded her head. 'I reckon you could give our Gracie a run for her money and no mistake. You're wasted in the chorus.'

'She's not that good,' carped Sally, stepping up onto the chair. Mary raised her eyebrows at Jessie, loaded her mouth with another lot of pins and set to work on her next victim.

Jessie shrank. Maybe she was setting her sights too high.

Frances gave her a nudge. 'There's always one, isn't there? And she's the one.'

Jessie shrugged; perhaps Sally was right. She was tired and tetchy, and she knew she had taken it to heart, whereas Frances had taken not a blind bit of notice and didn't appear at all fatigued. Jessie yearned for Rita to call for a break; a little fresh air would be such a blessing. After all, they had been in the theatre since eight that morning, rehearsing to the sound of hammering as Bob created a set of treads that were to run along the back of the stage in front of the backcloth. He'd fashioned some curved posts from a sheet of plywood that with work – and a few lengths of four by two – would become a balustrade. Teamed with a painted backcloth, it would give the illusion of a terrace overlooking a grand garden. Matt, one of the stagehands, had been busy painting the patches of black on the flats that had chipped of during other productions. He had already used the same tin of paint to black out the windows including those in the dressing rooms that ran along at street level, thrusting the already poky corridors into even more darkness. The pace was ramping up as opening night drew closer.

During their fittings, a tall, distinguished-looking man walked into the auditorium. He had a petite brunette at his side who was hugging a clipboard and Jessie guessed it was the producer Jack Holland and his assistant. His dark hair was peppered with grey and he walked with a slight limp. The pair of them headed towards the middle section of the stalls and settled themselves, talking in low whispers. The brunette was busy scribbling notes as he talked, pausing to point at different areas of the stage. She would look up, nod and scribble again.

Now that they'd had their fittings and knowing Mary was satisfied, Jessie and Frances could at last take a break. Jessie picked up her bag. 'Fancy a cuppa in the café around the corner, Frances? The cakes look nice and it's my treat as a thank you for your help with getting my room spick and span.'

'Don't be daft. That's what mates do, isn't it? And we're mates, aren't we?' It wasn't really a question and Jessie was glad that the older girl had taken her under her wing. Some of her confidence had rubbed off on Jessie these last couple of days and she'd begun to feel more settled, less uncertain. There was something about Frances that made her more than her twenty-three years; Jessie didn't quite know what it was, but she didn't need to. She liked Frances and that was all that mattered.

'Friends,' Jessie said, and they each went to either side of the stage and tripped down the steps into the auditorium. Jack Holland called out as they passed. 'Nicely done, girls. I might get you to put that in the show. It looked great.' The girls grinned and dashed up the aisle and out into the light of the foyer where they bumped into Dolly, who was locking up the box office. She beamed when she saw Jessie.

'Jessie. How's it all going?'

'Great, better than I thought it would, to be honest.' She twisted to her left. 'Dolly, this is Frances; she got me a room in the same house in Barkhouse Lane.' She turned to Frances. 'Dolly's dad is George, the stage doorman and all-round sweetheart. They looked after me the first day I arrived at the Empire.' How her world had shrunken since then. She had fallen into bed each night, no time to do any of the things she had planned. She'd written to Harry, Grace and Eddie, keeping her sadness and insecurities to herself. She wrote of how she missed them – only not how much. It wouldn't do to have them think she had any regrets. 'Dolly lives in the street that runs along the back of the theatre.'

'I remember you telling me,' Frances said.

Dolly and Frances acknowledged each other with smiles. 'Dad told me you'd found a place to stay.' She popped the keys to the box office into her skirt pocket and patted it down. 'Ticket sales are going ever so well. We had a bit of a rush on this morning, I can tell you. Opening night is sold out.'

'That's good to hear,' Frances chipped in. 'It'll make my blisters worthwhile.'

Jessie winced at the reminder. 'Did you save me three, Dolly, near the front?'

'Course I did. I've put them in an envelope with your mum's name on it. That okay?'

Jessie nodded. 'Thanks, Dolly. I'll pay for them as soon as I get my wages.' It would take almost everything she had earned so far, once she had paid for her digs and new dance shoes, but worth every penny. She couldn't wait to see them all, but especially Harry. She recalled the extortionate price he'd paid for the tickets in Cromer and her heart fluttered. This time he would be in the audience watching her. Would he be proud of her? She'd hoped that the first time he saw her on stage she would be singing, but it didn't matter, did it, where she was now; it was where she was going that was important.

Dolly was walking towards the doors. It was lashing down with rain outside, the skies grey cloud.

'I'm just going to Joyce's for a break,' Dolly grabbed hold of the brass handle. 'I'm gasping for a drink, I've been yapping all morning as customers came in and bought tickets.' She laughed to herself. 'Not that I don't like a good gossip, but I'm parched now.'

'Is Joyce's the café around the corner?'

Dolly nodded. 'On Market Street.'

'Oh, we're going there too.' Jessie turned to Frances. 'I told Frances how good the cakes looked.'

'Do you want to join us?' Frances asked. Jessie was relieved not to be the one to suggest it. It was a thank you to Frances, but she needed to thank them both.

'I'd love to,' Dolly said, holding open the door, her eyes sparkling. 'Lead the way, Jessie. We're coming up the rear.' People had already found refuge under the theatre canopy, their clothing spattered with rain, waiting for it to subside so that they could move on. The girls didn't have time to wait; a couple parted to let them through, and they made a dash for it. The rain splashed at their ankles as it pounded the pavement but thanks to the ornate canopy that ran nearly the full length of the parade, they kept themselves dry until they turned the corner. 'Lucky the wind's blowing the right way, or we'd be soaked,' Dolly said, as they rushed inside to the warmth of the café.

A well-built woman was behind the counter frying eggs for a butty. She plopped the eggs onto thickly sliced bread slathered with a generous covering of butter, put another doorstopper of bread on top, drew the large knife over it and passed it over the counter to a thickset man in overalls. He had a newspaper folded under his arm and he took the plate and went and sat down at the back of the room. Joyce picked up a cloth and wiped the clean counter, her arms sweeping huge circles across the wooden surface. She was wearing a brightly coloured scarf on her head that was knotted at the front like a turban. Jet-black hair tufted from a gap at the front.

'Sorry, duckies. I'm a bit short-handed today.' She plopped the cloth to one side and adjusted the sides of her floral overall around her armpits. 'D'ya mind coming up and getting your order. I'll shout when it's done'.

Dolly introduced the girls.

'So, you're in the show, are you? With Madeleine Moore. I like her. She was on the wireless last week. I hear she's staying over the road at the Dolphin.' Joyce leaned on the counter, her ample bosom spilling through her folded arms. 'Nice to see the theatre opening up again. It's a big block to be shut up. Affects us all when the Empire shuts.' She cocked her head towards the door to draw attention to the card she'd stuck there. 'I hope someone answers that ad in the window for staff or I'll not be able to cope if we get a rush on. I've sent Vi upstairs to lie down; her ankles are like tree trunks, they are. She tried, bless her, waddling round like a constipated duck she was, I can tell you, but it don't do anyone no good when she's like that. I'll be as glad when that baby arrives as she is.' Joyce stood to attention and slapped the counter. 'Now, what can I get you, girls?'

Jessie's eyes grew round. Did the woman ever come up for breath? She checked the prices on the menu boards that hung at the back of the counter. The egg butty smelt delicious, but she didn't have the time or the funds to be extravagant. She quickly added up the price for three teas and three cakes. She could run to that, just. She smiled at Dolly and Frances.

'I'm going to have tea and a slice of fruit cake. What about you, Dolly?

'Same.'

'And me,' said Frances, opening her purse.

'Please, let me,' said Jessie, handing over a half crown to cover it.

'No, Jessie, you mustn't,' said Dolly, shaking her head.

Frances pushed herself forward. 'We'll be paying for our own orders,' she snapped, placing a shilling on the counter. 'Thank you, Joyce.'

Jessie's cheeks burned and stung as if Frances had slapped her on them. She must have appeared visibly shocked because Dolly stepped up to smooth ruffled feathers.

'I don't think Jessie meant to offend you, Frances. She was just being kind.'

'I know that,' Frances said, her voice firm. 'But kindness can be taken advantage of. I told you that you owed me nothing, Jessie, and I meant it. I don't want to be bought. I do things because I want to do them, not because I have to.' Joyce raised her pencilled eyebrows, quietly took their money and put their change on the counter. Frances took her own change and passed the rest to a stunned Jessie. 'Now put that in your pocket and save it for a rainy day.' She tipped her head towards the window. 'It might be summer season in Cleethorpes, but you can bet your life it won't be sunshine all the way. Now, let's get a seat and wait for that cake.'

They found a table by the window and watched the rain lash down. People hurried past, heads bent. A little boy in shorts and short-sleeved shirt was drenched from head to foot, his hair plastered to his head and, oblivious of his mother, jumped in puddles that seeped into his sandals and splashed up her legs. They could see her scolding him, pulling at his arm but he was having too much fun to stop. His little face was a beam of sunshine in the grey of the day. Jessie continued to look out onto the street. She didn't feel like talking any more.

Dolly broke the silence. 'Not long until opening night.' Her voice had a forced brightness and Jessie didn't want to make her feel uncomfortable. She mustn't sulk. It was childish, and it was too much like Aunt Iris.

'No,' she replied, paying attention to Dolly. Her blue eyes glittered with kindness and she berated herself for making her new friends feel awkward, even if it had been for the best of reasons. 'The other cast members are arriving today: Madeleine Moore, Billy Lane and the Duo D'or and one or two others, the magician – I can't remember his name, and the chap who plays the musical saw, Arthur something or other. We'll be able to rehearse our routines to a proper band as well. That will be so much nicer, won't it, Frances?'

Frances got to her feet and Jessie wondered whether she had offended her so much that she was about to leave. She walked to the counter where Joyce had placed three slices of cake and picked them up and brought them over, sliding them into the middle of the table. 'It will be heaven. It's all right rehearsing with Phil, he's a great pianist, but it gives you more oomph when you've got a brass section. I think Jack has done a great job with his choice of music, don't you?' She looked Jessie straight in the eye, forcing her to see there was no animosity between them. As far as Frances was concerned, it was forgotten.

Jessie pulled a plate of cake towards her and picked at a plump currant. 'I do, it's a happy and uplifting programme, exactly what we need.' She popped the dried fruit into her mouth. It was moist and succulent and she thought of her mum, suddenly feeling tearful. It wasn't that she missed home, because The Beeches would never be home, but it was the longing to have Grace and Eddie by her side, to feel as strong as she did the day she wrote to Bernie. She shook her head to blink the tears away just as Frances arrived back carrying a tray with three cups of tea, sugar and milk. She put it down on the table. When she saw Jessie her face fell.

'I didn't mean to upset you, Jessie.' She reached out, putting her hand on Jessie's shoulder, which made her feel even worse. She dabbed at her eyes with Miss Symonds hanky that she'd taken from her pocket when she knew she couldn't hold the tears back any more.

'You didn't.' She smiled; it was only partly true. Frances's sharp tongue had unsettled her, and she felt adrift again, out of her depth like one of the small boats bobbing about on the sea. 'I was feeling a little … I miss my mum's cakes.' She gave a shaky laugh, her eyes smarting. 'Well, I miss my mum, not her cake; well, I do miss her cake but … Oh.' She sighed. 'What I'm trying to say is—' she took a deep breath '—I miss her.' Her voice wobbled and Dolly put her arm around her. Her kind gesture made the tears fall harder and Jessie dipped her head and began to weep, the tears dropping into her lap, onto her hands. Her nose began to run and she wiped it, shaking the tears back, lifting her head. Her friends were sympathetic. Dolly hugged her.

'You're just a bit homesick, that's all. It's perfectly natural. I don't know what I'd do without my mum and dad. I really don't, so I can't even imagine how you must feel.'

Loneliness overwhelmed Jessie and she couldn't respond other than to give them both a weak smile.

'It gets better, Jessie, honestly,' Frances encouraged. 'I cried like a baby the first few weeks I was away from home. I still do sometimes, when I feel things are falling apart.' She sat down opposite Jessie and sipped at her tea. 'Now drink up. You don't want it to go cold; we've worked too hard for it.'

Jessie picked up her cup and drank. It had indeed cooled but was still hot enough to be enjoyable. She put her hankie back in her pocket; Frances crying? It was too hard to imagine.

'I'm so happy the theatre's up and running again,' Dolly said, changing the subject. 'When it closed the last time we thought that was it. Dad's as happy as a sand boy now he's back at the Empire.'

'How long was it closed for, Dolly?' Frances took a large bite out of her cake, squishing together the crumbs on her plate with her fingers.

'Seven or eight months, I suppose. Rumour is that Jack Holland has put all his own money in it and that's why his wife is such a grump. Have you met her?'

Jessie and Frances shook their heads, unable to answer for their mouths were full of food so Dolly went on. 'Apparently, she's a right old frosty face and he's so nice, isn't he?' Jessie and Frances shrugged, grinning at each other. Jessie relaxed back into her seat and listened to Dolly chatter on. Outside it was raining harder still and the rain bounced from the pavement and ran from the gutters above them.

The door of the café opened and Matt, one of the stagehands, stuck his head around the door. 'Rita's on the warpath looking for you two. I'd get a move on and get back on stage, girls. She's not pretty when she's angry.'

'She's not pretty when she's not.' Frances drank down the rest of the tea. 'Sorry to bail out on you, Dolly, but we'd best scarper.'

Jessie looked at her wristwatch. 'We've not been more than the fifteen minutes she said we could have.' She glanced at her half-eaten cake.

'Don't worry,' Dolly said. 'I'll get Joyce to wrap them in paper and bring them back for you.'

'You're an angel.' Frances pulled open the door. 'We'll have to do this again. When we won't be interrupted.'

Dolly's face shone with happiness. 'I'd like that very much.'

Jessie called out to Joyce who had her back to them, washing pots at the sink.

'Bye, Joyce, see you again soon.'

She waved a soapy hand in the air without looking up. 'I'll look forward to it, ducky.'

Chapter 9

The girls dashed back to the theatre and found everyone gathered on stage. Jessie could see Rita's furious expression from the back of the stalls. Frances led the way.

'Oops, looks like they've started without us.'

They hurried themselves and dashed up one set of steps this time, and Jessie felt a shiver of panic. Would Rita send her home? She snatched a look. Rita's scowl was ferocious, but Jack was all smiles beneath his moustache. He had a dimple in his chin like Kirk Douglas, and his green eyes were edged with creases from either lots of laughter or lots of worry. Jessie saw the shiny scar that ran down the left side of his face and part of his ear.

'Welcome, girls,' he said, as Jessie and Frances shuffled into the group, which opened up to let them in.

Rita nudged the pair of them muttering under her breath, 'Where the hell have you been?'

Jessie wondered whether she really wanted a reply and decided against it. The entire company was facing Jack who stood at its heart. 'I'm sure most of you know me, although I'm not flattering myself, merely stating the obvious, and I don't have any talent that would compare with each of yours.' He scanned them all, including Jessie and Frances, making them feel part of something greater than the show. Rita was still scowling.

'I'm Jack Holland, your director—' he spread his hands out at his sides '—and this is Annie Buxton.' Annie was stood beside him as always, the ever-present clipboard clutched to her chest. She greeted them with a gentle but serious smile. 'If you need anything or aren't sure of what we're doing, please let Annie know. I want this to be a cheerful show. A happy cast means you'll all perform better, and we'll get full houses that way. And we need full houses to stay afloat.'

Jessie looked around her; the dancers had automatically gathered together as one group, setting themselves apart from the others on the stage. There was an assembly of men, young and old, their shirt sleeves rolled up to their elbows. Jessie didn't recognise any of their faces and assumed they were the musicians. Everyone else in the cast had a photo displayed front of house so were easily recognised.

A heavily tanned man and woman were standing to Jack's left. He was resting his arm on her shoulder. His muscles rippled through his open shirt and she was standing so erect that Jessie knew without doubt that they were the acrobatic Duo D'Or. She searched the group for Madeleine Moore and Billy Lane, but they hadn't arrived. Wanting to make a grand entrance, no doubt. She smiled wryly and tipped her head so that she couldn't be seen, all the grand theatricals of the performers slowly coming back to her. Two middle-aged men had their heads together and Jessie thought they might be the magician and the man with the saw, Walter Earnshaw and Arthur Trott. She guessed the taller, thinner of the two older men was the magician, his bearing more suited to the sleight of hand that were his stock in trade. Arthur looked like a man who sat down a lot. He would be the musician, without a doubt. Was she right? She paid attention to Jack.

Jack held out his hand and Annie passed him the clipboard. 'I've put together a running order for the show but it's fluid, and subject to change. We'll see how it all hangs together first and I'll make adjustments as we go along. Okay with everyone?' People nodded but Jessie didn't see the sense in him asking. Who would say they weren't okay anyway?

'Rita?'

She put up a hand, stepping forward. Jack smiled and Jessie saw what a heartbreaker he must have been when he was younger. He looked at the clipboard. 'We'll start with you, Rita, and the Variety Girls. Let's see, the first number is "Let Yourself Go".' He turned to Phil. 'Okay?'

Phil nodded. 'We've got most of the dots, Jack. Just need the music for Madeleine and Billy.' Jessie was pleased to see she had guessed correctly as the musicians began to walk into the wings, Phil at their heels. They would have to go downstairs and access the pit through the door that led under the stage. Taking their leave, the other members of the cast made their way down the stage steps into the auditorium and sat in scattered places about the stalls leaving Jack and Annie on stage with the dancers.

'I think we'll go through all the dance numbers first so that I can get an idea of the choreography and how each routine presents. Is that all right with you, Rita?'

'Absolutely, Jack,' Rita gushed.

Frances looked at Jessie and rolled her eyes, and the two girls got into their positions beside Sally, Kay and Virginia and waited while the band settled themselves and began to warm up. There was a blast on the trumpet and saxophone, which made them all jump, causing them to giggle, a sweet refrain on the violin, the thump of a double bass.

Phil, the musical director, looked up to Rita from his position in the orchestra pit once they were ready and Rita gave the signal to begin. Jessie felt her skin tingle when they started to play. It was an entirely different experience dancing with the band; having the brass and string sections made such a difference and even though there were only eight of them, the sound was rich and round. The acoustics in the Empire were perfect and Jessie couldn't help but think what it must be like to sing in the theatre. Her thoughts drifted as she danced so she knew that she'd grasped the steps of the first routine. The girls smiled at each other as they moved across the stage. 'Let Yourself Go' was a tap routine and their metal taps jangled on the wooden floorboards. It was a high-energy routine with lots of high kicks, and Jessie threw herself into the moves they had rehearsed over and over that first week, finally feeling that she was equal to the others in pace, if not in style. Keeping up with them was still a struggle and test of her stamina, but she knew she was improving.

They had changed shoes and were well into the second routine when a young man swaggered into the theatre. The girls carried on dancing, but every eye was on him as he walked down the aisle; his jacket was slung across his back and he was holding onto it with his fore-finger. From the broad smile on his face it seemed he'd received the response he'd hoped for.

'Billy Lane,' Frances said out of the side of her mouth, as she glided past Jessie, her arms in a flowing stretch. 'And isn't he full of himself?'

Jessie twirled in a small circle. 'How can you tell from this distance?' Billy had settled himself into the row behind Jack and Annie and was leaning forward over the back of the empty seat beside Jack, who twisted around to shake hands.

'I can tell.' Frances brought both arms above her head in a sweeping movement and back down again and moved off to the other side of the stage.

Billy was leaning forward in his seat, talking over Jack's shoulder. Jack leaned back to catch what he was saying and laughed, nodding his head in agreement. Billy's hair was dark brown, a lot like Eddie's but he was much older, at least ten years on her brother as far as she could tell from this distance. More like Harry's age than her own. As the music came to an end, the girls waited on the periphery of the stage for the band to organise their sheet music.

'And again, girls.' Rita gave the nod to Phil who started again. 'One, two, three and—'

Jessie kicked her legs, stretching them as long as she could, following Rita's instructions as she stood before them, guiding, correcting as they moved across the floorboards. Jessie couldn't imagine life without music of some kind in it. It was the reason she struggled at her aunt's. Did Iris resent the music because it was Jessie playing it, or was music something that didn't touch her soul? Did she have a soul? The dance ended and the girls remained on stage awaiting further instruction. Jessie leant back on the proscenium arch. She was being unkind. Iris had her good points ... she tried to summon one. There, she had something. She had given them all a home, such as it was.

Jack turned his head to talk to Annie, and Billy sat back draping his right arm over the seat to the side. He looked over at the girls and waved, flashing them a smile. Kay and Sally responded with coy little waves. Frances leaned in to Jessie. 'He's sussing us all out, taking his pick. Those two have returned his advance; they're easy. They'll be no fun. Give him a wide berth, Jessie.'

Jessie frowned; how could she tell that from a simple wave? He looked all right as far as Jessie could tell. He was being friendly. After all, they were going to be spending the whole summer together; they needed to get along.

Jessie recalled her mum's words of warning about being on her own in the theatre. Maybe Frances was right. Rita signalled and they all got into place for the next routine. Jack watched them, talking to Annie, Annie scribbling notes. From what Jessie had seen there seemed to be a lot that would need to be ironed out – or maybe he was noting what was good about the show already. The band started up again and the girls went straight into their moves. What if the notes were about her? Was it obvious that she wasn't good enough? Oh lord, was that it? Frances knew, Rita knew and now they did too. She needed to keep this job, it would look bad to be sacked so early and then she'd never get another position. And Iris would love that. Iris. She lost her concentration and missed a step. Rita glared. She caught up, blushed, carried on. It was a relief when their routines were completed. The Variety Girls stood centre stage, awaiting Jack's instructions.

'Wonderful,' he called out, applauding them all. Rita beamed. 'Great choreography, Rita. Thank you. We'll chat later. Take a break, girls. Now, Duo D'Or, Bert and Hilda?' They stood up from their seats at the front. Bert passed his music down in the pit to Phil and followed Hilda up onto the stage. Hilda moved a small podium to centre stage, they got into position and began their routine. Jessie and the rest of the Variety Girls found seats in the stalls. Everyone sat in silence while the Duo D'Or performed, their bodies twisting and bending in time to the music, marvelling at Bert's strength as he held his wife on the palm of one hand, and Hilda's balance as she stood on her points.

'Gosh, that's absolutely amazing,' Kay said loudly. There was a ripple of applause as they finished, taking their bow as they would during a performance. Arthur Trott got up and played his musical saw then whistled Dixie on a battered metal teapot before finishing with a rounding rendition of 'Any Old Iron' on the spoons. The girls laughed and applauded.

'That will get them nicely warmed up for, Billy,' Jessie said.

'You're not getting any ideas about warming him up, are you, Jessie?' The girls were sat on the front row. Frances had folded her arms and crossed her long legs in front of her and Jessie thought Billy would have a hard time if the audience was full of people like Frances when he hadn't even begun.

'Stating a fact,' Jessie said, insulted. 'As if I'm that forward.'

Frances sighed. 'I didn't think for a minute you were, Jessie my friend. Just marking your card. I've met men like Billy before. You're homesick, it's your first time alone and a man like Billy Lane will take advantage. Wait until you've been round the block a few times. Then you'll know exactly what I mean.'

Jessie folded her arms in a mirror of her friend and stared straight ahead. Frances must think her a fool. She'd make sure not to cry again – not in front of Frances anyway.

Billy bounced up onto the stage brimming with exuberance. He smiled at everyone showing a set of white teeth that looked far too big for his mouth. His dark eyes twinkled with mischief and Jessie couldn't help but return his smile while Frances remained frosty-faced.

He came to the front of the stage, leant forward into the pit and spoke to the musicians.

'All right, lads? You'll be able to have a bit of a rest while I'm on. I'll only need my intro music and then if the drummer can keep an eye on me, I'll need a few boom booms on the bass with the pedal.' The drummer obliged with a demonstration. 'Perfect. And the same music going off.' He stood back, rubbing his hands together. 'That's me done, Jack.'

'Bloody comedians, they're all the same,' Frances mumbled to herself.

'How long do we have your spot down for, Billy?' Jack was conferring with Annie, who was pointing to something on her clipboard.

'Depends how much they're laughing.' He winked at the girls and the ducklings giggled. Billy held out his hand to them. 'There you go.'

'Keep it to twenty then, Billy. If we overrun, the late house will miss the last bus home and we won't be popular.'

'Twenty it is.' He put his hand in his pocket and pulled out a packet of cigarettes, flipped one into his mouth and caught it, pulled out a lighter and lit up, then bounced back down to the stalls with a spring in his step.

'Cocky little devil, isn't he?' Frances sniped. Jessie couldn't grasp why her friend was so irritated by him.

'He seems all right, Frances. He hasn't really done anything, has he?'

Frances sniffed. 'He will.'

Jack called for them all to break for lunch. The girls had made sandwiches at home, and sat and unwrapped them, sharing tea from a thermos, having an impromptu picnic on the stage. Dolly came in bearing their leftover cake in paper napkins.

'I saw some of the cast leave through the foyer so I thought you might be on a break.' She handed the cake over, and Frances and Jessie took it from her. 'The rain's stopped. I thought you'd like to know in case you wanted to get some fresh air.'

'Thanks, Dolly. I forget what time of day it is in here and what the weather's like. It's easy to forget everything, isn't it?'

'Most things,' Frances agreed.

After they'd eaten, they decided to take Dolly's suggestion and go for a walk. Dolly led the way, the pavements wide enough for them to walk side by side. They went down to the promenade and strolled the full length of the pier, past the concert hall, past the benches heavy with holidaymakers watching the world go by. They leaned over the railings at the end and looked down into the water. The wind had blown the rain away and the sea was made grey and murky by sand that had been stirred up. Waves crashed on the metal stanchions that were underneath them and the wind blew their hair about their faces. The air was heavy with the tang of salt and it lingered on their lips and tightened their skin.

'Gosh, this fresh air is doing me the world of good,' Frances cried above the wind.

They studied the long line of trawlers that sat in the estuary. 'I've never seen so many ships before, Dolly. They must be queuing to get in and out of the docks.' She recalled the train stopping there on Sunday. The warehouses and yards, the myriad of masts and funnels as ships gathered in the docks.

'What's that tall tower, Dolly?' Frances pointed with her finger to the long thin construction that rose above the buildings to the left.

'That's the Dock Tower. You can't go in it. It's machinery but it looks good, doesn't it? It's modelled on something in Italy. Pete says when he sees that he knows he's home.'

'Pete?' Frances and Jessie said in unison.

Dolly blushed. 'My fella. He's out there somewhere. He's a deckhand on the *Stalberg*. They should be docking in the next couple of days.'

'That must be hard, not seeing him for weeks while he's at sea.' Jessie thought of how much she missed Harry. At night, when she fell into bed, exhausted, her mind drifted to Harry, back to the lanes outside The Beeches, when he wouldn't hold her hand.

'You get used to it. It might get a whole lot worse soon enough.' Jessie and Frances leaned their backs to the railings. 'He's talking of signing up for the naval reserve if we go to war with Germany. They'll probably turn the trawlers into mine sweepers again, Dad said, like they did the last time.' It was the first time Jessie had seen Dolly without a smile on her pretty face.

'I've only been apart from Harry – my boyfriend – a little more than a week. I didn't realise how much he meant to me until I came here.'

Dolly nodded.

'Absence making the heart grow fonder. Or disappear altogether – out of sight and all that.' Jessie frowned. Frances's voice held no tone of bitterness. It was more of a question, spoken out into the sea air.

'I hope it's the former and he's not forgotten about me, Frances,' Jessie said, wondering if she should really be here, away from those she loved, especially with the future looking so uncertain.

Jessie and Frances made sure they were on stage well before anyone else drifted back, to make up for their absence earlier that day, and to avoid giving Rita any ammunition with which to berate them. Jessie was waiting for a rollicking because she had messed up in the routine in front of Jack, but Rita came back all smiles, Phil on one side, Billy the other, and she'd either forgotten or was so besotted at being the centre of male attention that it had paled into insignificance.

They gathered amongst the stalls waiting for Jack to join them and find out what they were to do next.

'I wonder when Madeleine Moore is going to arrive,' Sally said, saying what Jessie assumed they were all thinking.

'Probably waiting to make a big entrance,' said Billy, a sneer on his lip.

'And so she should, Billy Lane.' Arthur sat back and folded his arms. 'She's a big star. She's been to Hollywood; she's been in films.'

'I saw her in *Heavenly Angels*,' Hilda joined in. 'She's such a beauty.'

'So did I,' Kay chipped in. 'Wasn't she wonderful? I'd have loved to have seen her in the West End. I wonder why she came back? And why Cleethorpes?'

'Don't you know?' Billy grinned with satisfaction. 'Her husband went off with another actress, Minnie something or other. A lot younger than him ... eighteen, nineteen. Rumour has it that he spent her money on the gaming table while she was working from six in the morning on set.'

'How awful. That must be heartbreaking.' Jessie couldn't think of anything worse, being rejected so harshly – and so publicly.

'The movie studios tried to cover it up but a friend of a friend ...'

'... is a gossip,' said Wally and the rest of them in earshot smiled at his putdown.

Billy frowned. 'No, she isn't. But hey, I don't have to explain myself, do I?' Jessie thought he looked genuinely hurt. 'My friend,' he emphasised, 'said she's keeping her head down for a while. It explains why she's come here, out of the way. She probably wants time to get another act together.'

'Fancy your chances then, Billy?'

'Not for me, Frances. I'm perfectly capable of making the big time on my own. I don't need to live off a woman.'

'You do surprise,' Wally said tartly. 'You've gone up in my estimation.'

'Flattered, I'm sure,' he quipped, winking at Jessie.

Jack arrived with Annie and the pair of them walked to the front of the stalls and started going over what the cast were going to be doing that afternoon when they heard the click of heels across the stage. Everyone looked up and Jessie made her first acquaintance with Madeleine Moore. It had to be her, because the woman she was looking at was every inch a star. She was tall and slender with dark-blonde hair that cascaded in Rita Hayworth waves about her shoulders. She was wearing an emerald-green dress that accentuated her neat waist and then flared at her hips. It was beautifully cut; Jessie had seen similar in one of the magazines that was on the shelves of the newsagent's back home. On her head sat a jaunty little green hat that pulled the whole outfit together; she looked sensational. She continued walking to the front of the stage, put the flat of her hand up at her eyes as a shield and peered down at them.

'Am I late?' she said, and Jessie knew she didn't care if she was. She had that aura about her that Jessie knew so well, that indefinable 'it' that set the stars apart from the bill-fillers. The confidence of being the name that would bring in the crowds.

Jack made his way briskly to the steps to greet her. 'Not at all. Not. At. All.'

She leant forwards and he kissed her on both cheeks like a continental, then took hold of her hand and led her down the stairs. She stepped down gracefully in her high heels, her shapely calves showing as the dress flared with her movement. You could have heard a pin drop, and, as she came towards them, they were engulfed in a cloud of her perfume.

'Ladies and gentlemen,' Jack announced proudly, 'the star of the show, Madeleine Moore.'

Madeleine tipped her head slightly in greeting and there were murmurs of 'Hello' and 'Welcome' from those assembled and much shaking of hands from the rest of the cast.

'Lovely to meet you all.' Madeleine's voice was husky. 'I'm sure we're going to have a wonderful summer together.'

Jack put a hand on the small of Madeleine's back. 'Rita, if you and the girls would like to use the stage for the afternoon and rehearse with the band, then I'll take this opportunity for everyone else on the show to get acquainted.'

Rita looked disappointed not to be included but plastered on a smile and ordered the girls to get on stage. The band picked up their jackets and headed back into the pit and they spent the next two hours going over their routines. Jessie was tired, they all were, but having more people around brought a new energy. She was delighted to find that she could now keep up with everyone else and noticed that the other girls were getting things wrong as well. She had been so self-absorbed that she thought she was the only one making mistakes.

Jack returned with Annie, and Madeleine. The Duo D'or went up the steps and into the dressing room but there was no sign of Billy or anyone else. Madeleine took a seat next to Annie, while Jack watched the girls from the side of the stage. When they had finished the

routine he walked over to Rita, applauding gently. He
looked happy with things so far.

'You've all worked so hard and it's looking great,
girls. I'm going to work with Annie tonight and get a
few things in place and we'll do a dry run of all your
routines tomorrow afternoon from the top.' The girls
looked at each other, relieved that he wasn't disappointed by anything they'd done so far.

'Now then—' he smiled '—I want you to go home
and get some rest so that you're fresh in the morning.
Thanks, Rita.'

Rita clapped her hands and told everyone to break.
Frances raised her eyebrows. Jessie went to get her bag.

'Jessie?'

She turned to find Jack a few feet in front of her.
He was rubbing his chin. 'I noticed your surname –
Delaney. Any chance you're related to Davey Delaney?'

Jessie was speechless for a moment. She nodded. 'He
was my dad.'

'Was? His face was sombre.

'He passed away almost a year ago.' Jessie's voice
was quiet. The months had seemed like years.

'Well, I'll be.' He shook his head. 'I'm so sorry to
hear that, Jessie. I knew him so well. We were in the
same regiment.' He stared into the mid distance. 'When
I saw your name, then you … Well, I thought you had
the look of him, his smile definitely.' He smiled at her
now, taking her hand and patting it. 'He was such a
marvellous musician, a marvellous man. We must talk.
We'll have more time once the show's up and running.'

He walked away and Jessie couldn't move. It had been so unexpected, and she turned to seek Frances but instead caught the furious scowl on Rita's face. Even so, a look couldn't dampen her joy. She went to get her bag that she'd been stopped from collecting. As she bent down Rita leaned into her.

'Don't get above yourself, Delaney. You still have to prove yourself. As I've already said, you can be replaced.' She turned on her heel and walked off, draping her arms around Dally and Virginia as they left the stage.

'I heard what she said.' Frances took her arm. 'And if there's any funny business I'll be first in the queue to tell Jack Holland.' The pair of them left through the auditorium, their arms linked as they went into the foyer.

Jessie was elated. Meeting Jack Holland had been a sign from heaven, leaving her in no doubt that she was meant to be here. She didn't care what Rita said; there was someone here who knew her dad and it was a link, bringing him back into her life, and she felt strong again. He was with her and always would be, and she could put up with whatever Rita threw at her.

Chapter 10

Jessie and Frances had risen early, making time for a good breakfast before they set off for the theatre and the final dress rehearsal. Once they left they wouldn't be back until late that night or the early hours of the following morning. It had been a hectic week, the days in the theatre long, the breaks short as they were put through their paces by Rita, but Jessie felt like she was finally earning her place as one of the Variety Girls. Her mistakes were fewer, her timing more precise.

Frances battered the top of her boiled egg. They had enough for two each and had made some toasted soldiers to dip in. It reminded Jessie of times with her mum when they had eaten tea before they left to accompany their dad to a show. In later years, when travelling up and down the country had been limited by his poor health, he'd earned a meagre living performing locally when he could and taking in pupils for music lessons; Grace had taken in sewing. They had lived frugally but not poorly. 'Poor is a state of mind,' her dad often said, 'and if you have music, love and laughter, you'll be the richest woman in the world. Remember that, my darling girl.' Sitting here with Frances, she did indeed feel wealthy. She had friends, good friends, even though they had known each other only a short time.

'Are any of your family coming tomorrow night, Frances?'

She took a mouthful of egg and shook her head.

'No, they're all in Ireland.'

'That's a shame.'

'It is,' Frances agreed, 'but this is where the work is, and I'm content. They write. They'll send cards.' She sprinkled more salt on her egg.

Jessie persevered. 'Will they come later in the season?'

'No.' Frances was abrupt. She dipped one of her bread soldiers in her yolk and bit down on it. 'What time's your ma arriving tomorrow? Is she coming on the train? I'll walk down with you.' Frances had deftly flipped the conversation back to Jessie.

'Harry will bring Mum and Eddie in his car. They're staying until Sunday so if we don't get too many notes I'll be able to spend most of Saturday with them.' She couldn't help smiling even though she was aware that Frances wouldn't have such luxury. Being apart from Harry had made her realise what he meant to her. Absence did make the heart grow fonder after all.

'What about your aunt and uncle? Will they come?'

'I wouldn't think so. My aunt is such a snob. She thinks the theatre is common.' She regaled Frances with Iris's reaction to her coming back to the theatre.

Frances took the last bit of white from her egg and turned the empty shell upside down in the cup. 'She's not alone. Lots of people are of that opinion.' She modulated her voice so that it sounded upper class. 'Terribly, terribly louche, isn't it, Charles: all that exposed flesh.'

157

She wiggled her eyebrows up and down and the pair of them giggled. 'She sounds an absolute dragon.'

'She is.'

They were laughing when Geraldine joined them.

'Are you talking about me again, Frances?' She was neat as always, and Jessie imagined she arrived home exactly the same, as if no hair on her head would dare to stray. They had met only briefly in the week or so since Jessie had been at Barkhouse Lane. Jessie knew little about her other than that she worked in offices at Grimsby Docks, an accountant and deputy head of a department. She was of similar age to Grace but much more robust. She had an open face and kind eyes, but her manner was brisk and efficient. Jessie knew she wouldn't stand a moment's nonsense and it made her feel safe.

Frances turned. 'Caught red-handed, Geraldine. You get me every time.'

She patted Frances on her shoulder. 'Good to see that you're taking care yourself.' She went to the wall cupboard and took out a tea caddy and put it to one side, took the kettle to the tap then put it on the gas stove. 'Would you girls like a top-up before you go?'

Jessie looked at Frances; she would take her lead. 'Yes, we have time, that would be lovely, Geraldine. Thanks.'

Frances and Jessie washed the plates and egg cups and tidied them away. When the kettle sang out, Geraldine filled the teapot, got herself a cup and saucer and sat down at the table with Frances. Jessie elected to stand and leaned against the wall by the window that looked out onto the narrow backyard where the washing they'd done earlier that morning swung out on the line. It was cloudy but dry; she hoped it would stay that way. Geraldine poured and handed a cup to Jessie. 'I must ferret out another chair or two now that we're getting things sorted.'

'We'll have time to help once the show's started.' Frances examined her nails then looked up. 'The pressure will be off a little.'

Geraldine smiled. 'I must say, girls, it's nice to have some company. It's been a long time since I shared a morning brew.'

'Haven't any of the other lodgers ever joined you?' Jessie tipped a little milk into her tea, contemplating how well-equipped the house was. It might be a little tired and in need of a lick of paint, but the china was pretty, and the rooms must have been homely once. Overall, there was little to complain about and at least it was clean, mostly. Far removed from some of the rooms her parents had rented in later years.

Geraldine spooned two sugars into her cup and stirred briskly, placing the spoon on her saucer. 'Reg hasn't been renting it long enough for me to notice. He lived here with his mother; it was the family house. When she died, he inherited it.' She picked up her cup, blew gently over the top of her tea and sipped a little. 'He's at sea most of the time but didn't want to sell it, so he lets it out. On the QT, I think he's taken up with a woman in Hull so he's not so inclined to dash back here. He keeps the front room for himself, but it seems unlikely we'll see much of him. I get a reduced rate for taking care of things. It suits us both.' She got up and went to a cupboard, brought out a packet of biscuits and offered them around. 'As there's only the three of us, how about we each have a cupboard and we can have a kitty for things like tea, milk and bread. That way there'll be less waste. I can't eat a whole loaf and I do enjoy a slice of toast now and again.'

'Fine by me.' Frances checked with Jessie, who indicated her agreement with a nod.

'We'll be here more in the daytime when the show gets going.' Jessie looked around the kitchen. 'We'll even get time to do a little baking.' She could make the fruit cake from her mum's recipe. She would write and ask for it. It would be a sliver of connection to Grace.

'Speak for yourself, Jessie. I'll be chief taster and washer upper, but I've never been a cook. My cakes turn out like cardboard.'

'You're on. I hate washing up anyway.'

Jessie looked at the clock that hung on the lintel over the kitchen sink. There were still the traces of home. Reg's mum didn't have much but what she had was obviously well loved and cared for. One day Jessie would have a home of her own, with Harry. She imagined the curtains she would have and decorated the little kitchen in her mind. Lemon paint on the walls and pale-blue cupboards. She would have a plate rack over the gas cooker and ask Grace to make some curtains to cover the gap by the sink where all the cleaning cloths and buckets would be stored. Sewing was not her forte, her time had been spent practising piano and so many of her mum's skills had not been passed on to her. But there was time to learn. She grinned to herself. It was easy to dream but reality took effort.

'We'd better get off, Jessie.' Frances got to her feet and picked up her empty cup and saucer. 'Rita will be on the warpath if we're late.'

Jessie sprang away from the wall at the mention of Rita's name. It was guaranteed to keep her on her mettle, and she didn't want to give her the slightest excuse to complain.

The girls collected their bags and went out into the street. The sky was thick with cloud and gulls soared above them, their cries drifting across the air. It was good to have a landlady like Geraldine, and Grace would be pleased to know that an older woman was around. Jessie had come to realise the precariousness of the situation she had thrust herself in. Had her aunt been right to make a fuss? What she was doing was respectable but to come away and live on her own, amongst strangers? She hadn't thought it through.

She had been unkind to her aunt, hadn't she? And the longer she was away from home, the more she came to think that perhaps Aunt Iris really did have her best interests at heart. She linked her arm into Frances's and they sauntered to the theatre in the fresh air. The streets were still relatively quiet. Shop keepers outside their premises opening up the awnings called ''Ow do' and 'Morning' as they passed by. Once they had got the first few shows underway, she would send Uncle Norman and Aunt Iris two tickets. If they came, they'd see that she'd not been foolhardy. Geraldine was not unlike Miss Symonds and as such was a sort of chaperone. She looked up at the sky, found a patch of blue and grinned, her heart full of her good fortune.

Winnie and Doris, the theatre cleaners, were busy in the foyer. Doris was mopping the tiled floor and Winnie was halfway up the stairs to the dress circle, buffing up the brass handrail as the girls walked in.

'Morning, girls. I hope you've got your best knickers on today for all them high kicks you'll be doing later.'

'I hope you've got yours on, Doris. Sure, I can get a grand view of your backside from here.'

Doris sat back on her knees. Her hair was covered in a knotted scarf and her face was red with exertion. She was wearing a dark-plum apron edged with gold that crossed over her generous bosom, her sleeves rolled up to her elbows. 'You cheeky monkey.' She was as round as Winnie was long and Jessie had already thought that they would have made a good double act themselves. Doris was jolly, Winnie morose, and they made perfect foils for each other.

'We're coming in to watch when we've finished.' Winnie was putting little effort into her buffing, and Doris rolled her eyes at Jessie who bit at her lower lip to hide a smile.

Doris had already confided in Jessie that, 'Winnie needed a bullet up her backside but she was a good sort.' Watching Winnie slowly rub up and down the rail made Jessie feel close to laughter. Winnie's droopy eyes and long chin reminded Jessie of one of the donkeys she had seen on the beach. She made for the door to the stalls and held it open for Frances.

'I'll kick extra high so that you can check my drawers, ladies,' Frances said as a parting shot, leading the way into the auditorium. Jessie followed her.

Rita was already there, along with the other girls, but being as they were all sharing the same digs it was inevitable that Rita would make sure they were on the ball. Not for the first time, Jessie gave silent thanks that Frances had rescued her. Mike, Bob and Matt were walking about the stage with Jack and Annie. It looked like most of the work was done and they were ready for the dress rehearsal. They had carried out the technical the previous evening, checking that everyone was happy with the lighting for their respective spots on the show. It had been a late night; today would be even longer.

Frances and Jessie went through the pass door at the side of the stage and went downstairs to the dressing rooms. They had brought sandwiches and snacks with them and at some point planned to call in at Joyce's. It was getting to be a habit but a rather lovely one. All the rooms had been allocated when they arrived; there had been no dissent. The girls were opposite the band. Next door to them were Bert and Hilda, then Wally and Arthur who were sharing a room. Madeleine and Billy had their own rooms at the end, nearest the stage door. Kay waltzed in with her arms draped with clothes. 'Rita wants us to get our costumes down here ready for the run-through.

Sally and Virginia are already on their way. You better get up to Wardrobe sharpish.'

Jessie moved quickly, Frances dawdling behind her as they went up to Wardrobe on the first floor. The costume fittings had been finished the previous morning, and Mary would have worked long into the night to get things ready. She might have been dead on her knees, but she was still sharp as a tack when the girls found her.

'Thought you two would be the last to turn up.' She reached across to the rail. 'Jessie, get your dress off and put this one back on.' She held up the dove-grey dress that would be used in the finale. 'I want to check the sleeves are right; they looked cockeyed yesterday.' Jessie did as she was told, quickly slipping out of her skirt and blouse and into the satin grey. 'Get a kick on, the other lasses will be back for their shoes in a minute and I won't have too many of you in here at once.' Frances took her own clothes and called to Jessie over her shoulder.

'See you on stage.'

Mary tugged gently at Jessie's sleeves, stood back, squinted, leaned forward then back again. 'You'll do, off it comes. Must've been my eyeballs.'

Jessie handed the dress back to Mary who slipped it onto a hanger while Jessie got back into her own clothes. 'I should think your eyes are sore, Mary. It's been a lot of close work and the light in here isn't good.'

Mary gathered Jessie's other outfits and handed them to her. 'It's not just the light, Jessie. My eyesight's not what it was. Still—' she patted Jessie's hand as she clutched at the brightly coloured costumes '—I'll keep going as long as I can. We all will, won't we?'

She nodded and dashed back downstairs. In the dressing room the girls were getting into their costumes – black shorts and cream satin blouses – for the opening.

'Jack's taking it from the top.' Virginia was fastening her shoes, her red hair cascading about her shoulders. She pulled it back with two combs, then checked the mirror. 'I'm off to sit in the wings.' Jessie squeezed herself in and got ready as quickly as she could. She would need full make-up; it would be as if they were working to a full house.

The girls watched from the stalls or the wings when they weren't needed. Arthur was a corker, playing his saw, spoons and a metal teapot. Wally was slick, his sleight of hand deft as he made lit cigarettes appear and disappear. Jessie wondered that he didn't burn his suit. They went through their dance that opened the second half without a hitch and came off into the wings. Billy was on next.

'Are you going to tell your gags this time, Billy?' Kay asked as they hung around in the prompt side.

'No point, you won't find them funny. My act needs an audience.'

'We all need an audience, Mr Lane.' It was Madeleine. She had been standing behind them. Her dress was the palest green, decorated with beads and edged with marabou feathers that had been dyed the same colour. Her hair curled in soft waves, her make-up immaculate.

'Of course, Madeleine, of course we do. I didn't mean that. It's just hard to be funny when the house is cold.' Madeleine gave a slight tilt of her head. She didn't say anything, but Jessie got the impression that she didn't agree.

'You look stunning,' he said. 'As always.'

She smiled. 'Don't miss your cue.' Billy turned and tripped out onto the stage, swinging his arms flamboyantly.

The Variety Girls whispered quietly amongst themselves while Billy walked through his act. He talked flatly through his patter putting no effort into it whatsoever and Jessie wondered how he could be so relaxed about it all. Madeleine walked into a dark space at the back of the stage and turned her back to everyone. When she heard Billy's play-off music she walked towards them, deep in concentration. Virginia and Sally stood back to let her past, smiling broadly but Madeleine was too focused to respond.

Her music played and she walked on as if the theatre was full. Jessie watched her work, first from the wings and then into the stalls where she sat entranced, observing the way Madeleine made use of the stage and performed to the handful of people that were her audience. Jessie turned her neck and saw Doris and Winnie leaning in the front of their seats in absolute raptures. They applauded loudly when she finished. Everyone did, and Jessie felt a surge of determination within her. One day, yes, one day, that would be her, Jessie Delaney.

They finally broke at half-past nine, all relieved that there hadn't been an audience present. One of the strings went on the violin and it screeched wildly. A backcloth was dropped in and narrowly missed knocking one of the stagehands unconscious. Wally sneezed and dropped half his cards, but worst of all Jessie's heel broke on the final walk down and she had to limp off into the wings.

'Bad dress rehearsal, good opening night. That's what they say,' Wally said cheerfully as they all trooped into the stalls to wait for Jack's report. 'Not your fault, lass, and you were a trouper and got yourself sorted. Not much you can do in the circumstances.'

She shrugged. Why did it have to be her shoe? She slumped down into a seat. Her ankle was throbbing like the very devil.

'How's your ankle, Jessie?' She turned to find Madeleine behind her. 'I saw that it fell awkwardly as your heel went. Are you hurt?'

'No, I'm fine. Thank you, Miss Moore.'

The woman smiled and Jessie warmed to her. Since she had arrived the other day she had kept herself apart from everyone else, but then she hadn't needed much rehearsal. None of the acts had; they came with their own music, their lighting scripts and all they needed to know was how long they had and where they were in the running and a general awareness of the stage they were to perform on.

Madeleine settled back into her seat. She'd changed from her costume into a white blouse with a Peter Pan collar showing over a navy jacket and pencil skirt, looking absolutely impeccable. One day Jessie would be able to afford such clothes.

Jack walked on stage with Annie close at his heels. She handed over the clipboard and proceeded to give his notes, asking for few changes. It hadn't been too bad. He spoke softly to Annie and she disappeared into the wings. Jack waited while the crew members came out onto the stage and sat on the treads in front of the backcloth, and Annie made her way down the steps at the front of the stage and sat with the cast.

Jack began to speak. 'Before I let you go, I'd like to say a few words. A lot of people tried to dissuade me from taking on this theatre and putting on a live show. There will always be the naysayers; I'm sure you've met many of them yourselves.' He paused. Everyone nodded their heads. So, they all had their disapproving aunts then. 'If war comes, and every day it grows more likely that it will, people like yourselves will be needed more than ever. I saw action in the Great War and let me tell you that at the end of a long day's fighting many of us would cobble together our talents, poor as they were, and entertain each other, a song, a tune on a mouth organ. If we found a piano in a bar we would play it. We craved anything that cheered us. I'm sorry to bring things to a sombre tone but it's important to be aware of it.' There were mumblings throughout the cast as they indicated their agreement. He cleared his throat; he smiled. Jessie remembered her dad again. Always leave them smiling. 'You're all in the cheer-up business,' Jack said, spreading his hands out towards them. 'Don't ever forget how important it is.'

Chapter 11

The main bedroom at the front of the house was cool and dark. Grace had drawn back the curtains and opened the window to let in the much-needed air. Harry had returned from the kitchen with a glass of water and handed it to Grace who stood by the side of the double bed. The three of them had been in the hallway getting ready to leave when there had been an almighty thump and Eddie had rushed upstairs, two at a time, to find his aunt on her bedroom floor. Harry and Grace had swiftly followed, Grace instructing Harry and Eddie to help Iris onto her bed.

She was now lying stretched out like a corpse on the green eiderdown, the back of her hand against her eyes, moaning softly. Or was it whimpering? Harry couldn't tell. The room was dark with heavy furniture, which obscured most of the delicate floral wallpaper behind it. Perfume bottles and a silver-backed brush set was set out neatly on the dressing table under a large round mirror. Through it, Harry watched the scene playing out between Grace and Iris.

'You must've got up too quickly, Iris,' Grace said, plumping up the feather pillows, urging her to sit up. 'You'll feel better more upright. The blood would have rushed to your head.'

Iris let out another moan and kept her eyes firmly shut. Harry didn't think she looked ill. Pale, yes, but then she was white-faced to begin with and the darkness of her hair only accentuated it. She remained resolutely still. It didn't appear that she was going to do anything Grace suggested. He looked at his watch. They should have left twenty minutes ago and every minute that passed meant less time with Jessie. He tried not to get frustrated watching Grace as she patiently tended to Iris.

'Iris, dear. Take a little water. It will help.' Grace cradled Iris's head in her hands, but Iris was unresponsive. Harry didn't know how Grace could still find it in her; hadn't she had enough of caring for people? It seemed that no one ever cared for her and Harry guessed she wouldn't particularly like it if they did. She was a self-contained woman and he admired her for it. It couldn't be easy losing your husband and then having to live with relatives, and distant ones at that. He could barely remember his own mother and after she died, he saw little of his father and step-mother – which was as he liked it.

Grace passed the glass of water to Eddie who stepped away from the window, took it, and stepped back again, keeping as flat against the wall as he could. He was awkward in his aunt's room but then so was Harry.

'Harry?' Grace stood at one side of the bed by Iris's head. She indicated for him to go around to the other. 'Put your arm through Iris's armpit and hook her in the crook of your arm.' She demonstrated and he copied. Iris whimpered. 'On the count of three we'll lift

together and put her up on the pillows. One, two, three.'
They moved in unison and Iris was propped up whether
she liked it or not. Grace smoothed the pillows either
side of Iris's head then ran her hand over her brow,
turned her palm upwards and held it there. 'You don't
feel hot, Iris. You don't have a temperature.' The colour
was returning to Iris's cheeks. Grace reached out for the
glass of water and Eddie gave it to her. Grace held it to
Iris's lips. 'Sip this, Iris.' She was firm. It was an order.
Harry noticed the change in her manner.

Iris flickered her eyelids.

'Would you like me to get someone to sit with you
until Norman gets home? I could ask Nelly to stay on.'

Iris moved her head from side to side. 'Not that girl. I
need a doctor, Grace. Would you call for Dr Bellamy?'
Her voice was feeble, and Harry had to strain to hear.

Grace took Iris's hand and felt her pulse, counted the
beats against her wristwatch. 'You don't need a doctor,
Iris. There's nothing he can do. You need to rest. Have
you eaten anything today? Shall I get Nelly to bring you
some soup?'

Iris turned her head away. 'I couldn't eat a morsel.'

Grace's shoulders sagged. Harry looked to Eddie who
had stayed by the window. Neither had sat down, waiting on Grace as to what to do next. Harry was desperate
for them to get on the road but didn't want to hassle her.
He looked at his watch again. They really should leave
now if they wanted to make the start of the show. Jessie
had said she'd meet them in the café around the corner,
Joyce's, but they'd missed that opportunity already. If

they didn't leave soon they would miss Jessie's opening routine. Harry heard 'Let Yourself Go' in his head. He felt he knew every part of the show from her letters and was desperate not to miss any of it. He closed his eyes and pictured Jessie's smiling face, the little dimple to the left of her lips. He would be kissing those lips soon enough.

'Harry?'

He opened his eyes.

'Could you call for Dr Bellamy,' Grace said calmly. 'The number is five one two. I can sit with Iris until he arrives.'

He looked at her, silently pleading, but she shrugged. What else could they do?

He hurried down the stairs and dialled the number from the telephone in the hall. He could hear Nelly whistling in the kitchen as she washed the dishes, the sound clattering around the scullery and into the hall, making the most of her freedom while Iris was out of earshot.

The call was put through. Mrs Bellamy answered and said her husband was with a patient but would be with them directly. Harry sighed and trudged back up the stairs to report to Grace wondering how long 'directly' meant. In his brief absence, Grace had pulled up a chair and was sat beside Iris, indicating a long wait.

'He'll be here as soon as he can.' Harry jerked his head at Eddie who followed him out of the room. They went outside into the front garden. Harry had had enough of the house.

Eddie thrust his hands in his pockets. He'd slipped his sweater off when it was obvious there would be a delay and tied it about his waist. Harry leaned on the gate and stared down the lane, straining to hear a car engine. If Norman arrived, they could leave. He took out a cigarette, almost offered one to Eddie before thinking better of it. He lit up and took a long drag to get the nicotine, tilted his head back and blew the smoke out in a long exhale.

'I don't think she's ill at all,' Eddie said, slipping his hands out of his pockets and leaning next to Harry. 'She's doing it on purpose.'

Harry flicked his ash over the gate and onto the verge. The two of them faced forward. 'You don't know that,' Harry said, cautiously. He'd thought the same himself, but it wouldn't do to speak his thoughts. Norman was his boss and effectively so was Iris. It wouldn't do to tittle-tattle.

'I do.' Eddie was adamant. 'She's been perfectly fine all day. Then as soon as me and Mum started to get our things ready, she said she felt ill. It's because we're going to see Jessie. She doesn't want us to go.'

Harry was thoughtful. He took another drag on his cigarette, using it as punctuation to their conversation. Careful, Harry, he told himself. It won't do to jump to conclusions and Eddie here, well, he just wants to see his sister. He patted his arm. 'It's all right, old chap. We'll still see Jessie. The doctor will be here soon enough to check your aunt over, then we can go. I'll push the Austin to make up the time.'

Eddie huffed in frustration and Harry felt for him but there was nothing to do but wait.

Dr Bellamy arrived twenty minutes later and pronounced Iris fit and well, as Harry knew he would. Satisfied that Iris was not in any great danger, Grace gave instructions to Nelly to wait until Norman arrived home. Harry put their overnight bags in the car, leaving Grace to write a quick note for Norman. He went back in and Grace grabbed her coat from the stand in the hall and followed the boys into the drive. Eddie climbed into the back and Harry held the door while Grace got in the front, closed it and walked round to the driver's side. He glanced up one last time and saw the curtains of the upstairs room move. He was certain Iris had been standing there. Or had it been a trick of the light? The sun was dropping in the sky, bathing the lane in a soft golden glow. Midges hovered over the flowers and a Cabbage White danced amongst the red-hot pokers. They would hit the traffic leaving this late, but he would get there as fast as he could.

'I'm sorry,' Grace said as they left the village behind. 'I couldn't leave her.' She paused. 'Just in case.'

'There's no need to apologise, Grace.' He indicated, turned right. 'It wasn't worth taking the risk. At least the doctor has checked her over.'

Eddie leant forward and stuck his head and shoulders between the two front seats. 'She was acting, wasn't she, Mum? She didn't want us to see Jessie. She wanted to hurt her.'

'Now, now, Eddie. That's a bit harsh.'

He slipped back into the back seat. 'But it's true.'

Harry saw him through his rear-view mirror, slumped back, staring out of the window. The boy was right. He knew it, they all knew it, but they were trapped by Iris and Norman's so-called goodwill.

Harry pushed the car as hard as he dare. When they reached clear stretches, he put his foot down but the road didn't lend itself to speed, too many twists and turns for that. He checked his watch continuously, aware of the minutes ticking by, pressing his foot harder on the pedal, wanting with all his heart to make the curtain. He'd almost convinced himself that they could make it when smoke started pouring from the engine and they had been forced to pull into a layby. Harry and Eddie got out. The bonnet was too hot to touch, and they had no option but to wait until it cooled down.

Grace got out too. 'I saw a call box a little way back, by those two shops. I'll try and get a message to Jessie. Tell her we might be a little late.'

The ground was damp, the sky heavy with clouds and Harry hoped that they would be able to get back on the road before the rain started again. He looked down the road, no sign of Grace. Eddie was leaning over the engine, the bonnet popped up and secured. He held his hand over the radiator cap and tested for heat, put the cloth in his hand and tried to take it off. It had cooled sufficiently for him to grip and release it, twisting and lifting, the hot air gasping free. He turned to Harry.

'That should help cool it down a bit quicker.' He rubbed his hands on the cloth, stuffed it into his trouser pocket and settled himself on the verge next to Harry.

'No sign of your mum. Do you think one of us should have gone with her?'

Eddie shook his head and leaned back on his elbows.

'Mum's fine. She always walks when she's uptight.'

Uptight? He hadn't noticed. Whatever inner turmoil she was suffering was not evident as she had sat calm and resolute in the front seat. Even when smoke had poured from the engine, she'd not uttered a word of frustration – unlike Harry who had hit the steering wheel with the flat of his hand and muttered a few choice words. Why now, why when they were so close? Another half hour and they would have been there for Jessie. He leaned back on his elbows alongside Eddie and the pair of them watched a plane soar overhead. They must be near training airfields because they had seen quite a few go up and do loops and circuits.

Harry was continually amazed by this boy, so laid-back and matter of fact that he seemed older than his years. He was as different from Jessie as it was possible to be. What was his girl doing now? Getting ready in her dressing room, talking with her friends, going over her routines? He was furious with Iris; he'd thought of nothing else as they had raced along the roads, trying to make up for lost time. As the lanes turned into streets, and then to roads he remembered the fuss Iris had caused not wanting Jessie to go; to be fair, neither had he – but for different reasons. Iris appeared to be hell-bent on making her unhappy. Harry pulled at the strands of damp grass behind him. He'd found an old newspaper in the back of the car and sat on it to protect his flannels but was beginning to feel the damp through the seat of his trousers. A small plane buzzed above them.

'When the war starts, will you sign up, Harry?'

He thought of when Jessie had asked him the same question and he'd not wanted to talk about it, to spoil their evening, but the mood in the country was changing daily reluctance but an acceptance too. It was hardly worth bluffing now. He sought to reassure the lad, at the same time wondering whether that was a kindness or not. It was the unexpected that shocked – as it had done when he'd discovered Jessie was leaving. How much nicer it would've been to have talked it over with her first. He erred towards kindness. 'We don't know that there will be a war yet.'

Eddie sat up and leant on his knees. 'Yes, there will. People are different. They talk differently. Serious.'

Harry watched a number of cars pass them by. Lucky beggars. He sighed. No use softening things as far as Eddie was concerned. 'I'll join the RAF, if they'll have me. I'd rather be up in the air than on land or sea. Free as a bird.'

'Being shot at ...'

Harry nudged him with his elbow and grinned. 'I'll be shot at wherever I am so I might as well choose for myself.'

Eddie turned to him. His face was earnest, his voice firm. 'I want to choose for myself too, Harry. I don't want to push papers at Uncle Norman's office. I want to be an engineer.' He looked at Harry. 'Jessie has done the right thing, you know.'

'I know.' He paused. 'I miss her though.'

'It was good that she went when she did. Before Iris crushed her like she's crushing Mum.'

'Your mum doesn't strike me as someone being crushed. More as biding her time.'

It was at that moment that Grace came into view, carrying a brown paper bag.

'I brought some apples.' She gave them one and they polished them on their trousers before biting. 'I tried to call the stage door from the kiosk in the village, but it was engaged. I couldn't wait any longer. Has the radiator cooled yet?'

Eddie got up and felt the metal. 'We can put the water in now, Harry.' Harry handed over the can of water he kept in the car and Eddie poured every drop in, shaking the can a few times for good measure. 'Good job we waited, the radiator would've cracked.' He screwed the cap back on, wiped his hands. 'We should be there for the second half.'

'This is my fault,' Harry apologised. 'I should have checked the water before we left.'

Grace put a gentle hand on his shoulder. 'No apologies necessary, Harry. Our delay was in no way down to you, so don't give it another minute's thought. Please.'

He agreed, albeit reluctantly. Iris had a hand in it, but they might at least have made curtain up. He saw the flowers he had bought for Jessie lying on the back seat looking rather dejected and worse for wear. Not wanting to waste any more time the three of them got back into the Austin. There were few cars on the road as dusk fell, and Harry silently prayed that no other mishaps would befall them.

Chapter 12

It was cosy in George's office at the stage door, and Jessie sat with Jasper the theatre cat curled up on her lap. The walls were studded with leaflets, lists and scrappy notes that George had scribbled with his dark, stubby pencil when someone left a message for cast members. He would tear them off and hand them over when appropriate. He prided himself on not forgetting anything and this was his fail-safe system. The dressing-room keys hung beneath a set of pigeon holes. A pile of cards and letters had arrived in the late post and were waiting to be sorted. Jessie had already opened a bunch of hers from Grace and Eddie, Harry and Miss Symonds; even dear old Nelly had sent one. She'd been surprised to receive cards from some of Cole's clients. She hadn't told anyone – Norman had asked her not to, not unkindly, and she had respected his wishes – so it must have been Miss Symonds.

She ran through the routines in her head, which side of the stage she needed to exit on, where she needed to be for the finale. Yesterday's dress rehearsal hadn't been too bad. Everyone had been tense, nervous about their performance, and, knowing she wasn't alone, she'd slept a little better. But now that the minutes were ticking away to curtain up, she was feeling sick with anticipation, hoping she'd remember her steps, terrified she would fall flat on her face. Some dealt with it by being very quiet, others by being snappy but mostly they were all just concentrating as hard as they could to get it right. She'd made it this far. Could she hold onto her job after all? There was still a long way to go. What she was earning was enough to keep herself and save a little, but not enough to look after three people. Not yet. And there would be shoes to buy, and make-up when her own ran out. These were the random expenses that made it hard for her savings to amount to much. Once the show was bedded in, the other routines rehearsed, she would seek other income. If Joyce's hadn't been in such close proximity to the theatre she could have filled the position she was advertising, but it wouldn't do for her to be serving in a café and then pop up on stage in all her finery. It spoiled the illusion and the illusion had to be maintained at all costs.

'Ready for the show tonight?' George said, slipping the last card into the correct slot. Jessie moved to get up and let him have his chair back, but he stopped her with a shake of his head and held out his flat hand. 'Stay there, old Jasper's enjoying that quiet time with you. He doesn't take to everyone. He's a very fussy cat.' The cat purred again as if agreeing with George.

The door opened and Billy walked in. It was lashing down outside and, if it kept up, Jessie wondered if anyone would want to turn out to see the show. The rain was dripping off Billy's hair and he smoothed it back with his hand, blinking away raindrops that had fallen onto his eyelashes. He grinned when he saw Jessie. 'Things are looking up. You're the prettiest stage doorman I've ever seen. I like Jack's style.'

George reached into the pigeon hole and handed Billy his mail and his key. Billy flicked through the sheaf of cards. 'I must tell my mum to stop sending me so many.' He tucked them into his inside pocket, jangling his key. 'She doesn't want anyone to think that I'm not loved.' Jessie gave a wry smile. George cleared his throat.

'Oh, I'm sure your mum doesn't think anything of the sort and by the look of the handwriting they're all from different people.'

Billy slicked his hair back again. 'You spoil all the fun, George.' He winked at Jessie.

'Hmpff.' George put himself between Billy and Jessie and busied himself, reading every bit of paperwork on his walls. Billy reached around him, ducking into the gap between George's head and shoulders. Jessie concentrated on Jasper.

'Waiting for someone, Jessie?'

She looked up; he wasn't teasing now, simply making polite conversation.

'My mum and brother are coming to the performance. My boyfriend Harry is bringing them in his car.' Boyfriend: she liked the sound of the word and its attachment to Harry. She couldn't wait to see him, to see them all. She'd remained at Joyce's as long as she could before deciding to make her way to the theatre. They should have arrived an hour ago and as the minutes flew by she tried to dismiss the wild imaginings that were beginning to fill her head, of things that might befall them as they made their way to her.

'That's good. You're lucky to have someone out there for you. My old mum can't get about much these days. She'd love to come and see her little Billy perform.' He pushed out his bottom lip.

George sniffed, rather loudly Jessie thought. The stage door opened again, and Bert reached his arm over. George handed him a key and checked for post, shook his head. Bert ambled down the steps to his dressing room.

'Oh, what a shame,' Jessie said, ruffling Jasper's fur with her finger and scratching the back of his neck. The cat purred in ecstasy.

'Lucky cat,' Billy said under his breath. George grunted, clearly irritated by Billy's loitering in his doorway.

'Can I help you, Billy?' He was curt. 'Only I'm rather busy in here. Everyone's coming in now and you're in the way, if I may be so bold.'

Billy put up his hands and backed away. 'Sorry, George, old mate.' He peered around the old man's head. 'See you later, Jessie.' She smiled and gave a gentle wave. 'Bye, Billy.'

She watched him follow Hilda down the stairs who was carrying Duke, her little dog, and rubbing him with a towel. Billy reached over and ruffled the dog's head, said something to Hilda and then they were gone.

Jessie stood up and laid Jasper on the cushion that was on top of George's chair. 'I'd better go and get ready too, George. Will you let me know if my mum arrives before curtain up?'

'Of course,' George smiled warmly at her. She frowned. He was different again now that Billy had gone. Didn't he like him? 'I'll send one of the stage crew down with a message, don't you worry.' She gave him a peck on the cheek. 'Thanks, George.'

'Don't you worry, lass. I'll make sure they know exactly where you are.'

She went to the door and peered outside for one last look, hoping to at least see Harry's car parked in the street but was disappointed. Nerves were getting the better of her; she wished with all her heart they'd been here as planned. She'd looked forward to introducing them to Joyce but she just hoped that they were safe. Please let them be safe.

Down in the corridor she met Jack coming out of Madeleine's room. He wore smart evening dress and his hair was slicked back with oil so that it looked much darker than it had during the day. He smiled but his face was pinched with tension. He stood to one side to allow her to pass. The corridor bristled with the electricity of combined nerves and ego, the cast primed for performance, the smell of nervous sweat permeating backstage.

'All right, Jessie?'

'Yes. Thank you.'

He put a hand to her shoulder. 'Don't look so worried. If you go out there and enjoy yourself you'll knock their socks off.'

She grinned. It was kind of him to consider her feelings when he had the full weight of the show on his shoulders. 'I will,' she said, hoping she wouldn't let him down, that she would remember her steps, that her heel wouldn't break again. He knocked on Billy's door and she felt his eyes on her as she made her way down the corridor.

The other girls were already in the cramped dressing room. It was the largest one in the building but with six girls, their costumes, make up and personal belongings, there was very little room left to move. They'd decided to leave some of their headdresses and props in the wings to give them a little more space. Mirrors ran along two walls, each one set with light bulbs around the edge. The other wall was filled with rails of clothes. In the far corner was one easy chair that Rita had first dibs over. Thank goodness there weren't any quick changes and they had time between each routine to get ready without too much stress and panic. Jessie undid her cards and pinned then in the space above her mirror. There were plenty of them and she was buoyed by the amount of goodwill that she'd garnered. Frances sat to her left beside the wall and Virginia to her right. She was a sweet girl; Jessie liked her, although she spent most of her time with the other ducklings in Rita's entourage.

'More cards, Jessie. You must be very popular back home.' Jessie pushed in the final pin and sat down on her chair. 'I am lucky, but then so are you. Virginia's cards were greater than Jessie's small pile. She kept one from Grace and Eddie and another from Harry propped right in front of her, leaning on the mirror. Grace had obviously warned Harry against sending anything with the words 'Good Luck' on them as his card carried a picture of a leafy lane, much like the one outside The Beeches. Inside he'd drawn a small sketch of a man hobbling on a walking stick, his leg bandaged up to the knee. 'Break a leg' scribbled to the side of it. She ran her fingers over the drawing. In a few hours they would be together.

The room became quieter. Kay threw a lipstick across to Sally, Rita leaned into the mirror, creating big eyes by melting some black greasepaint in a spoon over a candle and blobbing it on the end of her lashes with a matchstick. Jessie noticed how much her hands were shaking. She hadn't for one minute thought that Rita would be nervous and it surprised her – but then these were Rita's routines. She felt for the girl and was glad she didn't have the responsibility. Virginia was already made up and sat back filing her nails.

Jessie read Harry's words over and over again. 'Missing you, darling Jessie. Can't wait to hold you in my arms.' She couldn't wait either. Were they here yet? Were they out front in their seats? She dabbed some greasepaint on her face, rubbing it in, layering a darker shade on top. Her hands were shaking but she managed to paint a perfect face. Bright-red lips and big eyes that could be seen from the back of the theatre, overdone so that the lights didn't bleach the colour from her face and make her look pasty and ill. Frances was sat in her red silk dressing gown, her legs crossed, fishnet stockings already in place, her face complete, reading a magazine she had borrowed from Virginia. How could she be so calm? Jessie's stomach was turning somersaults.

Matt walked down the corridor, banging on doors. 'This is your fifteen-minute call, ladies and gentlemen. Fifteen minutes.' There was no message from George. Why did she feel so sick? She squeezed out of her chair and dashed upstairs to the side of the stage. The crew were busy pulling the finishing touches to the set and props, and Mike was standing in the prompt corner going over the lighting cues. She squeezed past them and, pressing her eye to the peephole on prompt side, she looked out into the auditorium. The audience were dribbling in now, lots of seats already taken. She looked for Grace, but their three seats were empty. Someone came and stood close behind her, too close. She tried to move but couldn't.

'Any sign of your boyfriend, sweet Jessie?' Billy breathed into her ear.

She wriggled and turned, blushing, glad that it was in the shadows and he couldn't see. 'Not yet.' He stared into her eyes. They were darker still in the dim light and they held a mischievous twinkle. He smelt of cologne, an overpowering musk mingled with the smell of his minty breath. She wanted to get away but there was barely room to move and she was quite safe, she told herself, there were people all around. So why was her heart pounding so fast?

He grinned. 'You're not afraid of me, are you?'

She shook her head and squeezed around him, dashed from backstage to the stage door. Her legs were weak; she felt them trembling. George looked up as she came towards him and shook his head.

'No one yet, Jessie love.'

Tears pricked her eyes. She mustn't cry, it would ruin her make-up and she didn't have time to renew it. She searched down the street in case Harry had parked there but there was no sign of his car. She looked upward to stem her tears. The air was damp; it would make her hair frizz and she didn't need to give Rita any excuse to find fault. She took a deep breath and went inside just as Matt was calling the five minutes.

Rita was already in her costume, checking her make-up one last time. Everyone was ready, except Frances who was putting on her tap shoes.

'Delaney, get dressed and on stage, pronto,' Rita barked, leading the way. Overtures and Beginners was being called as they made their way out of the room.

Jessie hurried into her outfit of satin shirt and shorts. 'You all right, Jessie? You look a bit shaken.' Frances gave a flick of her taps.

'Fine,' Jessie swallowed, plastering on a smile. 'Well, actually I'm getting a bit worried. Mum and Eddie still haven't arrived, what if something's happened to them? They could have had an accident.' She pushed images of Harry's car overturned in a ditch out of her head.'

Frances checked her teeth in the mirror for lipstick stains then ran her tongue over them.

'Don't be daft. They're probably out in the foyer. It gets a bit stuffy in the stalls.'

For once Jessie envied Frances, expecting no one. There was no need for the extra nerves and that was a good thing. Jessie pulled the door behind them and went up on stage.

Behind the curtain, the girls could hear the buzz of audience as they waited in anticipation, the sound of seats clicking down into position becoming less frequent. Jessie stood tall in her Cuban heels, facing forward, her dad's words from long ago echoing in her head. 'Smile, Jessie. Always give them your brightest smile.' She felt the firmness of the wooden floor beneath her feet and began flexing her fingers and jiggling her arms.

'Eyes and teeth, girls, eyes and teeth.' Rita said, leaning forward from the line. Jessie stretched her mouth into the widest smile she could summon and murmured to herself, 'This is for you, Dad.' The stage crew stood poised in the wings, lit by the blue of the working light, watching the girls ready themselves to open the show. Jessie heard the musicians settle in the orchestra pit, Ron plucking two strings on his violin. The hum of sound beyond the curtain subsided. Rita looked along the line and smiled.

'Right, girls, let's show this town what we're made of.' They waited for the overture to strike up and looked straight ahead. Mike gave the signal. There was a round of applause from the audience, and an off-stage announcement introduced the Variety Girls. The band played the opening bars of 'Let Yourself Go', the curtains drew back, and Jessie threw herself into the routine.

They had opened to an almost full house – only three seats were empty.

Chapter 13

When Jessie came offstage at the end of the first half, she found flowers in her dressing room. A small delicate posy of larkspur and a brief note in what she now recognised as George's hand. *'From your young man. Your mother and brother are here.'* Jessie was elated, tears sparkled in her eyes, but they were of happiness – and relief. No need for Miss Symonds' handkerchief now. 'Frances, they're here.' She placed her hand on her heart. 'I was so worried. I thought they might have had an accident.'

Her friend was matter of fact. 'Well, all that worry went to waste, didn't it? Save your energy for the second half.' Frances had tilted her chair against the wall and managed to stretch her legs out and prop them on the dressing table. That was why she'd insisted on the place next to the wall, Jessie now realised. Having the legs up was good for the circulation when the ankles tired and Frances knew how to pace herself. These were all the tricks Jessie needed to learn and Frances was a good teacher. She didn't have any qualms about looking after herself and making sure she was comfortable.

Jessie embraced her performance for the second half with a full heart. The audience were receptive, warm and generous applause given at every entrance and exit, and Jessie found it wonderful to be on stage, especially knowing that Harry, Grace and Eddie were out there. She wanted them to see that she'd made the right choice, that she could make a success of her life and subsequently make a life for them all, away from Iris and Norman, away from sadness and bad memories, and into a life filled with good friends and kindness.

The Variety Girls were dressed in their walk-down costumes, long evening gowns in palest grey, with a split at the leg and covered with silver sequins that shimmered in the light. They wore long satin gloves of the same colour with paste bracelets that glittered like diamonds under the lights. Three of them stood each side, and thankfully Billy was opposite prompt. He stood between the black fabric legs that kept the wings shielded from the audience with his arm around Virginia and winked to Jessie and Kay. There wasn't much room to move as Madeleine finished her last song and walked into prompt side to rapturous applause.

She stood straight-backed facing the stage, and waited for the applause to ring louder before walking back on. She gave a low curtsey to the right, to the left, then centre stage, then gave a nod to Phil in the orchestra pit and began to sing her closing song. The audience sang along, and no one would imagine that people were worried about a war that might be hovering around the corner. The world outside the Empire was going along as it always had and this ... this was what Jessie wanted. The perfect escape from the world, not just for the audience but for herself.

Madeleine finished, took her call and walked off to do a quick change, Mary standing to one side as Madeleine slipped behind a screen to pour herself into her finale costume. The girls dashed to the back of wings and as the final piece of music began, the Variety Girls walked down the newly constructed steps from the back of the stage to the front and took their bow. The applause increased as the audience let the cast know who they had enjoyed the most.

Billy Lane scampered down the stage with aplomb, almost skipping to the front and taking his bow. The audience had loved him, and he stepped back into the line, holding out his arm like everyone else as Madeleine Moore walked down the stairs like the star she was. As she came right to the front of the stage, blowing kisses out into the audience, taking another bow, the rest of the cast came into line and waved as the curtains came together, and quickly opened again. Jessie was beaming and she looked along the line to see a reflection of her own happiness writ large amongst the rest of her colleagues. This truly was the beginning and she wanted to enjoy this special moment.

As the last curtain fell, it was a race to get off the stage and into the dressing rooms. Jessie wriggled out of her costume and into her paisley pattern robe, slathered her face with cream and wiped her heavy make-up from her face with a clean rag. She was desperate to see Grace. Had her mum been proud of her? Had Harry?

She'd spied them through the peephole before the curtain went up for the second half. Being on stage tonight and having the affection come in waves from the audience had filled her with an energy that she recognised from long ago. For the times she'd been there with Dad, taking the applause, for making people happy. She wanted to do it for the rest of her life.

It was all sharp arms and elbows as the girls hurried to change into their everyday clothes. Jack stuck his head around the door and found some of them half in, half out of clothes and didn't blink. 'Well done, girls, fabulous show. You were amazing. The audience loved you. I hope you'll all join me in the bar as a thank you. Family and friends are welcome.'

There were eager squeals of excitement from the ducklings and a gracious acceptance from Rita. Frances merely nodded. Jessie was torn. She wanted to join in with the joy and reward for a job well done – they'd got through the first show without any major mishaps and it could only improve from now on – but she'd missed Harry so much and she simply wanted to be close to him. Would it be enough for Harry after he had driven all this way? Without him, Grace and Eddie would have found it difficult but not impossible to get to opening night. And opening night, in her very first show was special. It had been harder than she'd imagined, and she still had a lot to learn, but she had done it.

She dressed quickly, slipping on her shoes, pulling at the heel, wobbling on one leg.

'Shall I see you in the bar?' Should she wait? Frances had been so kind to her. It was awful, this constant turmoil. Frances was still in her robe and in no hurry to move.

'Off with you, wench. Go see that man of yours.' She flicked her hand and grinned through the mirror at Jessie who needed no further encouragement. She raced up the stairs, squeezing through the crowd that had gathered there waiting for autographs, spilling onto the street. And there was Harry, lit by the street lamp, leaning against the wall, a waft of smoke drifting from his cigarette.

She stood at the edge of the crowd and watched him, hardly able to breathe, hardly able to wait, until he turned and saw her, threw his cigarette on the ground and rubbed it with his shoe.

'Harry.' It came out as a whisper and she ran towards him. He scooped her in arms and swung her around, and she felt as if she was flying, soaring in the heavens. Her heart was full, and as he released her onto the pavement he held her face in his hands and kissed her full on the mouth. His lips were warm and tinged with the smell of smoke and she closed her eyes and melted in his embrace before she had to pull away from him, laughing, trying to catch her breath.

'Oh, Jessie, I can't believe we're together again.' He ran his hand over her glossy hair, the side of her face, took her hand in his and squeezed it tightly, as if he would never let her go. 'Grace and Eddie are waiting in the theatre bar,' he said, leading the way.

'Your mum's desperate to see you.' He stopped walking, turned to her. 'She's missed you so much, Jessie. We all have. Especially me.' His eyes were shining with happiness and she leaned on his shoulder as they walked to the corner and around to the front of the theatre.

Jessie saw Grace and Eddie before she and Harry had even got through the entrance of the Empire bar. They were seated at a table by the window, their heads turned away from her, and she smiled to think she would have the element of surprise. It was wonderful to be with them again. She paused and took a deep breath to calm herself before pushing the door wide, squeezing past Ronnie and Ted and others from the band who were standing in a huddle, until she got to where her mum was waiting. It took her the briefest of moments to regain her composure at what she saw, then she rushed to embrace her mum, trying not to let the shock show on her face. Grace was so pale and drawn. In just a couple of weeks she'd changed so much.

'Mum.'

Grace got to her feet and Jessie held her as tightly as she dare without hurting her; she was so thin. As they embraced, tears pricked in Jessie's eyes. She could see the lights reflecting in the window, the crowd gathered behind them, and suddenly wished they were alone, just the four of them. Grace pulled back from her grasp, kissed Jessie on the cheek and whispered in her ear. 'Darling girl, my darling girl.'

Grace sank down onto the seat and it was Eddie's turn to hug his sister. He seemed to have grown, although Jessie knew he hadn't. 'You were brilliant, Jessie. I was so proud.' He threw awkward arms around her then quickly pulled away, head down in case anyone should see.

'What can I get everyone to drink?' Harry said, grinning now that they were all together again. Her mum waved her hand, indicating the drinks already on the table. 'Not for me.'

'A stout would be good.' Jessie slid into the plush velvet seat next to her mum.

Harry grinned. 'That's a new one on me.'

'It's meant to be full of goodness. According to Joyce.'

'Who's Joyce?' they all said at the same time, causing them to erupt into laughter. It was so good to be with the people she loved most in the world. Her happiness seemed to have no end.

'Get the drinks, Harry, and I'll tell you when you come back.'

Harry waded through the crowd to the bar and Jessie clasped her mum's hand.

'You were wonderful, my darling,' Grace said softly, leaning into Jessie. 'So very wonderful. Your father would have been so proud.'

It was heaven to have her here, to hear her tender voice. Jessie swallowed to dislodge the lump in her throat. Close to, Jessie could see the pallor of Grace's skin, the purple under her eyes. She appeared much worse than she'd been when Jessie had left Norfolk. She squeezed Grace's thin hand once again and listened to her talk about the show, all the time vowing that after tonight she would spend her energy on working out a way to get Grace and Eddie away from The Beeches.

Harry brought Jessie a stout and put his pint on the table, sliding in next to Eddie.

'We loved the show, Jessie. It was like old times, wasn't it?' Eddie was doing his very best to bring back the good memories and Jessie wasn't going to disappoint him. It was too blissful sitting here with them, knowing how difficult it would be when they had to leave. She pushed the thought away; why spoil what she had in this moment.

The four of them were going over the show, song by song, act by act, when Jack Holland came and stood at the end of their table. He placed a hand on Jessie's shoulder. The conversation stopped and Grace looked into the gentle face of Jessie's boss.

'I'm sorry to interrupt your evening, please forgive me. Mrs Delaney?'

Grace gave a slight tilt of her head in acknowledgement. He held out his hand and she took it. 'Davey and I were in the same regiment.' Grace's eyes brightened at the mention of Davey's name.

'You knew him?' Grace was instantly more alert.

'He was a dear, gentle man. I was so sorry to hear of your loss, Mrs Delaney.'

Harry slipped out of his seat and gestured for Jack to take it, which he did. Grace seemed to grow a little in Jessie's eyes, a little burst of energy reviving her. Oh, how she'd been diminished by the loss of her husband.

Jessie watched her mum lean in as Jack told of how they met, the tilt of her mum's head, the smile that played on her lips, the sparkle that came to her eyes as Jack talked.

'I can see Davey in Jessie, Mrs Delaney. What a talented man he was.'

'Please, call me Grace.' Her mum reached out and touched his arm. Jack took her hand and pressed his lips to it.

'Are you here for long, Grace?' He leaned forward to hear Grace above the general hubbub of the bar, cupping his hand about his ear.

'We leave on Sunday. Harry kindly brought us, but he has to be back at work on Monday.' Jack acknowledged Harry.

'I don't suppose there's any possibility we could meet tomorrow. I would dearly love to chat with you, about Davey.'

Grace looked askance at Jessie who nodded her assent. When had her mum last looked so happy? This brief conversation had given her a little boost and if Jessie had to share her precious time, she couldn't think of anyone she would rather share it with. Jack knew her dad. It was almost like having him here. Almost.

A curvaceous dark-haired woman in a long black dress, which clung in all the right places, sidled up to Jack. Jessie noticed the dazzling emerald drop earrings before she saw the sour look on the woman's face. Her thin lips were a dark, venomous red and her black eyes narrowed when she smiled. 'Jack, darling, the mayor would like to speak to you.' She pressed her mouth into another phoney smile, took hold of Jack's arm to lead him away. He looked apologetically at Grace.

'I'm so sorry ...'

'You don't have to explain, Mr Holland. Your show has been a success; you need to talk with people. I understand perfectly.' Jessie could tell that he appreciated her foresight as he was led away.

'Is that his wife, Jessie?' Eddie pulled a face. He was obviously of the same opinion as Jessie.

She shrugged. 'I presume so. I haven't seen her before tonight, and she looks very much like she owns him.'

Harry grinned. 'It makes him sound like a dog or something.'

'She might very well treat him like one.' Jessie looked over to where they were in the crowd, the mayor with his gold chain over his generous stomach. He reminded her of Uncle Norman. Did all businessmen acquire such rotund bellies? Was it part and parcel of being 'respectable'. If so, she hoped Harry didn't develop the 'belly'.

'Don't be unkind, Jessie.' Grace was gentle. 'People love each other in different ways.'

Jessie apologised, suitably reprimanded. How her mum could consistently think so well of everyone was beyond her. She must try to be more forgiving herself.

Her mum gave her a gentle nudge. 'You mustn't sit here with me, Jessie. You need to mingle; people will want to talk to the stars of the show.'

'I'm not a star, Mum.'

Grace clasped her hand and squeezed it. Her hands were still cold despite the warmth in the room created by too many bodies gathered in a too small a space.

'But you are, darling. And you must talk with everyone here who has seen the show. It's all part and parcel. These landladies and dignitaries are the ones who will bring your audience, night after night. They will sing your praises or warn people off and send them elsewhere. Go and sell the show. We can see each other all day tomorrow. I prefer to watch.' She let go of Jessie's hand and gave her a gentle push.

Reluctantly, Jessie slid out of the seat, searching for Frances, who had finally appeared from backstage and was standing in a corner talking to Hilda.

'Go and be with her, Harry.' Grace urged. 'Make yourself known.' She leaned close to him as he got to his feet. 'Let people know she has someone.'

Jessie reached her hand behind her and Harry took it as she led the way through the gathering, smiling to everyone as she went. She came to a stop beside Frances and introduced Harry to the two women.

Frances shook Harry's hand. 'Ah, now I know for definite that Jessie is the luckiest girl I know. Good to meet you, Harry.' Hilda greeted them both then said she needed to find Bert. 'He'll be at the bar with a pint, or two, or three. I always know where to find him.'

'Aren't you afraid he'll drop you one day if he doesn't sober up in time?'

'He has dropped me,' she called over her shoulder, 'and more than once.'

The three of them grinned. 'Glad I'm not his partner,' Frances said, accepting one of Harry's cigarettes and a light. They moved places so that Jessie wasn't in the way of their smoke.

'Haven't you ever smoked, Jessie?' Frances was curious.

Jessie shook her head. 'I have to take care of my voice.'

Harry put his arm around her and drew her close. 'And so you should. It's a beautiful voice and deserves to be looked after.' She wanted to melt in his arms, she felt so thrilled to be with him. She truly had everything. Her mum and brother, the man she loved and the beginnings of a stage career. Nothing could dull the happiness. She put her hand to Harry's chest and watched the merry-go-round of the bar as people moved from group to group, talking and laughing, checking intermittently that her mum and Eddie were all right.

Jack stood head and shoulders above them all and Jessie couldn't help but notice that he was doing the same: looking at Grace, getting his attention diverted by conversation, searching her out again. If she stood on tiptoes she would occasionally catch her mum smiling back at him. Grace's eyes shone and her face appeared more animated. Jessie relaxed.

Chapter 14

A gentle breeze blew up from the sea as Harry left the Dolphin Hotel and waited on the steps for Jessie to join him. The tide was coming in and waves rolled towards the shore. A long line of trawlers moved along the horizon, exactly like Jessie had described in her letters. Harry was glad that his feet were firmly on the ground and not on the rolling waves; that life wouldn't do for him. He thought of his conversation with Eddie. He would definitely choose the air, if he was given a choice.

It was almost eleven o'clock and the promenade below was already full of holiday makers. He rolled his shoulders back and forth to ease the pain, rolled his neck from side to side. He couldn't remember a time he had ached so much but then sleeping in the car hadn't been part of his plans for the weekend. He'd walked Jessie home last night only to find the door of the Bluebird Boarding House locked. Unable to wake anyone the only alternative had been to make for his car. He had dallied along the deserted promenade with only the moon and the stars for company. The landlady had opened the door to him at six and he'd had chance to wash before breakfast when Jessie joined them. He didn't want to waste a moment and he'd do the same again tonight if it meant spending one more precious minute with Jessie. He turned as the door opened and she sprang down the steps to join him.

'Where to?' he said, taking her hand. She was wearing her blue print dress and short red jacket, looking exactly as she had the day she'd caught the train. How slowly the days had passed since she'd left, and how the minutes flew by, now that he was with her again.

'Shall we head down towards the pier? We can walk right out to the middle of the sea and view the entire promenade from there.'

He took her hand. 'Is your mum okay with us sneaking off like this?'

'I think she's glad.' Jessie grinned, looking about her, taking it all in and enjoying the moment. 'I can't get a word in edgeways as it is. She and Jack have really hit it off.' She turned to Harry, pecked him on the cheek, squeezed his hand. 'You know, Harry, it was so good of Jack to come and see us like this, talk about Dad, especially after his first ever opening night at The Empire. He must have thought a lot of Dad.' She looked so proud. It was obviously of comfort, and would no doubt be to Grace too. As such he felt they had permission to go off and leave Grace where she was.

He allowed Jessie to lead the way, crossing the road and walking down the pier approach. He really didn't mind what they did or where they went as long as they were together. He listened as Jessie chattered on, her excitement infectious, as they crossed the road and onto the pier. The promenade was thronged with people, photographers milling amongst them, taking snaps that would be sent on to them after the sunny days of freedom ended, capturing memories that would be cherished when they were all back at work, noses to the grindstone in factories and shops. Would this be the last holiday before war? He hoped not but all the indications were that it would be. He pushed away thoughts of what might come. Best to treasure what they had now; there would be plenty of time when he was back in Cole's to ponder more serious problems. Today belonged to Jessie.

'I haven't really seen much as we've been in the theatre all day. Other than Joyce's, and my room at Barkhouse Lane. It's good that I get to explore it all with you.' She snuggled close to his side, holding on to his arm with both hands. He wrapped his hand over hers.

'You and Eddie make me roar with your "exploring". I wonder what he'll discover this afternoon.'

'Oh, engines of some sort. He's probably over the railway station, getting in the way,' she said, wafting a hand in the air. 'He'll be having a fascinating time discussing pistons and carburettors or whatever those bits and bobs he goes on about, driving some poor engine driver potty.'

Harry laughed. 'Don't let him hear you talk about his bits and bobs.'

'He'll be fine. He'll be happy.' She paused. 'Mum was happy, wasn't she, talking to Jack?' She looked up at Harry, her face serious, more thoughtful now. 'It must be lovely to have someone to share memories with, to talk about Dad when he was younger. He was only ever Dad to me but, well, he was a person in his own right too. When there was just Mum and him. Much like me and you, Harry.'

His heart missed a beat. Could he dare to think that she was seeing a future for them both? She ran her hand along the railings as they walked, skipping her fingers over the joints, around the lamp posts. The breeze caught at her hair and he was reminded so much of that day in Cromer, when he'd asked her to make a decision. He longed to ask again but fought against it, knowing that now wasn't the right time. He wanted to have a taste of happiness and he could with Jessie. He knew it, just as he knew he must wait.

The doors were open to the concert room and music flowed out into the air as they passed. Jessie pointed to a poster. 'Don Twidale and his Augmented Orchestra this afternoon at two. It's a dance, Harry. How lovely. It must be a rehearsal.' She swayed from side to side, her hands and arms stretching wider and wider as the music captured her attention. Harry caught hold of her hand to draw her back and she pulled herself closer still, taking his hand and daring him to waltz with her.

'Idiot' he said, grinning awkwardly. What would people think? Then suddenly, he didn't care what 'people' thought, he only wanted Jessie to be happy. The waves were beneath them, the clouds above and she didn't take her eyes off him. He held her gaze, wanting the whole world to melt away and there to be but the two of them. The music ended and she gently pulled away from him, and curtseyed. A smattering of people had stopped their promenade down the pier to watch them and burst into applause. The smile on Jessie's face was everything he could have hoped for and he caught hold of her hand again.

They walked in silence for a time until Jessie said, 'How is Miss Symonds?'

'Glum without you there singing and cheering her up. There is a new girl, Beryl, but she's not a patch on you.' Because she wasn't, and he was glad of it. Jessie was special.

'I'll bet she makes fewer mistakes than I did.'

'Possibly.' He grinned. 'Well, definitely, but that's not everything in life is it, Jessie?'

She nudged him and he staggered away, exaggerating to make her laugh.

'It's okay to make mistakes,' he said, taking her arm again.

'Depends what mistakes they are.' Jessie was serious. 'When I make a mistake in the dance routine, it sticks out like a sore thumb. Rita's watching me like a hawk, and I can't cover it up with a bit of glue and paper. It's out there for all to see.'

'Hmm, you have a point. I'm trying not to put a foot wrong at the moment so you're in good company. Norman has roped me onto a committee. We're in the process of transferring many of our documents into strong boxes off the premises.'

'You don't strike me as a committee man,' she teased.

'I'm not.' Her tone unsettled him. Was he turning into someone he didn't want to be? How many things had Norman coerced him into since making him junior partner?

'Sounds like you might be becoming one.' She lowered her voice and wiggled her fingers in front of his face. 'You are slowly morphing into a Norman. Oh, dear, when you promised me you wouldn't, Harry Newman.' He turned and walked backwards so that he could see her properly. Her eyes were sparkling and she looked so happy. God, how he missed that beautiful face. Seeing it every morning when he opened the door to Cole's was the very best part of his entire day; life was so very dull without her. It was simply work and even his promotion, which was once something he coveted, meant nothing without Jessie.

'Come back and save me then. You know I don't want to be a Norman.'

'I will,' she laughed. 'But not yet, Harry. Not yet.'

He knew better than to press her. She would come back in her own time. Grace said that she would come back when the life had lost its glitter and turned to a dull shine that could be found anywhere. But how long would that take?

They left the pier and walked along the promenade, down towards the open-air bathing pool. They peered between the turnstiles at the entrance, catching glimpses of bathers enjoying themselves, the sound of splashing and squealing floating out over the water. They admired the glass construction of the Café Dansant and decided they would bring Grace for a special lunch before they crossed over and read the posters on display in the foyer of Olympia. The Olympian Follies were playing there for the season with featured singers. Harry knew they wouldn't be a patch on Jessie. He checked his watch. 'Time we got back. I don't want to leave your mum too long.' She huddled close to him.

'Thanks for being so thoughtful, Harry. Mum wouldn't have made the show if it hadn't been for you, I doubt miserable Iris would have let Norman bring her.'

'I'm sure he would have.' He wanted to believe it, for her sake, but couldn't get it out of his head that Iris had made them almost miss the show.

'She doesn't look well, does she, Harry? I thought Mum would be feeling less of a strain now that I wasn't there to annoy Iris but ...' She studied the ground and he waited for her to speak. 'Will you keep an eye on her for me?'

'Of course I will.'

'Promise?'

He squeezed her hand. 'Promise. You didn't even have to ask.'

She paused. 'I wish I didn't have to leave her at all, but I couldn't stand another day with Aunt Iris. I'm sure Mum and Eddie feel the same.' He understood now when he hadn't before. Should he mention Eddie's suspicions? He didn't want to spoil the day for something that he wasn't certain of. No, it was best if he kept it to himself and do as she'd asked; he would watch over Grace and ease Jessie's troubles for as long as she needed him to.

He glanced towards the sea again as they crossed the roads to walk along by the floral displays, enjoying the colour of begonias and bizzy lizzies against the emerald green of the grass. Two defence forts built in the Great War stood sentinel against any possible invading forces, but would they be enough when war would come from the air this time around? The country had only just recovered from the scare last year when Chamberlain had arrived back from Munich so full of hope that many had thought they'd avoided war and not deferred it. He swallowed hard to disperse the bitter taste that had settled in his mouth.

He put his arm around her shoulders and looked ahead as the road sloped up towards Ross Castle, an odd-looking stone structure that wasn't a castle at all, merely a stone fort built as a tourist attraction. 'I'm looking forward to seeing the show again tonight. Well, the parts we missed anyway. It was good of Jack to offer us free tickets.'

'You never did tell me why you were late and missed the opening number.'

'My fault entirely. The radiator over-heated and we had to wait for it to cool down.' A car rushed past and tooted its horn as a family dawdled across the road. 'I pushed the Austin too hard in a hurry to get to you.' It was only partly a lie and he was willing to take the blame if it eased her mind. He wouldn't deny her happiness, for how long would it last for any of them? If Churchill was right, and there was no reason now to think that he wasn't, war was almost on the doorstep. They should enjoy this freedom while they had it.

As they came to the entrance of the Dolphin Hotel, they saw Eddie heading towards them from the Market Place. 'I can spot his grin a mile off,' Jessie laughed to Harry. 'I wonder what he's been up to.' They waited for him by the door.

'It's brilliant here, Harry. I've had such a good time.'

Harry ruffled the boy's hair. Was that a spot of oil on his sleeve?

'You can tell us all about it, Eddie. By the look of you it has something to do with engines.'

He checked his shirt. 'Oh, heck. Mum's going to kill me.' He spat on his hand and rubbed at the mark, making it worse. Jessie gave him a gentle shove.

'Mum's used to it, Eddie. She's been getting grease stains off your clothes for years. Another one isn't going to make much difference.'

They found Grace in the hotel lounge talking to someone who Harry didn't recognise from behind. Grace smiled as she saw them, and the person she was with twisted in their seat. Harry recognised her as the star of the show they'd seen last night, Madeleine Moore. Grace didn't need looking after; she was like a magnet to all the nice people in the world and that was because she was a nice person herself. She would never have to feign illness like Iris. Madeleine got to her feet when she saw them troop in.

'Jessie,' she said. Her smile was quite disarming, and Harry was struck by how vivid the woman was, exquisitely dressed as she was in a plum-coloured fitted suit, her dark golden hair in neat waves about her head. It was the first time Harry had ever seen anyone so glamorous close up. Was this careful elegance what Jessie aspired to, and if she did, would he be enough, a small-town solicitor with few prospects?

'I'll leave you to spend precious time with your mother,' she said, her voice husky. She slipped her clutch bag under her arm. 'Goodbye, Grace. It's been lovely talking to you. I hope we get chance to do it again sometime.'

Harry was aware that they weren't the only ones watching as she walked towards the lift. Conversations dulled and heads turned before a waitress swooped across to the table to clear away the debris.

'You all look like you've enjoyed yourselves.' Grace handed plates to the waitress as she gathered up the dirty cups and saucers, piling them on a small silver tray. 'Especially you, Eddie. Have you been down the station?'

Eddie hung his head. 'Sorry, Mum.'

'It doesn't matter. I know you've had a good time. As have I.' She gathered her bag and got up from the plush upholstered sofa. 'Shall we get some lunch?'

Jessie hurried to her side, linking her mum's arm in hers. 'We've found the perfect place. The Café Dansant. It's so lovely, Mum. A real treat for us.'

Harry thought Grace looked a little disappointed.

'Do you mind if we go to Joyce's café, Jessie? You've told me so much about it and I want to be able to imagine where you are when I'm at home. Don't you, Harry?'

He smiled. It was exactly what he wanted to do. To be where Jessie was, in his thoughts if he couldn't be there himself. They gathered their things and walked over the road to acquaint themselves with the legendary Joyce.

Chapter 15

Jessie should have been feeling elated; the press reviews had been positive and the word amongst the landladies was that the show at The Empire was the one to catch, but she was fighting back tears as Grace, Eddie and Harry prepared to leave.

The lump in her throat was so big that she couldn't speak, and yet there was so much she wanted to say. Most of all, 'Don't go.' But the words were held back along with the tears until she knew they were safely out of sight. It had been a magical couple of days, a perfect capsule of all the things and all the people she loved in the world. They had been with her at her brightest moment and she longed for them to be here for the rest of it.

Grace took hold of her arms and held her away, brushing her hair from her face and pushing it back over Jessie's shoulders. She felt like a small child and managed a grin.

'That's better.' Grace kissed her cheek. 'This is only the beginning, Jessie, but it's a good beginning and one to be proud of. After this first week is over, you will have time to think. More of your day will be free so use the hours wisely, darling.'

'I will,' she replied. There had been no time to think about anything other than her routines with the Variety

Girls. It had taken all her concentration, but Jessie knew from past experience that things would fall into place once the show was bedded in. It would be easy to drift from day to day and not make the most of the opportunity she had carved for herself. She wanted to work on an act that Bernie could sell to other theatres; she would make a start when she'd waved them off.

Harry was fastening the last of their bags to the rack at the rear of the car, and when he'd finished, he stood back, waiting for his turn to say goodbye. Eddie had already hugged her and climbed into the back, and Grace gave Jessie another quick hug and kiss before lowering herself into the passenger seat. Harry dashed forward, closing the door for her, then turned to Jessie.

'I'll be back as soon as I can, Jessie.'

She tried to summon a smile, but her mouth kept collapsing and wobbling and she really didn't want to cry, not yet. She didn't want her mum to see her weak and lost, she must be strong.

'I'll write, Harry. Every day. I'll write because it keeps me close to you.'

He put his fingers under her chin and lifted her face to his, kissed her forehead. His lips were warm, and she wanted for all the world to surrender and get in the car with him, but it wouldn't do; it wouldn't give them the life she wanted.

He kissed her again, full on the mouth and held her so tight that she could hardly breathe. She didn't want it to stop but he drew away from her, holding her firmly from him with a fierce but gentle grip. He wouldn't hurt her, she knew that. 'I love you, Jessie.' He stared deep into her eyes, gripping her arms. 'So now you know.' He released her and hurried around to the driver's side.

She was shocked and it must have shown on her face as she watched him from the other side of the car. Had her mum heard him too? He'd never said those words, even though she knew that he did indeed love her, because of what he did. But to hear him say it out loud? She couldn't suppress a smile when seconds earlier she had been fighting back tears. She touched her lips, feeling his kiss imprinted there.

He got into the car and started the engine. Grace wound down the window and Jessie leaned in. 'Thanks for coming, Mum. I'm so glad you got to see the show.'

Grace touched her hand. 'Keep safe, my darling.'

'Bye again, Jessie.' Eddie leaned forward as far as he could, squeezed his burgeoning body over the small gap between the front seat and the rear one. He looked so funny, bursting out of the car as Harry drove away, and she couldn't help but be cheered by the sight of his waving as they slowly disappeared down Isaac's Hill and onto the main road out of town. She kept waving long after she lost sight of them, her hand dropping limply to her side. What now?

People passed by her and she struggled to hold back long overdue tears, not wanting to cry in the street. Where could she go to walk away the pain of their parting? She turned for St Peter's Avenue, away from the seafront, looking in the windows of shops that were closed for the day. Tears glistened and dropped quietly down her cheeks and she pretended to be interested in window displays to avoid being seen. Harry had told her he loved her. What was she doing here, away from them all, away from him? She'd thought it would make her happier having them near, but it only left her feeling odd and disconnected, and she didn't know what to do with herself. Frances had left early that morning before Jessie had even risen and she knew that Geraldine was visiting friends somewhere. The last thing she wanted to do was go back to an empty house.

Worshippers in their Sunday best were coming out of St Peter's Church and she sat down on a bench on the other side of the road, admiring ladies' hats and children's straw boaters, little girls in their pretty summer frocks. It was the clusters of family and friends that left her suddenly feeling adrift. It hadn't been like this all week, so why now? She got up and walked again, through College Street and Sea View Street, passing schools and houses, pubs and shops until she was on the sea front again. Should she turn right and head back to her room or left for the theatre? Across the road, children were running to the top of Ross Castle. It proved a popular viewing point, children delighting at waving down to their parents on the promenade below. Families, couples, friends. Together.

So, it was to be left then. Someone would be at the theatre Sunday or not. She walked down the hill, taking her time, studying the trinkets in the souvenir shops, viewing more than her share of postcards. She would buy one to send to Miss Symonds, it would make her smile and she'd pick one that showed some of the views she saw walking to work every day. She was studying the racks when she felt a tug at her sleeve and looked down to see a blonde-haired girl who looked surprisingly familiar.

'Hello, Jessie. I told Mam it was you.'

'Hope.'

The girl was confused, and Jessie quickly realised that it wasn't her real name. 'You gave me a penny.' The girl nodded and Jessie patted her pocket and took out the coin. 'See, I have it on me all the time.' The child's face brightened, and Jessie looked up to see her mother holding the baby.

'Lord, she was so excited to see you. She insisted we walk past the theatre today. I told her it was y'er day off but she wouldn't have it.' Another jiggle of the baby in her arms to keep it quiet. 'An' she was right, wa'nt she.'

'I saw your photograph.' The child was beaming. 'You look pretty in your pretty dresses.'

Jessie smiled. 'Why, thank you kindly.'

The girl grinned shyly, dipping her head. 'Did you dance and sing for people?'

'I danced for them, but I didn't sing – not yet.'

'I'm going to come and see you with Mam. Auntie Ethel's going to look after Julie because she'll cry in all the wrong places, Mam says.'

Her mother raised her eyes heavenward and took her daughter's hand. 'She's such a chatterbox. I said we'd get tickets if she could be quiet for five minutes. I don't know who's worse, her or Julie.' Jessie put the penny back in her pocket.

'Your penny has brought me luck already. And it's bound to bring me lots more, and it's all thanks to you.'

The mother gave the child's hand a gentle shake of encouragement. It reminded Jessie of the many times her mother had done the same thing, her firm yet gentle grip issuing strength and security.

'We won't keep you,' the mother continued. 'We've to get on for my Fred, but good luck, duckie. Nice to see you again.'

They moved off, up the road from where Jessie had just come, and she watched as the child turned and waved with her free hand. Jessie waved back, then returned to the postcard rack, choosing one with a view of the pier and went to pay for it. The special penny would remain safe in her pocket and she would make sure it was doubled and trebled before too long.

The chance meeting cheered her, and she strolled along the remainder of the shops in better spirits than she had been only minutes ago. The sun was still shining, and she could smile again now. Trippers passing by smiled back, men lifting their hats in polite acknowledgement. Across the road in the gardens, people filled the benches, tilting their faces to the sun and kids skipped along the paths that wound through the ornamental flower displays, happy and carefree. Back on her side of Alexandra Road, people queued in long lines outside the cafés, and the air smelt of fish and chips and vinegar. There was no need for her to rush anywhere today, and she loitered on the steps of the Empire, gazing at the photographs that now filled the glass showcases at either side of the doors. She hadn't taken much notice before but now she studied the images that filled the boards – of Madeleine, Billy, and the other members of the cast. Production photographs had been added, and she saw herself, standing next to Frances, Rita, Virginia, Sally and Kay. It was real, wasn't it? It wasn't a dream – merely the beginning of a dream becoming reality; she belonged, she was part of something. She was a Variety Girl.

She tugged at the doors and went inside. June was in the box office and she waved a greeting before going through to the stalls. Bert and Hilda were rehearsing a new move. They put their hands up in greeting but didn't stop. They had a booking for the third week in September when the season ended and were going on to Paris. Their passage was already booked. She admired the dexterity and flexibility they possessed. The way they worked in synchronicity. Bert balanced on one hand, Hilda doing the splits. The way they talked it over and worked things out, trying a move again and again until they perfected it. Hilda was going to make some new costumes, sewing fabric onto leotards. She listened as they discussed which music would suit the new routine. A lot of work for a ten-minute chance to shine. She must start doing the same.

She sat in the stalls as they rehearsed but instead of seeing them she was imagining the show as it ran, her first dance routine, the feel of the lights on her face, the music floating up towards them as they went through their carefully choreographed movements, the applause. It was a slim comfort, but worth the sacrifice. The feeling of loneliness would pass; she would get used to it just as she got used to other things. The difference was that this was her choice, her decision, to give her family a better life. Inertia wouldn't improve her lot; she had to take action, make it happen.

She got out of her seat and walked down to the orchestra pit, sat down at the piano and began to play. Bert and Hilda gave her a thumbs up, and she smiled and carried on, watching them walk through a new part of their routine as she played. This was her solace and always would be, to have the gift of music, the precious gift from her dad. She played classical and old favourites, some of the songs from the show and was in the middle of 'Little White Lies' when someone began to sing along with her. Billy was leaning over the band rail. His voice was nothing special, but he could hold a tune well enough.

'Don't stop. It was beautiful.' He stood up again. 'I thought it wasn't Phil's style.'

She continued where she'd left off and finished the song. Bert and Hilda were perfecting a balance and carried on while she played an accompaniment. Virginia came from the wings and walked past them, giving the

Duo D'Or a wide berth in case they were distracted, came down the steps and stood next to Billy.

'I didn't hear you come in.' Jessie said to them both when she'd finished the song.

'You were playing. We didn't want to stop you. It sounded so lovely.' Virginia looped her hand through Billy's arm. 'I came to get a change of shoes from the dressing room. We're going for a walk along the beach; I didn't want to ruin my heels.' She lifted her leg, showing a shapely calf.

'Join us if you like.' Billy said, smiling. 'Now that you're on your own.' Virginia's face reflected her disappointment. Jessie wasn't going to play gooseberry for anyone and she really didn't need any more enemies. Keeping Rita happy was challenge enough. 'Thanks, but no thanks. I haven't played for a while and it's not often I get chance to practise.' Virginia visibly relaxed and she gave the girl a smile.

'Doesn't sound like you need to practise. Your voice is wonderful. Very easy on the ear – as you are very easy on the eye. It's quite a combination.'

Jessie felt uncomfortable with his compliment and noticed Virginia didn't seem too pleased either. But what could she do?

She turned away from them and continued to play, practising scales until she heard the doors swing shut. She would play a few more minutes then head for Barkhouse Lane. Hopefully, Frances and Geraldine would be back home, and they could settle down and listen to the wireless for the evening.

Chapter 16

The week had flown by, although Jessie was still lonesome for Grace and Eddie – and for Harry. How she missed him.

It had taken her by surprise when he'd told her he loved her; it had kept her awake at night when she'd at last fell into bed. It made her smile, made her heart tingle but she was still unsure of her own feelings. She missed him but was that enough? She had been so busy that there never seemed enough time to think about it. He'd planned to visit her again at the weekend, but she had written to him, telling him not to come. Sundays were the perfect opportunity to put in the extra hours of rehearsal and it was beginning to pay off. He'd replied, writing of his disappointment, but she was aware of her priorities now. Yes, she missed him, but keeping her job came first.

The Variety Girls rehearsed new routines each morning, Rita putting them through their paces until the routine was polished to her satisfaction. She still barked orders, still singled Jessie out for sloppy moves but Jessie knew she was improving – and she was never going to quit. Not now. The girls then had a couple of hours free in the afternoons before they needed to be at the theatre for the half-hour call. Firm friendships and alliances had already started to form, and Frances and

Jessie had taken to leaving the house earlier than necessary in order to call in the café. Joyce liked the company – and the gossip.

Dolly joined them most days before the first house went up and today, as always, they sat at their usual table in the window of Joyce's café, chatting easily, watching people go up and down the street. The closed sign was showing at the door and Joyce was busy mopping the floor. The last clients had left, and they'd got into the habit of sitting in the café until it was time to get to the theatre. Across the road they had a direct view of the rear lounge of the Dolphin Hotel and its side entrance onto Market Street.

A black taxi pulled outside and the driver sprang out to open the door. He was almost bending himself in half as first one long leg appeared and then another. It had to be Madeleine. No one else would render such humility from a taxi driver, not in this town. She gave him a warm smile, shook his hand and he closed the car door and ran up the steps to open the door to the hotel.

'Must be nice to stay somewhere like that.' Dolly stood on her tiptoes to watch as Madeleine sashayed up the steps and disappeared into the lobby.

'We will, one day.' Jessie said, draining her cup and pouring herself another from the teapot on the table. It was stewed, and she ladled in another two teaspoons of sugar and stirred it dreamily. One day she would be getting out of a taxi instead of relying on Shanks's pony.

Frances raised her eyebrows. 'Keep on dreaming, love. We're not going to get there anytime soon on our pay.'

'We're only just starting out, Frances. She had to start at the bottom. She's old now. She must be nearly forty.'

''Ere, less of the old, you cheeky beggar,' Joyce shouted across as she swabbed the black and white tiled floor of the café. 'She's years younger than me and I'm not old. Not yet.'

'Sorry, Joyce. No offence. I was just ...' She clamped her mouth shut and the three girls grinned as Jessie squirmed and tried to backpedal. She was saved by an almighty clutter from the back room and the sound of gushing water.

Vi called out. 'Oh, hell, Mam. Me waters have gone.'

Joyce dropped the mop in the metal bucket with a clang and ran through the back. The girls got to their feet. Dolly was ahead of them. 'I'll get Mam.' The door banged heavily behind her as she dashed out into the street. Frances was already rushing to the kitchen and Jessie followed, wondering what help she could possibly be.

Joyce's daughter, Vi, was balanced precariously on a stool, one hand on her belly, another on her back, legs apart and water still trickling to a puddle at her feet.

'Bleedin' 'ell, Vi, your timing's a bit off. You could'a give me chance to finish the floor and lock up first.' Joyce grabbed hold of Vi's hand just as her daughter let a long groan that made Jessie shudder. Was the baby coming now?

The groan turned into a strangled laugh. 'Don't, Mam. It's not funny.'

'You're telling me. How far apart are the contractions?'

Vi grunted again. 'I wasn't taking much notice. Twenty minutes, maybe more,' she wailed. 'I don't know.'

Jessie leaned further in through the doorway as it was rather squashed in the room with Joyce, Vi and Frances. Jessie didn't want to stand in the puddle of water and get in the way.

'Dolly's gone to get her mum,' she offered. It sounded so pathetic, but she had no idea what to do, whereas Frances was at Vi's other side, holding her hand, calm and collected.

Joyce tilted her head. 'Run round, there's a love, and tell her not to bother. This baby isn't about to come yet.' She looked at Frances. 'Can you help me get her upstairs? We'll be able to manage then.' Frances straightened herself. 'Lead the way, Joyce.'

'I'll be back as fast as I can,' Jessie called as they made for the narrow staircase. She felt like a lemon, having no idea what to do or how to help. She dashed out and caught Dolly in the street, her heart pounding in her chest, and gave her Joyce's message before heading back to the café.

The shop floor was a mess now and so was the back way. The best thing she could do was help Joyce finish the job. She mopped the rest of the floor, freshened the water and cleaned up the back room where Vi had been only minutes earlier. When Frances came downstairs all was ready for Joyce in the morning

'She could be ages yet, all night by Joyce's reckoning. It's her first.' She checked her watch. 'We'd better get to the Empire; we've already missed the call for the half.'

They shouted upstairs to Joyce, reminding her that they were only around the corner if she needed anything. Joyce scrabbled down the narrow stairs, her knees akimbo. Her face crumpled into a grin when she saw that the shop was spick and span.

'Thanks, you lasses. That's a big help. When I see you tomorrow there might well be another member of my tribe to welcome.'

Jessie was relieved to discover that she'd been of use in some small way and said, as they departed, 'We'll look forward to it, Joyce.'

Frances and Jessie rushed down the street, flying past George and thundering down the steps into the dressing room. Rita was applying her eyeliner and stopped mid eye when the two of them ran in and began pulling off their clothes. Frances leapt in before she could utter a word.

'I know we're late, Rita, but it was an emergency. Vi went into labour. We'll catch up.'

Rita continued to finish her eyeliner as Frances slid into her seat and started slapping the pancake on her face. Jessie quietly did the same, amazed at Frances's attitude. No apology, a simple statement of facts, and Rita had been soothed. It was quite an art and Jessie vowed to follow suit.

'I'll let it go this once, because I like Joyce.' She pulled on her satin shirt and shorts for the first number. 'Don't let it happen again.' She picked up her cigarettes and matches and went upstairs to the stage door.

'How do you do that, Frances?' she said to Frances's reflection as she continued to apply her own make-up.

Frances winked. 'Never complain, never explain.'

Jessie giggled and the two of them busied themselves getting ready. The girls had strung up a makeshift washing line above their heads and various pairs of stockings dangled above them. Virginia pushed them aside and peered at Jessie as she continued with her make-up.

'You sing and play beautifully, Jessie. I'm very envious. I'd love to be able to do either.' Virginia's face was luminous, her skin unblemished and her large green eyes glittered in bright lights of the room. She really was an attractive girl, Jessie thought, no wonder Billy had snapped her up as his girlfriend.

Jessie said, 'Thanks, Virginia. That's kind of you to say so.' She reached across the table and picked up her rouge, patting it on her cheeks. Virginia was still behind her and Jessie watched as the girl checked her hair and ran her tongue over her teeth, checking for lipstick smears.

'I wondered why you were here dancing when you can play so well. Most especially the classical pieces.'

'It's a long story ...' Jessie smiled, sensing an opportunity to talk about her dad.

'And one you haven't got time for, Delaney.' Rita was back, her voice sharp. 'You're already behind.'

Virginia leaned across her shoulder. 'Tell me later perhaps?'

Jessie nodded, licking at the lipstick on her lips. She got to her feet to slip into her costume. It was getting easier, more comfortable now. She wasn't so afraid of Rita, or of losing her job, understanding that Rita had to keep them all in check or they'd drift and get sloppy. It was far too easy to get distracted from all the things vying for attention. Kay and Sally wriggled past.

'Perhaps we can have a sing-song after the show one night if you fancy it?'

Jessie agreed, fastened her tap shoes then followed them upstairs. The girls found their positions on stage bending and stretching, taking deep breaths, smiling exaggeratedly to warm up their facial muscles. There wouldn't be anyone in the audience for her tonight, but it was easy to pretend that Harry, Grace and Eddie were sat at the back.

On the Wednesday of the second week of the show, after morning rehearsals, the Variety Girls trooped around the corner to see baby Frank who'd arrived at five o'clock on Tuesday morning, born in the one of the bedrooms above the café. The door had been wedged open and the café was crammed with well-wishers. Vi was sat at the table nearest the counter looking tired but happy, and Frank was being passed from woman to woman, each one of whom gurgled and cooed at the plump newborn.

Joyce was clucking about like mother hen, her face as red as the cherries on her Bakewell tarts. Dolly was behind the counter, passing over steaming mugs of tea. She waved when she saw the girls and pointed to the baby as if they couldn't have found him by themselves. The room rang with chatter and bursts of laughter.

'Nine pounds and seven ounces. I ask you. He's gonna be a big lad, our little Frank. We builds 'em big in our family don't we, Vi?'

Vi agreed, taking a bite of toast, keeping a watchful eye on her boy. The café was bustling with customers wishing them both well, pushing silver coins into the child's tiny hand, which Vi then tucked into the corner of the bassinette that was placed on the table. It was noisy and warm, the air full of joy and goodwill for the new arrival and at first Jessie was glad to be part of it but after a while she began to feel melancholy. Watching Joyce fuss about Vi with such pride and joy made her long to be with those she loved. She slipped away unnoticed, and went back to the theatre by the stage door. George was on the phone, so she mimed letters by making a scribbling action. He shook his head and mouthed, 'Not yet.'

She made her way to the stage. The rest of the girls wouldn't be back for a while and she could use the quiet time to play the upright piano, which had been left on stage from their earlier rehearsal. It would be pushed back into the wings before the evening's performance. Her hands were sweaty, and she took out her handkerchief to wipe them before she touched the keys and, as she did, Hope's penny flew across into the darkness of the wings. She watched as it rolled under a wicker trunk and heard the hollow ring as it came to a stop. She scrabbled on her hands and knees and peered into the darkness, reaching with her hand, not quite able to touch it.

'Nice view.'

She knew it was Billy without looking and was glad of the darkness as she felt her face burn. She leant back on her knees.

'Lost something?' he said, as she got to her feet.

'A penny,' she said. He didn't need to know anything more than that.

'You can have one of mine.' He put his hand in his trouser pocket and jangled the change, pulled out a penny and offered it to her.

She pulled a face. 'It's a special penny.'

'Aren't they all special?' His eyes were twinkling, and he was struggling to keep his mouth from curving upwards.

'Someone special gave it to me.' Her voice faltered; she was being ridiculous. All pennies were the same, weren't they? They didn't possess any magic but Hope – no, not Hope – the child, had given it to her, and it had become her talisman. Good things would happen for her as long as she had that particular penny.

'Ah,' he said. 'That's different. You should've said.' He hitched up his trousers. 'Here, let me.' He got down on his knees and reached into the dark corner, pulled it out and handed it to her, folded his hand over hers. 'There you are. I can't deny a special girl a special penny.' His trousers were covered in dust and he brushed it off with a few swipes of his hand.

'Thanks, Billy. I'm sorry you got in a mess.'

'Can't abandon a lady in distress, can I?' He put his arm across the flats, blocking her way. 'What are you doing here again anyway?'

'I wanted to play the piano. I'm not doing anyone any harm.'

'I never said you were. In fact, I'd say you do quite the opposite.'

She heard the clatter of metal pails. Winnie and Doris were mopping the aisles. She wasn't alone. She shrugged. 'Please yourself.'

He pulled a sulky face. 'That's no way to treat a knight in shining armour.'

'You reached for a penny in the dark.' It was her turn to tease.

'Ah, but it was a special penny, wasn't it? Not a run-of-the-mill copper like the others in the world. Rather like you, Jessie.' Billy leaned on top of the piano, watching her every move. She avoided his gaze, sat down on the stool, lifted the lid and began to play. In a few bars he'd ceased to exist along with everything else. She could let her thoughts wander wherever they wanted as her fingers moved along the ivory keys, lost in the music, letting go. When she finished there was a smattering of applause from the back of the theatre. Winnie and Doris had stuffed their cleaning cloths under their arms and settled themselves in the stalls to listen, fags at the corner of their mouths.

'Beautiful, ducky,' they called across the empty seats.

Billy came out from behind the piano. 'Would you like a little tap dancing to go with it, ladies?' He did a couple of time steps.

'No, thanks, Charlie, the music'll do us nicely, ta.'

Jessie suppressed her giggles as Billy turned to her, shrugging his shoulders, hands upturned, the wind taken out of his sails.

'Well, that told me. Worse still, they don't even know my name.'

Jessie sat on her hands and crossed her ankles, leaning into the piano. 'I rather think they do.' It was their way of bursting his bubble; she felt giggles fizzing and bit at her lips to suppress them. He scowled at the cleaners as they went back to their work and he jogged down the steps into the auditorium. 'One day everyone will know my name. I'll make sure of it.'

'No need to take it so serious, Billy. They don't mean anything by it.' He'd changed so quickly from being playful.

'Maybe.' He pushed down a seat on the front row and settled himself while she played again. After a while she heard the bang of the doors and clatter of buckets as Winnie and Doris left, then she only heard the music.

When she felt sated she closed the lid and got up from the piano stool. She needed a walk, fresh air. Her mind was busy now, ideas dancing in her head, possibilities. An act was beginning to take shape – songs she could sing ... a dress she could wear. Possibilities would become reality if she worked at it. Why was she wasting time playing the piano when there was so much to do? She got up and raced down the steps, walked as quickly as she could down the aisle at the side and out of the door into the foyer.

Billy ran after her.

'Where's the fire?'

'What?' She stopped.

He was frowning at her. 'You rushed out, all of a sudden. I thought something was wrong.'

'No, nothing wrong. Everything seems right for a change.' Because it did; suddenly things felt different. She'd been concentrating so hard on not getting the sack for lack of dancing skill that she'd forgotten that it was a stepping stone. She'd allowed herself to be distracted. Even Vi's new baby was a distraction, lovely as he was.

'That's good to hear.' He pulled back the glass door for her. 'I'll come with you. I'm just kicking my heels here.'

She dithered. She was going to buy some sheet music and manuscript paper and here he was, another distraction. She smiled wryly. He'd found her penny, hadn't he? 'What about Virginia?'

He bounced next to her. 'We're going for a walk, Jessie. You're reading too much into things.'

She reddened. 'I wasn't.' It was awkward. 'I don't want her to get the wrong idea.'

'There's nothing to get the wrong idea about, is there? And she doesn't own me, nor me her. Jeez, you women.' He shook his head, stuffed his hand in his jacket pocket and jangled his change again as he had done when he found her penny. 'She's cooing over that baby and then going shopping with Rita and Kay somewhere in Grimsby, so I'm not wanted.' He hung his head and she felt sorry for him again. He was being friendly, and he'd been gallant, saving her from scrabbling about on her hands and knees.

'I was going to the music shop in St Peter's Avenue, nothing spectacular, but you're welcome to join me.'

His face brightened immediately. 'That sounds quite perfect.' He swept out his arm and she led the way.

They walked up in front of the Dolphin Hotel and round by the way of the main road. Billy was good company and he made her laugh, talking about all the quirky little things that went on in the theatre.

'Mind waiting while I pop in here a sec?' He indicated the bookies.

'I'll wait, but not here; I'll walk further down, and you can catch up.' It wouldn't do to linger outside a betting shop; Grace would be horrified.

She was admiring a pair of beautiful blue evening shoes with a velvet bow at the front when he returned. 'Ta for that. I'm feeling lucky today.' He got into step beside her as she started walking again. 'Must be your lucky penny, having an effect on me.'

'Oh, please don't. No.' She was aghast. 'The penny's lucky for me, not for anyone else. It's a silly thing for me to do.' It was wrong of him to suggest anything else. 'What if you lose your money?'

He shrugged. 'Some days you win, some days you lose, but you've got to have a go, haven't you? Take a chance?' He grinned, nudging her as they walked along. 'Don't take heart. My risk, my reward. Nothing to do with you – unless I win, of course.'

What could she say? She taken a risk by coming here but it wasn't the same.

'Anyways, I reckon you're lucky for me – like your penny is to you.'

She was glum as they strolled along, trying to forget, hoping he hadn't wasted much in the betting shop. Money was far too hard earned to waste. She remembered the muted conversations between her parents when they discovered that another talented friend had gambled away their fortune before finding solace in the bottom of a glass; she was well aware of that slippery slope. It was Billy's bet, but somehow she felt tarnished by it.

Chapter 17

When they got back to the theatre, George came out from his office at the stage door and handed her a note, telling her what was on it. Billy stood there with his hands in his pockets, waiting for his key while George fussed over her.

'Your brother called. He said your mum was ill. He asked you to call back.' He paused. 'He sounded a bit distressed, Jessie love.'

Jessie took the note and stared at it. If she'd been here she could've spoken to Eddie, but now it was too late to make a call or she would have Rita on the warpath. She cursed herself. She'd allowed herself to be distracted by Billy far too easily. If only she'd had the courage to say no in the first place. She pushed the note into her pocket. Billy pulled his hand from his pocket and held out some change for the phone. Jessie shook her head.

'I'll get ready first and then come back and use the telephone.' She left Billy where he was and ran down the steps into the dressing room, her hands patting the walls either side to steady herself. Virginia and Rita were already sat in front of the mirror doing their make-up. Virginia took the band from around her hair and shook it out, picked up her hairbrush and began attacking her glorious red hair with ferocious sweeps, flicking it out with her free hand.

'Enjoy yourself this afternoon?'

'I did, thank you, Virginia.' Jessie bent down and put her bag under the table and started shrugging out of her jacket. 'Did you get anything from the shops?' She looked around for bags but couldn't see anything. Her heart was beginning to race, and her fingers trembled as she undid her dress and let it fall to the floor, stepped out of it and reached for her robe. 'I went for a walk.'

Kay and Sally squeezed past Jessie and took their places at the other end of the room. Jessie smiled at them and sat down on her chair and began pulling off her shoes.

'With Billy, yes; Sally told me she saw you down the Avenue.'

Sally shrugged and carried on with her make-up, avoiding Jessie's gaze.

'I wasn't doing anything wrong, Virginia; we were talking, that's all. Billy said you were shopping. I was going down the Avenue and he asked to tag along.' Her head was spinning; she really didn't need this – not now. Why would Eddie call? Was everything all right at The Beeches? Her mum ...? She tried to concentrate on her make-up. There wasn't time for mistakes. She looked across to Virginia through the mirror. 'Did you get anything nice?' she asked again.

'Much you care.' Virginia smacked her hairbrush down hard and Jessie winced.

Jessie steadied her hand, hovering over her lips with a pencil. 'Look, Virginia, I'm not interested in Billy. I have Harry.' It was a walk; she'd only thought to be friendly. Why did the simplest things have to be so complicated? She hadn't thought to be soothing someone else's hurt feelings. She needed to prepare for the show; she needed to get to the phone. She rummaged in her purse for pennies.

'Better not be.' Virginia sniffed, pulling her robe about her and tightening the belt with some force.

Jessie sighed. She didn't have the energy to battle with Virginia, nor did she have the inclination. All the sour glances and sniping remarks reminded her of life at The Beeches and she didn't want to drag memories of that around wherever she went. Frances sauntered in and began to get herself ready, she pulled a face at Jessie, obviously aware of the atmosphere, but Jessie shook her head. What was the point? She quickly finished her hair and make-up, got into her costume, picked up her coins and ran back upstairs, only to find Hilda hogging the line, deep in conversation with who Jessie soon discovered was her sister. She leaned against the wall waiting, checking the time by the clock in George's office.

'You all right, love,' George said, kindly. 'Do you want to sit down while you wait?' He gestured to his chair, which Jasper was keeping warm.

'I'd love to, George, but not in my costume. Wouldn't look too good going on stage covered in cat hair.'

He peered over his glasses. 'No, now that you mention it.' She patted his chubby hand.

'Thanks though, George.'

He clasped his other hand over hers. 'Any time,' he said, removing Jasper from his chair and taking it for himself.

Hilda hung up and Jessie fed her coins into the slot on the phone. It rang a couple of times before connecting. Her heart sank when Iris answered. 'Can I speak to, Eddie? It's Jessie.'

'I'm quite aware of to whom I am speaking,' Iris replied.

Jessie stuck out her tongue, delighted that her aunt couldn't see it.

'Can I speak to him?' she repeated, keeping her voice firm, glad that the woman was miles away. But then so was Grace. She put her hand to her throat.

'He's out on an errand for your uncle.' Her voice was clipped and sharp, and Jessie had to bite her cheek not to snap at her aunt. She took a deep breath, exasperation beginning to get the better of her. 'Can I speak to Mum then, please, Aunt Iris?' Oh, it was awful having to be nice to this dreadful woman. Why did she have to be so damned difficult?

Iris sniffed. 'She's having a lie down.' Silence. 'Do you want me to wake her?'

Jessie glanced up at the clock. By the time Iris woke her and Grace got to the phone her money would have run out and she'd be due on stage. There was no time for games. 'Eddie said that Mum was really ill. He was worried enough to call me.'

Iris snorted with derision. Jessie gritted her teeth. 'Your family are so over the top. I thought Eddie had more about him but he's obviously prone to exaggeration as well.' She paused. 'Your mother is a little unwell but nothing that a lie down and rest won't fix. I offered to call a doctor, but Grace said not to fuss. So, I didn't.'

'I'll bet you didn't,' Jessie muttered, her hand covering the mouthpiece as Iris went on.

'Your mother is perfectly sensible, as you well know.'

Jessie shook her head, looked up to the ceiling, knowing that Grace would keep suffering in silence. She would have to try again later, try and speak to Eddie if she couldn't speak to Grace.

The pips started and Jessie spluttered a quick thank you and hung up. Matt was calling the Overtures; only five minutes to curtain up, no time to get back to the dressing room so she dashed onto the stage. She was the first one there. Virginia walked up and stood next to her and Jessie felt the icy blast from her cold shoulder but what could she say? She and Billy had only walked into town together, nothing more. Was it so wrong to walk with someone?

The other girls came on stage and got into position, ready for the show to start. She tried to blank her mind and focus but couldn't help worrying about her mum. It wasn't like Eddie to exaggerate but then perhaps he had begun to hate it at The Beeches as much as she'd done. Her mum would never complain, and so Eddie must be concerned to call her when she was so far away. Butterflies of panic filled her stomach. She would ask Harry to go and check, she knew he wouldn't mind. He'd promised. She looked across to Rita as they heard the orchestra start up. Billy was in the wings watching, grinning at them as they waited for the tabs to open. Behind him, Bert and Hilda were going through their stretches. Jessie turned, eyes in front in case Virginia thought his smiles were for her. Focus. Harry would know what to do. She would call him at Cole's in the morning.

The Wednesday house was light on customers, but they gave them a warm reception and Jessie managed to get through the routines without making the slightest mistake. It was enough to have Rita on her back but to carry Virginia as well was more than she could bear right now. Jessie managed to tell Frances what all the fuss was about while they hung about in the wings waiting to go on. 'Best to front it out, Jessie. It was a bit daft of you, if you ask me, being Billy an' all, but you haven't done anything wrong. Have you?'

Jessie was horrified and stepped away from her friend. Frances caught at her arm. 'I thought not.' Frances shook her head. 'You're far too naïve for this game, Jessie. You've such a lot to learn.' Jessie was close to tears and Frances put her arm about her and pulled her close. 'It's all right, girl. You've got me to keep you on the straight and narrow.'

The atmosphere in the dressing room was sub-dued; Frances tried to make conversation, but Jessie's thoughts kept drifting to Grace and, in the end, she apol-ogised and turned to her pen and writing pad. Frances picked up a magazine. Jessie wrote the postcard to

Miss Symonds and a letter to Harry. She wrote one for Grace, and another for Eddie and slipped them inside the same envelope to save on postage. When she looked up, Virginia pushed past and glared at her through the mirror before leaving the room. The girls could hear raised voices from across the hall as Virginia and Billy argued. Frances glanced at Jessie and Jessie felt her cheeks burn. When Virginia eventually came back her eyes were red, but she was holding her head high as she sat down to retouch her make-up. No one said a word.

Glad the show was over, Jessie hurried to get changed and out of the theatre as fast as she could. She picked up her bag.

Frances caught her arm. 'Are you going to the bar?'

Jessie shook her head. She didn't want to spend another minute in the awkward atmosphere. 'I'm going straight home tonight.' It had been a terrible evening. She'd tried to get hold of Eddie, but Iris had answered again and Jessie daren't try a third time.

Frances pulled her down to whisper in her ear. 'You can't go home. You must go to the bar or it will look like you were up to something with Billy this afternoon.'

Jessie was horrified. 'But I wasn't.'

'I know that, and you know that, but if you do something different tonight Virginia will be suspicious. You have to come, whether you want to or not, or it'll cause you all kinds of problems. Let her lord it over you in the bar. Just one drink, then home.'

Jessie sighed. She'd promised Grace that she would go straight home after the show and she meant to keep that promise. Breaking it was the last thing she wanted to do. But Frances knew the ropes better than she did and so she waited while Frances got changed and they went into the theatre bar together, going out through the auditorium and not the stage door as she always did. Grace would understand.

Even though the theatre had not been full the bar was busy, mostly with patrons but many of the cast were there too. Madeleine would no doubt still be signing autographs and chatting to people at the stage door as she did each night; Billy preferred to hold court in the bar. And there he was, surrounded by a coterie of people laughing uproariously at his tales of other shows he had worked in and the top-line names that were, of course, personal friends of his.

Sure enough, Virginia was at his side, leaning close, pouting and preening. She looked stunning, her long legs peeking out tantalisingly from a very tight-fitting green skirt. Had she bought it that afternoon? Jessie got a seat by the window, turning her back so that neither Billy or Virginia could see her, nor she them. She had enough to worry about without Virginia spitting feathers. The room was a heavy with cigarette smoke and Jessie knelt on a stool to open the window, taking a couple of gulps of fresh air before sitting back down again.

Frances put a glass of stout in front of her. 'Get that down you.' She nudged her from her seat with a sharp elbow. 'Sit there.' She pointed to a stool that backed on to the window. 'Face them. Smile. Be happy for her.'

Jessie did as instructed and shuffled her body to where she could be seen, moving her drink to her new position. Virginia gave her an imperious smile and Jessie returned it. Virginia pulled Billy closer, holding her head higher, showing a little more leg, which Billy twisted briefly to admire.

Jessie took a mouthful of stout, fiddling with the beer mat on the table.

'I am happy for them, Frances. I don't want to be with Billy. I love Harry.' How she wished he was here. She must call him as soon as she could. What a fool she was.

'Indeed, you do, and you don't want to do anything silly to jeopardise things and lose him, do you. If you do, you're a dolt.'

Jessie put her glass down on the table. 'You think so little of me.'

Frances leaned back into her seat. 'Not at all.' She paused. 'You are as green as a cabbage, darling Jessie. Look at Virginia. She thinks she's made her catch.'

She observed Virginia enjoying being Billy's girl. Her arm was twined around his and she laughed too loudly when he made jokes. Occasionally, she glanced across to where Frances and Jessie were seated. It was the merest flicker of her green eyes, but she was checking them out all the same.

'So?' Jessie wasn't sure what Frances meant.

'Now, look at him.' Jessie took another sip of her stout and watched him over the rim, trying not to be obvious. He wasn't taking the slightest notice of Virginia, playfully punching the punters who were listening intently to his stories.

'She's jewellery, Jessie. A pretty bangle for his arm. What he's offering is just for the summer. Don't get sucked into the trap.'

'What trap?' Jessie was curious.

'Of the sunshine, stage, seaside, summer.' Jessie watched the scene at the bar playing out as Frances talked. 'It's sleight of hand of the best order. He wants company for the summer and then he'll move on without a backward glance. Virginia will have a broken heart. And let's hope that's all she's left with.'

'And Billy?' Jessie ran her finger over the rim of her glass. The thick creamy froth clung to the sides.

'Another girl, another show.' Frances opened her bag and took out a compact and lipstick and reapplied a vivid red cupid's bow.

'You sound like you know what you're talking about.'

Frances paused, eyeing Jessie, opened her mouth, then closed it again.

'Some other time.' She snapped the compact shut. 'Just marking your card – as a friend.'

Gosh, she was a dark horse. Jessie was only too glad that Frances was on her side, she wouldn't want her as an enemy. She was strong and she was astute, everything Jessie felt she was not. It had been a long day and tiredness was beginning to sink into her bones now. Had she eaten? She couldn't remember; she'd had quite the day. She hadn't expected it all to be so hard. How naïve she had been, expecting to leave all her problems at The

Beeches, thinking everything would fall into place once she'd escaped from Iris.

Jessie drained her glass. 'Thanks, Frances.' She sighed and looked around the bar as people drifted in and out. Bert was sat on the banquette that ran along the back wall, in his usual spot, talking to Wally and cradling a glass of whisky. Ronnie and Arthur were in a group with Kay and Sally. Rita had already left with Phil.

Hilda walked towards them carrying a glass of sherry and a bar of chocolate.

'Can I join you, girls?' Jessie got to her feet. She didn't need to sit here any longer to make a point for Virginia's benefit. Her mind was on other things. Grace and Eddie for one, Harry another. They would all be sound asleep, early to rise, and she realised how quickly she'd adjusted to this topsy-turvy living of late nights and even later mornings.

'I think I've stayed long enough?' She looked at Frances, who checked on Billy and Virginia, then nodded her head.

'See you later.' Frances took out a cigarette and tapped it on the packet, looking around for somewhere to cadge a light.

'Something I said?' Hilda settled herself down on Jessie's vacant seat.

'Oh, I ...' Jessie hesitated. What should she do now? Hilda flicked her hand at her. 'I was teasing.'

*

Jessie was glad to get out in the fresh night air. The moon was fat and round and smiled down on her from its place amongst the stars, but it didn't cheer her as it usually would. The day had started out so well, fussing over Vi's baby, and now she felt clumsy and wrong footed. And she had her mum to worry about too. Iris had said her mum didn't want any fuss, had refused a doctor – but then she would. She wished they weren't so far away … that she wasn't so far away.

There were still plenty of people on the streets, those coming out of the Nottingham pub and the Cliff Hotel as she came up to Sea View Street. Someone wolf whistled and she pulled her jacket about her and folded her arms, feeling vulnerable, her bag in the crook of her arm. Hurrying off the main road, she wound her way down towards Barkhouse Lane, fumbled for her key, opened the door and ran straight upstairs. Safe at last she threw herself on the bed and burst into tears, her body racked with sobs that seemed to come from the pit of her stomach. She pressed her face into her pillow. What a fool she was, a damn silly fool. Iris had been right. If she hadn't gone to Cromer with Harry, if she hadn't written to Bernie, if she hadn't had a dream … She punched the pillow hard and sobbed again, fear and panic taking hold until she was aware of a persistent knocking on her door. She made a half-hearted attempt to stem her tears.

'Are you all right, Jessie dear?' It was Geraldine. 'Can I come in?'

Slowly, she got to her feet and opened the door. Geraldine was there with open arms, her face wrought with pity and Jessie couldn't hold back any longer and fell into them, sobbing again as Geraldine led her to her own room. She settled Jessie in her armchair and poured her a glass of brandy. 'Sip it, Jessie. Slowly.' She did as she was told, coughing and spluttering as the spirit hit her throat. Geraldine smiled kindly, taking the glass from her hand as Jessie searched in her pocket for her handkerchief. Miss Symonds' parting gift was getting more use than she'd ever envisaged. Another sob was building in her throat and it hurt to swallow. She spluttered again.

'I know, it tastes dreadful, but it will help calm you, my dear.'

Jessie relaxed as the warming sensation tingled in her throat. She dabbed her eyes and blew her nose. She must look a fright and when she caught her reflection in the dressing table mirror, she did indeed look ghastly. Her face and eyes were red and swollen, and she hung her head to hide it from Geraldine who was having none of it. Geraldine settled herself at the end of the bed facing Jessie.

'Don't be ashamed of your tears, my dear. I'm not judging.' She took her hands in hers. Geraldine's hands were warm. A book she had been reading lay on the candlewick bedspread and an oak standard lamp with a chintz shade had been placed by the chair. A framed family photo and one of a man in uniform sat along the mantle of the cast-iron fireplace. There was a dressing table, a chest of drawers, a small wardrobe and a writing desk in front of the window. It was a little cluttered but perfectly cosy and comfortable. Jessie settled into the chair feeling foolish for such an overwrought display of emotion.

'I'm sorry, Geraldine.'

Geraldine put up her hands to silence her. 'No apologies necessary. Are you feeling a bit better?' She smiled, tilting her head and Jessie was reminded of her mum, which made her want to cry again but she swallowed and the lump in her throat finally shifted.

'Sit there. I'm going to make us both a nice warm drink. Don't move.' She rose from the bed and left the room. Jessie heard her in the kitchen, filling a pan, the gas popping to life.

Geraldine returned with two mugs of hot milk, handing one over to Jessie. It tasted odd after the brandy, but Jessie welcomed the warmth and comfort it offered.

'I'm sorry I disturbed you.' She hugged the mug in her lap.

'Not at all. It's wonderful to have company. An unexpected delight.' She was so gracious that Jessie felt more guilt rise. 'Do you want to talk about what's troubling you?' she said kindly. 'I'm happy to listen and it will go no further than this room.' She smoothed her hand over the bedspread, swirling her hand over the floral pattern. 'It helps to untangle the knotty thoughts, I find, don't you?'

Where to start? It all sounded so trivial but sitting in this cosy room she did feel calmer. She began to tell Geraldine of baby Frank, walking out with Billy, the girls giving her the cold shoulder and the phone call

from Eddie. 'I've been ridiculous, Geraldine. I thought
it would all be so simple, that I was brave enough,
strong enough ... that I could make a different life for
us all.' She let her head droop again. How childish she
sounded.

'It sounds as if you had quite a day, all in all, and
worry for your mother must have made it appear much
worse. You girls are young, and life is very complicated when you're young. Believe me, it gets so much
easier when you're my age.' She didn't seem that old.
Was she in her forties like her mum?

'Frances said this was your first time away from
home?'

Jessie nodded, taking small sips from her drink. The
milk was hot; she wrapped her hands around the mug.

'It's not that I don't know the ways of the theatre, I
do, but it's different on my own. I was always with Dad,
Mum in the wings. I would occasionally go on stage
depending where we were. But I see now how shielded
I was from everything.'

'That's understandable, a parent is an effective shield,
don't you think?'

Jessie thought of Iris and how Grace had come
between them, keeping things on an even keel. She
hadn't grasped the full extent of Grace's protection until
now. Her lip began to quiver again.

'More than that. My mum is such a strong woman;
she wouldn't want me to be weak and silly. She nursed
my dad.' It all came tumbling out, now that she felt
safe, now that she didn't have to consider anyone else's

feelings, trying not to upset them. It had been awful, truly awful. Dad had to give up his piano teaching and Jessie managed to keep on most of his pupils for a time. Grace had taken in sewing, more than she could manage, but she sat by his bedside day and night, talking and stitching. It was the thought of her dear, strong dad, wasting away in his bed, getting weaker until he was but a pale shadow, the brilliant light of him dimming slowly – and then he was gone. Gone. Big fat tears dropped on her cheeks. And she'd left Grace, hadn't she, fading away too. Images of her mum came to her, vividly now, sitting in the chair, slowly suffocating while Iris slept the afternoons away. Why had Eddie rung? Her heart was pounding, and she began to tremble.

Geraldine clasped her hand. 'Jessie, my dear, you are resourceful and strong just like your mother. Remember that and it will help.'

They heard the front door open and Frances's steps on the stairs, a knock on Jessie's door, the soft call of her name, the realisation she was elsewhere. Geraldine had left the door to her room ajar and Frances knocked and stuck her head around it. Geraldine beckoned her in.

'You all right?' Frances put a hand to her shoulder, her face was pinched with concern. Jessie nodded. Her own face felt like a balloon, her eyes swollen and sore, her body leaden but oddly, she did feel better. 'I am now. Thanks to Geraldine.'

Frances grinned at her. 'That's good, because we've got an early call tomorrow. And you thought you had problems.' She rolled her eyes.

Geraldine patted the bed. 'Sit down, Frances. You can't leave me in suspense now.'

Frances complied, leaning into them both, her eyes flashing with excitement. 'Bert fell down the stairs; they think he's broken his wrist. Mike – the stage manager,' she said for Geraldine's benefit, 'took him off to the hospital to get it checked, but, just in case, we're all at the theatre for nine so that they can rearrange the show – or at least sort something out.' She leant back on her arms, relaxing on the comfort of Geraldine's bed. 'Might be your big chance, Jessie. You can play the piano and you can sing. They might use you in a new number.'

Her head felt fit to explode. She should be excited, there was so much she could do, but all she could think of was Grace. The two women sat on the bed smiling at her and she tried to smile back, her head spinning. She felt exhausted, as if she could lie down and sleep for days and days.

'It'll be the brandy; you're not used to it.' Geraldine got to her feet. 'Come on, sweetheart, let's get you to your bed.' She took hold of Jessie's arm. 'You need to get your beauty sleep. It could be a big day tomorrow.' Frances took her other arm and the two of them helped her to her room, settling her gently on the bed. She was aware of someone taking off her shoes and swinging her legs onto the mattress then a blanket being placed over her before she gave in to oblivion.

Chapter 18

Harry placed the receiver down on the cradle. Hearing Jessie's voice so early in the morning had brightened his day but left him with a dilemma. He'd promised to look in on Grace to put her mind at rest, yet he couldn't just call in as he used to when Jessie was there. Things were different now.

He'd been unaware of anything untoward when he'd been helping Eddie with his exam prep, although he hadn't seen Grace. She usually stuck her head around the door but now that he thought about it, he hadn't seen her since they'd come back from Cleethorpes. He slumped at his desk and rested his chin on his fists. His head was full of too many things and he knew from past experience that the best way to resolve problems was to start dealing with them, one by one. He got up and went into the reception. Miss Symonds looked up and took off her glasses so that they hung around her neck by their chain. Neither of them spoke.

Beryl was working through his notes at her desk with great efficiency and didn't look up when he came into the room. Her neck was long, her mousey hair held firmly in place with numerous pins. She was a bright, clever girl and her shorthand skills were impeccable, but she didn't light up the office as Jessie had done.

He put his hands in his pockets and went over to the window. He couldn't talk while Beryl was there. It wasn't that he didn't trust her, but she didn't know the ins and outs of the situation at The Beeches, nor should she. If he could talk to Miss Symonds, he was sure it would help. What was the best way to approach this?

'Beryl?'

She looked up immediately. Her forehead was covered in angry red spots and it appeared the poor girl had another corker about to erupt on her chin. He smiled at her.

'Would you mind going to get me some of those lovely bath buns from the bakery at the end of the High Street? Do you know the one I mean?'

'Burtons, Mr Newman? Yes, I know it.'

He drew coins from his pocket and put two bob in her hand. 'Could you get me four, please.'

'Of course, sir.' She got to her feet, pulling on her jacket.

'No need to rush, Beryl. And thank you.'

The bell over the door chimed as she left. Harry pulled up a chair beside Miss Symonds.

'What can I help you with, Mr Newman?'

He grinned. 'Nothing gets past you, does it, Miss Symonds?'

'I try not to let it,' she said, pushing back into her chair. Jessie's postcard of Cleethorpes Pier was displayed on her desk, leant up against her lamp. Harry looked at it and smiled. It instantly brought back memories of him dancing with his girl in the sunshine.

'I'll get you another card when I go at the weekend.' It was an odd way to start the conversation, but he felt the need to skirt around it before diving in with Jessie's concerns. After all, Norman was his boss and he needed to get things right. He hadn't made any decisions, not yet, and when he did, he wanted them to be made in his own time. He thought again of Jessie; would she ever decide?

'I didn't know you were planning a trip so soon, Harry.' Harry shook his head. He would have been there every weekend if he had his way, but Jessie was always busy with extra practice and he had to let her have her head for as long as she needed it. He couldn't push but had to be there for her in whatever way he could. It seemed today was one of those times. Miss Symonds got up and closed the door to the main office that Beryl had left ajar. There was the soft click as the latch caught and she returned to her seat.

'Neither did I, but Jessie phoned this morning.' He lowered his voice and relayed exactly what Jessie had told him.

'It's a very tricky situation, Harry.'

'I know.' He rubbed at his head, messing his hair. 'I can't go barging in, making things worse.'

Miss Symonds nodded thoughtfully, running her finger round the neck of her fine knit sweater. 'Grace is a lovely woman, but I must say she's never looked in the best of health. Not that I've seen her many times, of course, but you get a feeling for these things. And that cough.' She shook her head. 'Not good at all.'

Harry sighed, rubbing his jaw with relief. 'I knew you'd understand.' He relaxed, leaning forward, resting his elbows on his knees.

'Do you think young Eddie might have exaggerated the situation to Jessie?'

Harry shook his head. 'He doesn't strike me as that kind of boy.' He knew she had to ask; he'd asked himself the same question, wanting to be sure.

'Hmm, me neither.' Her agreement convinced him. They were both silent for a while.

'Why not pay a visit on Jessie's behalf, for something totally unrelated.' Miss Symonds clasped her hands together and made a moue with her mouth. 'Let's see, that she has sent something, and you are checking that it arrived?'

'But what?' They both sat in silence for a minute or two, weaving a lie.

'A parcel,' Miss Symonds said brightly. 'You don't have to know what's in it. Jessie didn't say, did she?'

'That's perfect; why didn't I think of that?' He sat back, the weight dropping from his shoulders. He knew Miss Symonds would come up trumps. She was a wily old bird. He could've kissed her.

'But you did, Mr Newman.'

'Did I?' He laughed. 'I'd thought to take the bath buns but that's even better – and we can eat the buns.'

'Marvellous.' Miss Symonds put her glasses back on her nose and checked the paper in her typewriter, her help no longer needed. Harry got to his feet and replaced the chair he had removed and stood by Beryl's desk, scrutinising her work. It was immaculate, the papers orderly, pencils sharpened, and not a smudge to be seen.

'Cakes will make the afternoon all the sweeter,' Miss Symonds said, beginning to type again. 'Beryl will like that.'

'It will,' Harry agreed. 'And Beryl's a good girl. I like her.' He ran his hand over the edge of the desk, hoping to attract a little of Jessie's essence that might have lingered there. 'Very efficient,' he added, tapping the desk with the flat of his hand.

'Not like Jessie.'

He looked across. Miss Symonds was smiling and so was he, now that he had a solution to at least one of his problems.

'No, but then no one is like Jessie. She's a one-off.'

Harry pulled up outside The Beeches. He paused, looking down the lane that he and Jessie had walked along together. Was it only weeks since he'd heard raised voices in the kitchen, when Jessie had lost her temper, the words floating out of the house through the open window? It had been such a shock to hear of her leaving that way – that she hadn't told him of her plans hurt more. Far, far more. Still, there was no time for regrets. She was gone and he'd better take it on the chin and wait, and be someone worth coming home for. He was getting out of the car when Eddie came down the path to meet him.

'I heard your engine, I knew it was you.' He was lacking his usual grin; looking untidy and uncared for.

Most of all, he looked afraid. His shirt was hanging out from under his tank top and his blue trousers sagged at the knees. He rubbed his hand across his face and Harry put a hand on his shoulder to comfort him, hoping it would help.

'Jessie rang. Asked me to drop in.'

Eddie made fists with his hands. 'I called the theatre, Harry but she didn't call back.' The boy was agitated, moving from foot to foot, looking to the house and frowning. 'I think she's forgotten all about us.'

As they walked up the path together, Harry said, 'I'm sure she hasn't, Eddie. Not for one minute; you're too important to her.' Jessie might forget him, but he knew how much Jessie loved her family. 'Perhaps the message wasn't passed on.' It was more than likely, given Iris's attitude to Jessie's departure but if her nephew was worried, surely she would seek to put his mind at rest?

'Mum needs a doctor, Harry. I'm sure of it. She says not to fuss. She always says that.' He gave a sad half laugh. 'But Aunt Iris should take charge, shouldn't she? I can't call a doctor. Aunt Iris would ...' The anger made his voice catch. Harry understood the boy's impotency. 'I don't want to upset Mum, but someone needs to do something, Harry!' They stood facing each other at the front door and Harry put a hand on Eddie's shoulder and squeezed it.

'That's what I'm here for.'

The boy looked doubtful as he opened the door and let Harry into the house. Hearing voices, Iris bustled into the hallway to greet them.

'Harry, how lovely to see you.' A smile lit her face, softening the angles. She appeared genuinely pleased by his presence and Harry began to wonder if Eddie had been mistaken. If Grace was that bad surely Iris would be worried sick – but here she was, looking perfectly composed. He was wrong footed for a moment but then swung into the lie that he had been perfecting all afternoon.

'Mrs Cole, how wonderful you look this evening.' She preened, patting her hair and smiling at him, suitable flattered.

'How very charming you are, Harry,' she trilled, her voice becoming girlish. 'What brings you out here on a Thursday? Not that you're not welcome, you're always welcome. Norman didn't say anything so I wasn't expecting you.' She swept her hands down her brown skirt, adjusted her stance, another pat of her hair.

Harry smiled. 'I was wondering whether I could have a quick word with Grace. Jessie wanted me to check whether her parcel had arrived. I won't take up too much of your time.'

'Not at all, Harry, not at all. Do come through.' Harry followed Iris into the sitting room. Grace was sitting in a chair with her back to him and he was shocked when he caught sight of her. Her pallor was grey and when she coughed he could hear the rattle in her chest. She was covered with a blanket even though the room was warm, stifling, in fact. The window would be better open to let in the fresh air, but he couldn't go into someone's house and start suggesting things, could he. He glanced across to Eddie who hovered by the doorway. Poor boy, how awful it must be for him. He sat opposite Grace and she struggled to smile. He wondered how much effort it was taking just for her to remain upright. The skin under her eyes was dark purple and the veins protruded on her forehead.

'You don't look well, Grace.' It was a grave understatement.

Iris tutted. 'The journey to the coast last week was too much for her. I keep telling her. Wasting money she doesn't have on trips to see that wayward child of hers.' She sat down in her chair. 'Can I get you a drink, Harry?'

A drink? How he wanted to shake her. Couldn't she see the woman was suffering? Where was her compassion? Harry cleared his throat, choking back the words he really wanted to say.

'Not for me, thank you, Iris.' He forced a smile that she returned. He needed to remain calm and considered if he was to be of any help at all. He sucked at his cheek in frustration, remembering Miss Symonds' advice. He took Grace's hand in his.

'It's good to see you, Grace.' He looked directly into eyes that had lost their sparkle. How could she have gone downhill so fast? What could he tell Jessie? 'Jessie asked me to come. She wondered if you'd got her parcel?'

Grace feebly shook her head and he was incensed that he had to burden her with such a stupid, stupid lie. Eddie came further into the room and stood behind the sofa, watching Harry. Harry raised his head to smile at him, hoping to give the boy courage. He got to his feet.

'I won't keep you, ladies; I merely came to see if the parcel had arrived.' He smiled broadly at Iris but there was no warmth in it. What was wrong with the woman that she couldn't find it in her heart to care for anyone but herself? He signalled to Eddie to go outside and Eddie slipped quietly from the room. He clasped Grace's hand lightly, fearing she would break if his touch was too firm. She was burning with heat. A doctor should be called immediately but he couldn't barge in and take control. Miss Symonds was right. It was merely a fact-finding mission and he'd seen enough to know that Jessie needed to be aware of how very ill her mum was. What did Norman think of it? He was puzzled. Surely he knew the situation?

'I'll let Jessie know, Grace. I'm so sorry to have troubled you both. Perhaps it was premature of me to come.' Grace pressed her hands to the arms of the chair and attempted to stand. Harry gestured for her to remain where she was. The words wouldn't come, they couldn't get past the lump in his throat.

Iris got to her feet. Harry found a smile from somewhere and gave it begrudgingly to Iris. 'I can see myself out. Thank you so much. I'll leave you ladies to your evening.'

Outside, Eddie waited on the path, his face crumpled with misery and fear. 'Jessie needs to know. Mum needs the doctor.' He hung his head, hands in pockets, heavy with despair.

'She does, Eddie; she does on both accounts.' What could he say that would bring comfort? The poor lad was trapped. 'It's a difficult situation to say the least. I don't want to make things worse. I can't call the doctor, much as I'd like to, but I will call the theatre. Then I will go and get Jessie and bring her home.' The boy had managed to keep strong but now fat tears fell down his cheeks. He opened his mouth, but words escaped him, and he shook his head in anger and frustration. Harry patted him on the back. 'Don't worry, old chap. You can hang on until Saturday, can't you?'

He nodded, then drew his arm across his eyes. 'Mum made me promise not to worry Jessie, but I think she should know. I want her to come home.'

How Harry wanted her to come home too, but not like this. He put his arm around Eddie's shoulder and hugged him. 'Be strong, Eddie.' Eddie nodded again, following Harry down the path and out into the lane. The sun was dropping on the horizon, the clouds tinted with red, and a warm breeze troubled the leaves on the beech trees that surrounded the house. Harry got into his car and drove away, seeing Eddie in his rear-view mirror frozen on the kerbside, head hung low, and he began searching for the first call box along the way.

Chapter 19

Jessie's head felt fuzzy and her eyes were still a little swollen from her tears the night before, but she hadn't been late for the morning call. Geraldine had taken charge, waking the girls in plenty of time, so that all three of them could sit down to breakfast before scooting off to work. They had parted with Geraldine at the bus stop and Frances had waited outside the phone box while Jessie made a call to Harry, then the two of them had carried on to the Empire.

The entire cast, and crew, apart from Madeleine, were scattered amongst the seats in the stalls watching Jack, Phil, and the stage manager, Mike, discussing how to rework the running order of the show to take up the slack left by Bert and Hilda. Frances and Jessie moved along and took a seat, joining in on the general chit-chat as they waited. Rita was flicking through the latest issue of *The Stage*, her legs resting on the seats of the row in front of her.

'Did anyone hear how Bert got on last night at the hospital?' Sally leaned forward moving her head from side to side, searching for an answer from anyone who possessed information. Arthur turned his neck and said from the side of his mouth. 'It's a fracture, they reckon. Him an' her have had to clear the digs and go home.'

'Oh, poor things.' Sally sank in her chair.

'Poor they will be.' Arthur was matter of fact. 'Neither of 'em will be able to work 'til his hand gets better. Might keep him off the juice in future.'

Jessie wondered how they would manage; it wasn't as if Hilda could do the act on her own. She supposed they must have money set aside for such an occurrence. She hoped they had, and she must make sure to do the same herself. 'What a worry for them both,' she said to Frances.

Her friend pursed her lips. 'It could happen to any of us, Jessie. I can't remember how many times I've danced with injuries; we all do it. Best to have something put by, just in case.'

Jessie nodded. That would take some doing. She'd not been able to save much at all so far.

'Always glad I'm not a speciality act with all the props and paraphernalia that goes with it. Glad I'm not a juggler, or ruddy dog act,' Billy said flatly. 'I can do my jokes sitting down.'

'Might be funnier if you did, lad.' Arthur ducked in expectation of a flick to the neck that didn't come – until he had sat upright when Billy delivered a playful blow. Virginia was next to Billy, filing her nails. She'd greeted Frances and Jessie when they arrived, and Jessie was glad that Frances had made her stay in the bar the previous night, even if her head didn't feel the benefit. The animosity the girl had shown to Jessie had all but disappeared.

'Why isn't Madeleine here?' Virginia asked.

Billy put his hands behind his head. 'Because she's the star of the show and doesn't have to be concerned with things like this. The whole audience is waiting for her to come on at the end, she can't spoil it by coming on sooner. The punters will get up and go home, then what will us poor buggers do – play to an empty house?' He yawned, patting his hand across his mouth.

Jack walked forward to the front of the stage and addressed them, Annie at his side with her trusty clipboard. He was smart in his dark suit and waistcoat, his shirt open at the collar, his tie undone about his neck. The lines on his forehead ran deep and he looked as if he hadn't slept at all. Jack cleared his throat. 'As you may have heard, Bert had an accident last night and he and Hilda will be going home to Sheffield.' He clasped his hands in front of him. 'Which means we are ten minutes light in the show where their spot would have been.' He walked a few steps to the left, head down before looking at them all again.

'I don't want to bring in anyone else at this point – Bert's hand might repair before the end of the run and I would like them to have a job to come back to. I understand how precarious these things can be.' He pursed his lips, running his hand around his chin. 'So, if you are in agreement, and we can work things out musically and so forth, I wonder if any of you would be willing to do something extra to fill the gap? On a temporary basis, until we know what's what.'

'Don't think I've ever heard anything like that before,' Arthur said, turning to talk to Billy. 'Keeping a turn's spot open. Mind you, it'll save him a bob or two, won't it?' But Billy wasn't listening; he was already on his feet.

'I've got an idea or two, Jack.' He began pushing past Virginia, making his way up onto the stage.

'Cripes, the lad don't let the grass grow under his feet,' Arthur said. No one else moved, leaving the way wide open for Billy to monopolise Jack. Frances folded her arms across her chest and sucked in her cheeks. 'I smelt the ground burn under his heels, Arthur.'

'That was his arse, dear heart,' Wally chipped in, not looking up from his crossword. He took his pencil from behind his ear and marked his paper.

Jessie watched as the two men on stage talked, lowering their voices. Jack took off his jacket and Annie stepped up and took it from him, slipping it over her arm. She thought she'd heard her name mentioned and immediately stiffened. Billy put his hand on Jack's back and guided him towards the rear of the stage. Jack leaned in to Billy, listening as the comic expanded his idea, gesticulating, bobbing his body as he talked. Jack stood straight, rubbed his chin, slapped Billy on the back. They returned to the front of the stage, all smiles. Both men looked at Jessie. Virginia was staring at her now, then back to Billy, and Jessie could only look down at her lap. Virginia shifted in her seat and Jessie became uneasy.

'Phil, can you come back up, and Rita, we'll need you too.' Rita let the newspaper drop to the floor and began making her way down the row towards the stage, while Jack addressed the rest of them. 'Arthur, Wally, no need for you to stay now, but could you come back early tonight, say five o'clock?'

Arthur, needing no excuse, picked up his trilby and left, quickly followed by Wally, while Rita and Phil got up onto the stage. Frances shoved her in the ribs, and Jessie sat bolt upright, staring at her friend, surprised by her sudden aggression.

'Jessie.'

Frances nudged her. 'They want you.' She pointed up to the stage. Jack and Billy were looking at her, Billy's grin wide.

'Yes, you Jessie.' Jack was smiling. 'Can you come up here, please.' Jessie stood up and Frances gave her a gentle push. She was going to squeeze past Virginia, but one look and she decided against it, turning instead to wriggle past Frances and take the longer route. Her legs had suddenly become weak. As she walked on stage Jack was holding out his hands to her and she took them. His hands were strong and firm, and it steadied her. Her heart was thumping and she daren't look out into the auditorium in case she caught Virginia's scowl, but she so wanted the courage that Frances gave her. She focused on Jack's face. Up close she could see the kindness in his dark eyes and there was comfort for her there.

'Billy has a fabulous idea for a routine for the pair of you.' His voice was smooth ... enticing. If he believed she could do it then she must at least try. 'Phil already has an arrangement and Rita is going to put together a simple routine that you and Billy can do together.'

Was she dreaming? She'd opened her eyes, hadn't she? She dared to look back to the stalls. Frances was grinning, giving her the thumbs up. Sally and Kay were deep in conversation, and Virginia was stewing nicely, as her mum would have said. Jessie hesitated. Why hadn't Billy put Virginia forward for this – but then, this was her chance, wasn't it? And she'd be a total idiot not to take it. If Virginia took umbrage she'd just have to grin and bear it.

Mike and Bob pushed the upright piano on stage from the wings and brought on the stool. Phil settled himself on it. She heard her name again. It was Jack. She turned.

'Could you sing something for us, Jessie? What would you like Phil to play?'

She put her hand to her head, brought it down over her hair.

'Sing "It Had to be You",' Billy gestured the go-ahead to Phil who waited for Jessie.

'This key all right for you?' He played the opening bars.

Jessie nodded. Phil began again and she came in on the right note and began to sing.

When the song ended, she looked at Jack. The whole theatre had fallen silent. Winnie and Doris had stopped mopping and were leaning on the back rail, fags hanging out of their mouths, turbans on their heads.

'Well, I'll be darned. What a voice, Jessie.' Jack took her hand. 'What a voice.' He was shaking his head in disbelief. 'My God, you are your father's daughter, aren't you?' He squeezed her hand again, shaking it in his.

She could sense his excitement and it seemed that time had frozen and the voices about her mingled into garble. There was more discussion between Jack, Rita and Billy. She looked for Frances and they exchanged grins. Frances settled herself in her seat and folded her arms across her chest, and Jessie knew she wasn't going to leave. It gave her courage to know someone was on her side.

Jack gathered them around. 'Right. Rita, opening of second half of the show, first routine. Without Jessie, of course, so five of you and you're featured front. Can you adapt?'

Rita was a tight spring. 'Of course.'

'Good. Then, as Billy has suggested, he and Jessie come on and sing "I'll String Along with You". I'll need you to put something simple together for the two of them. Is that possible? Sorry to dump all this on you, Rita.' He touched her forearm.

Billy did a couple of flowery time steps to demonstrate his skills.

Rita screwed up her nose.

'It's only basic, Rita, but I know how to sell it.'

He was desperate to get this, Jessie thought. She studied the energy he put into taking this chance and making it his. Watch and learn, she told herself; watch and learn.

Rita wasn't impressed. 'You'll need to work your arse off, Billy but if anyone can get away with it you can. No playing for laughs, though.' She was firm and Billy, for once, didn't argue.

Jack was pleased. 'Good, good. Then we'll have Jessie sing solo ...'

'Me?' She was shocked.

Jack took her arm. 'Yes, you. What a talent you have. We mustn't waste it.' He thought for a while. 'What about "The Sunshine of Your Smile"? Do you know it?' Did she know it? Her dad had sung it to her mum so many times, mostly when they'd fallen out and he needed to make her smile again. He was with her – not just in her heart, but in the very fibre of the theatre ... in the ether around her. He was here. She shivered. She wouldn't ever let him down; his name and talent had to live on through her. This was her opportunity too, and she must be like Billy if she wanted to seize it for herself.

'Yes, I know it.'

Jack looked down to Phil who gave him a thumbs up. Jack ran his hand through his hair.

'Strewth, that's the first part sorted.' His face changed now that things were moving forward. 'Now we need to make it happen.' He checked his watch. 'We have four hours. Let's get to work.'

The band took their positions in the pit and Phil stepped down to join them. The piano was moved offstage, and, while Billy and Jessie went through the music with Phil, Rita concentrated on getting the rest of the Variety Girls to adapt the opening routine for the second half. They were dismissed once the routine was sorted so that Rita could focus her attention on Jessie and Billy's duet. They opted to stay, lighting up cigarettes and settling themselves in the stalls, watching Billy and Jessie go over and over the steps, Rita taking hold of Billy's arms at times, stretching them out to get a better line.

'Now stand behind her and hold her around the waist.'

'With pleasure,' Billy said under his breath and Jessie glanced at Virginia who was watching every move they made with intense scrutiny. Jessie tensed.

'Relax,' Rita barked. 'This is no time to be prudish, Jessie. It's not as if he's going to try anything on with a full house, is it.' She slapped Billy on the backside. 'And you behave yourself. We'll have none of that.'

'None of what?' he said, putting up his hands and laughing.

Rita gave the nod to Phil who began to play, and they went through the routine again. And again. And again. Jessie was picking up the steps easily enough, but Billy kept making mistakes and they had to repeat until it was as good as it possibly could be, given the time they had to rehearse.

Jessie was glad when she heard the rattle of crockery as Annie came down the aisle closely followed by Winnie pushing a trolley that held a tea urn, and was laden with biscuits and a pile of sandwiches.

Jack got up from his seat on the front row and applauded them all. 'We'll take a break now or you'll not be fit for the show tonight. We don't want you flagging and all this hard work to be for nothing.'

They trudged down the steps and got themselves drinks. Jessie's clothes were soaked with sweat, so much more than they'd ever been when rehearsing the dance routines. She pulled her top away from her skin and shook it, letting the breeze cool her skin.

Frances came and stood beside her. 'You were brilliant, Jessie.' She jabbed at her arm. 'I'm so thrilled for you.'

Rita helped herself to biscuits and mug of tea. 'Good work, Jessie.' She dunked a digestive in her mug. 'I wouldn't want to be in your shoes.'

Jessie had expected Rita to be awkward about her moving out from the chorus but there was none of it, and Jessie realised it was because Rita's love was dance and nothing else came close. It was a huge relief to have that knowledge, for it was obvious Virginia was resentful. Kay and Sally stuck close by their friend. While Jessie rehearsed she'd seen them, sitting either side of Virginia in the middle of the stalls, where they could get a balanced view of the stage, heads close, whispering. It was unsettling. But it wasn't going to stop her.

'Looking good, kid. Make the most of it.' Billy offered her a sandwich and she took it. She'd hardly eaten anything the day before and that probably contributed to her feeling so adrift yesterday.

'I'm so grateful to you, Billy. I know it was you who put me forward.'

'How grateful?' He teased.

She shook her head, disappointed. 'Not that grateful, Billy. I hope you did it because you know I have talent.'

Frances pushed past him and moved Jessie away. 'Give it a rest, Billy. Aren't you ever offstage?' She manoeuvred Jessie to a seat. 'Eat that and I'll get you another one.' Jessie was glad to sit down. Her head was a muddle of steps and words, of music and movements, and it all needed to be in the right order. It was difficult to keep stopping and starting when Billy made mistakes but as long as she remembered her part, it would be okay.

Frances came back and handed Jessie a mug of tea and another sandwich. 'This could be the break you're looking for, Jessie, and you don't want to pass out in the middle of it.' She sat next to her friend, leaning forward and resting her arms on the seat in front, looking up at the stage.

Jessie took a large bite out of the sandwich. It was only a few minutes but offered so much potential. She glanced across and Billy put his foot up on one of the seats and chatted away to Virginia. He kept looking at Jessie and smiling and she couldn't help but smile back. If he hadn't heard her playing the piano that day, he wouldn't have put her forward. She'd been so sad, but something good had come from it.

The afternoon was difficult, and she began to tire more easily. Her limbs were aching and her head was swamped with directions from Rita and Jack, hoping to get everything right but worrying about getting it all wrong. Going over the song was a dream; she'd always found learning lyrics easy, and Phil was great at coaxing the best from her. His arrangement was effortless and simple for her to follow. Billy sat back in the stalls, Virginia trying to get his attention, which Jessie knew was fixed firmly on her. She was aware of his eyes watching her every move and she tried not to look at him, or at Virginia whose eyes had narrowed to thin slits.

After a while, Jack took her to one side. 'Enough now, I want to you rest. Don't worry if it's not perfect, Jessie. We'll get through tonight and then we can work on it some more. And I will make sure that you get a raise in your pay packet for this. Make a note of that please, Annie.'

She hardly knew what to say so she just grinned at him like a loon. It was worth the hard work, every damn bit of it, if it meant more money. She didn't want Bert and Hilda to suffer hardship, but it had opened a door for her, and she was ready to walk through it.

'I'm going over to the hotel to let Madeleine know what's happening and I'll be here tonight, in the wings.' He smiled again. 'I know you'll be just wonderful.'

After he left, she lingered on the stage, not sure what to do, where to go.

'Do you need anything, Jessie?' Annie asked. 'Mary is making a skirt that can go over your original dress for the routine to make you stand out a little more. All very simple really, we don't have time for anything else, but at least it sets you apart.' She was kindly. 'Something less to think about. Your head must be spinning.'

It was, but they had gone over things as much as they could. She would simply have to remember as much as possible and hope for the best.

*

The first half ran as normal, albeit ten minutes shorter for the absence of Bert and Hilda. For the entire interval Jessie scarcely sat down, pacing in what little space there was, going out into the corridor, back in the room again. She sat and she stood until Frances pushed her into a chair and instructed her to 'sit' like a dog. Rita was brisk and professional, talking over Jessie's moves with her, and making sure the other girls were confident with their new positions for the opening number. She showed no sign of fatigue or nerves, and Jessie had a renewed admiration for her. Kay and Sally were quiet, but no one could ignore the tension in the confines of the dressing room. Virginia simmered with a silent resentment that was hard to ignore. It was all too much to deal with, nerves were getting the better of her and the last thing she needed was an argument. She could talk to her after the show, let her know that she was most *definitely* not interested in Billy.

'Right, madam. Sit still and don't move.' Frances sat down next to her. 'You have to remember to breathe. In. Out. In. Out.' She placed her hand to her chest and demonstrated the long inhale, the even longer exhale and Jessie began to do the same. 'That's better; easy, isn't it?' Jessie was so glad to have Frances beside her. If her lucky chance ruffled the ducklings' feathers, then she would have to let them squawk for the time being.

Jack came to see her before she went up on stage for the second half. He'd been at the theatre for most of the day and was still wearing the same suit, only now his tie was fastened and he smelt of cologne. 'Smile, relax, enjoy yourself, Jessie. I'll be watching from the back. Break a leg.' He took her hand and planted a light kiss on it, smiled encouragingly. She was desperate to repay his faith in her.

Mary bustled in, taking what little room there was left. Draped over one arm was the wrap-over skirt she had fashioned and fitted for Jessie.

'Time for me to go.' Jack left Mary adjusting Jessie's skirt until she was satisfied. Overtures was called and the Variety Girls minus one went up to the stage. Mary pinched Jessie's cheek. 'I can hear your heart thumping away like a big old drum, lass. You go out there and enjoy yourself and the audience will enjoy it too. It's infectious, let me tell you. That's all there is to it.'

Jessie hugged her tightly. Mary patted her bottom. 'Up you go. Have fun.'

Jessie blew her a kiss and made her way upstairs. She remained in the darkness of prompt corner when the curtain went up and watched the routine that she was once part of. Rita had done a brilliant job of rearranging the format and Jessie found it incredible at what the woman had done in such a short time and under such pressure. There she was, leading the troupe, smiling broadly with not a hint of the stress that had lain on her shoulders. Jessie must do the same. Billy was standing in the wings the other side of the stage ready for his entrance, and the rest of the cast had crowded either side to cheer them on.

Jessie closed her eyes. Her legs were jelly; she didn't want to walk out and fall flat on her face. She was aware of movement behind her and, opening her eyes, turned to see Madeleine beside Mike. Jessie's stomach somersaulted.

The curtains came forward as the dance came to an end, two stagehands placed an ornate bench centre stage and the backcloth of a park was flown into place as the dancers ran off.

Jessie pressed her feet firmly on the stage to ground herself and then stepped forward to sit on the bench. The orchestra segued into their song, the curtains opened, and Billy strolled onto the stage to join her, singing the first line. Her heart was beating furiously, but when she saw him it was the most natural thing in the world to begin her own movements and sing her own part.

He stood before her, holding out his hand and she took it as he drew her to her feet, and they stepped along together. His arms were around her waist as Rita had designed and they strolled over the stage, smiling at the audience, singing together, singing solo in turn, and then together for the final verse. Their song came to an end and as the audience applauded their approval, Jessie felt her chest expand to allow for the greatness of the feeling in her heart. She was home, she belonged, she was complete.

Billy took hold of the microphone. Through the brightness of the stage lighting, in the semi-darkness beyond, she could see smiling, happy faces on the first few rows before everything disappeared into blackness. This was what her dad had hoped for, trained her for, why he'd spent the hours coaxing and honing her voice, and now, at this very moment, in this small theatre, in the most glorious seaside town, she was singing again. At last.

Billy announced her with a flourish and a wink that was only for her. 'And now, ladies and gentlemen, for your own delight, the wonderful, dazzling songbird that is Miss Jessie Delaney.' He backed off the stage and into the wings, holding his arm outstretched as he did so.

Over his shoulder, she caught sight of Madeleine in the shadows. The lights changed to soft pink as Billy had advised and the spotlight shrank to focus on her and her alone. She briefly closed her eyes, breathing deeply as the band started playing the intro to her song. This was her moment and she wanted to remember every second. She hit the note at exactly the right time and everything in her heart and body told her that this was the one true love of her life. Nothing else made her feel as she did this very moment. She smiled as she sang, reaching her hand out into the darkness as a request, drawing the audience along with her.

In her mind's eye she could see her dad in the front row, along with her mum, Eddie and Harry, and she sang to them with every ounce of love and joy she possessed. Through the half shadow she could see the first few rows of the audience and they were with her, she sensed it, they were holding on to every word and she sang for them, each and every one, but most of all she was singing for herself, for all her hopes and dreams, because now she knew they would all come true.

The applause was rapturous, and she felt the warmth coming over the orchestra pit and wrapping around her.

It was if she was floating. She bobbed a small curtsey and backed off to the right. Billy took her hand and dragged her back onto the stage, taking her by surprise. It wasn't in the running order, Billy was supposed to go on directly after her, straight into his act.

'Ladies and Gentlemen, what a girl, let's hear it once more – Miss Jessie Delaney.' He whispered into her ear as he led her back on, 'Wonderful, they'll be putty in my hands.'

The crowd carried on applauding, clapping harder, and Jessie gave another curtsey then pulled away from his hand and into the wings. Madeleine had gone but the Variety Girls were there in the semi-darkness, all smiles – even, she was pleased to notice, Virginia.

Arthur patted her shoulder, his old eyes twinkling in the dim light of the prompt corner. 'Well done, gal. You were ruddy marvellous out there.' She grinned as she was swept along by the rest of the Variety Girls and down to the dressing room. If only Harry had seen her, and Grace, then it would have been perfect; it was a bittersweet triumph without them. She drifted down the stairs on a cloud of joy.

Frances was grinning wildly, Rita graciously protecting her fledgling as she took the first steps that would help her leave the nest. The others changed into their robes to relax while Billy and Madeleine did their acts, having a full half hour before they needed to be ready again. Jessie wanted to keep her costume on a little longer, wanting to stay in the moment of her success, feeling that if she disrobed a little of the magic would fall away with it. Virginia had left shortly after they got back to the room but returned with a tray holding mugs of tea. She passed one to Jessie. 'I know you'll be a big star one day, Jessie. Talent always comes to the top.'

Jessie was taken aback. 'Thank you, Virginia; that means a lot to me.'

The girl gave her a small smile and passed around the other mugs. The chatter subsided as they settled down to pass the time as best they could.

Billy's applause drifted through the floorboards and down into the dressing room beneath the stage as they waited for the walk down and final curtain. Madeleine's intro music played, and Jessie could pinpoint the moment that the star stepped out into her spotlight. The audience would erupt, giving her the warmest of welcomes as she made her entrance. One day, that would be the sound that greeted Jessie as she walked onto the stage. She knew it. It was not a dream but a reality that was within reach, if she worked hard enough.

Billy stuck his head around their open door as he came offstage. 'Bloody brilliant, Jessie. They loved you. I knew they would.'

She got to her feet. 'I have you to thank for that, Billy.'

He wafted a hand, batting the compliment away. 'Nope, I might have paved the way, but you had to come good, and you did.' He leant on the door jamb and winked at Virginia who blew him a kiss. Billy made a clicking sound with his tongue and disappeared into his room. Virginia put down her magazine and followed.

The girls settled down with their knitting and letter writing, and Jessie was left with her thoughts, her mind racing with all the opportunities that might come calling because of tonight. It was awful that it had come from someone else's hardship, and she truly felt bad for Bert and Hilda, but she needed to grasp every chance from now on.

The Variety Girls were in their finale costumes when Jack came into the dressing room. His eyes revealed his tiredness, but she could immediately tell from how he looked at her that he was happy with her performance. He stood behind her chair, placing his hands on her shoulders, talking to her reflection in the mirror.

'Well done, young lady. A fabulous performance, and I hope the start of many good things. I don't think we've seen the best of you yet. Will you be in the bar after you've signed your many autographs?'

She nodded. This deserved a small celebration, a marking of her progress. She wouldn't be able to sleep anyway, and she was certain that Grace wouldn't mind, just this once.

They rushed offstage as always, wanting to get out of their clothes and into the bar. Jessie's head was reeling, her heart skipping with the delight of it all. This was a breakthrough moment, a time when her fortunes could turn. The noise and laughter filled the dressing room and she wanted to make sure she looked good and presentable because there would be autographs tonight. She wasn't just a Variety Girl any more; she had a place on the bill. Granted it was only one song, but it put her on a different standing. As she followed Frances out of the room they could hear Madeleine's voice the length of the corridor. It was harsh; Jack's was calming, placating.

'I know exactly what Billy is up to,' Madeleine snapped 'It has to be changed.' Frances looked at Jessie and shrugged.

'Wonder what he's been up to now?'

Jessie didn't want to know. It didn't matter. As they walked past the star's dressing room, Madeleine came to close the door. Jessie smiled at her but it wasn't reciprocated. She frowned at Jessie, her face set in hard lines. 'Some people are getting above themselves,' she spat, closing the door. They could still hear her arguing with Jack as they went up the stairs.

Jessie turned to Frances. 'Do you think that was aimed at me?'

'Don't be daft,' Frances said, pushing in front of her. 'Let's celebrate your success. The first drink's on me.'

Chapter 20

Geraldine waited up until the girls had got home to hear all about Jessie's performance. They'd sat and talked into the small hours before they'd all drifted off to bed. Jessie had been unsettled by Madeleine's comments, but Frances said she was reading too much into things and she'd eventually let it go, not wanting it to spoil her happiness. She'd lain awake, going over and over her performance. How thrilled she was, how quickly her time had come. It was a comfort to think that her choice to strike out on her own had been justified. She'd heard the rattle of milk bottles before falling asleep.

The first thing she did after getting dressed was to call Harry from the telephone box on the Kingsway. He wasn't exactly evasive, but she felt he wasn't telling her the whole truth. He'd promised to come on Saturday as planned but instead of staying over would take Jessie back to see Grace. She swung her arms as she sashayed back to the house, her heart brimming with happiness.

Grace would be delighted, she knew it, and it would cheer her to know that Jessie was succeeding. As she reached the top of Barkhouse Lane, she heard someone call her name and turned, shielding her eyes against the sun that was climbing over the rooftops. Dolly was

284

walking behind her, a brown paper package in her arms, another two balanced on top, a grin on her face. Jessie retraced her steps.

'Let me help.' She held out her arms.

Dolly shook her head. 'If you move one thing the whole lot'll tumble.'

Jessie grinned. 'Are you coming to us?'

'Am I ever. Got a few things to share.'

Jessie walked up the short path and opened the front door. A waft of Jeyes Fluid greeted them. It was Geraldine's day off and they'd all agreed to help clean the front room so that she could let it if Reg changed his mind. Dolly was still chattering as they walked into the hall. 'We told Mam all about last night, me and Dad, that is. Oh, wasn't it wonderful, Jessie? And Mam told Joyce, you know how it is, and ...' She put the parcels on the table in the back room. 'Joyce asked her friend Betty to make extra. She's sent a tea loaf.'

Frances grinned. 'That woman is the sweetest and you'd never guess it to look at her. Joyce and her stale cakes.'

Geraldine fetched a plate, which Dolly took, unwrapping the fruit loaf while Frances moved the old newspapers that were spread over the table and made space for it.

'You can never tell what anyone is like from looks alone, girls,' the older woman said, looking pointedly at Frances, then walking back to the sink. 'Good or bad.' She shook the water from her hands and rubbed them with a tea towel.

Jessie put the kettle on the hob and rinsed their mugs, popping outside to drop the used tea leaves on the soil. When she came back into the kitchen, Dolly had opened the remaining parcels. She was shaking out a flower print dress in blue and Frances was holding a red wool one in front of herself, looking down and kicking her legs to flick out the material. Dolly handed the blue dress to Jessie.

'Yours if you want it. And the other two on the table. They were our Lizzie's but she's on her fourth pregnancy and she's given up hope of ever getting back into them. I can alter them to suit.' She hesitated. 'If you'd like.'

Jessie gripped her arm. 'I'd very much like, Dolly.' What a godsend the girl was. Her wardrobe was so small that she had been able to bring almost everything with her when she left The Beeches. How delicious it would be to have something new – well, new to her. Frances was equally delighted. The two girls held them up against themselves, admiring the style.

'Don't you want them, Dolly?' Jessie asked. 'They're lovely quality.'

Dolly shook her head and moved to let Geraldine slice the cake.

'I've got three sisters. I'm forever getting dresses from them. More than I could ever wear. Take 'em.'

The two girls hugged her. 'That's so thoughtful of you.' Frances took a dress from the table. 'Okay if I have this one, Jessie?'

Jessie nodded, taking the other dress that Dolly had brought with her, fingering the delicate lace of the collar. 'They're lovely, Dolly. Really lovely. We must give your sister something for them.'

'Lizzie doesn't want anything. Well, maybe she'd like a couple of tickets to the show next week. Yes. She'd like that. Dan, her hubby, he'll be back on shore in a couple of days. They love to catch a show.'

'Consider it done,' Frances said. It was sweet of Dolly to suggest such repayment, knowing that, now the show was up and running, the girls had a small allocation of free tickets as long as it was for early in the week when there might be spare seats. The kettle whistled and Jessie laid the dress carefully on the table and began to warm the teapot. When tea was made the table was cleared and they sat and enjoyed Joyce's gift.

'Is Dan on the trawlers too, Dolly?'

Dolly nodded, her mouth full of the fruit loaf. She put her hand in front of her mouth while she chewed quickly and said, swallowing the last mouthful. 'He's skipper's mate. Wants to take his ticket this year so he can get his own boat.'

'Is Pete with him?' Frances asked. 'The same boat, I mean.'

Dolly shook her head. 'No, he's with another company. Not sure if he'll switch owners.'

'It must take some getting used to,' Jessie said, 'being married to a fisherman. They must spend more time at sea than they do on land.'

'They do,' Geraldine agreed, 'and it's a hard, hard life for the men when they're out in the heavy seas.' She glanced across to Dolly. 'And harder still for the women left behind to bring up the children on their own.'

Dolly tipped her head to one side. 'I suppose I'll have to get used to it because I love him. And if other women can do it, so can I. You get used to it – them being away an' all.'

'I hope I get used to it too.' Jessie was thoughtful. 'It's not as if Harry's in danger, not like Pete or Dan, but hearing his voice this morning was so wonderful. At least I can speak to him – and I'll see him at the weekend.'

She told the others of her plans, of how delighted she was to be seeing Grace and Eddie, and how she hoped that Grace would be on the mend.

Geraldine got to her feet and began clearing the plates. 'I'm sure you'll be just the medicine she needs.'

After the show on Friday night, Jack took Jessie to one side and invited her to take afternoon tea with him at the Café Dansant the following afternoon.

She had been at sixes and sevens as she'd got herself ready, wondering whether to have her hair up or down, if she should wear lipstick or go without. In the end, Frances had taken charge, tying her hair back with a bow and slicking on a little lippie.

'I can't imagine what he wants to talk about, Frances,' Jessie said as the two girls linked arms and walked along the Kingsway. 'Do you think it's about the show. Do you think he wants me to do something else, another song?'

'I've no idea, my love. It must be good news – he wouldn't take you out to somewhere quite lovely if it was to be bad.' They waited for a horse and cart carrying trippers to pass, avoided a car, skirted around a few cyclists and sauntered to the other side of the road. 'He did say he wanted to chat about your dad. It's probably about that. You're a lucky girl, Jessie Delaney.'

Jessie leaned on her friend and they touched heads. 'I am, Frances. You know, when I first came here, I thought I'd made the biggest mistake of my life. I'm so glad I stuck it out.' Frances withdrew her arm as they parted ways by the entrance to the Café Dansant.

'So am I, girl. So am I.'

The waiter showed her to a table by the window and Jack got to his feet when he saw her, smiling warmly.

'Jessie,' he said, moving forward, kissing her on the cheek, taking her hand and leading her to a chair. The waiter pulled it back with a smooth sweep, waiting for her to sit down, before artfully sliding the chair forward. From their position they could both see out of the window and watch the dancers twirling past them. The orchestra occupied a small podium at the back of the room and the floor was full of happy couples, twirling about the floor. The waiter leant close to Jack and took his order before disappearing amongst the cloud of dancers.

'Do you like it?' Jack pressed his palms together, resting his elbows on the table.

'I do,' Jessie gushed, enjoying the music, the light-heartedness of the atmosphere. 'We were going to bring Mum here.' She smiled, turning back to him. 'But we didn't quite make it.'

He nodded. 'Then next time she visits we must make sure she gets to see it for herself.'

The waiter came with a tray laden with teapot and china cups, and a waitress moved swiftly to his side, placing a three-tiered cake stand onto the table. The bottom layer was laden with sandwiches cut into delicate fingers, the middle layer with scones, cream and jam and the top plate held the most exquisite cakes Jessie had ever seen.

She looked out of the window as the waiter poured from the silver teapot, watching people pass by, the ladies in summer dresses, the men in their shirtsleeves. The weather was warm but cloudy, a cool breeze blowing in off the sea. She turned back to Jack and he smiled at her again, the wrinkles deep about his dark eyes. 'The sunshine has deserted us but luckily the crowds haven't.'

She took up her cup, holding the saucer beneath it. 'That must be good for business.'

He heaped two spoons of sugar into his tea and stirred. 'Yes, too hot and the crowds stay on the beaches and too wet and they don't want to come out at all. I'd say this weather is perfect for us.'

'Ticket sales are good then?'

'They are, couldn't be better.' He showed her the palm of his hand, inviting her to help herself to the sandwiches.

She couldn't ask what his plans were; it wasn't her place. She would find out soon enough but it all sounded good. Perhaps the season would be extended.

She helped herself from the display, taking her time, savouring the taste of cucumber and butter.

'Are you enjoying being in the show, Jessie?'

She nodded, her mouth full of food. He hadn't eaten at all. He cleared his throat.

'I don't quite know where to begin, Jessie.' She looked away from the dancers swirling elegantly about the floor. His mouth was twisted as he sought the words. 'I feel so bad about all this.' He glanced out of the window, back to her, held her gaze. 'This is my first theatre. One day I hope to have many more.' He smiled at her again. 'It's been rather a huge learning curve for me, getting to grips with running a show. I had the opportunity and I took it, God only knows why. It was a mad impulse.'

She nodded, knowing only too well where impulsiveness could lead.

'I might not have the experience like other theatricals,' he went on, 'but I have the passion, and I can learn. We can all learn.' He paused. 'I made a mistake, Jessie.' His voice was soft, apologetic.

She looked back at him and his eyes were sad. He fiddled with the teaspoon on his saucer, let it drop, interlaced his fingers, rested them on the table. 'I'm so sorry to have to say this, Jessie, truly I am. I'm afraid I have to cut your solo. It makes the show unbalanced, one female singer after another. Madeleine is the big draw and ...'

She didn't hear the rest of what he said. Had Madeleine forced his hand? She recalled her harsh words with him after her performance. This was down to her, wasn't it? She'd heard of stars making demands, the jealousy, the bitchiness – and Madeleine had been so nice to her, or she had until Jessie had had her small moment in the spotlight. It was obviously Jessie whom Madeleine thought was getting above herself. Her spikey comment the other night had been aimed at her, not Jack. Jessie had to be put in her place and Madeleine had the power to do it. Geraldine was right: you couldn't tell what anyone was really like.

'But you still have your duet with Billy.'

She nodded, trying to smile. Tears brimmed in her eyes and she turned away to look once again at the dancers swirling past until the overwhelming need to weep disappeared. A single tear ran down her cheek and she caught it discreetly with her finger. She wouldn't cry. Not here. She turned back to him.

'I understand, of course I do.'

'It was all spur of the moment. I heard you sing "The Sunshine of Your Smile", and I was taken out of myself and that's a good thing ... but ... that song. So many memories, Jessie. Forgive me.'

'Oh, please, Mr Holland. There's nothing to forgive.'

He shook his head. 'Please, call me Jack.' He cleared his throat again, adjusting his tie. 'You're a talented girl, Jessie. I'm sure there'll be other opportunities for you to shine. It's just not the right timing for me at the moment. Of course, your agent might have you contracted to something else?' She could see how uncomfortable he was. It was her turn to comfort him.

'I don't have a contract with Bernie. He was a friend of my dad's. I have his word that he'll get me work and that's good enough for me.' She tried to eat more of her sandwich but now it didn't taste so good.

'Then is my word good enough for you too?

'Of course.' The disappointment was painful. She felt a fool but there was nothing she could do. Perhaps if he hadn't known her dad it would have been different, a curt word at the side of the stage, or a note left on her mirror. He was only being nice because of her dad, feeling that he owed her. Yes, that was it. All the kind words meant nothing at the end of the day.

The orchestra segued into a waltz, the tempo slowed. It was all so lovely. He'd promised to take her out for tea right at the beginning but now it smacked of pity, of keeping her quiet and a small consolation for having her number cut from the show. She studied his face. No, he wasn't that kind of man. She could tell from the set of his face, the tenderness in his eyes. He was doing his best to keep his show afloat – they all were.

He held out his hand. 'Shake on it?'

She put down her sandwich, wiped her hand on her napkin, took his hand in hers. His grip was warm and strong. He wanted to explain further but she said, 'Please, can we talk about Daddy instead?'

He seemed relieved as a smile broke across his face.

'"The Sunshine of Your Smile".' He leaned back in his chair, rubbed at the face of his wristwatch. 'That song. Your father played it when we were in Rouen. We found a bar with a piano. He played and we sang, thought of our loved ones back home. How good it would be to be home.' He swallowed, looked down at the table. 'It wasn't the world we expected to come back to. I couldn't do the work I had done before … couldn't settle.'

She nodded, remembering her dad saying the same thing. Nothing was ever what you wanted it to be. You had to make the best of what was laid before you. And that was exactly what she intended to do.

Chapter 21

Harry pulled the car into a space along Dolphin Street at the back of the theatre and waited, mulling over how to break the severity of Grace's illness to Jessie. Starlings hugged the trees then swept out like confetti as he opened the door. When he'd spoken to her on the telephone he'd been able to traverse the fine line of alerting her without distressing her, but now that he was here he needed to reconsider. He chewed at his lip. Perhaps he should break it to her bit by bit on the drive home.

He leaned on the roof of the Austin, tilted his head, squinting against the sunshine as a plane soared over-head. The sorties in Norfolk were more frequent now as fledgling pilots stepped up training, and talk of scare-mongering was almost non-existent these days. More or less, everyone in the country had accepted that war was a matter of not 'if' but 'when'. It seemed to be bad news all round but best that it was faced head on.

'No bloody good burying your head in the sand, Harry, old lad,' he told himself. 'Get the boil lanced and get on with it.' God only knew how much Grace had deteriorated in the last couple of days. He only hoped that Eddie had been able to persuade his aunt to call a doctor – or that Grace had requested one, even though he very much doubted it. He walked round and opened the door on the passenger side, took out the flowers he had picked for his girl. Another posy of larkspur. She loved the blue-violet flowers of summer. They would be small compensation.

As he approached the stage door, George got to his feet and shook his hand with ferocity. Harry had spoken to him on the phone the day before when he'd called to speak to Jessie previously and gently explained the situation, hoping that the girls would rally round and support her, whichever way things panned out.

'She's like one of me own, that little girl,' George said when Harry quickly updated him on how Grace's health had deteriorated. 'I wouldn't want a drop of harm to come to her, or her dear mother.' He shook his head in dismay, running his hand about his chin. 'She'll be down in the dressing room, son. You know the way.' He patted him gently on the back and Harry felt strengthened by his kindness. Jessie was in as a good a place as she could be.

He rattled down the steps, holding on to the rails either side, strode along the corridor, knocked on the girls' ever open door. The smell of different eau de toilette and perfumes greeted him. He caught a glimpse of Frances, her long limbs stretched in front of her, and smiled wryly. It was all exactly as Jessie described in her early letters; cards pinned in a patchwork across the wall, the light bulbs that framed the mirrors, the costumes spilling out over the rails, stockings on a makeshift line strung across the room. The sense of family.

Virginia looked up from filing her nails and frowned. 'Harry, isn't it?'

He nodded.

'Three doors down.' She cocked her head to indicate the direction he should go before adding, 'She's with Billy.'

Was there a hint of malice in her voice? Harry felt uneasy. What was Jessie thinking? He didn't want her to get a bad reputation. He quickened his pace.

Billy's door was wide open, and Jessie was sat on a spoon back chair. He was relieved to find that she wasn't sitting about in her robe but wearing the flowery print dress that was so familiar to him. It was the dress she had worn when they drove into Cromer to celebrate his partnership. It gave him a bitter taste in his mouth. Her legs were stretched out in front of her, ankles crossed, arms folded across her chest, scowling. Billy was in his shirtsleeves and grey flannels, his hair slicked back with oil. Here too, many cards were wedged around his mirror, and Harry took in the towel laid in place, sticks of greasepaint in neat rows, his comb at the top like a spoon. His suit was on its hanger on the back wall. He was smoking a cigarette, his hands low as the smoke drifted towards the open door. Harry knocked on it and Jessie looked up in surprise.

'Harry. You're early.' She was flustered, dragging her hands across her face. She got up and took hold of his hands, planted a kiss on his mouth. He took hold of her chin and tilted her gaze to him. God, she was beautiful. She was smiling but there was such sadness in her eyes.

'Come on in, Henry.' Billy beckoned with his hand, wafting smoke at him.

'It's Harry.' He hesitated. Where should he stand? Instinct made him want to take Jessie's hand and bring her out of this man's room, but he fought it. Play it cool, play it cool.

'Sorry, chum.' Billy smiled and Harry wanted to knock those big white teeth out of his stupid head. He wasn't his chum; not at all.

'Jessie's had a bit of a setback. I was giving her the benefit of my professional advice.'

Good excuse, Harry thought, fair enough. He was clever, this chap. Grace had been unsettled by him from the start and had said as much in the car on the way home from the show – but what could any of them do? If he said anything Jessie would dismiss it as jealousy. Play it cool, Harry.

He tried to appear relaxed. 'Why?' he asked, calmly. 'What happened that she needs it?' He didn't want to stay here, they could go out, she could tell him any- where, but he knew he must handle this carefully. He was in no doubt that Billy was enjoying this more than he should.

Jessie slumped back down on the chair and Harry leant against the wall so that he could see her fully. 'I've had my song cut out of the show. It was all so good and then … nothing. I was so excited for you to hear me sing solo, Harry.'

Billy gave another puff on his fag. 'She was bloody wonderful, mate; that's the top and bottom of it.

Madeleine got the wobbles. Too insecure. I told Jessie; it's dog eat dog in the theatre. She's too sweet, isn't she, chum?' He flicked ash into the saucer to the side of him, and took another drag.

Harry felt the muscle in his jaw twitch. Keep smiling, Harry, be friendly. Not for the fool's sake but for Jessie's.

'Let's go and get a drink of tea or something. We can talk as we walk. It will only take a few minutes.' Harry was cool. He held out his hand and Jessie took it. He pulled her to her feet and shot a warning glance at Billy in case he decided to invite himself.

Billy smirked. 'Great idea, Henry. I'm off to get myself a man's drink in the bar. Catch you later, sweet Jessie?'

Jessie pressed his arm. 'Thank you, Billy. I'll get my chance again; I know I will.'

Harry's heart ached that he wasn't here to protect her. Couldn't she see what Billy was doing, a spider slowly drawing her in? He longed to warn her but instead he put his arm around her shoulder and the two of them headed out into the street.

She threaded her arm through his. 'I can't believe Madeleine would be so petty, can you, Harry? She's top of the bill. It was one song, just one song.' She snuggled close and, God, it was so good to have her near. How he'd missed her.

'There'll be other chances, Jessie. You'll get another opportunity. Your talent needs to be shared.'

'That's what Billy said,' she replied, innocently.

Harry tensed. His cheek twitched again. He wanted to change the subject, talk about things that Billy had no knowledge of. Like Grace – and he couldn't help but notice that Jessie hadn't mentioned her.

'Have you packed a bag, Jessie? Have you got it with you?'

She shook her head and the glorious copper tones shone in the summer light as they had that day long ago when she leaned out of his car window, when she had been full of joy and expectation. He hated seeing her so glum and now he had to make things worse for her. But slowly, he decided, little by little to break such news.

'I left it at home. So stupid of me. I wasn't thinking properly; I was too angry about my song being cut. Too worried about Mum. Could you go and get it for me, while I do the first house, or shall we get it before we leave?' She stopped walking and turned to him, as if she had read his thoughts. 'How bad is Mum, Harry?'

He couldn't tell her the truth, not when she had a show to do. How could she smile and dazzle out on the stage if she knew? He looked down at his watch, tapping the face avoiding her gaze. 'We can talk about it after the show. You need to get ready.' He looked up again but she was waiting for an answer.

He pursed his lips. How could he lie to her, this girl who had his heart? 'Bad, Jessie. She's very ill. I wanted to call a doctor, but Iris was adamant, and I couldn't interfere.'

She studied him, her eyes serious. 'So now you know what I mean?'

He nodded. 'I do.'

*

In the end, Harry opted to get Jessie's bag while she worked the first house as it would save time at the end of the evening. He would catch her routine with Billy in the second house. He crossed over the road and headed down towards the sea. The resort was busier now and he wandered down towards the pier, retracing their steps when they had danced along the boardwalk. How happy they'd been then. He walked on, his brain busy with thoughts, longing for the summer to end so that Jessie would come back to him. Please God, she would come back to him.

Geraldine was outside as he turned into Barkhouse Lane. He could see her rubbing at the window frames with a cloth, the glass glinting in the sun, the net as white as a sheet of Cole's headed notepaper. Her hair was covered with a bright headscarf, her sleeves rolled up to her elbows, clothes protected by a brightly flowered apron. At her side was a large metal pail and another by the door was full of weeds, the dandelion and plantains piled high. As she dropped the cloth into the pail she lifted her head as she wrung it out; she smiled when she saw him. Her face was flushed and she pushed a strand of hair away with the back of her hand, threw the cloth back into the bucket and wiped her hands on her apron. 'Harry.'

He took her outstretched hand and shook it. 'I'm sorry to stop you working.'

She put her hands to her back and leaned into them, stretching herself. 'I'm not. It's quite enough for one day.' He stood in the gutter to let an elderly man pass by.

''Ow do,' the chap said in thanks, touching his cap to Geraldine.

Harry got back onto the pavement. 'It looks totally different.'

'Cared for?'

He grinned. 'Spot on.'

She folded her arms and stood beside him. 'I should perhaps have tackled the outside first, but I considered the inside more important. If prospective lodgers could see past the surface, then I knew we would get on.' She put out her hand, 'Come in, come in. Are you here for Jessie's things?'

He nodded. 'I thought it would save time.'

She stepped inside the house. 'Very wise.'

The hallway smelt of disinfectant and any dirt that had once clung to the walls and floors had been scrubbed and buffed to submission. She opened the door of Jessie's room and stood back to let him pass. Jessie's small bag was on the chair in the corner. On the chest of drawers, she'd set out her photographs. One of her dad, Davey, wearing his evening suit, holding his violin, another of the whole Delaney family, and he was cheered to see the one of himself that he had given her. Beside it was a pile of letters tied with a red ribbon. He wondered if they were the ones he'd sent and hoped that Jessie missed him as much as he missed her.

As if catching his thoughts, Geraldine asked, 'How is Grace?' He knew from her expression that she didn't expect a positive reply.

He shook his head slightly. 'Not good. Not good at all. She's very weak. And grey.'

Geraldine frowned. 'Are they not looking after her well enough, Harry? Jessie did mention what a harridan her aunt was. I thought she didn't look too well when she was here.' She paused, perhaps sensing his unease. 'But it didn't look too serious. Weary, more than anything. I think, mostly, that she's still grieving her husband. It's early days for her, poor woman.'

A shaft of sunlight pierced the darkness of the room as the sun began to sink down the horizon and fell soft on the woman's face. She couldn't have been much older than Grace, but they were miles apart. He hadn't been able to pinpoint what it was before but now he did. Geraldine had vigour, she embraced her life, whereas Grace seemed to be letting go of it bit by bit.

He turned to the window and thrust his hands in his pockets. A cat strode along the partition wall and dropped down into the backyard. The glazed tile path was littered with weeds and the shrubs were wild and untamed. He supposed Geraldine would make a start on that soon enough. She was of the same ilk as Miss Symonds, possessed of fierce practicality wrapped up in kindness. She was reliable. It was an immense comfort to know that Jessie was under her protective care.

'I hope you're right.' He gripped Jessie's bag.

'Grief is a strange animal, Harry. It comes in waves, an ebb and flow. Perhaps a visit from Jessie will brighten her again.' She put a hand to his shoulder. 'As much as it will brighten you.' A smile lit her face and he found himself relaxing, the earlier tension and doubt forgotten.

'I'm sure it will,' he grinned as she led the way downstairs.

He had more of spring in his step as he walked back to the Empire and called in the bar off the foyer. He bought himself a pint of bitter and sat nursing it. He'd already put Jessie's bag in the car so all he had to do was wait. It was quiet in the bar when the show was on and one of the barmaids, Vera, was leaning on the counter, taking the chance to have a crafty cigarette. The second half had already started and he went to the door to the left where Jessie had told him Dolly would be.

He opened the door when he heard applause and stuck his head around it. In the dim light he saw Dolly dressed in her plum and gold usherette's uniform and caught her eye. She nipped across, pulling back the curtain, and closing it as he slipped in. He leaned on the back screen to watch the show. It was no fun being in the audience on his own and he was glad when Dolly stayed next to him. It was a full house, as he'd discovered it was every night. Although the entire country's thoughts were directed at the uncertainty of war during the day, they flocked to the theatres and picture houses to escape it during the evening. Perhaps the laughter and songs made them forget. He smiled, ruefully. Jessie had been so right; her dad's words so perceptive.

The opening routine for the second half came to a close and as the applause died down, the band began to play 'I'll String Along with You'. The silver curtains drew back to reveal Jessie sitting on a white bench. The backcloth was cleverly painted with trees in full leaf and in the centre a wrought-iron arch was decorated with the letters *People's Park;* a path wound into the distance and led to a pond. His Jessie. He leaned deeper into the screen, resting his chin on his folded arms when he saw her sitting there, waiting. The intro music played and Billy came on. Harry had to admit his voice wasn't too bad – for a comedian – but he'd never make it as a singer. He walked towards Jessie, and Harry felt every muscle in his body tense as Billy held out his hand and drew her to her feet. The two of them strolled along, holding hands, until he stood behind her, sliding his hands about her waist. They smiled at each other, then out to the audience as they sang. Harry felt himself burn with heat, his ears stinging as he watched them move together. He tried to tell himself it was all part of an act, but it looked real enough to him, and even if Jessie thought it was all innocent, Harry knew that Billy would be making the most of being close to his girl. Jessie was his girl. He didn't want to watch but he couldn't take his eyes away from her. Her voice was as sweet as a lark, and she'd become more confident in the days since he'd seen her last, her voice more true as it travelled over the audience, and into every corner of the theatre. Yes, she deserved to be given the stage to herself. He'd wished that this routine had been cut instead, and not her solo.

As the song ended Dolly nudged him and whispered, 'Isn't she wonderful, Harry? She lights up the stage, doesn't she?'

It was hard to speak, hard to smile but he did. 'She does,' was all he managed in reply. He couldn't stay here any more and pretend he was enjoying it. He indicated to the door, using his finger to let Dolly know of his intention, turned on his heel and left, the sound of their applause ringing in his ears. He'd seen enough.

He stayed in the bar until the show came down and the audience began to burst out of the doors into the foyer. He saw their smiling faces, heard their chatter as they spilled out onto the streets, their laughter as they repeated jokes that Billy *bloody* Lane had told. He drained his glass, put it down on the table, studied the foam that clung to the sides, watched it slowly fall to the bottom while he waited for Jessie.

At the stage door he squeezed past the autograph hunters and stage door Johnnies that hung around waiting for their chance with the pretty girls. George was standing guard as always and, as soon as he saw Harry, he beckoned him to his office. Harry stood in the doorway watching as, one after the other, the acts came out in their civvies to sign autographs before they went home for the weekend or back to digs. He noticed that Wally and Arthur were barely disturbed for their signatures but that the girls were much sought after. Again, he felt another pang of jealousy that now he was sharing Jessie and so many others adored her now too. George handed him a parcel wrapped in brown paper.

'Olive sent something for the journey. A pork pie, a bit of cake, like.' He handed over a pale-blue thermos flask. 'I dare say you'll be in need of something hot as well. It's a fair old drive you'll have to do again, lad.'

Harry was overcome. 'How very kind, of you both, George.' He shook his head. 'I'll make sure you get your flask back.'

'Give the dear lady my best wishes,' George said, pressing his hand.

'I will, George. She'll need them.'

The old man frowned. 'Is it that bad?'

Harry nodded, feeling choked. He mustn't think about Billy wheedling his way into Jessie's affections. It wasn't important. Jessie was all that mattered, supporting her, getting her back safely to Grace and Eddie. He was the man she relied on and he wouldn't dream of letting her down. Someone tapped his shoulder and, as he turned, Jessie planted a kiss on his lips.

'Ready?'

He held out his hand and she gripped it, leading the way, squeezing past the crowd that had swelled since Harry arrived. She let go to sign as people pushed autograph books under her nose and he carried on without her, waiting on the pavement while she signed some more. She had a beaming smile and he was filled with pride. He'd never seen her look so happy, or so lovely as she did right then.

The coast road was soon behind them as they began the long journey back to Norfolk. Jessie had twisted herself, so that her back was to the passenger door and she could look directly at him. From time to time he took his eyes off the road and looked at her, happy for the two of them to be reunited. Her hair was down about her shoulders and her green eyes sparkled with energy. After a while, she settled down into her seat, staring out into the darkness of the country roads. It was black as pitch, only a few lights here and there, in upstairs windows of cottages as they wound down endless roads, clocking off the miles.

'I should have trusted my instinct, Harry. I knew Eddie would only phone if things were serious.' She squeezed his hand and drew it over to her lap. 'I let Iris talk me out of making a fuss because I hate her so much ... I couldn't wait to get her off the line. I wanted to speak to Mum and I've been so thoughtless. Mum needed me and all I could bother about was getting a song in a show. I'm just a stupid girl who's forgotten what's really important in life.'

'Hey, don't beat yourself up about it, Jessie. How were you to know?' He let go of her hand to wind down the window and let some fresh air into the car to wake himself up. There was still a long way to go. The wind ruffled his hair as they sped along and he took a few deep breaths to refresh himself, leaning his arm on the window frame as his hand steadied the steering wheel. How could he be so petty, upset about Billy putting his arm about her, when there were far worse things to worry about? He took her hand again. 'It will all be fine, you'll see.' He glanced at her. 'Your mum will be so glad to see you, Jessie. And Eddie.' He gave her hand a gentle shake, hoping to comfort her in some way, knowing the worst was yet to come.

When they were done talking, she laid her head on his shoulder and put her hand over his as he changed gears, and they drove along the winding country roads. The moon was bright and lit up the flat landscape. When they hit the open roads, he put his arm around her shoulder and drew her to him and she put her hand over his heart. He was tired; it had been a long day.

Jessie was asleep when he pulled into the lane where The Beeches stood silhouetted in the semi-darkness, surrounded by the large black outstretched limbs of the trees that gave the house its name. A fox darted in the hedgerow as Harry got out of the car and somewhere in the distance a pair of owls called to each other. In a few hours it would be dawn, and, as Harry gently shook Jessie awake, he wondered what the new day would bring.

Chapter 22

Jessie stood on the lawn, arms wrapped around her, staring up at the front of the house. The two bedrooms over the front door were in darkness and as she walked around to the back, she saw the soft glow of a lamp in Grace's room. Was she awake? She scrabbled around in the half-light for pebbles to throw at Eddie's window, found a couple of small stones and threw them, heard the gentle tap as they hit the target. When he didn't appear, she sighed, whispering to Harry, 'I'll have to wake them all up. We can't stay out here all night.'

He caught at her arm. 'Jessie, darling.' He was stumbling for the words. 'It might be a bit of a shock when you see your mum. She was very frail when I saw her last and I've no idea if she ... well, prepare yourself.' His eyes locked onto hers, wanting to make sure Jessie understood.

Her stomach tightened, her pulse racing as she tried to remain calm, but time could be of the essence. She sprinted round to the front door and rattled the knocker, the sound bouncing around them in the still air. She paced back and tilted her head. There was no sign of movement in the rooms above her, so she attacked the door with force and panic, hammering with her fists and calling out.

'Open the door,' she shouted through the letterbox, then repeated it up at the windows.

'Keep it down, Jessie.' Harry's voice was soft. 'It's late, remember.'

'What else can I do?' she hissed.

He sighed, shrugging his shoulders, and stepped back from the front door. 'Give them a chance to wake up. They might well be dazed, wondering what's going on.'

'Why? They knew we were coming.'

He shook his head. 'I didn't tell them. Did you?'

She froze, his words slowly making sense in her brain. She hadn't told them either. She'd been so wrapped up in her success, and then Maddy's spitefulness, making Jack cut her song for the show, her own misery, that she hadn't thought of alerting anyone. They stepped onto the lawn again, saw the landing light go on through the half-moon over the front door, heard the thunder of footsteps on the stairs. The bolts were hastily drawn, the key turned in the lock, and the door flung wide by Eddie, already fully clothed. Behind him, Norman, his brown dressing gown over his striped pyjamas, rubbed his face and returned his glasses to his thick nose. At the top of the stairs loomed Iris, wearing a hairnet that scraped the hair from her face making her appear more sour than usual – although Jessie wondered whether that was possible.

Eddie threw himself into his sister's arms, his shoulders shaking with silent sobs. Jessie hugged him fiercely as he bent into her, taking in Norman and Iris over his shoulder. They would indeed wonder what was going on. It was her fault; she could easily have phoned. She ran her hand over his head and pushed him gently away. He wiped his nose on the back of his hand, sniffing, trying to shake off the tears that had betrayed him.

'Oh, Jessie. I didn't know what to do. I've been so scared for Mum.'

She took hold of his hand and squeezed it. 'No need to be scared any more, Ed. We're here now.'

Norman was beside them. 'Can someone tell me what the hell's going on?' He glanced at the grandfather clock at the back of the hall. 'Good God, it's almost two in the morning. What on earth were you thinking of, Jessica?' He tightened the cord of his dressing gown. 'Harry,' he muttered by way of acknowledgement. Jessie felt Harry shift uneasily behind her, his shoes scratching like sandpaper on the stone doorstep. 'You'd better come in so we can close the damned door. I thought the ruddy war had started.'

Harry did as he was told and closed it quietly behind him. Iris remained at the top of the stairs watching it all playing out before her. It reminded Jessie of paintings she'd seen of Queen Elizabeth in her school books, red hair drawn back from a white face, imperious and unforgiving. Jessie bridled. How Iris would be revelling in all of this. If she hadn't been so self-absorbed she would have thought to call but then, she asked herself, would things have been any better? Iris would not have left a key under the mat, far too common a practice, and she would have enjoyed making Jessie feel guilty about keeping her up all night, waiting. There wasn't a good way, Jessie decided, rapidly calculating her next move. But where in all this commotion was Grace? The thought made Jessie's heart pound harder. She put her hand on the newel post at the bottom of the stairs.

'I'm truly sorry I didn't call ahead, Uncle Norman. Aunt Iris.' The woman looked coldly down at her but remained as a statue bearing down on the scene below. 'Eddie was concerned about Mum and I wanted to come back and make sure she was well.'

Iris folded her arms. 'A proper little Florence Nightingale, aren't we, arriving in the dead of night. You do so like your dramatic entrances, don't you, Jessica?' She switched her gaze to Harry. 'I'm so sorry Jessica has involved you in all of this, young man. A waste of your weekend as well as your petrol.'

Jessie eyes flashed a warning for him not to answer and she saw him chew at his cheek. That he was involved wouldn't help his position at Cole's, and neither her aunt or uncle needed to know that Harry was concerned enough to come and collect her himself.

'What a sorry to-do this is,' Norman grumbled. 'Now that you're here, Harry, we might as well get you a drink.' The older man ushered him into the sitting room and Jessie bounded the stairs, Eddie close behind.

Iris stood to one side as they made for Grace's room.

'That you should drag that young man into your she-nanigans is unforgivable, young lady, but then what do you care about anyone other than your own spoilt self?'

Jessie's skin prickled and she stemmed the abuse that would erupt from her mouth if she lingered any longer. She took a deep breath, turning her back on her aunt. She tapped lightly on her mum's door and peered around it. It was no use thinking that her visit would be a surprise, the commotion accompanying her arrival had put paid to that, but Jessie suppressed a gasp when she saw Grace.

For a moment she couldn't move, hanging onto the Bakelite door handle with such fierce grip that her knuckles whitened. Her mum was tiny in the bed, cheeks sunken, her skin pale. Grace attempted to turn her head towards the door. It was obvious the effort was too much for her and Jessie was galvanised into action. It felt as if her bones had melted away, her legs shaking as she moved swiftly to her mum's side. Images of her dad, lying in his bed, flashed into her head and she didn't want them to take residence. Again. Would it happen again?

'Jessie.' Grace's voice was thin as a needle, her face twisted in a question. Jessie forced herself to smile, her lips trembling; she pressed them together so hard that it hurt. Settling on the edge of the bed, she took hold of her mum's thin hand and gently ran her own fingers over it, holding back tears, squashing down the fury that was rising within.

'How are you, Mum?' She brushed the hair away from Grace's face. The heat from her head was intense and Jessie bit at her lip as Grace tried to smile.

'Fine.' Grace's voice was again a whisper. The smell of stale sweat rose off the bed and mingled with the stench of urine from the pot underneath it. How long since she had been washed, the sheets changed? The heavy curtains were only half drawn, and through the gap she could see stars dotted about the creeping pale darkness of the summer sky. Her mum's navy dress hung on the front of the wardrobe, covering the long mirror, and a soft pink blanket was draped over a chair, the cushions squashed and flat. For a split-second Jessie thought that Iris must have been keeping watch until she realised why Eddie had been fully dressed. She rocked to and fro, suppressing the urge to flee from the room and drag Iris in. She wanted to shake the woman with such violence it frightened her. An elephant was sitting on her chest, her breath so hard to find. She needed to think. Think. Anger was of no use, not yet. She pushed it deep down inside her, kissed her mum's hand, placed it at her side. Eddie had been a shadow behind her, and she got to her feet, pressed his shoulder, saying, 'Stay here, Eddie. I'll be back in two ticks.'

Iris had gone from the landing, her door slightly ajar. The old bitch didn't want to miss anything, did she? Jessie gritted her teeth. Her mum came first, everything else could wait. Slowly, she descended the stairs, holding onto the cold wood of the banister, jaw clenched, staring straight ahead of her, taking in nothing. She picked up the phone.

'Dr Bellamy, please.' She was surprised how calm and even her voice came out for she'd never in her life felt such rage. She ground her nails into the palm of her hand as she spoke to the doctor, apologising for the lateness of her call but stressing the urgency. Grace had waited far too long already. If anything should happen ...

She replaced the phone in the cradle and went into the sitting room. Harry was nursing a glass of whisky, as was Norman. The older man had calmed somewhat, and Harry shifted uncomfortably in his chair. She looked bleakly at him. Were they too late?

'Did I hear you call the doctor?' Norman's tone was challenging as he sat in his nightclothes, swirling the whisky around in his glass before taking a sip. The room was even quieter, and she recalled the silent hours she'd sat with Grace, watching the hands move about the clock, ticking, ticking, like a bomb ready to explode. She glanced at it now anxiously, waiting for Dr Bellamy to arrive.

'Yes, you did, Uncle Norman,' she replied, emboldened. She had no doubt that Dr Bellamy would share her outrage. 'When he arrives, would you be so kind as to show him up to my mum's room.' He stiffened, no doubt annoyed that she was giving him instructions in his own house, but she was beyond caring.

Turning to Harry she softened her voice, taking hold of his free hand. 'Thank you for bringing me, Harry. You must be exhausted. I'm going back to sit with Mum, and I think it's best for you to go home and rest.' He'd been wonderful, but she didn't want to crowd her head with thinking about how the next few hours would play out, wondering whether he would hear her make another exhibition of herself.

He got to his feet, folding her hand in his and it gave her such strength to feel the warmth of him. 'I'd rather stay a while, if that's all right. Until the doctor has visited.' He held her gaze and she nodded silently, kissing his cheek before going back upstairs, using the rail to haul herself up the mountain it appeared to have become. She heard her uncle speak to Harry as she ascended. He was gentler now.

'I'll get you a blanket, old chap. It could be a long wait I'll be damned if she couldn't have waited until the morning, calling the doctor out in the middle of the night.'

Harry cleared his throat. 'To be honest, Norman, Grace looked dreadfully ill when I called earlier this week. Eddie was concerned enough to phone Jessie.'

She closed her eyes, stopping on the stairs. 'Thank you, dear Harry,' she whispered to herself. 'Thank you for defending me.' His quiet support gave her wings.

'Hmph.' Norman growled. 'Iris didn't mention anything and to be quite honest I've been too busy to notice what goes on the house. I leave it all in her good hands.' He muttered something that Jessie couldn't quite catch, and she was aware of Harry's silence. Possibly the best and only response.

Back in her mother's room, Eddie had settled himself in the chair, the blanket pulled over his knees and he smiled wanly as she came into the room. How awful it must have been for him, to be so helpless in this house. She went over and bent to him, rubbed his arm, kissed his cheek. He looked so small again, like a little boy instead of the half man he had been that day on the station. She paused by the window, raised it a little and let the sweet air wash over her. She closed her eyes, her heart thundering wildly. Let her do everything right. Let it not be too late. Please, God, don't let it be too late.

She opened her eyes, rested against the window frame, steadied herself, then pulled herself upright. There were things to do. She twisted on her heel and forced herself into action. The pot was taken from under the bed and she emptied it down the toilet in the bathroom next door, swilling it with water, opening the window to get rid of the stench, washing her own hands, the smell lingering in her nostrils that left her feeling sick and furious. She took up a clean flannel and soaked it in cool water. Back in the room she settled at Grace's side, gently mopping her head. Her eyes were closed, the sheets barely moving as she breathed, and with every laboured breath her mum took, Jessie's fury grew.

The pair of them got to their feet when they heard a car came down the lane, Eddie agitated, running his hand through his hair, which left it sticking on end causing Jessie to smile fondly. He looked awfully young and afraid, but she could be strong for both of them. There were voices as the door opened and she was aware of movement in the front of the house. Iris? Then the men coming up the stairs. Dr Bellamy entered the room, followed by Norman who couldn't keep the shock from his face when he caught sight of Grace. He looked at Jessie, such pity in his eyes, but it was far too late to be of consolation.

'Good evening, Jessie.' The doctor looked at his patient and then to Jessie. He didn't attempt to hide the disdain from his face, his dark eyebrows raised in a silent question. She shook her head.

'I've only just got back, or I would have called you sooner, Doctor.'

He touched her arm. 'No explanations needed, dear girl.' His words were comforting. Many times she'd witnessed his suppressed contempt at being called out for Iris. But she was paying and that was his job. He put his bag on the end of the bed and Grace opened her eyes. He smiled kindly at her and Grace did her best to return it. 'Good evening, Grace. Now what have you been up to?'

Eddie shifted uncomfortably in his chair.

'Why don't you go down and keep Harry company, Eddie,' Jessie suggested, sensing his awkwardness. 'You've done a fine job here. Let me take over for a while and you can have a rest.' He got to his feet, dropping the blanket back on the chair. Norman put out a hand as he passed, draping it over the boy's shoulder.

'Good idea, Jessie,' he said, as Dr Bellamy put his stethoscope about his neck and began unbuttoning Grace's nightdress. He guided Eddie from the room and Jessie felt much of her fury ease, only to soar again as Iris swanned into the room. Her hair was minus the net and she'd made up her face to greet the doctor.

Jessie glared at her, clenching her fists, digging her nails into her flesh. The urge to scream at her to leave was less than the obsession to protect her mum. Overcome with the violence of her feelings, she moved away, as the woman whined while Dr Bellamy examined Grace.

'I am so very sorry that you have been called out like this, Dr Bellamy.' She craned towards him, speaking directly to his ear. The doctor continued to examine his silent patient, dropping the stethoscope from his ears so that it hung around his neck.

'Thank the Lord that someone did call me.' He turned his back on Iris even though his words were meant for her, Jessie was certain. 'Another few hours and the situation would be more serious than it is already.' Iris took a sharp intake of breath and, had the circumstances been less grave, Jessie would have rejoiced at his slight, but the severity of her mum's health dulled the triumph. 'I can't imagine why you didn't call me, Mrs Cole, especially when I attend to you so often.' He put his hand on Jessie's elbow and led her away to the window. In the pale darkness of the summer night the beech trees spread their arms and fingers to the sky.

'I don't need to tell you how ill your mother is, Jessie.' His voice was low, gentle, yet tinged with anger.

She closed her eyes to the pain of his words. How could any woman be so uncaring as to let a fellow human being suffer like this? A mixture of rage and pain wrestled inside her chest, tears balancing on the edge of her lashes. She blinked them back.

'What do I need to do?'

He glanced at Grace, then Iris. 'Not here.'

Jessie leaned into him. 'Let me get Eddie.' She made for the door.

'There's no need,' Iris said quietly. 'I'm here.'

Jessie bit back the venom surging inside her. 'I'll get Eddie,' she said again to Dr Bellamy, brushing past Iris as she left the room.

Dr Bellamy talked over Grace's diagnosis and treatment in the sitting room. He scribbled a prescription and handed it to Jessie. Eddie had gone back upstairs at Jessie's instruction, and Norman sat in an armchair, hands clasped, a grave expression on his face.

Harry had raked the fire and disturbed the embers, put on a little kindling and more coals and the beginning of a good fire now pushed warmth into the room. He'd got to his feet as Jessie came in and offered his seat, which Jessie declined. She felt stronger standing. Tiredness was long gone and she needed to pay attention and ask the right questions. A plan was forming in her head and she needed to make sure that the actions she was contemplating would harm no one, least of all Grace.

'Your mother has walking pneumonia, Jessie. If it had been left much longer, well ...' He turned to Norman. 'That poor woman has suffered unnecessarily, Norman. Tantamount to severe neglect. It doesn't look well, especially from a man of your standing in the community.'

Norman harrumphed. There was nothing he could say in challenge; he wisely kept his mouth firmly shut. It made Jessie think a little better of him and he did appear genuinely remorseful. Jessie was glad. So he should. And as for that witch of a wife upstairs, Jessie would deal with her in time. But her mum's welfare and recovery surpassed every other thought and action.

Norman offered the doctor a drink, which he declined. 'I will get back to my bed and would suggest all of you do the same.' He picked up his hat and bag, and Jessie showed him to the door. She followed him down the path and out to his car, her eyes quickly adjusting in the darkness of the lane. She heard the muffled sound of a hedgehog snuffling along the hedgerow.

'Thank you, Dr Bellamy. I am so sorry for calling you out so late but—'

He put a hand on her shoulder. 'No need to apologise, Jessie. It possibly saved your mother's life.' He sighed. 'Grace is ill, but she has a good chance of recovery, and with your love and care I'm sure that won't take long.' He opened his car door, leaned across and put his bag on the car seat.

That was the point. With *her* love and care, not Iris's. But how, when she had a contract, and keeping it was the only way to get them out of this damned house, away from the sour old harridan? There was a decision to be made and it was an easy one, and one she must take alone, for Grace was not fit to decide, and Eddie too young.

'Would you send the bill to me, at the Empire, in Cleethorpes?'

He shook his head. 'You'll get no bill from me, Jessie. I've lost count of the times I've been called here for no good reason. I am only sad that it had to be your mother who is suffering so much.'

She sucked in her cheeks, and nodded, grateful. Tears would come, but not now. There were questions to ask.

'I can't care for my mum here. My aunt makes things impossible. I'm thinking of taking my mum and Eddie with me.' Dr Bellamy had one hand on the roof of the car, one on the door frame, ready to step into the driver's seat. 'You can see for yourself that I can't leave her here.' Her voice wobbled and she was cross with herself.

He paused and she held her breath, watching his brow furrow as he calculated the risks to his patient. It didn't matter what he said anyway, it was her beloved mum. She'd already lost one parent and she would fight with every bone in her body not to lose another.

'I agree with that, Jessie. But it's a long journey. I cannot stress how fragile your mother is.'

'It is obvious to everyone except my aunt, Dr Bellamy. I have no real option.'

He nodded, stepping into the car. 'I can't argue with you.' The engine started abruptly breaking the stillness of the night. He wound down the window. 'Hopefully, your love and care will give her the strength she needs to fight this.' He smiled at her, 'If anyone can do it, you can, my dear.'

She waited while he turned his car around in the lane and headed back towards his own home at the other end of the village before going back through the gate. It was Harry's help she needed once more, and she knew it was a lot to ask. He must be exhausted. He had taken the long, round trip in one day, and now she would have to ask it of him again.

By the time she entered the house, Iris had settled herself in the sitting room and was standing at the back of the chair occupied by Norman. Harry was looking decidedly dishevelled, his sweater draped over the arm of the chair, his shirt stuffed lazily in his waistband. His sandy hair was in disarray and she wished the two of them had some semblance of privacy, but it was not to be. 'Harry, go home, get some rest.' She pleaded with him again. 'I'll call you later.'

He held her gaze. 'I'll stay here – or in my car.' He looked at Norman who shook his head.

'Here is fine, Harry.' He tipped his head back to Iris. 'We men could do with a hot drink, Iris. Tea okay with you, Harry?' Harry nodded. 'Jessie?'

She hauled herself upright, shaking off the last vestiges of weariness. Her plans for the day were already firming in her mind; the alternatives if Harry was not willing to support her. Looking at him now she had no doubt that he would do as she asked – whether he agreed with her or not – and she loved him for it.

'Not for me.' She was parched but she wasn't going to give Iris any chance to make amends. 'I'm going to get some hot water and bathe my mum.' Another flash of her eyes at Iris. Did she shrink slightly? God, she hoped so. She hoped the old cow would shrivel up and disappear entirely.

In the kitchen she took a pitcher from the shelf and filled it with warm water, appreciating the luxury. But what was luxury in the absence of kindness?

Iris bustled into the room, filled the kettle with water and stuffed the cap on top.

'I shall bring one up for Grace,' she said to Jessie as she made to leave the room. 'I think she would like that.'

Jessie stiffened, gripping the handle of the pitcher so hard she thought it would shatter. She turned to face her aunt who had diminished somewhat these last few hours, perhaps not physically, but she no longer loomed so large to Jessie.

'Don't you think it's too little too late, Aunt Iris?' Her voice was low. 'Do you think this can all be resolved with a cup of tea?'

Iris held her head high. 'I don't know why you are so hurt. Your mother insisted she was all right. I offered to call the doctor, but she wouldn't have it.'

Jessie heard the gas hissing, flames licking about the base of kettle. Her body was pulsing with so much anger that she couldn't move one way or another, her legs trembling with the effort of suppressing her rage, wanting to push the kettle away and shove Iris's smooth white hand over the flame to demonstrate what pain really was. She thought of her mum upstairs, her work-worn hands revealing every sinew, her grey face, the smell of urine and sweat that lingered despite the windows being thrust open. She made a move towards Iris and saw her flinch. Good! Let her be afraid. Let her suffer.

Jessie gritted her teeth. 'I will never, ever forgive you for this as long as I live. You don't have one caring bone in your body.' Spittle flew from her lips, and Iris made a show of wiping it from her face. Oh, the pleasure of small victories. Jessie spun on her heel and left before she lost all control.

Back in her mum's room, she placed the pitcher on the dressing table. Her dad's photo was always pride of place. Jessie kissed her fingers and ran it over the glass. Grace hardly looked in the mirror when she brushed her hair, choosing to stare at the photo of her beloved. If he'd only made provision when he was well, if only he hadn't instilled the love of theatre, she would have been content with her life at Cole's and marriage to Harry. She wanted to be angry with him, but she couldn't. He'd shown her something else and she'd wanted so much to be a success, for all of them. It had all been going so well, the extra song, the extra pay. And now? She steeled herself. It was the only way out, and she had to make it work.

She caught sight of herself in the mirror. What a sight she was. Taking up her mum's brush, she took a ribbon and tied her hair back, hearing her dad's voice so clearly in her head. She was a Delaney and Delaneys never quit.

There was so much to do, and it began with marching off to the airing cupboard on the landing for fresh sheets. No matter that Grace would only be in them for hours; for that brief time she would be comfortable.

All was quiet downstairs save for the muffled sound of Eddie and Harry talking. She strained to hear Norman and Iris but there was nothing, merely the chink of china. She felt another surge of rage; obviously Iris was taking her tea before she brought one up for Grace.

Back in the bedroom, Grace had pulled herself more upright.

'Whatever are you doing here, Jessie? It must be late.' The effort started her coughing again.

'I've come to take care of you.' Jessie was brisk now, fired with the energy that would get them from this house for good. 'It is late, Mum, far too late for me to wake you, but if you let me wash you and change the sheets, you'll sleep better.'

'But the show?'

'Will go on, as it always does. And I will be in it, don't you worry about that.' She grinned as she placed the new sheets at the bottom of the bed, along with fresh towels. 'Don't worry about anything at all. All you need to do is concentrate on getting well. I'll take care of everything else.' She poured warm water into the cream china bowl and put it on the floor beside her mum. How many times had she helped her mum do this for her dad? How had Grace borne it for all those weeks and months, tending to him; the relentlessness of it all. It had been so frightening, willing him to be well, hoping, watching him fade away. She would not leave Grace's recovery to hope and prayer – she knew it didn't work.

Jessie was careful to preserve her mum's modesty as she removed her cotton nightdress, soaping the flannel and holding up a towel as Grace, with huge effort, freshened herself up, having no breath left to speak. Jessie took the fresh nightclothes from the end of the bed and pulled the chair as close as she could to the side of it. Gently moving her mum's arms, she helped her into the clean clothing and then onto the chair. Covering her with a blanket, she proceeded to strip the bed and make it anew while Grace looked on.

'I wouldn't want you to give it up, Jessie. Not when you're doing so well. A duet. A song.' Jessie scooped up the bedding. Grace didn't know of her disappointment, and what difference would it make? Best to keep her positive and hopeful. At least she was still getting paid. Jack had been honourable, stressing that it was hardly her fault – which it wasn't. Billy had been furious on her behalf but there was nothing to be done. She made a clean bed in minutes and gently helped Grace back into it. The expression of peace on Grace's face was sweet reward. She settled her mum on the plumped pillows and scooped up the soiled sheets.

'I'll get rid of these and bring back some tea.' Dr Bellamy had given her advice on Grace's care and she would follow it to the letter, keeping her patient upright, fluids little and often. And rest, plenty of rest. 'Do you feel hungry?'

'No. Perhaps – later.'

Jessie nodded and, satisfied that Grace was comfortable at last, hurried down the stairs to dispose of the sheets, stopping at the door to the sitting room. She stuck her head around it and the conversation came to an abrupt halt. 'I'll get Mum's tea then, shall I, Iris?' She was gratified to see the horror on Iris's face as the woman struggled to her feet. 'Don't bother,' Jessie snapped. 'Too late.' It was all too late, all of it. Iris would never be able to redeem herself in Jessie's eyes, not as long as she lived. She was relieved when Iris didn't follow her into the kitchen and tea was quickly made then taken upstairs.

She kissed her mum's forehead and was pleased to feel it cooler than it had been. Her skin felt fresh and sweet from the Camay soap. It was the little things that made a difference and Iris was lacking in all of them. 'Get some rest, Mum,' she said, patting the pillows about her head.

Grace took her hand. 'You too, sweetheart.'

She kissed her again, feeling strength flowing through her body as she descended the stairs. She needed to talk to Harry.

By mid-afternoon the sun was bright, the skies blue, the temperature in the high seventies but Jessie was chilled from lack of sleep. She pulled her cardigan tight, wrapping her arms around her. Harry was bent over the luggage rack securing their bags.

'Is that it?' he called over his shoulder.

'It's all you have room for. We'll have to come back for the rest some other time.'

He faced her, still grumpy. He hadn't taken it well, her decision for them all to go to Cleethorpes, but admitted he'd half expected it. Eddie handed him his small case and Harry placed it on top of Grace's, securing them with the leather straps.

'I don't need much, Harry. Blokes don't, do they?'

Jessie nudged him with her elbow. 'Hey, cheeky.' She was glad he was in good spirits – it made her feel that the decision she was making was the right one. After all, he was giving up his education, and the opportunity that Norman offered him would have given him a stable career for the rest of his life. Stability. It was crucial, wasn't it, and yet here she was, throwing everything to the four winds and uprooting them all. But it was a chance to build a home for themselves. She just wished she'd had a little more time to plan. Her hand had been forced and as such the destiny of the Delaneys rested entirely on her shoulders.

'Go and get me the pillow and blanket I left in the hall will you, Ed.' She raised her eyebrows and hoped he would understand her need to be alone with Harry. He dawdled up the path.

Harry came and stood beside her, the pair of them leaning on the roof of the Austin. Birds chattered amongst the branches of the trees around them and she squinted into the sun.

'How will you manage, Jessie?'

She shrugged. 'I will. I have to.' It was all she could think about as she'd sat by Grace's bedside, watching her sleep. 'Getting Mum well is all that matters. She can have my bed; Eddie and I can sleep on the floor. I can borrow blankets and pillows.' She reached across and rubbed at his hands that were resting on the car roof. 'Don't worry. We'll be fine. I have good, kind friends who will help me work things out. I'll sleep at the theatre if I have to.'

He took hold of her hand and turned her towards him. 'I don't want you to go.' His words were unnecessary, his pain and disappointment obvious, but she mustn't let wanting to be with him stop her from looking after her family. She brought his hand to her lips and kissed it.

'I know you don't, Harry but this is how it has to be. We can't stay here, and we have nowhere else to go.' The thought chilled her, and she wanted to break away from it. She drew away from him. Doing something, anything, took her mind away from the enormity of it all. 'I'm going to fill the flask and gather a little something for us to eat on the journey, then we'll be on our way. Is that okay with you, Harry?' She waited for his consent, which he could only give with a nod and a shrug of his shoulders. It pained her to hurt him, but she mustn't weaken. She went back to the house and he followed. Eddie passed them, clutching the pillow and blanket. Jessie called out. 'Back seat, Ed.'

Norman was waiting in the hall, fiddling with the umbrellas in the oak stand. Sunlight spilled onto the black and white tiles from the open door and Jessie was sure that The Beeches would be a beautiful house with more light in it, if Iris had not been so intent on shutting it out. He cleared his throat. 'All a bit of a sorry mess, eh, Harry.'

Harry shoved his hands in his pockets, non-committal.

Jessie knew he wouldn't be drawn. This was all her fault, and she could only guess how awkward things would be at Cole's tomorrow morning. How she wished she hadn't had to drag him into this debacle, but he wouldn't leave her. No matter how many times she'd urged him to go throughout the night, he had remained.

Norman turned his attention to Jessie. 'I'm sorry that it has come to this, my dear. Your aunt didn't mean to be uncaring to Grace. She simply took her at her word.'

She could see that he was tired, his face drawn in heavy lines, his jowls sagging, but there was something else there too. It wasn't fatigue brought on by the night, it was more than that – was he tired of life ... of Iris? She'd taken so much for granted, and now an inner awareness of the workings of other people's relationships was drawn into sharp relief. She pitied him.

'Please, Uncle Norman. Don't make excuses.' Her manner was gentle. There wasn't really anything he could've done. He was hardly ever home and left the running of the household to Iris – yet hadn't he had one tiny inkling that her mum was so ill? However, her energy was flagging, and she didn't want to waste any of what she had on useless arguments.

Norman gave a small nod. 'Your aunt and I will bring the rest of your belongings if you decide to stay ... as you said you might.' He was floundering, not wanting to upset her. 'We could come and see the show.'

Jessie shrugged. 'If you want to, Uncle Norman.' She didn't much care. In the beginning she had wanted them to come, to impress them, but she had little respect for either of them now.

He tried again. 'There will always be a home for you here.' Was it for Harry's benefit or did he mean it? His words followed her as she went into the kitchen to collect the sandwiches and fruit she'd already assembled in a string bag. Norman had said to take whatever she needed. George's flask was replenished with tea.

The dirty linen lay in a heap by the back door. Nelly would deal with it tomorrow – she didn't expect Iris would even find the grace to put them outside and she wasn't going to do it. Let the smell fill the house and go up their noses as a reminder. She wanted to weep but anger flared, and she swept out of the room. Iris was in the hall, having kept herself hidden in the sitting room. Had Norman made her come out? Jessie was brazen now; there was no way she was going to be contrite. It didn't matter if they thought she was wrong, ungrateful … it didn't matter at all. She squared up to Iris and to her satisfaction the woman seemed to cower. 'I did offer to call the doctor, Jessica. It was at your mother's request that I didn't.'

Norman let out a long sigh and because of it, Jessie held her tongue.

'I'm ready,' she said to Harry, handing the bag and thermos to Eddie. 'Would you help me get Mum to the car?' He followed her up the stairs.

'Let me help,' Norman said, spurred to action at last.

Grace was dressed, sitting in the chair, a blanket pulled across her legs. Jessie had helped her tidy her hair and that small effort had made her look so much better. Her pallor had improved slightly but she was still incredibly weak. When Jessie had told Grace of her intentions she had not disagreed. Perhaps she had little strength to do so. Jessie was of the opinion that her mum was too frightened to stay to argue – and that in itself infuriated her. There was not one utterance of recklessness or stupidity from any quarter, but Jessie had been well prepared to combat it if there had.

She watched as the two men tenderly helped Grace to her feet and down the stairs, causing her as little distress and discomfort as they could. That Norman could be so gentle and kind saddened her. Why had he left it so late? He could have cut short her mum's suffering if he'd only taken the smallest of actions. Iris was lingering in the hallway. Had Norman made her? She knew they'd had words earlier on, she'd heard his admonishment, her whiny excuses and muffled mutterings. Jessie unhooked her coat from the stand in the hall.

'If anything happens to Mum, I will hold you responsible.'

Iris stiffened but didn't reply.

Jessie stood in the open door and paused for a moment. 'I hope you and Uncle Norman do come to the show, Aunt Iris. You would be welcome in Cleethorpes – you might learn a little about kindness there.'

Iris gasped. 'We have given you a home. Is that not kind?'

Jessie paused. No need to spoil things this late in the day. Why make a scene? It would be what Iris expected of her, but she was wiser now.

'Kind? You wouldn't know it if it bit you on the backside.'

Iris's sharp intake of breath gave her immense satisfaction as she stepped out onto the path. Grace was already settled in the car, and Harry leaned over the roof at the driver's side. Eddie stood next to Uncle Norman, waiting for Jessie to take her seat next to Grace. He held out his hand to Jessie and she took it. He looked so embarrassed, and she felt for him again.

'Anything you need, Jessie, please ask.' Such a shame she thought, now that they were leaving. She nodded, determined never to take him up on his offer. He put out his arms and tried to hug her, but it was awkward, and she pitied him the lack of warmth in his life as she stepped back.

'Thank you, Uncle Norman.' She climbed into the back seat of the car and Eddie shook hands with his uncle and got in as well. Norman said something over the car that drifted away on the breeze and Harry got in and started the engine. Grace coughed into her handkerchief and Jessie patted her knee. 'Not long now, Mum. A fresh start for us all.' Grace could only mumble a quiet 'yes', and closed her eyes as Harry pulled out into the road.

The A17 was busy, the journey slow and Jessie hadn't banked on just how cramped it would be in the back of the Austin. Her neck and shoulders ached, and she kept getting pins and needles in her toes. She wriggled as much as she could to adjust herself, but Grace scarcely moved at all. Jessie poured water from a bottle and held a cup she had taken from the kitchen for Grace to sip from. She would send it back with Harry, wanting no reminders of The Beeches. As they drove through the countryside, and open fields disappeared behind thick verdant hedgerows, she considered the task that lay ahead of her. Lying back as much as was allowable in the tiny space, she closed her eyes.

'Tired, darling?' Grace reached across and took her hand in hers. Her skin was cooler now and Jessie smiled but kept her eyes shut. It had all been so upsetting and sitting in the car, with nothing to do but think, weariness came upon her like a cloak.

'A little. Relieved more than anything.' She opened her eyes and caught Harry watching her in the rear-view mirror.

'You did what I didn't have the strength to do.'

Was it down to strength? Or was it anger that drove her – and when it subsided, what then?

'We're together,' Jessie said. 'That's all that matters.'

Out of the window starlings swooped in murmurations over fields that were golden with wheat. Summer would soon be on the turn, and as the season drew to a close, so would her work in the show. She could no longer drift along, she would have to make a call to Bernie tomorrow and get something for when this show ended, something that paid better than being a Variety Girl. She sighed. There would always be offices to work in if not.

Eddie twisted in his seat. 'I'm glad we've left. I didn't want to be a solicitor anyway. No offence, Harry.'

'None taken, old boy.'

Jessie could see him grinning in the mirror. Their humours were slowly being restored the further away they travelled from Iris. They were leaving the nightmare behind them.

Chapter 23

It was early evening when they reached Cleethorpes. The road out of town was thick with coaches heading inland but there were still plenty of people milling around in their Sunday best, making the most of the splendid sunshine that had been with them all week. Not that Harry had seen much of it other than through his windscreen. His knees ached from sitting in the same position for too many hours. And to think he used to love driving. He'd had his fill of it this weekend, not that he minded, but it still bloody ached and his backside felt like a razor blade.

Eddie leaned out of the window and tilted his face to the sun as they drove up Isaac's Hill. 'Oh, I do like to be beside the seaside.' They all laughed, and he sat back in the car, grinning wildly. 'I do, Mum. It's going to be fun.' Grace's weak laughter had set off another coughing fit and through the mirror Harry caught the concern on Jessie's face. Harry was glad for the boy's optimism. He only hoped it was well founded.

A swell of people hovered by the kerbside waiting to cross and Harry let the car idle, gesturing them over the road. A couple strolled in front of them, arm in arm, giving him a wave of thanks as they went in front of the car. They were so cheerful, and he wanted some of

337

that. They all did. It had been in short supply these last few days. He saw Jessie again in his rear-view mirror. She had perked up in direct proportion to the way he'd flagged as they drew closer to their destination, but she looked pale and exhausted. He twisted his head from side to side to release the tension from his neck. His eyes were sore from concentrating hard and he still had the return journey to do; alone. Only hours ago he'd harboured hopes that having some of their belongings at The Beeches would bring the family back, but he knew in the pit of his stomach that this was the beginning of goodbye.

As Harry turned the car into Barkhouse Lane, he saw Frances walking towards number forty-one. She waved, waiting by the front wall as Harry brought the car to a stop. Jessie got out and Frances threw her arms about her, hugging her tightly. Thank God she had friends.

Frances held Jessie by the shoulders. 'Heavens, you look like death, my love. What on earth have you been doing to yourself?'

Jessie shook her head. 'It would take too long.' She took a breath. 'I've brought her with me. I had to.'

'Your ma? Jesus, Mary and Joseph. Whatever has happened?' She peered in the car and when she turned back to Jessie her face had paled. 'What hellish weekend have you had? I thought it was just a visit.'

Jessie was too tired to explain. It had indeed been hell but going over it would take energy, and she needed what little she possessed to get Grace inside. Her head throbbed and she rubbed at it, hoping to release some tension. She really hoped she'd made the right decision and hadn't made her mum worse with all the upheaval. And poor Harry – he must be exhausted from all the driving. Frances inclined her head, searching Jessie's face for an explanation. 'I've brought them both.'

Further up the street a tumble of kids were playing with a soap cart, running down the hill, shouting and squealing. Eddie got out of the car, looking up at the windows of the house. Harry waved a greeting and went round to help Grace.

'Let me.' Frances was swiftly at Harry's side and the two of them gently eased Grace from the back seat. She winced with pain and whimpered a little, but only a little. Jessie saw her friend's face and knew an explanation was no longer needed.

Jessie called across to her brother, 'Get Geraldine, Eddie.' Her instruction was unnecessary. Geraldine must have seen them from the upstairs window and was already at the door.

'Come inside, my dear. We must make you comfortable.' She took over from Frances. 'Go upstairs, Frances. My room is open. Move the things from my chair and the small table to the side so we can get Grace in without falling over ourselves. 'Young man, Eddie, isn't it?' He nodded. 'Kettle on the stove, please. You'll find a barrel of biscuits on the top shelf of the pantry.' Eddie disappeared into the house and Jessie could have wept, so glad to be with people who cared. Her tiredness dropped away.

'Let me, Harry,' she said, moving to take his place by her mum's side. Harry released Grace into Jessie's hands and went to get the bags. Geraldine looked at Jessie over the top of her mum's head and shook her head in pity. 'Don't worry, my dear,' she said to Grace. 'We'll soon get you comfortable.'

Grace slowly lifted her head. 'I'm so sorry to have put you all to such trouble.'

'Now, we'll have none of that nonsense, Grace.' Geraldine's tone was brisk but kind. 'I can call you Grace?' Grace offered a feeble smile. 'Good, then let's get you upstairs and into a nice clean bed.'

The three women took their time ascending the stairs and along the narrow landing to Geraldine's room. Frances had drawn the curtains and switched on the bedside lamp. 'I thought it might have been too bright.'

Geraldine nodded her approval and Frances patted the cushion on the chair, more from a need to feel useful than anything else. They settled Grace into the high-back chair and Jessie briefly closed her eyes with relief. Her mum looked exhausted, but her eyes told Jessie everything she needed to know. This battle was over. It was time to heal, and yet even as she thought it complications flooded into her head. How would they manage without taking advantage of her friends' kindness? Where would she find the money? They couldn't crowd into one small room for the duration. She ran her hand through her hair and wild strands fell about her face again. Her back ached with sitting twisted in the small space she'd squashed herself into on the back seat. She put her hands to her hips and leaned backwards to ease the muscle. How would she ever be able to dance tomorrow night?

'I'm going to put fresh sheets on my bed, Mum. I won't be long.'

Geraldine waved them away, and Jessie left with Frances following close behind.

Eddie was on his way upstairs with small tray bearing a cup of tea and half a dozen Bourbon biscuits. He'd foregone the formality of a saucer, which was provident, as Jessie wasn't sure Grace possessed the strength to hold one and drink so delicately.

Jessie leaned over the staircase. 'Mum's in the bedroom at the front of the house, Eddie.' He nodded, keeping his eyes on the tray.

It was good to be back in her own room, small and bare as it was. There was enough space for one of them to lie on the floor at least. It was all temporary, she told herself. It could be bettered after a night's sleep, but for now she needed to get Grace comfortable. Frances came in carrying a small vase of flowers from her own room, placing them on the dressing table.

Her friend helped her pull the sheets from the bed. 'Your poor ma. I had no idea.' Blankets were piled on the chair and the sheets made another pile by the door. Jessie flicked out a new sheet and Frances eased herself down the opposite side of the bed.

'Neither did I.' She tucked the corners of the sheets under the mattress and slapped her hands across, smoothing out the creases lest they dig into Grace.

341

She'd always been of slight build but there was barely any flesh left on her. Anger flashed again, giving her another burst of energy. If Aunt Iris were here, she would slap her. Holding back her rage had done nothing to help but at least it had saved Grace more distress. Satisfied that all was as it should be, they went back into Geraldine's room.

Grace was sipping tea, so small in the armchair. Geraldine was talking quietly to her, her hand hovering close to take the cup in case Grace's strength should fail her.

Downstairs had been a flurry of activity as Harry and Eddie went in search of a small armchair from the room at the front of the house to put in Jessie's room. They were to bring it upstairs, lifting it as high as they could to avoid marking the banister.

All things taken care of, Jessie led Grace to her room. It looked much cosier with the addition of the chair and the simple flowers that Frances had contributed. Grace's nightdress and gown were draped over the end of the bed, her slippers at the side ready for her to step into. Frances pushed up the sash to let the air circulate, while Jessie helped Grace into her nightclothes, having already instructed Harry and Eddie as to where to leave bags and directing them towards extra blankets, pillows and towels. Frances went downstairs with the dirty linen.

Geraldine bustled back into the room as Jessie pulled the white sheets and the pale green blanket over Grace and made her comfortable. 'We can make things easier tomorrow but as long as we're all in tonight that's good enough.' The breeze disturbed the net from time to time and it billowed into the room like a sail. Jessie felt that she could exhale at last.

Eddie had sat at the bottom of the stairs while the women fussed around, and Jessie heard Frances scoot him into the kitchen in search of something to eat. Grace was propped up on pillows and Jessie was relieved to see her mum more perky than she had been in twenty-four hours. Was that all it was? It had felt like days.

'What an inconvenience I've put you to,' Grace murmured.

Geraldine settled herself in the easy chair that Harry and Eddie had brought into the room.

'No trouble at all. It's nice to have someone my own age at last. These fluffy-headed girls are not much company.'

'Hey.' Jessie was sat on the end of her mum's bed. 'Fluffy-headed, me?'

Harry had come back upstairs and was leaning against the door frame, arms folded across his chest.

Her mum spoke, her voice a whisper. 'You must spend time with Harry before he leaves.' She beckoned Harry to her, reaching for his hand as he came close, clasping her own over his. 'Thank you for all you've done, Harry. For all of us. I should think you're just about done in.'

He shook his head. 'Don't even mention it, Grace.'

Jessie was torn. How could she leave Grace? They'd only just arrived and now she was supposed to go out and enjoy herself, and leave everyone else to take on the responsibility? She couldn't do it. It would be reckless.

Noticing her hesitation, Geraldine stepped in. 'I'll keep her quite safe, Jessie dear. Do as your mother says.' Leaning to Grace she murmured, 'I shouldn't think that happens very often.'

Grace grinned, and, knowing her mum was in safe hands, Jessie went to freshen herself up.

Harry perched on the low wall outside the house smoking a Navy cigarette. It was all they'd had at the King's Head when they'd stopped for a break. He could have murdered a pint, but it would have made him drowsy, and his priority had been to deliver them all safely. He must stink like a sty; there had been no time for the niceties of life. He blew out a plume of smoke as Jessie came outside. She'd washed her face and tied her hair back with a blue ribbon that matched her dress. She looked dog-tired, but he was so damn proud of her. He threw the cigarette on the floor and ground it out.

'Where to, Cinderella?'

She smiled and her eyes twinkled, and he didn't care how ruddy tired he was any more. He had her all to himself.

'I'm suddenly starving, are you?'

He stood away from the wall, tugging at the lapels of his jacket to smarten himself for her. 'Feel like my throat's been cut.' The little picnic Jessie had hurriedly assembled had been welcome but not enough to sustain them. Hunger tore at his belly. 'What do you fancy?

Waiters? White tablecloths?' He'd go to as much as his pocket would allow. His girl deserved The Ritz, but he wouldn't be able to stretch to that.

She held out her hand for his. 'I could murder a bag of chips.' He grinned, relieved. She was still the same Jessie.

He took her arm and hooked it inside his and they followed their noses to the nearest chip shop. The queue wasn't too long; a straggle of kids, shoving and nudging each other, a middle-aged chap standing in line while his wife sat on the wide window ledge that served as a bench. Blue and white tiles along the back wall were interspersed with pictures of local trawlers that landed fish in Grimsby. A panel above them declared: *Fish doesn't get any fresher than Fred's Fish & Chips.*

Harry and Jessie leaned on the metal counter, watching the women thrust the fish into trays of batter then into hot fat, the batter bubbling and bloating. They ordered two large bags of chips and shared a huge piece of fish between them, sprinkling them liberally with salt and vinegar, before the woman wrapped them in newspaper. 'There you go, ducks.'

Harry paid and they dashed over the road and into the gardens, the parcels hot beneath their hands. They admired the floral displays that depicted anchors, boats and shells, set squarely in blocks of green, punctuating the footpaths that led around the gardens, and managed to find an empty bench opposite the Empire.

He read bits of the newspaper to her as they ate, watching people as they passed, carefree and happy.

'Cor, look at this headline: "Empire show a hit. The Variety Girls are a cloud of glamour. Gorgeous Jessie Delaney steals the show."'

She laughed, trying to read his paper and he leaned away so she couldn't see. She put a chip into her mouth, wafted her hand in front of it to cool it.

'Where does it say that? Don't tease.' She was still smiling though, and he put his chip paper back on his lap. 'It might not say it now, Jessie, but one day it will.'

She kicked out her legs, and crossed her ankles.

'Wouldn't it be wonderful, Harry: to be top of the bill ... a star ...'

She was warming to the idea, he could tell, and, even though she was exhausted, she knew the dreams would give her something to hold on to. For Grace might well be with her but she was still frail and weak, and ... he gave those thoughts the elbow.

'Why stop there?' he asked. 'You could be starring in one of those hit shows in the West End. I'll get a partnership in a top London office and we'll live the high life, Jessie, you and me. What do you say?'

She nodded, her mouth full of chips. A huge Dalmatian sauntered past, his nose in the air, his owner too, and the pair of them giggled when they were at a safe distance. The main road was still busy with coaches and cars heading out of town, ready for work on Monday.

Work.

He hadn't given it a thought until now, but he wondered what the atmosphere would be like when he went into the office. And Norman ... how would that play out? He felt sorry for the old chap. He'd always been fair to him and generous. Business-like, of course, but that was as it should be. How could he have ignored Grace, though? And Iris. What a cold fish. He shook his head in disbelief. He broke off a piece of fish that was hot in his hands, blew on it a little. 'Open wide,' he instructed. He popped it into her mouth, then leaned to her, kissing her lips, tasting the salt and the vinegar. 'So, you can do as you're told then.'

She dug him in the ribs. 'You're wasted as a solicitor, Harry. You should be a comedian.'

His mood changed. 'Like Billy?' He chewed, staring down at the floor. When he was gone, would she turn to Billy to make her laugh and forget about him? He looked away from her, shaking his head once again.

'What's wrong, Harry? What did I say?'

He shrugged. 'Oh, I don't know. I guess I don't like it that Billy gets to put his arms around you every night and I don't.'

She laughed and it irritated him. 'You know it's just acting. There's nothing wrong with helping the audience dream a little.'

Harry wasn't sure that Billy looked at it that way. 'Life isn't a dream though, Jessie. You have to keep your feet on the ground.'

'And you don't think I do?'

He sighed; she was getting irritated too. What a fool he was. He could have ripped out his tongue, but he was tired – and he would be leaving without her. He hadn't wanted them to fight.

They finished their chips in silence, sucking the grease from their fingers. He screwed the paper into a ball, gave her his handkerchief to clean her hands, took her chip paper and walked over to the bin to dispose of them. Hoardings across the front of the Empire advertised the Variety Revue, the words *Madeleine Moore* and *Billy Lane* writ large. He had to hope that she would still want him when the summer was over. He turned back and saw her, sitting on the bench, so sad and weary, and he wanted to scoop her up into his arms and never let her go. He'd loved her from the moment he'd set eyes on her. That would never change. Not for him, at least. He walked back, holding out his hand.

'Fancy a walk on the beach?' God, please let her say yes.

'It's getting late.' She looked about her, not at him.

The sun was dropping down into the horizon, the clouds backlit with red gold. 'So it is.' He grinned. 'Your mum's quite safe with Geraldine. She'll thrive here – just as you have done.' He caught her hand and pulled her up from the bench. 'Indulge me, one last time before I go?' The words stuck in his throat. When would he be able to see her again, hold her hand, kiss her? He squeezed her hand and pulled her, and she let him, and he felt reassured as they walked down towards the sea.

They trod the wooden steps down onto the beach, which was almost deserted now. The tide was in, lapping at the shore, sucking the shingle back and forth, and the gentle hush as the waves broke was soothing; he let his shoulders drop. He was worn out but he wanted to spend every last moment with her. He had to leave her happy. There were few people on the beach now, and they strolled along in silence for a while, Jessie intermittently bending down to collect shells that caught her eye. He found flat oyster shells, and they skimmed them along the water for a time until he led her away, towards the softness of the beach where they could sit down awhile.

Jessie jiggled the tiny shells in her hand like pennies. 'I'll never be able to thank you enough for bringing us all here, Harry. You must be exhausted with the driving.'

He took her hand, brought it to his lips, kissed it, enfolded it in his and kept it tight. 'It doesn't matter. I will do anything for you, Jessie ... anything.'

She smiled and he melted. 'I'll send you the money for the petrol as soon as I have it.'

He let her hand drop as if it had burnt him, for her words certainly had. 'I don't want paying, Jess; I did it because I love you.'

'I know you do,' she said quickly. 'I'm also well aware how much this is costing you.'

'You have no idea.' He looked up at the sky. Clouds swept by so fast that it was making him dizzy. 'I wish I'd called the doctor when I visited.' If he had he might have prevented Grace from getting so ill, and then this journey would have been needless; Grace would still be at The Beeches and Jessie would be coming back at the end of the season.

'Why didn't you?'

He paused. 'And lose my job?' He ran his hand over the sand, grabbed at it, letting the grains fall through his fingers.

'I could have lost my mum.' Her voice was flat. He knew that she wasn't accusing him, just stating a fact, as he had done.

'But you didn't.'

'No.' She rubbed at his arm. 'Thanks to you, arriving like a knight in shining armour and whisking me back to save my mum from Iris, the dragon.'

He put his arm about her shoulder, and she leaned into him, resting her head on his chest. He kissed her hair and whispered into it. 'I did everything I possibly could. I've already lost you; losing my job would leave me with nothing.'

'You haven't lost me.' She sat up, gazing into his eyes.

'Haven't I?'

She kissed him then and he released his arm, cupping her sweet face in his hands. He never wanted to stop kissing her as long as he lived. She pulled away.

'Of course you haven't.'

He wanted to believe her, but he felt her slipping away from him. The tide was on the turn now, the water moving back. He put his arm around her once more and she rested her head on his shoulder, her hand on his beating heart and they sat for a long time, watching the tide recede. She shivered.

'Cold?'

'A little.'

He took off his jacket and put it about her shoulders, got to his feet and pulled her to hers. 'Time to go home.' His heart was heavy, but he smiled because that was the last thing he wanted her to remember.

Chapter 24

Jessie had been desolate when Harry left, empty of tears, empty of good thoughts that drowned in the fears flooding into her head now she was alone. A car spluttered past the end of the road and she prayed that Harry would have an easy journey. Dear God, let him be safe. She'd made him promise to take breaks, to sleep in the car if necessary, and he'd given his word that he would. But would he? She shivered despite the evening's warmth and went back into the house.

Frances was coming down the stairs and Jessie followed her into the kitchen. Geraldine was rinsing a glass, which she dried and placed on the shelf above the sideboard. 'I made up the bed in the small room for Eddie,' Geraldine said, pushing Jessie down onto a chair and pouring her a cup of stewed tea. Jessie took a sip and pulled a face; it was bitter. She added another spoonful of sugar, not wanting to put anyone to the trouble of making a fresh pot. 'It's hardly more than a cupboard but he was happy enough.' She took a seat beside Jessie.

'I don't think the boy has it in him to be sad, so I do.' Frances yawned. 'I've checked on your ma; she is fast off, so no need for you to fret.'

Jessie was grateful. She hardly had the energy to make more than one trip up the stairs tonight. How would she ever be able to repay their kindness? They had made it easy for her, with not a murmur of the inconvenience it had caused them. She drank more tea, draining the cup, pushing it away. It was swiftly cleared by Frances who washed, dried and stored in seconds.

Geraldine's voice was soft, reassuring and Jessie was near to tears at their kindness. 'Now that she's here she will let go and her body will repair. I've seen it so many times. Love and care will give her sustenance. It must have been very frightening for you, my love.'

Jessie nodded, biting at her lip.

Geraldine placed a hand on her lap and said, her voice brisk, 'Get to bed, my girl. We can't have you ill too.' She took her hand, helping Jessie to her feet.

Jessie hugged her with what strength she had left, hoping the fierceness of her embrace would express her gratitude because words were beyond her now. She kissed her cheek and Geraldine seemed mildly embarrassed.

Frances turned off the lamp and the three of them went upstairs. Geraldine vetoed Jessie sitting in her mum's room, reassuring Jessie that she was in a deep restorative sleep and they should all do likewise. 'You can get in with Frances, no argument. We'll leave all the doors open, and Frances or I will see to your mother, should she need anything. You need to catch up on the sleep you've missed; you have work tomorrow.'

Jessie's nightdress and gown were already on the chair in Frances's room and Jessie had to smile at the way they had sorted everything out while she was out with Harry. The lump that it brought to her throat was so hard that she put her hand to her neck to hold it there. The two girls got into their nightclothes, and Frances made Jessie get into the side by the wall. 'In case I have to go to your ma.'

There was ample room in the double bed. They turned on their sides to face each other and Jessie recounted events to Frances whose gasps of horror and pity punctuated the telling until she fell asleep. Jessie turned on her back and stared at the ceiling rose, her eyes following the ornate pattern. Her body was exhausted, but her mind was active. It had been unbearable when Harry left. It would be a whole week, maybe more before she saw him again. Tears threatened but she swallowed them down. Norman had been kind, hadn't he, in the end, but ... She could have lost Grace, and the pain would have been worse than losing her dad, because then there would have been just the two of them: her and Eddie. Oh, poor Eddie. He wouldn't be a solicitor now, would he? And it was her fault. She closed her eyes. Harry was right, she would never go back to The Beeches again, so how would their relationship fare when the Variety Revue came to an end? Bernie would get her more work. Good old Bernie; he wouldn't let her down ... not like Iris, not like Norman. But would that work be here? She doubted it. How could she make more money to support them all if she remained so low down on the bill? Perhaps Grace could take in sewing like she used to ... yes, that was it. And Eddie ... and Harry ... and ...

Her breathing steadied and at last she sank into sleep.

Jessie woke to the sound of dustbins clattering in the alleyway and sat up with a start, struggling to get her bearings until she realised she was in Frances's room. She scrabbled around for her wristwatch and was shocked to discover that it was a quarter past eleven. Lord, she should have been up hours ago, and Grace? She'd neglected her care already. She threw off the bed-clothes and, pulling on her dressing gown, dashed into Grace's room to find her sitting up in the armchair and Frances on the spoon back. A bowl and pitcher were on the dressing table, a flannel and soap by the side. Grace's hair was brushed and held away from her face with pins. She was still in her nightclothes, but she looked so much better for a little bit of tenderness and care. Jessie was ashamed. It shouldn't have been down to Frances.

'I'm so sorry, Mum. I can't think why I slept so long.'

Frances grinned. 'Ah, she's fine. Me and your lovely ma have been having a chat.' She got to her feet, pressing Grace's arm with the lightest of touches. 'I'll get rid of this,' she said, taking up the bowl and water. 'Then I'm going to make us all a nice pot of tea.'

As Frances passed her, Jessie whispered, 'Thank you.'

Frances shook her head. 'No need.'

Jessie kissed her mum's cheek, which had taken on a healthier colour, and sat down on the bed, leaning over the rail at the bottom. The sun was streaming into the room and sharing its warmth.

'I'm so sorry I left you, Mum.'

'It's me who should be apologising, Jessie. Putting everyone to all this trouble.' She paused, gathering her breath. 'If I hadn't been so stubborn.' She paused again. 'I should have accepted Iris's help when it was offered.' Her face wrinkled in a half smile. 'It comes so rarely. It took me by surprise.'

Jessie tried to smile for her mum's sake but the thought of her aunt worthy of any praise made her feel nauseous. Instead she said, 'You're here now. That's all that matters.'

Grace patted her hand.

'You have good friends, Jessie.' Jessie was learning to wait between pauses, but, as her mum exerted herself to hold a conversation, Jessie felt she mustn't stay too long. She had an inkling that Frances had done all the talking this morning. The girl never stopped. 'And Harry. How wonderful he is.'

Jessie couldn't reply, so simply nodded. Any thought of him was painful.

Grace noticed. 'Love will find a way, darling. It always does.'

She wanted to cry now that her mum was here, be a child again and put her head on her lap so that Grace could stroke her hair as she used to. It all seemed so very far away. What on earth was she thinking of leaving things to Frances?

As if waiting for her cue, Frances came in with a tray of tea. Jessie shuffled up the bed and Frances poured, setting a cup down on the small table at Grace's side and passing one to Jessie. She took one for herself and leaned against the wall, cup and saucer in one hand, waving a biscuit around like a baton.

'I was telling your ma about your new routine in the show. She'll be able to see it for herself now.' Frances took a bite of her biscuit, munched away and began again. 'It's a pity they had to cut your solo, Jessie, but ...' Frances stopped, realising from Jessie's expression that she hadn't yet told her mum. 'Oh, me and my big mouth.'

Grace smiled. 'Don't apologise. I know this life. It's hard.'

Frances looked sheepishly at Jessie, shrugging her shoulders. What was there to say? Grace would have known sooner or later.

'What happened?'

Jessie explained Bert and Hilda's accident, and how Billy had put her forward for both the duet and the solo. Grace was thoughtful. 'And how is Bert?'

'Recovering.' Jessie was torn. If the Duo D'or came back she would lose her extra spot in the show, and the extra money. Well, this was not the time to be thinking about it, not yet.

'And Madeleine?' Grace sipped at her tea, placing the cup back on the saucer with great care and attention.

Jessie shrugged. She'd avoided her. It had been easy enough to do. Madeleine mostly remained in her dressing room while the show was on. It was the briefest of walks from the star dressing room to the stage and Jessie had made sure she was going in the other direction if Madeleine headed her way.

'Don't be bitter, Jessie. She will have her reasons.'

'Like jealousy,' Frances said. 'Jessie was so good, Grace. She has such a beautiful voice, the audience loved her, we all loved her – and do love her.'

Jessie grinned. 'My number one fan.'

'I think that accolade goes to Harry, don't you?' Grace said gently.

Jessie closed her eyes. Was he safe? Please, let him be safe. Was he at his desk in Cole's, with Miss Symonds taking care of him? Would Uncle Norman be kind?

The conversation returned to Madeleine and she opened her eyes again.

'She might be jealous. It's a tough business. Top of the bill one week and scrabbling for work the next.' Grace closed her eyes. Was she remembering the hard times or the good ones? She had no experience of how her parents had struggled in the beginning, only fragments of stories that had been told from time to time. It was the reason Grace was reluctant for Jessie to tread the boards, all the time understanding that it was something Jessie had to find out for herself.

They heard the outside door open and someone walk into the hall. Frances went to the top of the stairs and peered down.

'Morning, Dolly. Go through. I'll be down in two shakes of a lamb's tail.' Frances came back, gathering up the cups. Jessie got to her feet.

'I'd better get dressed.'

'Would you help me back into bed first? I'm feeling tired again. I'd like to sleep.' Jessie took her hands, helping her to stand, leading her slowly to the bed where she sank down. Jessie bent and scooped her legs up into the bed, waiting while Grace got herself comfortable before drawing the sheet over her. The window was open, the breeze clearing the air, and Jessie sat on the edge of the bed, holding Grace's hand.

'I'll be quite all right, darling. Off you go and get dressed.'

Reluctantly, she left.

Dolly was in the scullery, shaking salt and pepper into a large pan that was set on the stove. The smell of beef bones filled the air, transporting Jessie back to the rooms they had in Lowestoft when Dad was ill. There always seemed to be a pot on the boil, her mum sat beside him, feeding him with a spoon, wiping his mouth with the napkin that she laid across his chest, always white, so white. Jessie looked into the pot and wished she hadn't. The smell was intense and made her nauseous. Eddie's jacket was hung on the back of the chair. She hadn't given him a thought.

'Where's Eddie?'

Frances was standing in the doorway, the back door open to the yard, a cigarette between her fingers.

'Exploring. He said you'd know what he meant.'

Jessie grinned. It wouldn't take long for Eddie to settle. 'He'll be back when he's hungry then.' It was a relief not to have to worry about him. He'd always been curious, never holding back if he wanted to find out about something. He'd strike up a conversation wherever he went as long as it was about engines, and people seemed to take to him. He would have no problem finding something to do here. But he would have to go back to study, or get a job. Another pang of guilt made her clench her stomach, but she let it pass. He didn't want to be a solicitor and she wanted him to be happy more than anything. Having a roof over their heads and a steady income was something she'd never seen as the be-all and end-all of life. Now she wasn't so sure. It was all right following your dream, but you couldn't live on dreams. She'd been sharp with Harry, but he'd been right – she needed to ground herself in reality.

'Dad saw him in the market place this morning,' Dolly said, cheerfully, taking up a wooden spoon and stirring the contents of the pot. 'He was at the bus station with Mr Coombes. He told Dad that you'd brought your mum here. Dad called at the butcher's and got these, and sent me to help.' She put the wooden spoon on a saucer by the stove. 'That'll not be too much longer now, and when your mum wakes she can have a bowl or two, if she can manage. Mum sent a loaf she made this morning.'

'It will be full of goodness,' Frances said. 'My ma used to make it all the time. Mostly from lack of cash than anything else, but it will soon build her up. Never fails.' Frances took a draw on her cigarette and blew the smoke out into the yard. 'I've washed the sheets we took from your bed last night. When I've finished my ciggie we can do our clothes if you nip up and get them.' She flicked her ash onto the path. 'It's a fine day and it will be dry before we go to the Empire.'

'I don't know how I'll ever be able to repay such kindness,' Jessie said, wondering how on earth she could. 'And your mum and dad, Dolly. It's so good of them. Would you thank them until I can do so myself?'

'Don't be daft,' Dolly said, pushing her free hand forward. 'It's what folks do. Well, they do around here anyways.'

Jessie's heart was full and her voice trembled, but she didn't want to cry, there was nothing to cry about. She should be happy. She was happy; she was tired; she was scared. Her lip trembled. She glanced to the door where Frances filled the frame, her black hair piled on top of her head. She needed to be tough like Frances to get through this. Perhaps sensing her weakness, Frances threw her stub on the ground and stepped on it with her heel. 'Sleeves up girl, there's work to be done.'

For the next two hours the girls worked together, washing and rinsing until the line was heavy with newly washed clothes that swung on the line, billowing up occasionally. Dolly busied herself with the broth, then prepared a simple meal of ham hock and bread and butter, which the girls washed down with a bottle of lemonade Olive had put in the basket along with the beef bones. They took turns to check on Grace. Her coughing was less and mostly she slept, and, after the work was done, Jessie went to lie down on Frances's bed. The sounds of traffic and people talking in the alleyway at the back of the house were a distant hum, and knowing that Dolly and Frances were nearby, she closed her eyes and fell asleep.

Someone was shaking her gently and as she opened her eyes, she saw that it was Eddie. 'It's half past four, Jessie. You need to get up for work.' His face was smudged with grease and he smelt of oil, but his hands were clean, although his nails were not.

She felt like a garden roller had gone over her. Every bone ached and she struggled to sit up, Eddie gently hauling her upright, the two of them grinning at each other. She gradually swung her legs over the side of the bed and let her shoulders sag. From where would she summon the energy to walk to work, let alone dance when she got there?

He sat down beside her.

'Geraldine has made you something to eat. Mum's asleep and Geraldine is going to watch her tonight.' He rubbed his nose with the flat of his hand. 'I didn't get chance to give you this yesterday.' He pulled a clump of paper from his pocket that she soon realised were five-pound notes. She counted five of them, her heart hammering in her chest.

'What have you done, Eddie? Where on earth did you get this?' She dropped the crumpled notes in her lap, and he laughed.

'Don't panic. Uncle Norman gave them to me before we left.'

She looked down at the notes again, picked one up and straightened it. Yes, they were real notes.

'He said it was to help with Mum.'

She was speechless. Why support her now when they'd thought she was doing the wrong thing by coming here? But then it wasn't for her, was it? It was for her mum. 'We need to open a bank account, Jessie. I talked to Geraldine and she said she can help with that.'

Jessie smoothed the notes with her hand, flattening them, patting them into a neat pile. 'Well, it will take the pressure off for a good while.' It would help when they needed it most. Now was not the time for being proud. It could be paid back in time, when they got on their feet. 'I'll write and thank him,' she said, staring at the money. 'We both will.'

Eddie nodded. 'And I can take the pressure off a bit, Jess. I've got a job.'

'What? Where?' She was still tired; she had to get to work. How was Grace? What was Eddie talking about? She frowned at him.

'At the bus station. Remember when me and Mum came to see the show with Harry? Remember?' He was leaning towards her. 'That's when I met Mr Coombes, and, well he's taken me on.' He grinned, pushing her lower jaw with his hand to close her open mouth. 'Don't look so shocked. I won't let him down – or you.'

She leapt to her feet, clasped her hands and put them to her mouth, rocking back and forth. 'What about school?' Oh, Lord, what had she done. There hadn't been time to think, there still wasn't, but things needed to slow down. It was too much. 'You should've waited, Eddie.'

He set his jaw to her. 'I'm not going back, Jess. I'm done with school, and I'll be fifteen in September. I've always loved engines; you know I have.' He pulled himself more erect. He was going to be taller than Dad, more thickset too, but he was still a child; he needed direction. She pulled her hand around her neck, held it there ... trying to think, to decide.

Eddie carried on. 'You're doing what you love, Jessie – and so am I.' He walked over to the door. 'I'm the man of the house now, Jessie. We'll look after Mum together. It's as it should be. A fresh start for all of us.'

Chapter 25

Frances and Jessie linked arms and walked to the theatre along the cliff road. There was still heat in the sun, so they carried their cardigans in their free hands. The tide was out and the sand stretched for miles, the sea line barely visible, the air thick with seagulls that swooped and soared in the distance. Boats lined the estuary, waiting for the tide to turn so that they could make their way into the docks. The streets were somewhat quieter, the hotel dining rooms full of guests eating their meals before they headed out for the evening's entertainment.

Jessie glanced through the windows as they passed. How many would be coming to see their show? She threw her shoulders back, trying not to slouch, hoping she would somehow find the energy to get through their routines. She was glad she had Frances to hold on to. The wind was fresh off the sea and it made her feel more awake than she'd done all day, and the short walk to the theatre was helping to settle her thoughts.

'How are you feeling?' Frances asked.

'Tired, but I'll be fine.'

'Of course you will.' She patted her hand.

'The last two days have been a waking nightmare, Frances. I find it hard to believe how so much could

change so quickly. I thought losing my song from the show was the end of the world but when I saw Mum ...'
She looked away from her friend, hoping to dislodge the image of Grace that burned in her head; the smell of that room, the stench of sweat and stale urine.

Frances tightened her grip on Jessie's arm. 'It's behind you now. You can only go forward, and at least you're all together.' Jessie stopped walking and Frances let go of her.

'I'm scared, Frances. My mum hasn't been herself for such a long time and I could somehow accept that, her diminishing weakness, but not the neglect.'

A group of lads wolf-whistled at them from across the road, and when Jessie scowled at them, they waved cheerily. Jessie turned her back. 'When I saw Mum, I lost my head. All I could think of was getting her away from my damned aunt—'

'And thank the good Lord you did.' Frances took up her arm again and they began walking down the incline to the theatre. 'She wasn't being cared for, and is too weak to care for herself. When she gets well, and she will get well, Jessie.' She faced Jessie as they carried on walking. 'When she gets well, she can decide for herself, but don't go doubting what you've done.' Her dark eyes were serious. 'Trust me, I know. Some decisions are difficult to live with, but you will adjust. No matter what lies ahead, I know you have spirit, Jessie Delaney. You have enough to carry your ma until she can fend for herself. As for Eddie ... well, the lad's a happy little sand boy now, isn't he?'

Jessie grinned, unable to contradict her friend. She couldn't turn the clock back and choose again, and maybe she wouldn't want to.

George sprang from his chair when Jessie and Frances walked through the stage door. He threw his arms about her and she hugged him tightly, feeling safer, like the old man was a wall against the world, holding everything at bay. Jasper wrapped himself about her legs and she gave him a quick pet but didn't have the energy to pick him up.

'He's getting fatter, George.'

'That's a good sign,' Frances said, taking her mail. 'Means fewer mice about to nibble our toes.'

George gave Jessie a letter. It was Harry's handwriting. Had he written it before Saturday? What day was it now? Monday, yes, it was Monday. The start of the week and a new beginning. Arthur squeezed past her on his way to the stairs, tipping his hat in greeting.

'Evening, George. Girls.'

George replied to him and Arthur said to Jessie, 'How's your dear mother?'

She hesitated. 'Better than she was, Arthur. Thanks for asking.' She wasn't well by any means, but she was safe, and that was everything. Frances touched her arm and indicated that she was heading down to the dressing rooms.

George smiled kindly, peering at her over his glasses. 'She'll be grand now that she's here. This fresh sea air will do her the power of good.'

'And the kindness more so.' Jessie was well aware that it took more than a person's surroundings to heal them, and experience told her that they were in the best place for that. 'She has the best of care, and the medicine the doctor gave her seems to be working well.'

The stage door opened again, and Billy breezed in, filling the space with his bubbling energy. He leant by the door, waiting for George.

'Don't fret yourself, lass.' George reached inside his room and handed Billy his key and a couple of postcards.

Billy gave the pictures a cursory glance, then flipped them over, grinning to himself. Jasper mewed again and George said, 'He's glad to see you back.'

'He's not the only one.' He bent down and tickled the cat under the chin. Jasper arched his back and straightened his tail. 'Ah, I still have the magic touch.' He grinned at Jessie, and George grumbled his distaste. 'How was your mum? Grace, isn't it?'

Jessie nodded. 'Better than she was. I brought her back with me.'

He raised an eyebrow. 'I thought Harry was taking you back for a visit.'

Jessie sighed. 'It didn't quite work out that way.' She looked at Harry's handwriting on the envelope again. He seemed further away than ever. 'Best get my slap on.' She smiled at George, waving the envelope, gripping the stair rail in her other hand. 'Thanks, George.'

Billy hurried behind her. 'Is your mum here for a holiday then?'

She turned her head slightly to reply as they went downstairs and into the long corridor. 'Not quite.' Why was he asking so many questions? She couldn't think. She paused at the open door of her dressing room. 'See you later, Billy. I'm too tired to talk.' Virginia was staring at the pair of them and Jessie hurried to her seat.

'Hi, gorgeous.' He blew Virginia a kiss. 'Come and see me when you're ready.' He slapped at the door with the flat of his hand. Virginia turned her back, nodded at him via her reflection in the mirror. Jessie sighed, dreading more animosity from Virginia. It wasn't her fault that Billy kept talking to her. They were doing a number together, after all. Jealousy was such a redundant emotion. What did it achieve?

She flopped down in her chair. Rita, halfway through her make-up, was in her red-and-black silk dressing gown that was decorated with a large golden dragon. She talked to Jessie through the mirror, drawing a line in lip pencil around her mouth.

'Sounds like you've had one hell of a weekend. Are you going to be all right tonight?'

Jessie froze. Was Rita looking for an excuse to get rid of her? Her shoulders tensed. She needed this job more than she ever had before. She flashed Rita the widest of smiles.

'I'll be fine.'

Rita's voice softened. 'I'm not having a go, you chump. I'm worried.' She pressed her lips together then pouted. 'If you can get through tonight, you'll be able to sleep all day tomorrow to make up for it a little bit.' She flicked her head. 'Frances told us what happened.'

Frances showed her backside as she bent down to put down on her shoes and Jessie laughed, they all did, and she felt lifted by them. 'We'll keep it down, won't we, girls?' Kay, Sally and Virginia murmured their support.

Rita got to her feet and peeled off her robe, stepping into her black satin shorts. 'After the first spot you can get your head down until the interval. Save your energy for the duet and the finale.' She checked herself in the long mirror, turning this way and that, running a hand either side of her head. 'That's me done. See you on stage, girls.'

Jessie picked up her greasepaint sticks and began making up her eyes, the white around the brow arch, the red dot in the centre that would make the eye appear larger, brighter. Tonight it would have to work extra hard, for her eyes were dull, the skin dark below them. Virginia stood behind her and Jessie froze, her pencil poised mid-air, looking at her through the mirror.

'I hope your mum gets well soon, Jessie. I understand how worried you must be. I lost my mum two years ago. I don't think I'll ever get over it.' She touched Jessie's shoulder and gave it a gentle squeeze. 'See you on the boards.'

Jessie lowered her hand to the table and rested it for a moment as the rest of the girls left the room. How strange people were, she considered, as she quickly finished her face and stepped into her costume. How had she got them all so wrong?

The girls were as good as their word and quickly changed after the first routine and sat quietly in the room, making sure Jessie settled in the only comfortable chair that was there for guests, but used primarily by Rita. She didn't sleep but closed her eyes, aware of their lowered voices as they whispered to each other. Strains of Arthur's musical saw drifted in and out of her consciousness. She managed to get through both of the routines in the first half without making errors, and was relieved to get back into the dressing room for the interval when the curtain came down. Eddie was sitting in her seat and his grin almost split his freckled face as the scantily clad girls filled the dressing room. Jessie smiled at his unconcealed delight.

'An intruder,' Rita declared. 'And a male one at that.' She turned left and right, putting her fists to her hips. 'What do you think we should do, girls?'

Eddie's expression changed to one of fear and they all burst out laughing.

'Don't worry. Only teasing, little brother.' Rita slapped his shoulder. 'Up out of that chair, your sister is in need of it more than you.' He leapt to his feet and stood back, ruffling his hair with his hand so that it stuck up when he drew it away.

'Face to the wall, Eddie,' Frances instructed as the girls took off their costumes and slipped on their robes. When they were dressed he turned around, his face red and hot. Jessie dipped her head so that he couldn't see her amusement. She twisted in her chair to him.

'You haven't left Mum on her own, have you, Eddie?'

He shook his head. 'Geraldine's with her.' His voice came out squeaky and she bit at the inside of her cheek to stop herself. The rest of the girls, noticing his embarrassment, began chatting amongst themselves.

Billy popped his head around the door. 'Well, well. Good work getting in here, Sonny Jim.' Eddie blushed even more. Billy looked around the room. 'What's he got that I haven't, ladies?'

'Where do you want us to start, Billy?' Frances started counting on her fingers. 'Charm, good looks, manners ...'

Billy held up his hands. 'Okay, okay.'

Eddie was getting flustered and Jessie felt for him. Billy was only teasing but her brother was only just getting his bearings. He hadn't moved from his position by the wall.

'I only came to see Jessie because I'll be at work before she wakes up tomorrow.'

Frances interrupted. 'Hey, you don't have to explain yourself to Billy.'

Billy cocked his head on one side and glared at her, before turning back to Eddie. Frances turned her back on him and retouched her lipstick, watching him through the mirror.

'Ah, a working man. Good for you. Say, Eddie—' he held out his hand and Eddie came forward to take it; Billy shook it vigorously '—why don't you come and sit with me while these ...' he paused '... ladies get themselves decent.' The two men looked at Jessie for her approval.

She shrugged her shoulders. What harm could it do?

When the curtain went up for the second half, Jessie made her way up onto the stage as the short overture played. It had been a case of going through the motions to get this show over and done with, and she hoped that, by the end of the week, things would be back to normal. She squeezed past Matt and Sid, who were sitting on her bench, ready to rush on with it when the Variety Girls finished their routine.

'Hi Jessie. How's your mum?'

'Good.' She smiled; did everyone know? 'She's good; thank you for asking.' The two men gave her a half smile. She couldn't be more supported than she was already, and the thought gave her another lift of energy; if she'd ever doubted it, she was wrong, because people cared. As she made her way to the prompt corner, she was surprised to find Billy standing there, Eddie at his side. Mike had his back to them, reading the *Evening Telegraph* by the prompt light. In the soft light that spilled into the wings, Jessie caught Eddie's smile as he watched the Variety Girls go through their moves. Billy tapped him on the shoulder and he turned to her. She stood beside them, all three huddled in the space between the tabs and flats that screened the wings from the audience.

Billy leaned into her and whispered, his arm still on Eddie's shoulder, 'Thought young Eddie would like to watch his big sister sing tonight.' He slapped Eddie on the back and the boy grinned, turning again to watch the girls, the light from the stage giving his face a glow. 'If you stand here, Ed you won't be in the way and you'll get the best view of your sister. Although—' he winked at Jessie '—it's actually me that gets the best view of all.' He tapped Eddie again and made his way along the rear of the backcloth to the other side of the stage, ready for his cue.

Jessie took her place on the bench that had been set. The first few notes of their song played, the curtains drew back, and Jessie waited for Billy to sing his opening lines to her. Eddie was almost leaning on the proscenium arch watching them both and his smile made every movement so much more worthwhile. The ghost of her dad hovered close by; he'd done the same thing so many times when she was younger, watching her, giving her cues to use her arms more expressively, to smile, to lift up her head so that her voice came true and sure. Her smile was just for Eddie as she came towards him, and his face brightened. Billy took her hand, wrapped his own around her waist and the two of them strolled towards Eddie, then away, and she was watching his enjoyment, which doubled her own. Tiredness fell away. Eddie was happy and so was she. Grace would get well; she was sure of it. It was going to work out after all.

At the end of the song, they tripped into the wings, waited for a beat of four, then onto the stage for a final bow. Billy left Jessie on stage to take the applause, and was standing beside Eddie as she came off before going back on to do his act.

The two of them stood side by side, watching Billy as he told his gags rapid fire, drinking in the roundness of the laughter as it filled the theatre.

'It's just like old times, isn't it, Jessie?' Eddie said, his face half in shadow.

'Almost,' she said, because it was. But not quite.

Chapter 26

It was half day and Geraldine was home for the afternoon. The doctor had again been to visit Grace and deemed her on the way to recovery. He left another prescription and thought that Grace might not be in need of another if she continued to respond as well as she had done so far. Jessie recounted his words. 'She's not a well woman by any standards but she is past danger. It's simply a matter of good nourishment and plenty of rest.' It was obvious to anyone who saw her that Grace had improved, but Jessie wasn't taking any chances.

'That's good news.' Geraldine unpinned her hat and placed it on the dresser in the small back room. 'And perfect timing.'

Jessie wasn't sure what she meant. 'Oh, we need to talk about the rent as well. There are three of us now.' She felt her cheeks burn. 'I'm sorry I haven't mentioned it before, Geraldine. I had no intention of taking advantage. It was all a bit—'

'Rushed?' Geraldine smiled kindly. 'That wasn't what I meant, Jessie. Although we do indeed need to sort something out.' She picked up the mail that Jessie has set on the dresser that morning, and scanned the envelopes before putting them back where she'd found them. Frances came in from the kitchen. 'Kettle's on,

Geraldine. I've been out and bought some cakes from Parker's to celebrate.'

'Wonderful. But before we settle down and enjoy them, I'd like you to come with me, Jessie. I've had the news I wanted myself today and want to know what you think.'

Jessie looked at Frances, who shrugged but twisted her mouth to avoid a smile creeping upon it. What exactly was going on? Jessie followed Geraldine who stopped at the door to the front room and took out her keys.

She put one in the lock and, before she turned it, said to Jessie, 'I've spent the last couple of evenings getting things in place, but I couldn't say anything until I got hold of Reg. His ship docked in Hull yesterday and I put a call out to him from the dock offices.'

She pushed the door open and stood back, letting Jessie walk in first. The room was so pretty, much nicer than any other room in the house. Blue wallpaper flecked with roses decorated the walls and a high-back navy velveteen chair had been placed by the window. Beside it was set a small oak table on which was placed a small pile of books, and a short vase containing pink chrysanthemums. There was a large fireplace fitted with a gas fire along one wall and a bed made up the opposite side. Light flooded in but privacy was maintained by the pristine white net at the window. Hadn't it once been grey? Somehow the house had been transformed and she hadn't been there to help. A wave of guilt swamped her. She'd been so tired, oblivious to almost everything except her mum getting well again. But what did it all mean? Frances stood by the open door, her smile no longer suppressed, her eyes twinkling. Jessie looked to Geraldine for answers.

'There's room for the small armchair that we took upstairs. It belongs in here. We could put it the other side of the window, by the fire. What do you think?' A smile was forming on her lips.

'It's very nice, Geraldine.' What else should she say? She had no idea what Geraldine was thinking.

'Do you think your mother would like it?' She walked over to the navy armchair, plumped the tapestry cushion and set it back down. 'It was Reg's mother's room; that's why it's a little prettier than the rest of the house. He always made sure she had exactly what she wanted. I wrote to tell him of your situation. He's met someone in Hull. I don't think he'll be back for a while and he agreed for me to let your mother have the room. I managed to get a bed in here without making it too cramped. It depends what you think. And if you're planning to stay, of course.' She leaned into the window and looked down both ends of the street then turned to face Jessie, who was still rooted to the spot. 'The rent is small because of the circumstances but when your mother is well she will be able to bring in work. You said she could sew. And Eddie's room – well, it's not really a room, is it? – I've agreed a price with Reg that I think you'll find acceptable.' She clasped her hands in front of her. 'Will it do?'

Jessie had been unable to move. 'Will it do?' she repeated, unable to think of anything else to say for it was beyond what she had expected and so very, very kind. She threw her arms about Geraldine who softened a little in her embrace.

'Now, now.' She smiled, peeling Jessie away. 'There's no need for that. I'm merely thinking of Reg. It will suit all round, and much nicer for your mother to receive her visitors here, don't you think?'

'If we get Grace settled quick sharp,' Frances said, 'we can have tea and cake with her in here. A little celebration, so it is.'

Jessie laughed at their conspiracy and gave Geraldine another hug. She would get used to it.

Grace was soon settled in the chair by the window, her teacup and a small slice of cake at her side that she picked at, the crumbs easy to swallow. She was dressed in her print frock, its white lace collar sitting over a green cardigan. Her skin was gaining colour and even though her hair could do with a wash, it was tidy and neat. Geraldine had suggested to Grace that they leave washing her hair until the weekend, when they would all be home and Grace a little stronger. The upholstered armchair had been brought down from Jessie's room and placed the other side of the small table. Geraldine was seated on it, and Frances and Jessie sat on the bed that was covered with a silver-grey paisley eiderdown. They balanced their plates on their laps and drank from mugs. Geraldine had pulled the top sash window down a smidgen and the occasional sound of dogs barking and heels clipping the pavement punctuated their conversation.

'It's so lovely being part of life again,' Grace said, turning from the window. 'I feel like I've been away from it for so long.'

'You've been very ill,' Geraldine said, picking minute crumbs from her skirt and putting them on her plate.

'No, not that.' Grace paused for breath. 'I thought The Beeches would be good for us. Only it shut us away from everything.' Another pause. 'I should've been stronger. But after Davey … it was too much.'

Geraldine took her hand. 'I understand. But you will get strong again, Grace.'

Grace swallowed. 'I don't know what I've done to deserve all this.' She tried to smile but Jessie could see that she was overwhelmed by their kindness.

Geraldine got up and began taking the plates and mugs and putting them on the tray. 'You don't have to have done anything, Grace. The room was empty. I am being practical on Reg's behalf. The more rent he has coming in, the happier he will be.'

Grace blanched. 'The rent.'

Jessie reached across and pressed her mum's hand.

'It's sorted, Mum. We have the money. Don't fret so. Geraldine has given us a special rate, in total agreement with Reg. Uncle Norman sent money, Eddie is working and so am I.' She pressed Grace's hand harder. 'You concentrate on getting well and leave the rest to me and Eddie for the time being.'

Geraldine picked up the tray and walked towards the door. She turned before leaving, 'I think you should do as you're told, Grace. The girl is bossy to a degree. It suits her, don't you think?'

Grace smiled, the anxiety leaving her face, and Jessie bent forward and kissed her cheek.

'That's my girl,' she whispered into her hair.

Geraldine did the washing up while Frances and Jessie went upstairs to bring down the rest of Grace's things and restore Jessie's to her own room. 'Thank the Lord I'm back in my own little bed. I might get some sleep now.'

Frances put Jessie's good shoes underneath the window. 'Haven't you slept? I thought you'd sleep like a log. You've been so exhausted.'

'I still am,' Jessie giggled. 'Your piggy snoring kept me awake.'

Frances drew a pillow from the bed and threw it playfully at her friend. 'Why you cheeky ...'

Jessie put her arm up to deflect the pillow and threw it back. Frances caught it and the pair of them fell on the bed laughing. They laid on their backs, looking up at the ceiling.

'Your mum looks much better already, Jess. And Eddie has a job.' She moved her head to look at her friend. 'You must know that you did the right thing.'

Jessie remained staring at the ceiling. She was still so tired, it was hard to think – and it was early days. They were a long way off being secure, but she couldn't argue with Frances's statement. For the moment, at least, things were looking brighter, but there was still much to do. The summer wouldn't last for ever and she needed to start working on putting her own act together.

When they went downstairs, Jessie stuck her head around her mum's door. Grace was laid on the bed, sleeping. She closed it quietly and went into the kitchen.

'What an upside-down life you live, girls.' Geraldine was tying an apron over her clothes. 'I'm coming in from work just as you're about to go out. How do you ever get used to it?'

Frances shrugged. 'Like you get used to anything, I suppose. You sleep when you're tired and wake when you're not.'

'I'm still not sure how that works,' Jessie muttered. 'I'm only just beginning to get over the weekend of no sleep.' She giggled at Frances who didn't bite at her jibe.

'Ah, but that's different,' Frances said. 'I think we have it the right way around anyway, Geraldine. We get the best of the day to ourselves.' She stuck her head in the pantry and rummaged around on the shelves.

Jessie sighed. 'That's when we're not rehearsing, practising or performing.'

'Ah, no rest for us wicked girls.' Frances picked up her bag. 'We need milk. I'm going to make us an egg custard before we go back to work.' She winked at Jessie. 'Your turn tomorrow.'

Jessie blew her a kiss and Frances flounced off. She knew quite well that both Geraldine and Frances had subtly tailored the meals for Grace. She picked up an empty envelope from the ones Geraldine had discarded from the morning's post, found a stub of a pencil and sat down at the table to write a list of expenses. She drew a line down the middle of the paper and wrote IN on one side, and OUT on the other. In the IN column she recorded their income. Their savings – twenty-five pounds from Uncle Norman, and two pounds, three shillings and sixpence that she had managed to save herself. What she'd put by had quickly diminished on the extra expenses incurred for Grace's medicine, and food for all three of them. To it she added her own wages that she would receive tomorrow, and whatever Eddie could bring in. When Grace was well enough, she could take in sewing or find something that would bring in extra cash, but Jessie was determined not to rely on it. Who knew how long it would take for Grace to get back to full health? She listened for movement in the next room, but all she heard was Geraldine pottering about in the kitchen, as she took the jars and dishes from the shelves and wiped them down before replacing them. She began writing down their expenses: rent that had been agreed with Geraldine earlier, food, a little for clothing and medicine. She tried to list every small expense she could think of. Her stage make-up wouldn't last forever, and, if she went out on her own, she would need stockings and definitely a better pair of shoes. If Grace was well enough, she could get some fabric and would be able to make her a dress quite cheaply. That would do for now. There was no need for an elaborate costume; something simple would be suitable. She wouldn't get in debt; just to think of it made her heart beat faster and she felt in her pocket for Hope's penny. It calmed her. She would always have that penny so she would never be in debt. She smiled, encouraged. When everything was written down in black and white it seemed more manageable. She drew a heavy line under her calculations and hunted about for another scrap of paper.

Frances came in with the milk, closing the door quietly behind her.

'What are you doing?'

Jessie twiddled the pencil between her fingers. 'Thinking of songs for my act.'

Frances peered over at the blank sheet. 'Sounds wonderful.'

'I haven't started yet. I need something that will make me stand out.'

'Go for the oldies. Folks love 'em.' Frances took the milk into the kitchen and came back followed by Geraldine.

'What about "Thanks for the Memory"? It's very popular at the moment.'

Jessie screwed a face. 'Not for an opening song, Geraldine. It's too slow. It's the kind of song you leave the audience with. I need something that will make them sit up.'

'Something lively, eh.' Frances wiggled her fingers on her chin. 'What about "Roll Out the Barrel"? That'll get 'em going.'

'Going straight to the bar.' Jessie dismissed that one outright.

'"All the Things You Are"? A beautiful song.' Geraldine was wistful and Frances and Jessie glanced at each other, raising their eyebrows, wondering who had inspired the sentiment in their friend.

The three of them threw songs into the melting pot that Jessie was stirring, hoping to come up with a powerful concoction that would please the audience and give her something to present to Bernie when he came. There was so much to do. Bernie had replied – or rather his secretary had left a message with George. He would be coming along in the next few weeks. Business was booming; there was plenty of work and opportunity for grafters with talent. For a split second the prospect taunted her. Did she have the talent? Her eyes were sore and she rubbed at them.

'I have plenty to choose from anyway,' she said to her friends, getting to her feet, tucking the list behind the wireless on the sideboard. At least she felt like she had a plan. It was easier having Mum and Eddie here, and more complicated too. She leaned her head on her hands and rested. Harry had a plan, they both did, but it had been forgotten in the mayhem. She really ought to write to Harry. She could do it at the theatre during the break between shows. Although it pained her, she knew it best to tell him not to come this weekend as they had arranged when he left. Was that only Sunday? No wonder she was still so tired. And he must be too. Dear Harry, God bless him, it was such a long journey; she'd asked so much of him, and he'd not complained. Not once. She owed him so much and longed to have him near, to smell his skin, to taste his lips. She hugged herself, remembering. But she mustn't be selfish. She must think in future, before she made any decisions. Not just of herself, but of Grace and Eddie – and, of course, Harry.

The three of them went into the kitchen and began to prepare the meal. Frances busied herself with the egg custard, Jessie peeled potatoes, while Geraldine stabbed some sausages and put them in a low oven. Jessie and Frances sang quietly as they worked, inspired by Jessie's list. The pair of them were at the sink, tapping their feet as they washed, and hands dripping with water, started to sing 'Side by Side'. They did a little routine for Geraldine who was leaning against the warm oven. Frances placed a damp hand on Jessie's shoulder, and they strolled like Flanagan and Allen, performing for their audience of one.

When Jessie checked on Grace, she was walking around the room, holding on to pieces of furniture for support.

'Mum, what on earth are you doing?' Jessie hovered about her mum nervously, but Grace flapped at her with her hand. 'Using my body before I lose use of it altogether.' She let out a long sigh as she settled back in the chair, using the table and seat cushion for support. 'Better than I thought for a first attempt.' Her breathing was rapid with effort and she closed her eyes, trying to slow it down. She coughed a little.

'Little and often, Grace,' Geraldine interrupted. 'Quite right.'

Jessie swivelled to find Geraldine gently applauding Grace. 'Your mother and I have had plenty of practice with invalids. Haven't we?' Grace opened her eyes. 'And no doubt will again. Not something I thought would ever happen.' Geraldine put the *Evening Telegraph* on the bed and patted it, saying, 'For later.'

Jessie saw the headline of the early edition. She seldom read the paper. What could she do with the knowledge? War would come or it would not. Geraldine left them, closing the door behind her and Jessie sat down in the small chair.

Grace looked out of the window. 'I like it here, Jessie. You made good choices.'

'Did I?'

Her mum turned back to her. 'Of course. When Norman offered ... it was meant to be temporary. When your dad died ... the debt ...'

'It doesn't matter.' Grace's breathing was laboured, and Jessie wanted her to save her energy to get well. Her mum had overdone it and she was cross with her, and yet loving her. And afraid. How would she get well if she didn't rest?

'But it does.' Grace stared into the middle distance, her face sad. 'I planned to take in alterations and sewing. To supplement my widow's pension. Iris wouldn't hear of it, having strangers come to the house.'

'They were hardly strangers,' Jessie said. Her mum didn't need to explain anything. 'Everyone in the village knew everyone else.'

'It wasn't only that.' She paused, considering her words carefully. 'She was afraid.'

Jessie felt her eyebrows almost rise off her face. 'Iris. Afraid?' There was nothing weak about Iris.

Grace leaned back into her chair, closed her eyes once more. 'If only I'd explained.'

What was there to explain? Her aunt was cold, uncaring. Cruel.

Grace's breath steadied. 'She had a child. Maisie. Diphtheria. Four years old. Oh, the loss. The grief. I understand grief, Jessie. It makes you numb, dulls life. No joy any more. To lose a child though … I can only imagine the pain.'

Jessie stared out of the window. A rag and bone man was heading down the street and she could hear him call, the clip-clop of the horse's hooves. Grief: she understood a little of it. How every thought of her dad was a sting in her heart that lingered. How laughter had disappeared. How her mum had shrunk, until she was a pale shadow of who she used to be. Would she get that mum back again? They'd all been changed since Dad died, Grace most of all. All her life Jessie had witnessed Grace bustling about, hauling trunks and cases on and off trains and buses, climbing God knew how many stairs in digs and rooms. She had the inner strength and the outer. Grace was the one who lifted Dad's spirits when his act had bombed, who reassured him that he would get work, that they would manage. Had it all been pretence?

'Your dad would like it here.' Grace said, jarring Jessie's thoughts. 'The house is full of warmth and laughter. You have good friends. All the important things in life.'

'Mmm,' Jessie said, smiling at her mum. 'Apart from Harry. If he was here, everything would be perfect.'

Grace sighed. 'Life is never perfect, darling. Never.'

Eddie walked past the window and Jessie got to her feet. 'Here's the working man now. Better get him his tea. He'll be famished as usual.' She pushed up the sash that Geraldine had opened earlier. 'Frances has made a lovely egg custard. I'll bring you some.'

The girls served up the meal while Eddie washed himself. He was beginning to adjust to a house full of women and joined in the conversation more easily. It was a joy to Jessie to see how quickly he'd begun to gain confidence, no longer hovering on the edges of the room as he'd done at The Beeches. Geraldine had the knack of putting him at ease and Jessie wondered how she'd developed the right touch, leading him gently into the conversation.

When Frances and Jessie got up to leave, he remained at the table, chatting to Geraldine. The girls made sure the dishes were washed and put away, and Grace settled before they left for work. Jessie knew that Eddie would not be far behind them, for he had taken to popping into the Empire each evening. George loved talking cars, the crew indulged him backstage, and Billy made him laugh.

Jessie picked up her bag. 'Will I see you later, Ed?'

He continued to explain the finer details of the combustion engine to Geraldine and merely nodded his head in reply.

As they walked down the street, Frances said. 'Aren't you a little worried about Eddie spending so much time with Billy?'

'Should I be?' They stood at the edge of the pavement while a cyclist passed them, then crossed over.

'I just think you should keep your eye on him, that's all. Eddie could easily be led astray by the likes of Billy.'

Jessie linked her arm. 'He's just being friendly.'

'Friendly my arse, Jessie. He's using Eddie to get in your good books.'

'Even if he is. So what? Eddie likes him. Lots of people do. The audiences love him.'

Frances stopped and Jessie paced ahead then waited, turned. Frances stood there, hands on hips, shaking her head.

'What,' Jessie said, laughing. 'Come on we'll be late.'

'Billy uses people all the time to get what he wants. I don't want to be right, but I know that I am – and you know it too, Jessie. I know you do.'

She waited while Frances caught her up and they linked arms again. 'I know what you're saying, Frances, but what harm can it do? Eddie lives in a house full of women and has done for most of his life. He craves male company. Besides,' she added, 'I'm not interested in Billy that way. I have Harry. I will always have Harry.'

Chapter 27

It had been a difficult week and Jessie's letter had just about put the tin lid on it. Harry folded it, shoved it back into the envelope and slipped it into the inside pocket of his jacket that was hung on the back of the chair. The room was stuffy and airless. He had taken to leaving his door open, appreciating the sound of typewriter keys smacking paper, as Miss Symonds and Beryl went about their work.

From time to time he closed his eyes and tried to imagine that it was Jessie working in the room across the hall, but it didn't work. Instead he pictured her on the beach, that last evening they'd spent together, holding hands, watching the tide recede. He'd been looking forward to doing it again this Saturday but now she had written and asked him not to go. He sighed bitterly and went back to the plot of land he was trying to locate the registry title for. He pushed the papers around, trying to make sense of them and failed. He shoved them to the far side of his desk. It was all so ruddy pointless.

His concentration was shot to pieces as he turned over the reasons why Jessie didn't want him to come, hoping it wasn't because she was tired of him, dreading that she'd started to find Billy more attractive. The telephone rang in the main office and he heard Miss Symonds ask Beryl to take some files to Mr Cole and to take a pencil and notepad for dictation.

He waited until he heard her knock on his door and Norman call enter before pushing his chair back and going into the main reception. Miss Symonds was answering another call and taking notes, so he sat on Beryl's desk playing around with a pencil until she put the receiver down.

'You look a little glum, Mr Newman.'

He sighed. 'Mmm.'

'How's Jessie? Did she say how her mother was?' He'd always had his letters come direct to the office, not wanting to wait until he got home at the end of the day. Sometimes they arrived in both first and second deliveries, giving him the chance to read and reread them throughout the long days at Cole's. Lately they had petered out, from being daily to almost non-existent.

Neither Norman or Harry had spoken of the weekend's events and Harry was unnerved by it. It left him wondering how to fend off questions that might come up regarding Grace and Eddie. Miss Symonds hadn't remarked at all when he'd arrived in the office on Monday morning, tired and dishevelled, but at coffee break she'd magicked up two thick rounds of buttery toast from the café across the road and placed them on his desk, along with the morning coffee.

Harry merely mentioned in passing that he had taken Grace and Eddie to stay with Jessie. That they thought the air would do her good. He didn't think for one minute that Miss Symonds believed him, but she didn't ask any further questions and he knew she wouldn't, wise enough to fill in the missing information by herself.

'Improved.' He nodded, looking down at the wooden floor.

'Jessie or Grace?'

He looked up. 'Grace is improved, much improved. I was going to travel up on Saturday, but it looks like I'm not wanted.' He told her of Jessie's letter.

Miss Symonds was quiet. 'I would think that she will be quite tired. They all will be. As are you. She's being quite sensible, don't you think?'

He nodded. She was right but it still hurt to think that she could manage without him.

'I never thought I'd be saying that about our Miss Delaney though. Sensible was not top of my list but she has changed. She has had to, Harry.'

He liked it when she called him Harry, not that she did when anyone else was around.

'I can't help thinking what she said about the theatre being her family.'

'I wouldn't worry too much, Harry. It's a figure of speech, that's all.'

If only he could believe it. He'd convinced himself that she would do the season and that would be the end of it, but Grace and Eddie being there put a different slant on things. And he had been the one to take them there.

'Families argue and fall out,' Miss Symonds said.

He couldn't quibble with that. He couldn't remember the last time he'd seen his father. Not that they'd argued, simply drifted apart.

'I would think it's all fleeting,' Miss Symonds continued. 'They are all thrust together and must get along for the duration. I suppose they have to rely on each other or the whole show will fall apart. And, as we all know, Harry, the show must go on.'

He tried to smile at her attempt at humour. Fleeting or not, it left him agitated. As much as things were between Russia and Germany. Who was in and who was out. Friends or foe. People were taking sides. 'How can people carry on as if nothing has happened, Miss Symonds?' He wasn't only thinking of Jessie now, but of Norman. Would everything be swept under a huge carpet? Surely the lump it made would be obvious.

'You can do nothing but wait and see how the cards fall. Jessie is strong-minded and spirited, but that's what you like about her – if I'm not talking out of turn.'

He shook his head. The old gal was bang on the money, she always was, but he couldn't sit around wishing and hoping that everything would pan out the way he wanted it to. Jessie hadn't waited. If she wanted something, she went for it, tooth and nail, no matter what. Perhaps it was time he did the same.

He heard the click of Norman's door as it opened and stood away from Beryl's desk. 'Why wait here twiddling my thumbs? Jessie won't come back. She'll learn to manage; it's who she is.'

Miss Symonds removed her glasses, holding them by the arms even though they were secured by the chain about her neck. 'And who are you, Harry? She may well have had her head turned by the bright lights, but she loves you. Hold on to that.'

Beryl came back down, slipped paper into her type-writer and began clacking away and Harry drifted back into his office, reflecting on what Miss Symonds had said.

At lunch he took off his tie, rolled up his sleeves and went out for a walk in the hope that it would clear his thoughts. It was warm but the sun was obscured by cloud, the patches of blue limited. He wandered down to the common land at Spout Hills to eat his lunch. As he crossed the road by the obelisk, a woman bustled by with a pram, her white-blond-haired son holding onto the handle that was only just within his grasp, his short legs going like the clappers to keep up with her.

Harry walked around for a while to waste time, then found space on a bench next to an old man reading the *Daily Mail*. The trees were in their full green glory and as Harry sat down in the shade they offered, the man folded his newspaper and placed it on his lap. Harry blew out over his lip. The old man wanted to talk, and Harry didn't feel like talking.

He unwrapped the potted meat sandwich he'd made earlier that morning and stared out across the water that trickled down into the brook. Sensing lunch was on offer, a team of ducks headed towards him, stewing about his feet. Harry chewed, tossing the crumbs to the floor, and the two men watched the ducks snatch at the crusts and fight over them.

The old man cleared his throat. 'Bah, looks like everyone wants to scrap these days, even the birds.' He tapped at his paper and Harry tilted his head. The old man rubbed at his whiskered chin, then peered at Harry, his eyes creasing at the corners. 'Looks like them buggers will have us on the run again, eh, lad. We'll have to sort 'em out good and proper this time round. What do you say?'

Harry shook his head. 'I wish they'd hurry up and make a damned decision, in or out.' He carefully smoothed the brown paper bag to use again. 'It's the sitting on the sidelines that does for me.'

The old boy nodded. 'You've hit the nail on the head there. It's the waiting that does you in. Holding yer breath too long makes a bloke light-headed, don't it?'

Harry laughed. 'It does. It does.' He slapped the old chap on the back, then got to his feet. The clouds had cleared a bit and the patches of blue had begun to outnumber them. 'I'd best get back to work. Enjoy the rest of the afternoon.' The chap touched the peak of his hat with his forefinger and Harry thrust his hands in his pockets and whistled all the way back to the office. He wasn't going to hang around to go where someone else wanted him to be. Grounded like the ducks, waiting for what was tossed his way then fighting over scraps that someone else tossed to him. If anyone was making a decision, one way or the other, it might as well be him.

Chapter 28

Jessie pulled the net back and peered down the street.

'He won't come any faster for you looking, love.' Grace was settling herself in the chair, the wireless on low. She'd slept for most of the afternoon and had woken feeling hungry. It was a turning point, and Jessie had been quick to respond. She let the net drop and came away from the window.

'I thought he would have raced home with his pay packet. He was full of it this morning.'

Grace reached for the local paper and placed it on her lap. 'He's probably with his work mates. Mr Coombes might be talking to him about how he's done. You know how it is – first week, first pay packet. Surely you haven't forgotten? That was you not so long ago.'

It felt like years. Time had skipped along at a rate since she'd first arrived at the railway station alone, and now here they all were, together again. The turnaround in Grace's health had been remarkable but it was her revived spirit that pleased Jessie more than anything. The distress of it all had been worth it for that alone. Still, although Grace was revived, her good health was not completely restored – that would take longer.

Jessie plumped the cushion behind her mum's back. 'I don't like to leave you.'

Grace leaned back into the cushion. 'I'll be fine. There's no need for you to worry.'

How she longed for a tap in her head that would allow her to turn the worry off. Geraldine wouldn't be home until six and she would rather Eddie be there before she left. If he didn't come in the next couple of minutes she would have to leave regardless. Frances had already gone on ahead and, as it was, she'd have to dash. 'I'll see him soon enough, I suppose.'

'Go, don't be late.' Grace urged. She lifted the newspaper and turned the pages. 'There's variety on tonight. Tessie O' Shea. Your dad worked with her in Liverpool.'

Jessie bent down to kiss Grace on her cheek. 'Is there no escape?'

Grace smiled. 'Did we ever want it?'

Jessie picked up her bag and threw her cardigan about her shoulders. It was so good to see a glimmer of the old Grace, the one who loved music, who loved to laugh. 'Did we ever leave?' she called out as she stepped into the hallway and into the street.

George had a letter. It was from Harry. Who else would it be from, apart from Miss Symonds? Everyone she loved was here.

'He'll be running out o' paper afore too long.' George laughed as she kissed the envelope. There was no time to read it, so she pushed it into her pocket and ran downstairs to the dressing room. At least she'd made it for the half-hour call.

The girls were all sat in front of the long mirror painting on their faces, apart from Virginia, who sat in the armchair, her legs slung over the side. 'Eddie was here looking for you,' she said, looking up from her magazine. Her face was already made up, her full lips painted pillar-box red.

Jessie shoved her bag under the chair and began taking off her clothes. Once she had her robe in place, she sat down and began her own routine. 'Did he leave a message?' her voice wobbled as she rubbed Leichner over her face and throat. She reached for her rouge. 'How odd that he came here first.'

'Still here as far as I know.' Virginia flicked a page and folded it back. Vivien Leigh pouted at her in black and white. 'Went off to find Billy.'

Frances didn't comment and the others were too busy getting their slap on to take any notice, so she finished her face, got into her costume and went off in search of Eddie. The door to Billy's room was closed but she could hear voices and laughter, Eddie's laughter. She knocked and Billy called out to 'Come in.'

Eddie was perched on Billy's table, the mirror bulbs lit around him, giving him an angelic glow. Arthur and Billy were sat in their shirtsleeves, lounging in the two chairs opposite him, and all three were drinking beer from the crate that Billy kept topped up in the corner. Eddie was red-faced and happy – whether from the jokes or the beer Jessie wasn't sure. Her fists clenched; she mustn't make a fuss. She glared at Billy. He grinned.

'Ah, here's your big sister come to celebrate too. Perfect timing.' He stood up. 'Take a seat, Jessie.'

She shook her head sharply. 'What are you celebrating?'

'Why, Eddie here, joining the ranks of the working man. His first week's work. His first pay packet.'

She tried to keep the disappointment from her face, but she knew she had failed. Matt paced down the corridor calling the fifteen. Eddie slipped off the table. He put the beer bottle on the table behind him, dipped his head a little then looked Jessie in the eye, aware of her disapproval. Arthur cleared his throat and struggled awkwardly to his feet.

'Better move myself. Cheers for the beer, Billy.'

He patted Eddie on the shoulder. 'Nice chatting, son.'

Jessie stepped back to let him pass. It wasn't the old man's fault, but words failed her. Arthur looked uncomfortable. Jessie didn't know why; this was definitely down to Billy.

As she heard the click of Arthur's door she said, 'When you've finished, Eddie, please go home. Mum was looking forward to seeing you. Especially today.'

'Sorry, Jessie. I'll go now.' He might have worked a full week, but he was still only a boy. She stepped back to let him pass and, as he did so, Billy reached out and took Eddie's hand, pumping it up and down. 'Well, done, Eddie lad. There'll be plenty more celebrations before too long.'

Eddie brushed past Jessie and out into the corridor. She would talk to him tomorrow, but he was hardly to blame – she knew exactly at whose feet that lay. She waited until Eddie was out of earshot before letting rip. 'Billy, how could you?'

He grinned at her through the mirror, pulling off his tie and tossing it onto the table. 'How could I what, sweet cheeks?'

'Don't call me that,' she said through gritted teeth. 'I am not your sweet cheeks, or anything else. Eddie shouldn't be drinking at all.'

'Give him a break, Jess. It's his first pay packet. I was just being brotherly. Men have to celebrate these things. Didn't you celebrate your first wage packet?'

She folded her arms, clenching her fists beneath them, determined not to be sweet-talked by Billy. 'With cake, Billy. Not beer. He's only fourteen. Mum would be furious if she found out.'

'Well, I'm not going to tell her. Are you?'

He began unbuttoning his shirt, looking at her through the mirror. 'That's yet another way men and women differ, darling.' He winked at her. Is that what her dad would have done? Would Harry have taken Eddie for a drink? She knew he wouldn't.

'What other celebrations were you talking about?'

He pivoted, slipping off his shirt and she looked away. He was smiling at her. 'Don't be so prudish. You girls walk about with your tits and arses half out so don't blush at my expense.'

'Don't talk like that, Billy. Don't lower yourself.'

He opened his mouth to reply, then closed it again, turning away from her.

'Thank you for marking his first week, Billy. But in future I'd rather you didn't offer him alcohol.'

'Yes, ma'am.' He bowed low, almost sweeping the floor with his arm, bringing it up with a flourish. Why did she feel so awkward when she was meant to be looking out for Eddie? He was entitled to a bit of freedom and fun after the last couple of weeks; they all were. She sighed. There wasn't time to haul it over the coals now, she needed to get up and take her place on stage. She left Billy and hurried down the corridor, colliding with Madeleine as she came out of her room. Damn and blast it. After Madeleine had cut her song, she'd made a concentrated effort to avoid her, not wanting to be rude. And yet wanting very much to be. She was flustered. 'I'm sorry, Miss Moore. I wasn't looking where I was going.'

'My fault,' she said, graciously. Through her open door Jessie caught a glimpse of her room, festooned with flowers from admirers, the obligatory cards and photographs on the walls, around the mirrors, the bulbs turned off to keep the room cool. A lamp on a side table gave off a soft glow and the delicate scent of roses drifted into the corridor, lending an air of luxury to the drab rundown tat that it really was. It was only the same as her mum had done, making the room a little home, using all the tricks to make it less of the windowless cell it really was. That's what Jessie wanted. One day. A sense of making things better than they really were. Artifice, but who cared. You made of it what you could.

Madeleine spoke again and Jessie looked at her and away from the room.

'How is your mother, Jessie? Well, I hope?'

Why did she have to be so nice to her face? It meant that she had to be nice too.

'Much better, thank you, Miss Moore.'

Madeleine reached out to her. 'Please, call me Madeleine. Or Maddy.' Her expression was soft, tender like her mum's, and for a split second Jessie felt the warmth of her, and then it was gone. Jessie nodded. Madeleine continued. She wanted to walk away but couldn't. She didn't trust herself to speak; she had enough on her plate without inviting any more problems. Madeleine might get her duet with Billy cut.

'I heard Eddie was with Billy.'

Jessie nodded again, looking at her shoes. The toes were scuffed; she should have polished them. Yet again she had been distracted.

'Can I give you a friendly piece of advice, if you'd take it?'

Ah, here it was, just as she had expected, something else to complain about. That gorgeous face was only a mask. At least Aunt Iris looked sour and bitter. What could Jessie say or do other than to stand and listen, and wonder why Madeleine would ever want to be nice when she was stabbing Jessie in the back with one hand, and so-called caring for her with the other. 'Watch your brother. Billy will use him if he thinks it will draw you two closer.'

Jessie scowled. She could take it from Frances – she was her friend – but not from Madeleine. 'It seems I can't trust anyone these days.' Her voice was sharp but she was too furious with Billy to care.

'Ah,' Madeleine changed her tone. 'If you let me explain ...'

Matt squeezed past them, calling Overtures. She heard the clatter of heels and turned away, watching the rest of her troupe making their way to the stage. Jessie flicked her head. 'I need to go,' she said, rushing up the stairs after them.

Chapter 29

Frances had gone off to her friend as she did every Sunday, and Eddie had walked down to the golf club to caddy for Jack Holland. Jessie and Grace discussed him as they walked arm in arm along the Kingsway and up towards the Cliff Hotel. The sun was high in the sky and seagulls soared and swooped across the water, their screeches mingling with the sound of voices and car engines chugging along the road. They waited on the kerbside to cross over towards the gardens, taking their time. There was no reason on earth to rush and Jessie was enjoying the slower pace that walking with Grace entailed.

'Eddie seems to have found his feet already,' Grace said, as they stepped onto the pavement. 'It hasn't taken him long at all.'

Jessie waited while Grace caught her breath before the women moved on. 'He's saving for a car. When he's old enough he wants an Austin, like Harry's.' They walked through the archway into the gardens, found a bench and sat down for a while so that Grace could rest before they moved on, starting and stopping, walking a little further each time. Their target was the part that overlooked the pier. It would be enough for one day. It was wonderful to be out in the sunshine with her mum and she wanted to enjoy every precious minute. To have been so close to losing her had been terrifying, and getting her well could not be rushed. These small triumphs were encouraging.

'How is Harry?' Grace said, when her breath had steadied. 'I thought he was going to visit this weekend?'

'I told him not to. We all need the rest – including Harry.' It was hard to take in that it was only a week ago that Jessie had taken the decision to bring them all here. One long week that had left her struggling with her conscience.

Grace was thoughtful. 'It's good to be up and about.' Jessie was pleased to see that her eyes had regained some of their light. Grace smiled. 'Well, do you think we can make a life for ourselves here, Jessie?'

She leaned back on the bench. Couples walked past and a young man pecked his girlfriend on the cheek; she tucked her arm tighter into his and they walked down the hill together. If only Harry were here. His reply had been curt; he was hurt but she knew it was the most sensible decision. She was trying so hard to think before leaping head first into anything. A klaxon sounded and a charabanc rushed past, bursting with children who were squealing with delight.

'I don't see why not. It's as good a place as any.' It was better than most places they had been to.

'It couldn't have worked out better, darling. I just wish it hadn't had to be this way. But ...' she paused. 'If it had been left to me, we would still be with Iris and Norman.'

'Would that be a bad thing?' Jessie shielded her eyes, looking up to the sky as a plane soared above them leaving white trails in the blue.

Grace frowned. 'Don't say you're having second thoughts.'

Jessie shook her head. 'No, never. I will never go back.' And she knew she wouldn't – no matter how hard she had to struggle, she would not go back to wither and die. Better to try and fail. 'But it was hardly fair on you, or Eddie.'

Grace pulled at Jessie's arm. 'Whatever you think, Jessie, the reality was we didn't fit in. We're used to a different way of life – and do you know what?' She leaned towards Jessie and whispered, 'I rather like it. Don't you?'

Jessie grinned. 'Why don't you sit here, and I'll get us an ice cream.'

Grace patted her hand. 'Sounds quite perfect.'

Grace watched Jessie walk down the path between the flower beds toward the kiosk by the waterfall. Her limbs were tired but there was no rush; she knew Jessie would sit on the bench all day if Grace wanted her to. And if she couldn't walk, Jessie would find a way to get her home. She tipped back her head, closed her eyes and pictured Eddie walking around the links course further down the road, carrying a golf bag on his shoulder, wiping the club heads with a towel before putting them away. Both her children were resourceful, and she was thankful that they could fend for themselves and come up with solutions.

It had been more than she'd been able to do. When Davey had died she'd wanted to let go of a life that she was tied to by the slenderest of threads. It was Eddie and Jessie who helped her cling on. She'd felt her heart torn from her body. After nursing him she had been left with nothing. No money, no energy, no spirit. All the hopes and dreams for the future had died with him. A future where they would grow old together. A song came to mind, about growing too old to dream, that she would still have him to remember. He would be so proud of Jessie, and Eddie too. Tears sprang to her eyes and she felt them run down her cheeks.

'Are you all right, Mum?'

Jessie stood before her, holding two cornets, silhouetted against the sun, which lit her glorious hair. Her beloved child. Their child.

Grace swallowed her sadness away, and held out her hand for the ice cream. 'I looked into the sun. Stupid of me.' She wasn't certain that Jessie believed her, but she said nothing, and the two of them sat quietly, enjoying the treat. When they'd finished Jessie handed over her handkerchief for Grace to wipe her hands on.

'Was Miss Symonds right after all?' Jessie tilted her head; such a serious little face, Grace thought. 'More for laughter or for tears?' She jiggled the handkerchief. Jessie took it from her, wiping her own hands.

'Happy tears – and sticky hands.' Jessie's eyes glittered with happiness and Grace felt her heart swell in her chest.

'I'm pleased. Let's hope it stays that way.' She put out her hand and Jessie took it, helping her to her feet. 'Shall we go a little further?'

'Can you manage? I don't want you to overdo it.'

Grace smiled. 'There's no danger of that with you and Geraldine hovering over me like wasps on a jam jar. Come on, darling, let's enjoy a little more sunshine. I feel so much better for it.'

It was good to be with people again, feeling part of life instead of holed away in a house that held not a whisper of happiness within it. It wasn't good for either Eddie or Jessie to expect so little from life. They deserved so much more, and Grace was sure that here, in this lively little resort, they would be certain to find it.

Later, when they had arrived back home, Jessie helped her mum off with her jacket.

'Have you heard from Bernie?' Grace asked her.

'He said he's hoping to make it in a couple of weeks or so. I want to be ready when he comes. I know he'll give me a chance because of Dad, and you, of course.' She left the room briefly to hang Grace's jacket on the hall stand. 'I don't want a leg up out of pity, though. I want it because I'm good.'

Grace lifted her needlework from her chair and sat down. 'You are good. No. You're wonderful.' She shook her head. 'All the old insecurities. Your dad was the same. You must never let the doubts get the better of you.'

Jessie put a light blanket over her mum's legs. The weather was warm, but Grace still felt the cold.

'Will you be all right if I leave you? I said I'd meet Dolly at the Empire. Frances said she'd join us later.' She picked up the song list that the two of them had worked on in the middle of the week. 'I want to start working on my act and Dolly has a good eye for these things; she's seen so many shows.'

'Only you will know what works, Jessie.' Grace said. 'It's in you, as it was in your dad. Instinct. Don't keep her waiting.'

Dolly was sat on the low wall outside her house when Jessie turned down the street. She sprang to her feet when she saw Jessie and hurried towards her.

'The box office is still open so we can get in at the front.' She sped up to Jessie's pace.

'Thanks for coming with me, Dolly. I wanted an impartial eye, someone with experience.'

Dolly put on her sunglasses. 'I'll gladly help, Jessie. But I'm no expert.'

Jessie nudged her. 'Don't be daft. How many shows have you see over the last few years? Hundreds, I'll bet.'

'Yes, but I only know what I like.'

Jessie pulled on the heavy glass entrance door of the Empire. 'That's good enough for me.'

Dolly hung back to have a quick word with June in the box office while Jessie went into the theatre and onto the stage. The working lights were on and the safety curtain lifted. Mike was cutting some new gels for the lamps at the back of the stage.

'Don't you ever go home, Mike?'

He grinned. 'The wife's got all her sisters round our place. A man can only take so much, and the pubs are shut. Might as well be here, catching up. Save me time tomorrow.'

She heard the doors open at the back and Dolly came up to join them. 'I've come to rehearse, if that's okay with you, Mike. We won't get in your way.'

He waved a hand. 'You won't know I'm here. Fill your boots.'

The girls grinned at each other. 'What do you want me to do?' Dolly asked, splaying her hands.

'I'm not really sure, Dolly. I'm just playing around with ideas at the moment. I haven't got anyone to accompany me, so I'll just sing a couple of songs and try and incorporate a few dance steps; well, sort of movements, I suppose.' She sighed. 'Really, I'm just making it up as I go along, but if you toss me a few ideas, and tell me what you think, it gives me something to work with.'

Dolly nodded and went to sit on the side of the stage while Jessie walked off to the wings and began to speak aloud her thoughts. 'The intro will play, da da da de dah and so on and I'll walk out like this ...' She walked to centre stage. 'Then I'll sing.' She began to move about the stage as she sang, trying to take in the invisible audience, moving her arms to the music in her head, remembering to use a variety of facial expressions, give some emotion. It was hard without the music, but she could keep good time without it. Dolly was smiling throughout, yet it all felt a bit of a muddle. Amateurish. She longed for her dad to be here. It felt so wrong without

411

him. She glanced up into the flys, the ropes that held the cloths dangling above her in semi-darkness. What she did had to be top-notch for Bernie. She wanted the top-paying theatres. Could she hope for the number three circuit and build her way up to the number ones – The Hippodromes and Palaces in all the cities? Bernie had the connections but was she setting her sights too high?

When she looked across into the auditorium, the doors at the back opened once more and Billy walked in, plonking himself down in the middle row. He didn't speak but watched them. Jessie went through another song, trying to ignore the fact that he was there. She sat next to Dolly, stage right and went back to her list. 'So, "Always" there, and should I follow it with "Tea for Two", do you think?'

Billy bounced up on stage, his heels clicking on the boards. 'Can I be blunt, girls?'

Jessie looked up at him. He was going to give his opinion whether she wanted it or not. She may as well listen; he'd been around a bit after all – and he was a professional. She nodded.

'"Always" would be all right, I suppose, but some of the others are old hat. You're better than that and your audience deserves better, Jessie Delaney. Think top of the bill. You're playing too small. It has to be big – you have to reach out to the back, and you're aiming for the middle. It won't get you anywhere.'

'What do you suggest then, oh great one?' She was irritated, still angry from the other night with Eddie.

He smirked. 'I'll take that as a compliment. Afternoon, Dolly.' Dolly flashed him a sweet smile and Jessie had to smile too.

'You're young, Jessie. What you need is something fresh and lively. When I was in the West End ...'

Dolly gasped. 'You weren't?'

'Course I was.' He swaggered a little, hand in one pocket, bending his knee, leaning forward to them. 'Anyway, when I was in the West End, I went to scc *Wild Oats, These Foolish Things ... The Dancing Years.*' He paused for them to be suitably impressed, but they were anyway, so he needn't have bothered. 'I had a mate in the chorus who got me backstage. I got to see a lot of the big stars working, met a lot of them. Lupino Lane, Noël, Gertie.'

'You don't mean Noël Coward and Gertie Lawrence?' Dolly's eyes grew rounder; she sat up, moving her hand so her arm was straighter as well as her back. She was hanging onto Billy's every word. Jessie had an inkling that his mate was 'female'.

'They're the kind of songs you need. Songs that bring the West End to the Empire while you're waiting for the real thing. You want some of that, don't you, Jessie?'

She nodded, and he laughed. 'So do I.' He studied his fingernails. 'Wanna know something else?' He paused, and the girls waited. 'These big stars? They're ordinary, just like me and you, Jessie. No different. Probably less talented, some of them. Especially where you are concerned; me, not so much.' She tried to protest but he held up his hand to stop her.

Dolly's grin got wider.

'Hear me out, sweet cheeks. It's down to luck. That's all it is. And you make your own luck in this business by getting the right songs, the right dress, the right jokes. Even the right name. It's being ready for when that lucky day comes along and making sure you're there—' he pointed forcefully to the floor '—smack in the middle so that everyone can see you.'

Dolly rubbed at Jessie's shoulder. 'You've got to be ready for that lucky day, Jessie. You've got what it takes.'

Jessie touched her friend's hand, got to her feet, brushed the dust from the back of her skirt. 'What songs do you suggest, Billy?'

He walked across and put his hand around her shoulder. 'You and me are going places, girl. I can see your name in lights.' He drew his hand across the air in front of them. 'Starring Jessie Delaney and Billy Lane. Can you see it?' He twisted to look at Dolly who clapped her hands in delight.

'Course I can. Jessie's going to be a star!'

Chapter 30

Harry put the last of the boxes in Grace's room. It had been a relief to see her looking well and vibrant; she was still very thin but so obviously happy. The bed was neatly made, a grey paisley coverlet over it, and the armchair that he'd taken upstairs when they first came was now back by the window. It was cosy and comfortable, and far more suited to her than the heavy darkness of The Beeches. Grace had immediately busied herself rummaging through the boxes until she found what she had been looking for. The photographs of her husband, her brothers, her parents. A picture of Jessie and Eddie when they were children. One photograph of her husband in his evening suit, posed with his violin, one at the piano. She chatted as she took them from the newspaper wrapped around them that shouted of Hitler and Russia and calls for volunteers for the ARP.

'These I have missed most of all, Harry,' She polished them with her sleeve, placing them on the cabinet that was tucked snugly to one side of the chimney breast.

Nelly, under Iris's instruction, had completed most of the packing by the time he arrived so there had been very little for him to do other than put things into the car. Iris had kept well out of the way, Nelly chuntering on about how they were well rid of the old witch.

'They look lovely there, Grace. The finishing touch.' She settled in the armchair and motioned for him to do the same. Harry put his glass on the table, hitched up his trousers by the knees and sat down. 'Norman sent his best wishes and said that he and Iris will come visit soon. They plan to bring Eddie's bike.'

'That's very kind of them.' Grace said, looking across at her photographs. He'd been glad he was able to bring them.

There was a gentle rap on the door and Geraldine stuck her head around it. 'Evening, Harry. How long have we got?'

Harry checked his watch. 'Ten minutes, fifteen? It depends how long you want to be sat in the stalls before the show starts.'

'Let's make it ten. I'd rather we had plenty of time.' She disappeared upstairs.

'Have you seen Jessie yet?' Grace asked. 'Or Eddie? I would think he's already mooching about down there.'

'I saw Eddie outside George and Olive's. They offered me a bed for the weekend when they knew I was coming. It's incredibly kind of them, and far nicer than staying at the boarding house on the hill. Jessie only briefly; she had to get ready.' They'd snatched a kiss and held each other before she'd had to dash back to her dressing room. It was enough to sustain him until the show was over.

Harry took a mouthful of his drink. It felt good after the long drive to be here again, although it was sobering to realise that he was now firmly on the edges of their lives and not part of it. He felt sorry for Norman. He must miss Eddie, Harry knew he thought a lot of him. They had a grand time when he caddied or took him out on his boat. He'd treated him like a son. Harry was certain that if Iris had been a little less overbearing, Jessie would have settled down to life there, if only for the sake of her mum and Eddie. It had been a good life for them all but none of them were happy, he could see that now. Grace looked like a different woman. Possibly the woman Jessie remembered but that Harry had never got to know.

They heard Geraldine hurry down the stairs, and Harry took Grace's hand and helped her to her feet. He held out her jacket while she slipped it on, and she put on her hat in front of the mirror that hung over the fireplace. Geraldine came into the room. 'Ready?'

'We are,' said Grace, taking Harry's arm. They followed her into the street and while she locked up, Grace got into the car. It was no distance to walk but Grace was still recovering, and the drive would be beneficial at the end of the night if not at the start.

'What have you been up since we saw you last, Harry?' Geraldine asked from the back seat.

Harry looked at her through his mirror. 'I signed up to the RAF. I've been accepted.'

Grace took a sharp breath.

'Well done, young man.' Geraldine patted him on the back. 'They don't take just anybody.'

'Must have made a mistake over me then.' Grace's silence was making him uncomfortable.

'And Norman?' Grace asked, after a pause. 'It must have been quite a blow for him?'

'Almost as if he had half expected it. Sooner or later anyway.' Which was true. Norman wasn't being defeatist by any means, but he was planning ahead. 'He's already advertised for a new clerk, and old Mr Cole is going to do what he can.'

'Good heavens, I thought he'd washed his hands of it all. He was a broken man when ...' She paused. 'No doubt retirement didn't suit him.' She paused again. 'How did Jessie take it?'

'I haven't had chance to tell her.' He looked at her as they waited at the junction ready to turn left. 'How do you think she'll take it?'

Grace stared straight ahead. 'She'll be upset. She'll be worried.' She touched his arm as he held the steering wheel. 'We all will be, Harry. It's all right while she imagines you waiting for her in Cole's, but if you're not there, well ...'

There was no way Grace could make him feel any better. He'd dreaded telling Jessie but if her mum could help him to soften the blow, it might help. He sighed. 'I haven't a clue where to start, Grace. What would you say is the best way to tell her?'

Grace shrugged her shoulders. 'You'll find a way, Harry. Just do what your heart tells you to do.'

Eddie stuck his head around the dressing-room door and the girls chorused, 'Hello'. He grinned, blushing. 'Harry's on his way, Jessie. He's gone to pick up Mum and Geraldine. I'll see them out front.' He looked at the posy of violets in the tumbler by her mirror. 'Oh, I see he's already been. I should have known.' He was gone again.

'Getting quite the regular, your little brother,' Rita said, pushing her feet into her shoes. 'Do you think he'll go into the business as well?'

'Not a chance,' Jessie replied, knowing he never would. 'Not enough engines.'

'You'd hardly think so the amount of time he spends with Billy,' Virginia said. She'd been quiet tonight; the girls had commented on it. She'd brushed it off with mutterings of a headache. 'If it isn't him, it's you,' she snapped.

'Virginia, that's hardly fair. I don't see Billy other than at the theatre and Eddie's just happy to have another man to talk to. He misses Harry. You'll have Billy all to yourself this weekend.'

Virginia sneered. 'I doubt it.'

Frances shook her head. 'Quit feeling sorry for yourself, Ginny.' She peered at Virginia through her mirror, then twisted in her chair. 'What's wrong with your lip?'

Jessie saw that it was swollen; she hadn't noticed earlier. Frances didn't miss a thing. Virginia had tried to disguise it with make-up but close up it was clear it had been bruised – as was her arm.

Ginny dismissed it. 'It's nothing. Billy gets carried away sometimes, holding me too tight, kissing me too hard.' Her neck had reddened, and she bent forward, looking for something under the table that wasn't there.

Jessie was appalled. 'Love shouldn't hurt, Virginia.'

'Oh, but it does,' Frances said. 'It frequently does.'

Virginia looked at Frances and Jessie caught an unspoken understanding flash between them. She turned back to the mirror. She was certain Harry would never hurt her – and if he did their love would be over.

Rita stood up and put one foot on her chair, checked her wet white leg make-up for smears, tilting her leg this way and that, scrutinising, and then checking the other. She adjusted her breasts in her blouse, pushing them forward and out, checked her bottom in the mirror. 'Right, that's me done. On stage, girls. And, Virginia, eyes and teeth, eyes and teeth. The punters haven't come out at the end of the week to watch you sulk.'

Jessie felt sorry for her, but nothing could spoil tonight. Grace would see her routine for the first time, Harry was out front, and word had come that Bernie would arrive at some point too. More than likely it would be Sunday afternoon. He had acts appearing in Filey and Scarborough, and was working his way down the coast. She had been practising the songs that she'd chosen with Billy. It was all gradually coming together.

'Come on, Virginia.' Jessie smiled. 'Let's go up together.' She waited while the girl got to her feet then followed her up to the stage. She could afford to let things go. She had everything, didn't she, and Virginia must be feeling lonely. She mustn't make her feel worse.

When the curtain came down, the cast raced off the stage. Some would go home for what was left of the weekend but most of them were staying. Those who were would find their way into the theatre bar. Virginia was taking her time, Frances was ready. Rita was going out to a club with the trumpet player, Phil having been given the elbow. 'He's such a good kisser, girls. Such a lovely embouchure.' She played an invisible trumpet and they all started giggling.

'Ooh, get you.' Kay laughed. 'What's that when it's at home.'

'The way he puts his lips together to blow, honey child.' Everyone laughed. Virginia remained stony-faced.

'Coming to the bar, Ginny?' Jessie didn't want to think of the girl being alone. She was happy and she wanted to share it. Frances raised her eyebrows.

'Later,' she said, her voice flat. She leaned back into the mirror and wiped her face with a clean rag. Frances pushed Jessie's shoulder. 'Get out there, girl. You've kept Harry waiting long enough.'

Harry was standing at the bar getting drinks for Grace and Geraldine, looking alternately at the door that led into the theatre and the one that led onto the street. Wally and Phil came in together, and he checked as anyone entered the room. He saw Frances's dark hair and eyes and then, behind her, Jessie. She eased between the crowd to get to him. Her face was alight with happiness and he hoped it was especially for him. She squeezed next to him as Frances went over to say hello to Grace.

'Did you enjoy the show?' She kissed his cheek.

'Every minute of it, but you were the best.'

She hugged his arm. 'I bet you were bored rigid.'

'Never, not as far as you're concerned – everyone else in the show ...?' He tilted the flat of his hand back and forth. 'Maybe.' She gave his arm a playful punch and he pretended it hurt. 'What shall I get you, half a stout? Same for Frances?'

'You remembered.' Her eyes shined with mischief and she snuggled closer. He could smell her scent. She was looking around again.

'Who's missing?' Was she searching for Billy?

'Eddie.' She waved. 'Oh, there he is.'

Eddie walked in behind Billy who put up a hand in hello to Harry and made straight for him. Harry's heart sank.

'Get us a pint, chum, and a shandy for Eddie. I'll get the next round.' He grinned at Jessie. 'How's my gorgeous singing partner? Good night tonight, wasn't it? We had the audience all the way.' He put his arm around Jessie, and Harry felt the muscle in his jaw tighten. He forced himself to smile. Jessie was glowing. 'She makes it so easy for me. The audience is warmed up when I go on to do my patter because this girl makes them so happy.' He hugged her to him again and Harry bit the inside of his cheek.

'Such a smooth talker and I don't believe a word of it,' Jessie said, as Harry handed her drinks for Geraldine and Grace. 'Take these. I'll bring the rest.'

Jessie took the glasses and wriggled through to where Grace and Geraldine were seated near the piano.

Arthur came and stood next to Harry in the gap left by Jessie and the crush at the bar eased as people were served, trying to get a drink in before time was called. 'Hello, son. Nice to see you back again.' He ordered his drink and quietly waited to be served. The barmaids were pulling pumps and Vera placed a pint in front of him with froth dripping down the side. Arthur ran his finger down the glass.

'How's Virginia, Billy?' Harry asked. 'I don't see her here.' He didn't want to be polite and ask him to join them.

'Ginny. She's fine. I used to call her Virgin for short, but not for long eh, Eddie?' The boy laughed and Harry felt his jaw tighten.

Arthur made a clicking noise with his tongue, took his pint and went to talk to a man Harry vaguely remembered as being in the band. Billy handed Eddie his shandy, while Harry handed over a ten-bob note.

'She's a nice enough girl, not a patch on Jessie though. Girls like Jessie don't come along every day, but you know that, Harry. She's a girl in a million. She's got everything, the whole package: looks, talent, and a genuinely lovely girl. The kind of girl you'd like to marry.'

Harry sipped his beer. Eddie shuffled his feet.

Billy didn't let up. 'Don't you worry about her being away from you? I would.' He looked at Harry while he took a swig from his glass.

Harry smiled. It wasn't worth an answer and he wasn't going to be goaded by a smart alec, tuppenny comic like Billy.

'Let's go and sit with the ladies, Eddie.' He put a hand on the lad's back and guided him to where Jessie was sitting with her mum. The women moved closer to make space for Eddie, and Harry stood behind Jessie. He touched her shoulder and she turned to look up at him, smiling, tipping her head slightly so that she touched him. He relaxed a little.

'Bernie will be here tomorrow.' Jessie couldn't contain her excitement. 'I was telling Geraldine the choice of songs I've put together for an act. My own act, Harry. I'll get my own billing.' Grace looked at Harry. He smiled, trying to be enthusiastic but Billy's words had unsettled him. And that had been the bastard's intention, hadn't it? He took another mouthful of beer. Billy was still at the bar, leaning with his back to it. He held up his pint in a toast and Harry dipped his head in reply.

'Get on the piano and play them, Jess,' Eddie said. 'I haven't heard you play for ages. Mum hasn't either.'

Grace laughed. 'Leave your sister alone. She's done performing for the day.'

'But a sing-song would be lovely,' Geraldine said.

It was all the encouragement Jessie needed, and she made her way to the piano and lifted the lid. The bar had emptied somewhat, and Harry had a clear view of her as she began to play. He sat down in her empty seat.

She began with 'On Mother Kelly's Doorstep', and a few of the customers began to sing, whether they could hold a tune or not. They began shouting out things for her to play, and Harry watched as she went from one old favourite to another. The room was in full voice when the door from the theatre opened and Madeleine Moore entered. She gave a small wave and a large smile to Grace and stood in the doorway watching Jessie play, nodding her approval. She came towards Grace and Frances, and Harry got to his feet.

'What can I get you to drink, Miss Moore?'

Her smile was quite disarming. 'Please call me Maddy. That's very sweet of you. A sherry would be perfect.'

He offered her his seat and went up to get her drink.

Billy was still at the bar, but his eyes were on Jessie. Harry leaned on the counter. Vera was giving it a brisk wipe with a cloth. 'I'll get these,' Billy said, turning his neck to Harry. 'My round.'

'No need,' Harry said.

Billy took another quaff of ale; Harry could see the grin he was not even trying to hide. He turned away from him, looking into the mirror that ran along the back of the bar.

'What can I get you, lovey?' Vera slapped the cloth on the counter.

Harry ordered a drink for himself and one for Madeleine and went back the others. As he did so, Billy moved to the piano. Jessie was playing 'It's a Long Way to Tipperary' and he whispered something into her ear. Harry saw Jessie throw her head back and laugh. He gritted his teeth. Grace looked at him and smiled reassuringly but it was no comfort. He was powerless to do anything at all but watch Billy wind him up. Billy leaned on the piano facing into the room and began to sing. Grace patted Harry's arm. Virginia came into the bar and Harry thought he would at least stop and get the girl a drink, but he merely put up a hand in greeting. She leaned to his ear and said something. He shook his head, pulled some cash from his pocket and gave it to her, slapping her on the bottom when she turned. She stood watching him while she waited for her drink, glancing at Harry.

Frances got up and went over to the piano, flashed the most enormous smile at Billy, then joined him singing 'Side by Side'. Billy didn't appreciate the competition. Frances winked at their table and Grace blew her a kiss. Eddie got up to join his sister.

Madeleine moved closer to Harry. 'Loathsome little man, isn't he?'

He nodded. 'I thought it was just me.'

'Not at all. The theatre has plenty of chancers like Mr Billy Lane. God, I even married one of them, so I know from bitter experience.'

He twisted to look at her. She was quite beautifully made up, and even though she was smiling at him there was a sadness about her eyes.

'Jessie's not a silly girl,' she said. 'She will see through Billy.'

'But she hasn't yet.'

'She will.' Madeleine sipped at her sherry and they watched as Billy got side-lined by Frances and Eddie. Grace and Madeleine grinned to each other.

'And if she doesn't? Will she learn from bitter experience too? I'm not here every day and he is.' It all seemed so pointless. A battle he couldn't win. Why couldn't Jessie see what tricks Billy was playing?

'But we are, Harry.'

It wasn't the solace it once would have been. Jessie was strong-willed; when she wanted something, she set out to get it. If only she had wanted him with such ferocity.

At the end of the night, people started to drift away; Jessie came and sat beside him, and Billy left with Virginia. Harry elected to take Grace and Geraldine home in the car. Frances was going to walk home with Eddie, but they would stay with Jessie until Harry came back. He was glad that Frances had an inkling of his unease. He parked his car in Dolphin Street outside George's house and went to get Jessie. The three of them were standing under the canopy outside the Empire. The bar was closed, the lights off. Jessie walked towards him and Frances and Eddie waved goodnight and made their way up the hill towards the Cliff Hotel. Jessie's face was shining, and he was thrilled to have her to himself at last.

'Care to promenade, Mr Newman?' Her hands were behind her back and she rolled back and forth on her heels.

He pulled at his chin with his hand. 'Hmm. Young girl out on her own? Late at night?'

She ran to him laughing. He held her and kissed her until someone called 'Oi, oi.' They pulled away from each other and saw a couple coming towards them. The woman gave the man a friendly slap on the arm.

'Leave 'em alone, Stan,' she said. 'We was like that once.' She tucked her arm into his as they strolled by.

'That long ago I can't remember, lad.'

The wife laughed and gave him another wallop, harder this time, but they cuddled closer and he pecked her cheek. Jessie watched them make their way over the road.

'I hope we grow old like that, Harry.'

'Less of the old, you cheeky blighter,' the man called over his shoulder and the pair of them giggled.

Harry loved her, how he loved her. How fragile they were, held together by the finest of threads that men like Billy took fun in snapping – like boys at school who gained pleasure from ripping apart butterfly wings.

He put his arm about her and they walked down towards the pier, along the planks, looking at the sea wash below them, the gentle hush as it rushed along the sand. Fishermen dropped lines along the end of the pier and leaned on the rail watching the trawlers move up and down the estuary. George had told him that many of the trawlers had already been bought by the admiralty for conversion to minesweepers. How long would men be able to fish?

'Sometimes it feels like we're at the end of the world, standing here. When it's dark and you can't see the other side of land.'

'Maybe we are,' Harry said.

'Don't say that, Harry. It's morose.'

He sighed. 'I was agreeing with you. It could be the end of the world as we know it.'

'That's a bit deep.' She turned to him. 'You're rather maudlin tonight, Harry.'

He shrugged. The pair of them stood in silence watching as a lanky man threw his line over the pier and leaned back and lit a fag. Harry did the same, blowing his smoke out over the sea.

'Jessie.' What was the best way to tell her? Now, when she thought it was the end of the world? Only hours ago he'd felt exactly the same. Jessie was his world and she was slipping away from him, a fish caught on a line – and Billy standing there with a hook in his hand. Grinning. He couldn't get him out of his head. The smugness.

She held onto the railings and leaned back. He looked out into the blackness. It was now or never.

'This could be the last weekend I get to be here with you.'

She pulled herself back, and let go of the rails. He drew on his cigarette. 'I signed up for the RAF. I've been accepted for training. I report on Monday morning at o-eight hundred hours.' The smile left her face and she stared at him, opening her mouth then closing it again.

'Aren't you going to say congratulations?'

She shook her head. 'And be happy that you're going to do something so dangerous?'

He shrugged and looked away from her. Along the promenade there were still lights showing on the station, carriages pulling away, steam billowing.

'I was happy for you, Jess, when you wanted to live your dream.'

'But my dream's not dangerous.'

'That's a matter of opinion.'

She spun on her heel. 'What's that supposed to mean?'

The lanky man shushed them then called in a loud whisper, 'Keep it down, you two; you're gonna frighten the fish.'

She walked away, hurrying down the pier and he ran after her, throwing his cigarette into the sea. He walked beside her, and she said again, 'What did you mean, Harry?'

He paused, mulling over what to say to explain himself but then there was Billy's grin looming up at him again.

'Billy. Billy's the danger and you just can't see it, can you? Everyone else can but not you, Jessie.' It sounded so cruel. Why didn't he just keep his mouth shut and wait, like Grace had said, like Miss Symonds had said, but he couldn't bear to wait. He couldn't just stand by and lose her, not to a louse like Billy Lane.

She balled her fists. 'That's because there's nothing to see.'

'If that's what you think.' He stood his ground.

'Harry?' She put her hands to her face, shaking her head in disbelief. Well, he had to fight, didn't he? Because he couldn't just stand by and watch her make a fool of herself. For Billy to toy about with her like he had with Virginia. That poor girl was besotted with him, and he treated her so shamefully, and he knew he would move in on Jessie as soon as he could. She was like a fish on his line wriggling about and he didn't want her to get caught and be tossed back into the sea.

'Jessie, I love you with all my heart. Tomorrow I'll be gone. I don't know when we'll see each other again. It might very well be the end of the world, our world. But I at least wanted to fight for you.'

Tears ran down her cheeks and she brushed them away with her hand.

'How could you do this, Harry?'

'Because I can't stand by and do nothing any more.' She marched off and he ran after her, pulling at her arm. She wriggled and tried to pull away.

'Jessie, I could wait to be called up, like I've waited for you and end up with something I don't want. I want to choose my own fate, just like you have done. The longer I wait the further you drift away.'

'I have done no such thing.'

'You have. Everyone you love is here. You won't ever go back to The Beeches, you said so yourself. Where does that leave me?'

'Not everyone I love is here.' She pulled away from him. 'But what does it matter now? You decided without me.'

She ran off down the pier, her footsteps on the wooden walkway sounding hollow in the still of the night.

Grace heard the front door open and relaxed. Jessie was home but there was no sound of voices. No Harry. She heard movement in the room next door and, pulling on her dressing gown, went to check that everything was all right. Her daughter was slumped at the table, her tear-stained face grubby, her eyes swollen. So, Harry had told her.

'What happened?'

'As if you didn't know. Harry told you, didn't he, and Geraldine too? He told everyone before he told me.' She knew as she said it that she was being childish. Hadn't she done the very same to him? And yet this was somehow different. His life was in danger. She couldn't bear to lose him.

Grace filled the kettle and lit the gas. 'Out of necessity, Jessie. He didn't want to tell you before the show. It's all down to timing.' She smiled gently and touched Jessie's head. 'Your dad always said everything was down to timing.'

'Well, he got it wrong.' Her voice wobbled. 'He got so many things wrong, Mum.' She shook her head and looked up at the ceiling, fat tears rolling down her cheeks.

'Tell me, sweetheart.' Grace pulled out a chair and sat down as close as she could.

'He was horrible. He thought I couldn't see what Billy was up to, but I could, of course I could. But what can I do about it? It's not my fault he likes me.' Her eyes were wide, and Grace took her in her arms, holding her as tightly as she could, rubbing her back as she'd done when she was a small child.

'Billy was goading him all night.' She kissed Jessie's head. 'We saw him. It was obvious, but he did it when you weren't aware of it.'

Jessie pulled away. 'We?'

Grace could have bit off her tongue.

Jessie rubbed at her face with the back of her hand.

God, that man had a lot to answer for, Grace thought. She had to choose her words carefully.

'Why blame Billy?' Jessie asked. 'It was Harry who behaved badly.'

'I'm not blaming him, Jessie. I'm telling you what happened. Madeleine tried to reassure Harry but ...'

'I can't believe you're taking Madeleine's side? She cut my song. It was Billy who made sure I got a chance. Billy.' She almost spat the words out, snot running down her nose. Jessie wiped it away with the back of her hand.

Grace reached out, stroking her hair, sweeping it away from Jessie's face, which was becoming puffy with tears.

'For his own ends, Jessie. For selfish reasons.'

'Didn't Madeleine cut my song for selfish reasons?'

Grace pulled Jessie towards her again and was relieved that Jessie let her, sinking back into her arms. Oh, to spare the child pain. There had been too much of it already. 'Darling girl, there's so much to learn. Madeleine wasn't being selfish; she was being professional. She is the star of the show. It's hard getting to the top, harder still to remain there. These are the things you will learn. Harry is good for you. He gives you wings. You'll work things out.'

'Harry was jealous.' Jessie was snivelling now. It didn't suit her. Grace was gentle, stroking her hair, over and over, soothing, cooing, her voice soft in the night.

'Harry is not that kind of man.'

Jessie was petulant. 'He was tonight.'

Grace sat more upright, griping Jessie by the arms. 'Be careful, Jessie,' she warned. 'This is exactly what Billy wants to happen. To divide you and Harry.' She sighed and got up to attend to the kettle that was on the verge of shrieking. 'It looks like he's succeeded.'

Grace made Jessie a sweet tea and the two of them sat quietly until Jessie was calmer. Crying would have tired her out. Grace got up and took the mug from her. 'Off to bed. You can talk it over with Harry in the morning. You don't want him going off to training with this between you.'

'I don't want him going off at all. Oh, Mum. What if there is war?'

She put her arm around her and held her close. 'There will be war, Jessie. There is no *if* any more. Only timing.' Davey's words again. Timing. She'd prayed with all her heart that there wouldn't be war, that her children would never have to suffer the heartache of loss, and the piteous sight of the tragic walking wounded that came home. And not to the better life they were promised. She didn't want Harry to be old before his time, for Jessie to suffer the heartache of losing him. Not now, nor ever.

Chapter 31

Jessie didn't know why she'd bothered going to bed. She hadn't slept, fearful that Harry would never forgive her.

She sat up and clasped her knees. Harry's picture was on the small bedside table and she reached for it. 'Oh, Harry. I love you so much.' She held it close to her heart. They must sort this out if he wasn't coming back until he got leave, and when in heaven's name would that be? She hadn't given him a chance, and she needed to make him see that there was nothing to worry about.

She left the photo on the bed, threw off the blankets, dressed and hurried outside. The pavement was wet and grey clouds swept overhead. She ran all the way, the rain splattering her hair to her face and she pushed it back not caring what she looked like. A paper boy was out on his bike posting the Sunday papers, whistling as he went, and she felt a little better for someone else's cheer. It was only seven and she slowed as she reached Dolphin Street before realising that Olive would be up, no matter what. She knocked on the door, and searched the street. There was no sign of Harry's Austin. Her heart was beating wildly as she waited, afraid to knock again, then footsteps, the tap of a stick.

'Hello, lovey.' Olive opened the door wide. 'Come in, come in, you'll catch your death.' She led the way through the short hall and Jessie followed.

'I'm sorry, it's so early,' she said, softly. 'I wanted to see Harry. Is he up?'

George came into the back room and she could tell by his face that she was too late.

'He left, Jessie dear. You've only just missed him. He said he had to report to his station tomorrow, early like. He wanted to get a good night's sleep.'

The breath left her body and she steadied herself, forcing a smile that didn't want to sit on her face. She nodded; of course he'd left. 'He's signed up. I was unkind.'

'It must have been a shock. You'll be worried. He's a fine young man.' George moved towards her and took her arm. 'Sit down, lass. You're white as a sheet.'

'No, I'm fine.' She wouldn't cry, not here. Olive and George had been kind enough already and she didn't want to weep and make them feel awkward. It was her own stupid fault. She should've come earlier. She should never have run off. She smiled as best she could, her voice trembling. 'I'll speak to him later. I'll call.' She turned her back and walked as steadily as she could out of the house, the sadness on their faces burning in her head.

Grace was at the window when she got back, and she went straight into her mum's room. She was drenched through and Grace picked up a towel, telling her to get out of her clothes. She did as she was told, a child again, as Grace wrapped her in the towel, pushed her into a chair and put a blanket over her.

'Oh, Jessie. What on earth happened?'

She looked up and Grace stared at her with pity.

'He's gone. I was too late.' Her face crumpled and she sobbed, great racking sobs that made her body heave.

'Oh, my darling, darling girl.' She sat down on the bed next to her, caught her hand and cradled it in both of hers. 'He'll be back.'

Jessie shook her head. 'He won't though, will he? Oh, Mum, what have I done? I've lost him.'

'Don't be silly,' Grace crooned, but Jessie could not be consoled.

'I might never see him again.' She leant her head on her mum's shoulder.

'You will. It's a lover's tiff. That's all. Your dad and I had them all the time.'

Geraldine peered around the door, her eyebrows raised in question. Grace shook her head. Geraldine's face fell and she left Grace to console her child.

'I wanted to make us safe,' Jessie sobbed. 'I thought I was so clever, didn't I? That I could have everything, all of us together, a career – and Harry.'

Grace held her tighter. 'No one gets everything, Jessie. You have to be certain that it is what you want. I loved your dad, I gave up my dancing to care for him and the two of you. I don't regret it at all. It can be such a lonely life. Look at George and Olive and what they have. That's something rare and true. Madeleine is alone. And Arthur.' She patted Jessie's leg. 'Look how

Bert and Hilda depended on each other? If you want the theatre and Harry, you'll find a way.' Grace stood up. 'Now, enough tears. You need to get dry and tidy yourself while I make breakfast. Bernie will be at the theatre shortly and you need to show him what you're made of.'

Bernie was already in the auditorium. They could tell by the smell of expensive cigar that washed over them when they opened the door to the stalls. He was standing with Jack and Grace was not surprised to see Billy there. The upright piano had been pulled mid-stage and Phil was leaning on the keyboard smoking a cigarette, waiting for instructions. Billy was hanging on Bernie's every word.

'Well, that man is determined to succeed one way or another,' Grace said, under her breath.

'There's nothing wrong with that is there, Mum? That's what I'm here for, after all?

Grace led the way along the back of the stalls. 'No, but it's how he uses people to get to the top. Remember that old saying of your dad's? It's nice to be important.'

'But it's more important to be nice,' Jessie finished.

'Yes, and when you're nice – you're important. It stood your dad in good stead. He may not have had a lot of money, but he had so much goodwill, so many friends. You'll get a lot of help and kindness from people like Bernie and Jack because of your dad. He was a good man. Like Harry.'

'You didn't need to say that, Mum. I know what an idiot I've been.'

Jack raised a hand in greeting and nudged Bernie's arm. The man beamed when he saw them, his round face a moon, and he stuck the cigar between his teeth to free his hands, walking towards them with outstretched arms. He was wearing a sharp navy-coloured pin-striped suit, a camel coat over his shoulders. His black hair was tinged with grey at the sides and his dark eyes creased with delight.

'Grace, good to see you.' He hugged her warmly then stepped back, smiling broadly. 'And Jessie.' He took hold of her hands, held her at arm's length. 'My, my ... such the young woman. And a star in the making, if I'm to believe Billy here.' He tapped his finger on his cheek, and she leaned forward and planted a kiss on it. 'Now then, what have you got to show your Uncle Bernie?'

Jessie took the sheet music from her bag and went up on stage presenting them to Phil, Grace watching her with a mixture of pride and anxiety, for the path she was taking would never be smooth.

Jack outstretched his arm and the two men waited for Grace to take her seat before taking theirs. Billy got in the row behind so that he could lean forward and take in the conversation. Grace tried not to react. It was pitiful really, how eager Billy was to leap at every opportunity, but this was her daughter's moment and Grace was going to make sure she got it. 'How's business, Bernie?'

'Wonderful, Gracie. Business is booming. All this talk of war is great for getting bums on seats. Every show I've got out there is packed to the rafters, night after night. We've never had it so good. People want to go out and forget. And I don't blame 'em. Most of us haven't got over the last one.'

'Some of us never will,' Grace said quietly.

'I'm sorry, Grace. I didn't mean to—'

She flapped a hand. 'Don't be daft, Bernie.'

He carried on. 'I've had to take on an assistant, and I've got three staff now. Got contracts coming out of my ears.' He nudged her arm. 'Not that I'm complaining, mind. Moving into wireless and television now that I've got the connections. That's very lucrative, I can tell you, and it beats slogging round theatres week in, week out. That's the way the game's going.'

'Wireless and television?' Billy interrupted. 'I like the sound of that, Bernie. Tell me more.'

'Always looking for good comedians, lad.' Bernie puffed on his cigar and leaned back as Jessie walked centre stage. 'When you're ready, darling',' Bernie called to her.

She turned to Phil who counted her in, then began to play. Jessie sang to the whole auditorium as if it was full to capacity. Her voice was pure and strong and Grace's heart soared. She had the talent and she had the tenacity, but was it what she wanted for her child? Would there be enough people looking out for her to keep her safe? The life was a good one, even better if you made it big, but it could be lonely. There were hangers on; there were the likes of Billy in every production, the chancers, the wastrels. She twisted to look at him. He was leaning so far forward he was almost at Bernie's ear. He was talking the whole time Jessie sang but she couldn't quite hear what was said. Bernie was nodding but he didn't take his eyes off Jessie.

The song came to an end and they applauded politely.

'Sing something a little melancholy, Jessie. Can you make an old man cry?'

Jessie turned to Phil who pulled another sheet of music to the front of the pile. Light came into the room as the door opened and Madeleine came down the aisle and quietly took a seat beside Grace. Jessie started to sing 'Danny Boy', so sweet, so wistful that, when she finished, Bernie got to his feet and applauded. He turned to Grace.

'Her father's daughter. What a talent she has, Grace. Something very special.' He nodded to Madeleine and put out his hand. 'Bernie Blackwood.'

'Madeleine Moore.'

He smiled, removing the cigar again. 'I was talking to Vernon LeRoy only last week. He said he was coming up to see you. Got you in the West End for a run of the new Noel Gay, hasn't he?'

Madeleine gave a graceful nod of her head. 'He has indeed.'

Bernie looked up at Jessie who was standing centre stage while all this was going on. 'Wonder what he'll make of this little lady.'

'I think he'll find her just wonderful, don't you?' Her smile was generous, and Grace was in no doubt that she was genuine. If Madeleine had caused Jessie problems, it was not for Grace to sort them out; it was important that she learned to do these things for herself.

'We all think she's damned wonderful, Bernie.' Billy was up on his feet now.

Bernie called up to the stage.

'That's great, Jessie. Get yourself down here.' He turned to Jack. 'Is there somewhere we can go and talk business? I need a quick word with Jessie and then we can talk about the future of the Empire, Jack. Are you hanging around, my boy?'

Billy's grin was so wide it was a wonder it didn't split his face. 'I'll get the drinks in,' he said, leading the way to the theatre bar.

Grace remained in her seat, as did Madeleine, and they waited while Bernie discussed business with Jessie. He put his arm about her shoulder and walked her back to Grace. 'Talk it over with your mum, Jessie, and let me know.' He shook Jessie's hand. 'I've plenty of work for a girl like you. Billy's right. You're going to be a big star. The biggest,' he said to Grace. 'Off to talk a bit of business with the boys, Grace. I'll see you again before I leave, will I?' She nodded. 'I think Jessie will make you proud.'

'She does that already,' Grace said.

Madeleine got to her feet. 'Would the two of you join me for lunch at the Dolphin Hotel? It would be so nice to have company.'

Jessie was putting her music back into her bag. 'That's really kind but—' She paused. 'I have a letter to write and I won't be good company today.' She had lost her sourness and Grace was relieved. Madeleine looked at Grace who responded with a smile.

'If the offer's still open, that would be lovely. Thank you.'

Jessie gathered her things and kissed her mum on the cheek. 'It's going to be a long letter.'

Grace touched her face. 'Best get off and get it started then, darling.' How she felt for her, torn between two loves, yet what could she do but be there to catch her if she should fall.

The three of them left the theatre together. The rain had stopped but the pavement was wet, water running into the gullies. The sun had broken through the clouds and, as Jessie turned right to go back to Barkhouse Lane, the two women turned left and made for the main entrance of the Dolphin Hotel.

Madeleine sat back as the waiter took her napkin from the table and placed it across her lap. As he left them, she said, 'I can't tell you how lovely it is to have someone to eat with.'

The restaurant was busy. They had been swiftly guided to a seat by the window. Heads had turned when Madeleine walked into the room and people had nodded their heads in recognition.

'How lovely to have you dine with us this afternoon, Miss Moore.' The maître d' couldn't hide his delight, and Grace acknowledged what a wonderful thing it was to light up people's faces with your presence. She hoped that Jessie would do the same one day. Life was hard

Tracy Baines

enough, and if it could be made more pleasurable for a short while it was such a gift. Grace was well aware of how lonely life could be for Madeleine, but others would only see the elegant woman who had the world at her feet, and beauty as well. Oh, how easily it could be dulled.

Waiters wheeled in a trolley bearing a large rib of beef and sliced it deftly onto plates, which they put before them in perfectly timed unison. A waitress delivered vegetables and faded into the background, far enough away for their privacy but waiting should they need anything.

'This is wonderful. Thank you, Maddy.' How good it was to have enjoyable company, and conversation. It reminded her how awful things had been at The Beeches. Why had she settled for less? Davey would not have approved.

Madeleine picked up her glass. 'Please, I am the one who should be thanking you. I usually take my meals in my room.'

Grace cut into her beef. It was tender and melted in her mouth. She couldn't recall the last time she'd eaten so well, and in such delightful company. Her face must have reflected her happiness.

'Wonderful food, isn't it?' Madeleine said, replacing her glass to the table. 'It doesn't quite taste the same when you eat alone' She paused. 'How do you think Jessie will cope, travelling alone? Will you go with her?'

Grace looked out of the window. People were flocking past the windows, some of them turning their heads

444

to see what was on offer to the diners. 'I have no idea. I don't think Jessie has either. She and Harry had a row.'

Madeleine nodded, understanding.

'She's not thinking properly – hence going off to write her letter.'

'He's a lovely young man. He reminds me so much of Marty.' Madeleine sat back in her chair and explained. 'We were engaged. He died. The Spanish Flu. I was distraught. A fellow much like Billy Lane came along. I married him because I knew I'd never find another love to match Marty. He spent all my money, gambled it away. I'm still trying to divorce him. It left me rather cautious – as you can imagine.'

They lingered over coffee. Eventually, Madeleine said, 'Would you come up to my room, Grace? I have some dresses I'd like you to take a look at.' She led the way to the stairs, her hand on the rail. 'I think one or two of them could be altered for Jessie. She'll need a new wardrobe if Bernie's true to his word.'

'There is no doubting that. He thought a lot of Davey.'

Madeleine smiled. 'Then I'd like very much to help. But please don't tell her, not yet.'

Chapter 32

Bernie was buoyant about Jessie's prospects and had sent word via one of his many secretaries that he had two or three openings for her when the season at the Empire finished at the end of September. However, he cautioned her to wait and not make any decisions as other irons were in the fire. There was no need for her to worry her pretty little head; Jessie's future was going to be bright. It didn't make her as happy as she'd thought it would. All she could think of was Harry.

Jessie sat in George's office, Jasper on her lap purring contentedly. She'd taken to sitting there each evening, hoping that the phone would ring in the absence of Harry's letters. The silence was deafening.

'Sweet cheeks. Why the scowl? It spoils your beautiful face.'

Billy was leaning by the door waiting for the phone. He tapped his hand to it. 'Gotta call coming in. Things are looking up.'

She didn't feel like speaking. She let Jasper down on the floor and went down the steps to the dressing room. Arthur was stood at the bottom of them, his bald head shining and he patted at it with a handkerchief. It was already so hot beneath the stage.

'Any news?' She shook her head. He moved to one side to let her pass. 'Probably being shouted at by an officer or two. It's his first week; he won't have a minute to write a note for the milkman.'

She smiled, appreciating his kindness but it didn't make her feel any better. She thought now of the times she had not returned his letters, when Grace was ill and she was so tired. Too tired to write. Perhaps there was something in it

By the end of the second week who'd all but given up hope. She'd called Miss Symonds who said she would try and find out what she could, but nothing had been forthcoming.

It was early afternoon on Saturday and the weather was beautiful. Norman and Iris were coming to see the first house and would be bringing Eddie's bike. He was smart in his best shirt and trousers. 'I'm going to see one of the lads then I'll see you at the Empire.' He grinned. 'It'll be easier going down to the golf club in the morning on my bike.' He kissed his mum who was still at her machine, shouting 'see you later' to everyone else in the house as he left.

Jessie went to the window and watched him saunter happily up the street, head held high. They'd used some of the money that Norman had given Eddie to buy a sewing machine and Grace had been able to take in alterations. She was working on a dress of rich blue satin.

'I used to be that eager,' Jessie said, letting the net drop and sitting in the armchair in the bay, the gentle treadle of the machine thrumming as Grace sewed.

'You will be. Give Harry time. He has a lot on his plate, Jess.'

'He's not thinking of me, though, and I can't think of anything else but him.'

Grace stopped, took her foot off the treadle. 'You don't know that.'

She sighed, pulling at the button of her cardigan, twirling it around and around.

'It will come off, Jessie.' Grace turned from her work. 'Keep yourself busy. Too much time to think isn't good for the soul. Remember how bad it was at The Beeches, Saturday afternoons, listening to the clock instead of the wireless. We don't have to put up with that any more and that's down to you. You need to get your best face on because I want your aunt and uncle too see how wonderful you are.'

Later, on her way to the theatre, she stopped to buy another postcard to send to Harry, thinking its brevity might elicit a response when nothing else had. It held a glimmer of hope and she felt more optimistic as she walked to work along the seafront.

That hope was squashed the minute she stepped into the dressing room. She peeled off her clothes and got into her robe, plonked herself down on her chair and took up her brush, sweeping back her hair to make-up her face. Kay was staring at her, pity in her eyes and Sally was repeatedly biting at her lip. None of the girls could hide the concern from their faces.

'What's up?' She fastened back her hair with swift twists of a band.

'Get ready first.' Rita was sharp. Virginia was agitated. Something was wrong but what? Frances shrugged. Rita's face was set firm and Jessie hurriedly made up her face.

'Now,' she said, turning in her chair, 'will someone tell me what's wrong?'

Rita spoke first. 'It's Eddie.'

Jessie sprang to her feet.

'What! Oh, God. What's happened?'

Frances put a steadying hand to her arm, pushing her back down in her chair. 'He's quite safe, only—' Rita pursed her lips. 'Better go see for yourself. He's with Billy.'

Virginia twisted in her chair. 'I tried to stop Billy, Jessie. But you know how persuasive he can be.'

Billy. It was always Billy, wasn't it? She hurried to his room, rapping fiercely on the closed door, dreading what she would find. Billy opened it wide when he saw who it was, revealing Eddie, who sat at Billy's dressing table, his head resting on his arms. Billy was smirking at her horrified reaction. 'He's fine. Or he will be in an hour or so.' She saw the half-empty whisky bottle, the two glasses. Beer bottles were lined up in front of him.

Eddie lifted his head and grinned into the mirror. He was unable to hold it up properly and kept lolling forward. 'Jessie.' He belched loudly, dropping his head back on his hands, giggling softly to himself.

Jessie was fired with fury. 'What the hell happened?'

'Hey, sweetness.' Billy's hands were on her arms and she shrugged them off.

'I am not your sweetness. I'm not your sweet anything.'

He pulled a face, which irritated her even more.

'Don't play the fool with me, Billy Lane.' She pulled Eddie to his feet and he stood for a moment, wobbled unsteadily and sat down with a slap, dropping his head onto the table with a thump.

Billy folded his arms and leaned back against the wall. 'Don't be so hard on him. He's a working man, not a child. It's unfair of you to treat him like one.' He brushed his trousers and sat down on the chair.

Matt ran along, giving the half to curtain. Eddie began hiccupping, his shoulders moving sharply, setting off another lot of giggles. Jessie wasn't at all amused.

'He was celebrating with me. That call I was waiting for the other night? It was from Bernie. I've got a slot on the wireless. The home station, prime time. We're going to be big time now, Jessie, you and me.' He took hold of his glass. 'Here's to bloody brilliant Bernie. Have a drink.'

Eddie held up his glass, his head still on the table, mumbled, 'Bernie' and put it down again.

Billy laughed. 'He can't take his drink yet, Jessie. It's all a bit of fun.'

She heard footsteps and the other girls were behind her. Frances gasped when she saw the state of Eddie. Jessie was close to tears from rage. If she'd been a man she would have punched Billy on the nose.

'I wasn't to know he would get like this, Jessie.' He spread his hands. 'I mean. Look. I was being kind, fatherly.'

'Don't you dare, Billy. My dad would never have done this.'

'Are you sure of that? Men like to have a drink.' He grinned and she could bear it no longer. She drew back her hand, slapping him good and hard. He put his palm to his face. 'Ouch.' He grinned again and fell into his chair.

'That was long overdue.' It was Virginia, and Jessie caught the look of satisfaction in her eyes.

Eddie belched again and Billy patted him on the back saying gently, 'All right, old chap.'

Jessie didn't know what to do with her anger. She clenched and unclenched her fists, over and over again. There was no air in the room and she felt light-headed.

Billy lounged back in his chair. 'Leave him in here with me. He'll sober up. Then he can go home.'

'Sober up!' Jessie spat out her words. 'Our aunt and uncle are coming to see the show. What in God's name are they going to think?' Iris would delight at Eddie's predicament. This was exactly what she expected to find at the theatre.

Billy spread his knees and let his hands drop between them. 'I'm sorry, Jessie. Don't be mad at him. Don't be mad at us.'

'You can't leave him here, Jessie.' Frances had squeezed herself into the room.

Rita took charge. 'We've got enough time to get him upstairs and into the fresh air. I'll get one of the stagehands to get some black coffee. Once we've done the first number we can look after him better.'

Virginia took one side of Eddie and Jessie put her arm under the other, and they struggled up the corridor, alternately pushing and shoving as he stumbled up the stairs and outside. The other girls followed. They were already in their opening costumes, and held Eddie as far away from themselves as they dare without letting him fall. George's face said it all when they got him to the stage door, and he leapt from his office and opened the outside door. The girls pushed him into the street and Eddie staggered as the fresh air hit him. He was promptly sick as the girls held him over the gutter. They held him at arm's length as he retched again.

A car pulled up and Jessie looked up to see a Ford with a bicycle tethered to the roof. In the passenger window was the distorted face of Iris as she recognised Jessie, and then, worse, Eddie.

Norman got out and hurried around to open the door. Grace got out of the back seat and rushed to Eddie, taking over from Rita. 'I'm afraid he's been sick on my shoe, Grace. I need to go and get cleaned up.' Grace nodded, looking at Jessie, her face showing more concern than fury.

'What happened?'

'Billy. Billy happened.'

Grace shook her head. 'Don't say another thing.'

Iris stood watching the spectacle that was playing out before them and Jessie's fury turned to shame.

She could see Norman untying the ropes that had held Eddie's bicycle firmly in place, heard the clatter as he placed it onto the street. Eddie retched again. Grace pulled out a handkerchief to wipe his mouth.

'Evening, Aunt Iris, Uncle Norman.' Jessie said, trying to straighten herself and haul Eddie more upright. It was a hopeless task.

'How demeaning,' Iris said finally, as Norman pushed the bike to the stage door and leant it against the wall. George came out with a glass of water and Jessie took it, and Eddie managed to lift his head enough to drink.

'Sip it,' she demanded. Vomit stuck in his hair and dribbled on his chin. He wobbled unsteadily but Grace and Virginia held him firm. Jessie made him drink again. Iris looked down her nose. George pushed past her.

'Bring him into my office, girls. I'll look after him while you get yourselves ready.' He shook his head. 'Billy Lane has a lot to answer for.'

'More than you could imagine,' Virginia said as they led the boy past the stage door.

Matt came out to tell the girls that the fifteen had been called. George sent him front of house for coffee.

Jessie lifted Jasper from George's chair and they settled Eddie in it.

Grace turned to the girls. 'Tell me what happened later, Jessie. You need to get yourself ready.'

'What about Uncle Norman and Aunt Iris?'

Grace let out a long sigh. Eddie was sat with his head forward and George had handed over a bucket of sand that was used to put out cigarettes backstage. 'He'll be fine here. I'll get Olive to make him some dry toast. Don't worry.' Grace followed Jessie into the street.

Iris was standing with Norman, gloating. Jessie could hardly bear to look at her.

'Well, Jessie. This is the life you wanted. Are you pleased with yourself? And to drag your poor mother and brother to it as well.' She tutted, shaking her head, smugness playing in her smile. Jessie pulled herself more erect.

Grace intervened. She was smiling at them, so dignified, as if nothing untoward had happened, while Jessie fought to stop herself from trembling with fury. 'I'll take you round the front to your seats, Iris, Norman.'

'Thank you, Grace.' Norman said, reaching out to take Iris by the elbow and guide her away.

'Oh, I don't think that will be necessary, Norman,' Iris said haughtily, causing Norman to let his hand drop to his side. 'I've no wish to stay and witness such debauchery.' She leaned to Jessie. 'I hope you're satisfied, young lady. You got what you wanted.' She huffed, turned on her heel and walked to the car, standing beside it, imperious, waiting for Norman to open the door, which he did, pausing while his wife got inside before coming back to Grace and Jessie.

'I'm so sorry, my dear,' he said to Grace. 'I know this has been some kind of misunderstanding. Eddie's a fine boy. I hope he's all right. Something has obviously gone terribly wrong.' He glanced at Jessie and her cheeks burned.

Grace shook his hand and he leaned forward and kissed her cheek. 'Goodbye, Jessie.' He put out his hand to her and she took it. 'I'm sorry we won't get to see the show. I was looking forward to it. Perhaps another time.'

Frances stuck her head out of the stage door. 'Calling the five, Jessie.'

'Go,' Grace said. 'You mustn't miss your entrance.'

She went back into the theatre. Eddie was quiet, George rubbing his back. George tilted his head and mouthed, 'He's okay', as they hurried past.

'You can't watch over Eddie twenty-four hours a day, can you?' Frances said. 'And he's going to have to learn these things for himself. Like we all do.'

'The sombre voice of experience.'

'It is.' Frances stepped up onto the stage. 'How I wish it wasn't.'

Chapter 33

There were no recriminations. How could there be? Billy had left that night, asking to be released from his contract, to which Jack had grudgingly assented, knowing that Billy would up and leave regardless. Jimmy Baker was doubling up in his place, working the first half at the Royal then coming down the road for the second half at The Empire. He was thrilled with the extra money and the opportunity to open the second half. His name had been printed on white strips that were plastered over Billy's on the playbills.

Older than Billy and a lot kinder, he had knocked politely on the dressing-room door on Monday evening before the show went up. 'Jimmy Baker,' he said, 'cooking up comedy and raising laughs, boom-boom.' He was as cheesy as they come but they all laughed.

'That joke just about takes the biscuit, Jimmy,' Frances retorted and he pointed a finger. 'You're wasted in here, girl.'

Virginia threw a make-up rag at him and he ducked.

The atmosphere backstage was flat and even Jimmy's corny gags couldn't lift the mood. Eddie had bitterly regretted his actions and had come into the theatre early to apologise to everyone for his behaviour, but it hadn't been necessary. No one blamed him. Everyone was glad to see the back of Billy, Virginia more than anyone, and she and Jessie had grown closer in the days following his abrupt departure. Jessie had reason to feel devastated but Virginia more so. Jessie had caught her being sick and the look of terror in her eyes was all Jessie needed to know. She'd sworn Jessie to secrecy, and she'd agreed, hoping it was down to something she'd eaten, the pair of them cursing the day they'd ever set eyes on Billy Lane.

On Tuesday lunchtime, Grace sewed the last button on the blue dress. She put it on a hanger along with the green and got herself ready. Jessie had been moping about. She folded another letter into an envelope and stuck her head into her mum's room. 'I'm going out to post this. Do you need anything?'

Grace was pulling on her jacket. 'What perfect timing. I'm taking these back to Maddy. We can walk together.'

They passed a post box and Jessie dropped in her letter.

'Does Miss Symonds know which base Harry is at?' Grace said.

Jessie shrugged. 'If she does, she's not saying.' She took the dresses from Grace and put them over her own arm, and they made their way through the back streets. The headline on the news boards declared that Hitler would talk with Poland. Would it lead to peace? Would war be averted after all and her fears for Harry unfounded?

They cut through the jitty between Albert Road and Dolphin Street, past the back of the theatre and crossed over the road to the Dolphin. Jessie stood by the entrance door ready to hand over the dresses to Grace. Grace kept her hands at her side as she mounted the steps. 'Come in with me. Say hello to Maddy.'

'I don't think so, Mum. I made a fool of myself, thinking Billy could be trusted. And Madeleine cut my song, remember?'

'Do you think that a woman like Maddy hasn't made a fool of herself over some man? Come with me.' She urged again and Jessie reluctantly followed Grace to the reception desk.

The man on reception smiled. 'Miss Moore left word that you were to join her in her room. Walter.' He beckoned to the young porter who led them upstairs and knocked on the door to Madeleine's suite.

'Your guests, madam.' They waited while Madeleine came to the door and as she let them in, the porter hurried back to his post.

The room overlooked the gardens across the road and down towards the sea. From the doorway, Jessie could see the crowds making their way to and from the pier. The sash windows were raised and the sound from the streets drifted in. It was laid out like a small sitting room with a door, which Jessie presumed led to the bedroom and bathroom. It was much nicer than any of the rooms she could remember her dad having, although when he was younger he must have once had rooms like this. Jessie followed her mum and laid the dresses over the back of an armchair. Madeleine walked over to them, running her hands over the fabric, admiring Grace's skill.

'They look marvellous, Grace. What a fabulous job you've done. I hardly recognise them.' She turned to Jessie. 'What do you think?'

Jessie nodded. 'My mum's a magician.'

It was good to see Grace being appreciated for her work. At least she and Eddie were happy here. Eddie would recover from the embarrassment of Saturday. He'd been mortified but who cared about Iris and Norman anyway? She lingered by the window, watching people below, touching the velvet curtains, appreciating the softness.

'Jessie?'

Madeleine was holding up the blue dress. 'Would you put this on for me?'

Jessie glared at her mother who folded her arms and glowered back at her. Madeleine was already walking towards the bedroom door and opened it, laying the dress out onto the bed then coming back into the room. The two older women waited for Jessie to move and, with an exaggerated sigh, her shoulders sagging with defeat, she marched ahead, pushing the door to, but not shut, hoping to grasp what they were talking about, their voices too low to make out anything useful. She hurried back into the sitting room and held up her hair while Grace did the fasteners at the back.

'Let me see.' Grace stepped back beside Madeleine and the two women looked Jessie up and down. 'Turn around.' Grace twirled her finger and Jessie did as she was told.

'Perfect.' Madeleine smiled. 'Don't you agree?' Grace nodded.

Jessie frowned. What was going on?

'Now try the green.' Her mum undid her fastenings and Jessie disappeared back into the bedroom, this time taking more notice of her surroundings. The bed was made with smart white sheets dressed with the plumpest pillows Jessie had ever seen. There were flowers on every available space. She went to the dressing table, drawn to the bottles of expensive scent and make-up. A tortoiseshell brush and matching mirror were placed to one side. How wonderful to have such lovely things.

Jessie went back into the room. Grace was sat on the ruby sofa, beaming. The two older women exchanged glances, Madeleine walking behind Jessie, smoothing her hands across her shoulders, which made Jessie bridle.

'Your mother chose it. Such a good eye.'

'I don't understand.' She looked to Grace for explanation but Madeleine spoke first.

'The dresses are yours. You'll need your own wardrobe. I'm sure Bernie has told you that.' She walked over to Grace and sat down beside her.

There was no doubt that the dresses were exactly what she needed, and her mum had worked her deft magic in transforming them. They fitted perfectly but she couldn't accept them – better to take them off and hand them back before she got used to the feel of the expensive fabrics on her skin. She put her hands behind her back and began fiddling with the buttons. 'I can't afford them.' It was galling, exposing their financial situation to Madeleine, wanting to spare her mum, but she wouldn't put them in debt, no matter how beautiful the dresses were.

Madeleine shook her head. 'They are a gift.'

Jessie forgot about the buttons, letting her hands drop. Why this change in Madeleine? She held her tongue, not wanting to embarrass herself, nor Grace. Her mum had had more than her share of that.

Madeleine carried on. 'Vernon LeRoy is coming at the weekend. I want you to sing the three songs that you sang for Bernie.'

It was confusing. 'Why? Why help me?'

'Because I can, Jessie. No other reason. I was young like you when I started out. I had no one to guide me. I made some silly, silly mistakes. Mistakes that not only cost me most of the fortune I made in films, but also the love of my life. I wouldn't want to stand by and watch it happen to you.'

'It's too late for that.' She looked across the room and out over the windows. The sky was blue with puffs of snowy white cloud drifting over the horizon. Was Harry flying somewhere in those bluest of skies?

'Haven't you heard from him?' Madeleine asked.

She shook her head. 'I don't suppose I ever will. I have no idea where he is. Just that he's in the RAF. How many people are in the RAF? How many airfields?' She sank down beside her mum.

'Harry is a good man,' Grace said, 'the best. He'll reply.'

'Perhaps he hasn't received them,' Madeleine said, kindly.

'Oh, I think he has.'

'Get up, Jessie.' Madeleine was suddenly forceful and Jessie jerked sharply. This was more like it. She was a bully, after all. Spoilt and used to getting her own way. Well, she had a shock coming. Jessie wasn't going to be pushed around by anyone.

'Are you a quitter?' Madeleine folded her arms, her eyes narrowed. 'You never looked like it to me. The first time I saw you I thought, here was a girl with fire and spirit. This girl is something special.' Jessie stared, confused. 'You've not lost that, Jessie. You've hidden it. Surely you're not going to be like one of those tired old nags that Billy Lane threw money at?'

Jessie glared at her. How dare she think that Billy would crush her. She fumbled for words. The last few weeks had been too much to take in. It had all been going so well and then ... and then. What? Was she going to let Billy spoil her dreams? Or Harry? Iris had been so happy that she'd failed, that she'd been right. And she had been, hadn't she, Jessie thought now. She was hot-headed. She didn't think things through. Some of the things she had done right, maybe not all of them, but they had a better life, didn't they? She looked at Grace. She was smiling, her eyes sparkling. Her hair had regained some of its lustre as had her skin, and no one could deny that she was thriving. And Eddie was doing what he loved. All was not lost; she was the only one who had given up. She tried to concentrate on what Madeleine was saying.

'You have great talent. Are you going to squander it because you've had a couple of knocks?' Madeleine opened the door. 'Come with me,' she said firmly.

Jessie looked to her mum. The two of them waited for Jessie to make a move and she realised there was nothing she could do but follow them.

Madeleine led the way, back down the stairs, into a room with a large dance floor. There was a baby grand piano in one corner and Madeleine walked towards it. Jessie got ready to play, but it was Madeleine who sat down and started to play the opening bars of a song that Jessie recognised from the repertoire she had sung for Bernie. She stood in the belly of the piano. 'I didn't know you played?'

'You never asked.' Madeleine stilled her hands. Jessie's head was reeling.

'Why do you want to help me? Because you feel sorry for me? Because I'm such a fool?'

Madeleine took her hand and held it gently. 'I've always wanted to help you.'

'But you had my song cut.'

Madeleine shook her head. 'Billy got your song cut. I was worried about you.'

How could she do this? Why would Grace stand by and let her twist things around?

'That's a lie. It was Billy who put me forward.'

Madeleine gripped her hand tighter. 'Billy wanted to get back at me. He put you forward for a solo in the first half – which would have worked nicely – but then he wanted the duet. You made him look better than he was, Jessie, and he liked it. I mentioned to Jack that it was too much for you. Jack is still new to this game; he shouldn't have put a singer following a singer. That's not variety.'

Jessie gripped the side of the piano. Grace didn't comment.

'Show business is a delicate balance of art and temperament,' Madeleine continued. 'It didn't do you any favours to dance with the other girls, then sing, dance again, duet, dance. It would have depleted you. It's so easy to jump at every chance that is offered to you, but that way you lose your passion. I didn't want that to happen to you. Losing your passion is the driest, loneliest place to be.' She paused. 'I suggested to Jack that you keep the solo and drop the duet. Billy wouldn't hear of it.'

Billy. What other damage had he done that she had not been aware of? 'I thought it was you.'

'That's because that's what he wanted you to think. He knew you'd never ask. You'd never be able to challenge me as the star of the show. And you could hardly complain to Jack. You might have lost your job.'

Jessie sighed. 'I am so sorry.'

Madeleine brushed her apology aside with a gentle wave of her hand. 'Don't be. It's a lesson. As long as you learn from it.'

'Oh, I will. You can be sure of that.' She paused. 'I've lost the duet anyway. Jimmy Baker can't sing a note.' Jessie's voice was bitter. She had lost so much more.

'Then sing for me now and we'll work together to polish this act you want so much. You've got to work at it, Jessie, and take the knocks that go with it. There are people like Billy around every corner waiting to live off your talents. You need to be sharp.'

She paused. Jessie was silent. Eventually Madeleine said, 'Are you willing to let me help you?'

Jessie looked at Grace who was smiling broadly. Jessie smiled too.

'I'd like that very much. Thank you.' She had a lot to learn about show business but even more about people, and perhaps Madeleine would be able to teach her that too.

Madeleine turned back to the piano. 'I'm ready when you are.'

Chapter 34

A reply arrived in the second post on Wednesday, a fine thread to which Jessie weighted an anchor. Harry was in Grantham; he doubted he'd get leave but hoped that Saturday would be everything she dreamed it would be. She picked up the letter and kissed it, put it in her bag and let out a long sigh. The whole country was holding its breath but at least she could breathe again. Chamberlin had issued an ultimatum to Hitler and the deadline was tomorrow at eleven.

Grace called up the stairs. 'Ready, Jessie?'

Frances was waiting on the landing. 'See you at the theatre. I'll leave you to walk with your ma.' Jessie nodded, suddenly unable to speak. She joined Grace in the hall.

Geraldine squeezed her shoulders. 'You'll be wonderful, and I'll be watching. We all will.'

Jessie nodded again.

Grace mouthed 'Nerves' to Geraldine and they set off down the street as she had so many times before. Jessie's head was full of the instructions that Madeleine had been issuing all week. She had arrived at the Dolphin every morning at nine, and they had worked through until three when Jessie was allowed to rest before the evening's show. Madeleine took her through music, notation, intonation – nothing had been left to chance.

They had been at the Empire earlier and Madeleine had called the orchestra in to go over Jessie's numbers, guiding her stage movements, when to come forward, when to hold back. She had sent her home to rest but Jessie was beginning to think that had been a mistake. Her brain was tumbling with what she must do, and what she should not.

'You have to be yourself, be natural but remember all these technicalities. It's so important, Jessie. But, most of all, let your love and passion for what you are doing shine through every word, every movement. Build that bridge into the audience and walk over it. If you can do that, I promise that you will never, ever want to come back.'

Grace linked her arm through Jessie's, bringing her back to the now. 'All right, my darling?'

Jessie gripped Grace's arm. 'Oh, Mum. What if I dry? What if I sing the wrong words? What if ...'

'What if you enjoy yourself, Jessie? What if you never want it to end?'

It seemed unlikely as the fear built in Jessie's body. The walk was a blur, she could barely remember the route they took, but when she arrived at the theatre, George was beaming.

'Olive's here tonight. And Dolly got the night off so she can be with Pete. He's home this weekend.' He was inordinately smart with a shirt and tie, and a waistcoat that hid his familiar braces. His hair was slicked back with Brylcreem, and he'd obviously had a liberal splashing of Old Spice.

Grace followed her down to the dressing room, but, when she opened the door, Rita put her arm across to stop her. Frances and Virginia, Sally and Kay were grinning, and Jessie was confused. 'Sorry, no admittance. This is the Variety Girls room. I believe yours is down the corridor on the left.'

Rita held firm, and Jessie looked at Grace, who shrugged, biting back a smile. Rita wasn't going to budge and as Jessie moved off, she heard the rumpus as the rest of the girls got to their feet and followed her down the corridor. She stopped as she came to the room Billy once occupied. On the door was a cardboard star, stuck with sequins and the words Miss Jessie Delaney written upon it. The girls were crammed behind Grace waiting for her reaction. She steadied herself for a moment, not wanting to cry, but her eyes filled with happy tears. Miss Symonds would approve.

'Open the door, for heaven's sake, Jess.' It was Frances. 'We've got a show to do.'

She did as she was told, gasping when she saw what her friends had done. All her costumes were hanging on a rail in the order that she would need them, the blue and green dresses at the back, her shoes placed neatly underneath. Her make-up box and hairbrush were neatly set out as she liked them and around the mirror were her cards. Photos of her dad and Harry took prominence. Harry, oh, Harry. If only he was here. She bit her lip to force the sadness away. The Variety Girls shimmied into the room, watching her through the mirror.

She could hear George's voice. 'Flowers for Miss Delaney.' The girls parted and let him past. He wriggled into the room with the biggest bouquet she had ever seen. 'Who could they be from, George?'

George blushed. 'It'll say on the card, but Bernie Blackwood sent 'em.' There was a burst of laughter and George wrinkled his nose, pushing his glasses up, only for them to slide down again. Jessie adjusted them onto his ears and planted a kiss on his cheek. George grinned. 'He wishes you all the best. We all do.' Tears dropped onto her cheeks now. What it was to have so many friends wanting her to succeed.

'Well,' Rita said. 'What do you think?'

Jessie threw her arms around Rita, then Frances.

'Thank you, thank you.' She stood in front of Virginia, wondering whether she would entertain a hug, but the girl opened her arms and Jessie responded with the warmest embrace.

'You'll be sensational, Jessie,' Virginia said into her ear. 'Don't let anyone hold you back.'

'I won't if you won't,' she whispered.

'Let's leave her to it, girls.' Rita lifted her arm and pointed towards the door, guiding the girls out of the room, calling over her shoulder. 'Don't think this means you don't have to perform your arse off in our routines, Jessie Delaney. You're still a Variety Girl and I will expect the very best of you.'

There was the rattle of heels as they rushed back to their own dressing room and Jessie was alone with Grace. Grace put the flowers to one side. 'I'll go and find a vase. If they haven't got one here, I'm sure Olive will lend us one. Or Joyce.' Jessie was still standing in the room trying to take it all in. Grace pulled out her chair and pushed her into it.

'You don't have time to daydream, Jessie. You need to get ready for the first half.'

Grace stood behind her, her hands gently resting on her daughter's shoulders. 'This is your beginning, darling girl. Are you ready for it?' Jessie put her hand up and took hold of her mum's, not wanting to let it go.

'As I'll ever be.'

Grace went in search of a vase. It was odd being in a room on her own and she missed the banter and idle chatter that filled the time before the show went up. It would take some getting used to, but if she wanted to succeed she would have to embrace the loneliness that came with being a solo artiste.

More flowers arrived during the first half and George did a valiant job of tucking them into the corners of her room, the scent of them intoxicating.

Grace came back in the interval, Eddie grinning over her shoulder.

'Everyone's in the audience, Jess. Joyce, Olive, Mr Coombes and the lads from the garage. I'm so proud of you, Jess. I could burst.'

'Well, don't burst in here, my lad,' Grace said, 'or you'll spoil your sister's costumes.'

Jessie was suddenly overwhelmed. 'Did you see Harry, Ed? Was he at the back too?' She tried to sound as bright as she could, not wanting to dampen his excitement. She exchanged glances with her mum, knowing the answer, and yet hoping she was wrong.

He shook his head. 'I saw Mr LeRoy though.' Eddie rambled on, his voice chipper, breaking the tension. 'He's sitting in the box. I knew it was him. He smells like money.'

Grace and Jessie laughed. 'And what does that smell like, Ed?' Jessie grinned.

'You know, filthy rich. He looks important. More important than Bernie.'

'Hmm.' Grace picked up the brush and began to tend to Jessie's hair. Jessie couldn't remember the last time her mum had done that. Was she nervous too?

Madeleine's reflection appeared in the mirror as she knocked on the open door. 'I like it,' she said as she fingered the star. 'Do you think the girls would do one for me?' Madeleiene was glowing. 'How are you feeling? Nervous?' Jessie nodded. 'That's good.' She smiled. 'I'd be worried if you weren't. Never take what you do for granted, Jessie. How are you doing, Grace?'

Grace wafted the air with the brush. 'Cool as a cucumber.' Her hand was trembling violently, which made them all laugh.

'See you on stage, Jessie.' Madeleine was gone.

Grace went back into the theatre, and the girls did the opening routine without Jessie, as they had done in the weeks when she performed her duet with Billy.

Jessie silently got into the blue dress as the girls danced above her, then stood with her eyes closed, slowing her breathing as Madeleine had instructed, visualising herself on stage, the audience applauding. In her mind's eye she turned to see Harry in the wings, hoping in so doing that it would come true.

Frances came into the room while Jimmy Baker went through his patter. They could hear the laughter in the dressing room. 'It's a fabulous audience, Jess.'

Jessie held up her hair as Frances fastened the buttons. Her voice was brittle with excitement. 'Bloody hell, girl. My fingers feel like sausages. Did your mum have to put so many buttons on this?'

They looked up at the ceiling, hearing the applause for Jimmy Baker. 'Madeleine next. You need to get up into the wings.'

Matt rapped lightly on the open door. 'Your call, Miss Delaney.'

Frances squealed. 'How divine. Let me walk with you.'

It was like walking to the gallows. Her body was leaden, and each step took so much effort. She slowed her breathing again, steadying herself, sensing her dad beside her, the lightest touch on her hair as she walked up onto the stage. He was there. She was not alone.

Eddie was already squashed in prompt corner, grinning like a Cheshire cat, and it warmed her to see his cheeky face. As she prepared to make her entrance, other members of the cast and crew gathered as close as they could, until there was hardly space to move. Madeleine finished her song and waited for the applause to die down, encouraging them by pushing down with her hands.

'Thank you, you wonderful people. I appreciate that you have come to see the show when tomorrow we will be in no doubt as to whether we will be at war or not. Many of you here tonight will have memories of the last one.' There were nods and groans. Madeleine lifted her voice, making it lighter, encouraging. 'What got us through was spirit, laughter and friends.' More noises of agreement. She nodded with them, leading them for Jessie's benefit. 'The young lady I am going to introduce to you tonight has such spirit. I'd like you to put your hands together and welcome on stage, the wonderful sweet sound of …' she paused '… Miss Jessie Delaney.'

Madeleine turned to face the wings, holding out her hand as Jessie stepped out.

The audience burst into rousing applause. Eddie was jumping up and down next to George and they leaned as far forward as they dare.

Jessie walked to centre stage as Madeleine exited the opposite side. The spotlight shrank to Jessie's head and shoulders as the applause died. Her heart was beating wildly as she began to sing to the darkness of the stalls, the dress circle, the boxes; smiling, smiling, and hoping against hope that Harry was out there somewhere. The audience applauded when she finished her first song and she went directly into the next.

By the time she'd finished, the audience were on their feet.

Madeleine walked on, clapping, as Jessie bowed centre, left, then right. In the box she saw Mr LeRoy on his feet, smiling down at her, lifting his hands in applause.

Madeleine took her hand. 'I think that means they like you.'

Jessie grinned, and the two women took a bow together. Jessie hurried off into the wings as Madeleine finished her performance.

Eddie's chest was puffed with pride and the girls swept her away into the light and privacy of the corridor to celebrate.

She had wings, she could soar way above the theatre and into the cloudless sky and float like a bird, like Harry in his aeroplane. Oh, Harry, if only he'd been here.

'Heavens, Jessie. You were wonderful.' George had his thumbs on his braces, his waistcoat discarded, his hair flopping over the side of his head. 'I was that nervous for you, lass. I'm glad it's all over. I can breathe again now.'

Jessie kissed him again and squeezed him tightly. 'Oh, George, you are so sweet.' His glasses slipped down his nose again and the girls laughed.

'Better get ready for the finale,' Rita barked. 'The show's not over yet.'

The finale was greeted with thunderous applause. Was it because they had been exceptional, or was it the thought that this could be the last show they would enjoy in peacetime?

Jessie walked on to take her applause on her own, not with the Variety Girls as she had done all season, delighted with the response from the audience. Madeleine came centre stage for her own applause, then took Jessie by the hand and brought her forward. The crowd cheered and Jessie felt as if her heart was soaring out of her body and into the darkness of the flies above them.

As the final curtain came down Jessie was hit with a tumult of emotions as the cast lingered on stage to congratulate her, before making their way back to their dressing rooms. It was everything she wanted, all she had dreamed of, and yet a small part of her felt empty and cavernous.

She lingered behind the curtain, listening as the audience left the auditorium; to the chatter and the excitement as they exited, the sound that she and Harry had made when they'd seen the show in Cromer. Had it been only weeks since then? Or a lifetime? Could this be enough for her, without him by her side?

Grace came onto the stage. Behind them the crew worked to strike the treads and backcloth, storing them until needed for the next performance.

'You need to get back to your room, darling. Mr LeRoy has sent word. He wants to see you.' Grace was glowing. This was what it had all been for, the risk – and to see such joy on Grace's face was reward enough.

Jessie took her mum's hand. 'We'll see him together.'

The girls shouted out from their dressing room as she walked down to her own. 'See you in the bar, you star.' Grace waved and Jessie carried on to her room. More flowers had arrived, there was hardly enough space to change and she gasped with delight, until her eyes fell on a small glass tumbler of violets in front of her mirror. She turned on her heel and rushed into the corridor.

Grace called after her. 'Jessie!'

'I'll be back.' She would be, but not yet. Her heart was leaping; she really could fly. Madeleine and Vernon LeRoy were walking towards her, but she couldn't stop. Wouldn't. This was more important. Fans were gathering about the stage door and George pressed ahead, parting them with his hands to allow her to escape. She put her hands to his cheeks and kissed him.

'Good luck, lass,' he called after her.

She stopped when she saw him, leaning against the wall as he had done so many times before, a cigarette in his hand. Just the same, her Harry, only this time he was in uniform. The same, but different.

'Harry.' It came out hardly more than a whisper, but he turned, threw his cigarette to the ground and stood away from the wall.

'Jessie.'

Every cell in her body was telling her to run to him but she wasn't sure of his reaction. Had he forgiven her childish petulance? He had come, hadn't he? That was enough. He held out his hands and she rushed forward and held them, his fingers entwining with hers. God, how she'd missed him. He pulled her tight towards him and tilted her face to his.

'There was not one second went by that I didn't think of you, darling Jessie.'

He kissed her and his mouth was hard on hers and she wanted the world to stop and hold on to him forever. Without Harry there was nothing. He drew away and she leaned against his chest, listening to his beating heart.

'Jessie.' Eddie had squeezed through the crowd waiting for autographs. Harry waved at him and Eddie grinned. 'Mr LeRoy wants you.'

There was only Harry, and she stared into his eyes, not wanting to let him go. 'I won't be long,' she called back.

Harry held her hand, and she felt like everything was connected exactly the way it should be. The perfect fit. 'You mustn't keep the big man waiting, Jessie,' Harry said, softly. 'This is what you've worked so hard for.'

'I kept you waiting, Harry. Too long. You were more important, but I didn't understand how much. Forgive me.'

He shook his head, put his fingers under her chin and tilted her face to him again. How she loved his beautiful face. 'Nothing to forgive.'

'Ask me again, Harry.'

He shook his head. 'I can't.'

She let go of his hand, dropped it to her side. So, she'd lost him after all. Well, it was only what she deserved, she'd been a fool. He took it again, brought it up to his mouth, kissed her fingers. 'Dope.' He grinned at her, and kissed her nose. Was he playing games?

'I can't, Jessie. Not now. It wouldn't be fair to you. Tomorrow we will get the news that we are at war. It won't be anything else.' He pushed her hair away from her face and she caught his hand, pressing it hard to her cheek.

'All the more reason not to wait one more second. I love you, Harry. I never knew how much until now. Mr LeRoy is waiting in my dressing room. I don't know how long he'll wait for me.' She paused. 'But I don't care. I can't let you go again. I won't.'

Eddie called again. 'Jessie.'

'Go and see him.' Harry was insistent. 'It's your big chance. The West End. I'll wait here for you.'

She shook her head. 'Come with me or I'll not go at all.'

His face was lit by the blue lamp of the stage door, and he looked so tired. She stood firm.

Harry looked across to Eddie and then back to her. His face creased into a smile and she felt stronger. Life was nothing without him, no matter how brief their time together would be.

'Ask me again, Harry.' She didn't want to plead. She wanted him to want her as much as she wanted him. 'Mr LeRoy could be waiting all night.'

He took her hands and pulled her close. 'Let's put Mr LeRoy out of his misery then.' He kissed her so hard, his hands either side of her face, that she found it hard to breathe. Her heart was beating wildly, and suddenly the world stopped. He let her go, he let her breathe. The crowd hushed as he got down on one knee. 'Miss Jessie Delaney, will you marry me?'

It was so easy to say yes and when she did the crowd by the stage door applauded. She flung her arms about his neck and as he got to his feet, he swung her around and she was once again as light as air. He put her down gently and she kissed him again. 'That's where I need to be, Harry. Both feet firmly on the ground, you at my side.' She held out her hand for his. 'Let's go and see what Mr LeRoy has to say.'

As they walked back to the stage door, their arms entwined, she knew that, whatever the future held, she would always love the theatre but her heart would forever belong to Harry.

ACKNOWLEDGEMENTS

The Empire Theatre still stands in Cleethorpes as does the pier. It was breached in the war and survived many incarnations. It is now a fish and chip restaurant, the theatre an amusement arcade; still places of entertainment, although not as they started out. But the important thing is that they are still here when many wonderful old theatres and piers have been destroyed.

The area I write about was my childhood playground, the characters my own, but the essence is of the warmth, fun and sense of community that surrounded me in my youth. And it all began with my wonderfully inspirational Nanny Lettie who wanted her stories to be told.

So, who to thank:

I bless the day I met Margaret Graham, the most marvellous writer and a magnificent mentor. She has both championed me and kicked me up the backside when I needed it. Without her guidance and constant nudging I don't think I'd ever have written this book. I can never repay the faith she had in me. She's an inspirational woman. A true star. Sparkly knickers and all!

Vivien Green for being an absolute constant and keeping me calm. I'm still counting my blessings.

The talented Katie Seaman, for her brilliant critical eye and kindness.

Gillian Green for listening to me prattle on about Battleship Grey. Thank you for sprinkling your magic my way.

All the wonderful creative people at Ebury who brought *The Variety Girls* to fruition and made it sparkle.

Ray and Janet Evans for their generous help with stories, research, coffee and laughter; lots of laughter!

Mia Carla, Talli Halliday and Dougie James – just a smidgen of all the wonderful entertainers who became part of our family. Their talent to entertain and let people leave their troubles behind is such a precious gift.

Cameron Watt, who sadly passed away before this book was published but who gave me my first job backstage on Cleethorpes Pier. The start of it all.

Maggie Moone, who shared her showbiz stories and was just as lovely as I remembered her to be.

Julie at Passion for Tap, who ran her eye over my dance sections to make sure I didn't put my foot in it.

To Chris Grant and Pete Rann, archivists at the King's Theatre in Southsea. Their passion for the theatre is infectious and I'm not surprised – the theatre is a beauty. If you get the chance, do book on one of their guided tours. You'll fall in love with it too.

Various local Facebook groups have been generous in sharing their knowledge, especially Dave Smith of Empire Theatre – Cleethorpes, Cleethorpes Memories,

Great Grimsby Memories, Variety, Summer Shows & Panto Past & Present.

Helen Baggott, our Monday Motivation led us both to finish our projects, and there's always been plenty of cake along the way. You've been the most marvellous support to me.

It goes without saying that I thank my wonderful family, Nick, Nelly and Ant. You're never too old to have fun and it's never too late to start. I'm so happy that you found wonderful partners with whom to dance through life.

My four entertainers – Elsie, Hadley, Huxley and California – the perfect quartet.

My husband, Neil, Mr Entertainment, who many times after an argument played 'You Only Hurt the One You Love' – and many times I wanted to smash the lid down on his fingers! Life with him has never been dull. He is the very essence of a variety entertainer, having worked in theatre since he was three years old. He is a constant source of inspiration and knowledge, my very own variety Google.

But most of all to my mum and dad who always believed in me when I didn't. Who encouraged me and told me and my sisters that we could do anything we wanted to do if we worked hard enough. I think we did all right, didn't we, girls!

Most of all they taught us the importance of kindness and forgiveness. They never stopped loving and sharing. My only regret is that my dad didn't live to see this book go out into the world, but I believe he was up in the clouds somewhere watching every word I wrote – and deleted. If it hadn't been for his entrepreneurial spirit and my parents' love of music and film I wouldn't have had such a rich source of memories to tap into. My greatest happiness is knowing how much my mum has enjoyed this whole journey with me.

I wrote *The Variety Girls* remembering all the Sunday afternoons watching old movies on the TV, all five of us together. Family. It was the highlight of the week. Happy times. I hope you find an essence of it here.

The Variety Girls will be back in the festive sequel

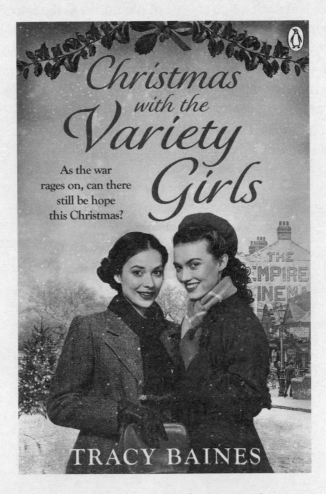

Keep reading for an exclusive preview …